ABOUT THE AUTHOR

Marianne Rosen is an emerging author of contemporary family sagas. She is a member of the Hay Writers' Circle, has performed at Hay Festival and is winner of the Richard Booth Prize for Non-fiction in 2018. *The Halls of Riverdell* is the second of the four-book Riverdell Saga, following her debut, *The Doors of Riverdell.*

For release updates: www.mariannerosen.com

CONTENT WARNING

This book includes scenes of a sexual nature, rape, domestic aggression, discussion of abortion and infertility, mention of abuse, and loss of a loved one.

If you wish to have more information to make an informed choice please view the author's website:

www.mariannerosen.com/content-warnings

THE HALLS OF RIVERDELL

MARIANNE ROSEN

ORIELbooks
www.orielbooks.com

THE HALLS OF RIVERDELL

ISBN 978-1-8380810-2-7

First published in Great Britain
in 2021 by Oriel Books
Copyright © 2021 by Marianne Rosen

Front cover design Amanda Hillier
Copyright © 2021 by Marianne Rosen
Incidental illustrations by Amanda Hillier
Copyright © 2020 by Amanda Hillier
Printed and bound by Clays UK

For Alex, and ALL the castles.

A Guide to the Characters of the Riverdell Saga

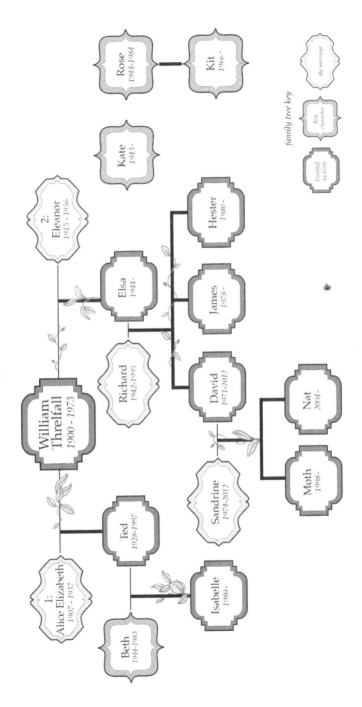

family tree key

By marriage

key character

Threlfall by birth

1

D earest Elsa,
We are married.
It is still unbelievable to say this.

We are married. On the twelfth, a few days before your birthday, and we missed you terribly.

I am now your sister-in-law as well as your dearest friend.

Rose left a few days ago. I'll wait to hear as soon as she arrives, please, for I'm sure she'll forget to let me know herself. She could have flown home but insisted on taking the boat again. The cost of air travel is extortionate, and she has taken with her the most monstrous India chest, which would have had to be shipped anyway. Plus, she said she had fallen in love with the oceans on our voyage out here. It was a wonderful, precious time. We were so close in those weeks. How sweet and devoted she was, so patient with what she termed my "outright idiocy". The time flew by.

Rose gave me away. She wore a dark morning suit with a silk blouse beneath, accessorised with a top hat and a silver topped cane, though I have no idea where she found either.

Ted's friends were agog at such a thing, especially when we danced together, as you can imagine. I didn't care, for I know I will not see her for far too long now, and Rose, well you know her, she never gives a fig. Will she ever change? I hope not. I'm glad she has been with me these last three months, though I think Ted is glad we are now alone. I know it is selfish, for she will have to wait another year to sit her masters, but her company has been the sole thing that helped me settle into this new and amazing life.

India, I can't believe it. I'm in India! And married.

The wedding was a simple affair. Rose and I couldn't face a huge to-do without you and Kate. Ted was happy to comply. His circle of acquaintances are mostly business friends, and his true 'family' out here is small, like ours. How I wish you and Kate could have been here, but I know we will see you again soon and can then celebrate together. Ted promises we will return at least every year or other for an extended stay at Riverdell.

It felt perfect, to be marrying in this sublime new place. I remember our talk about missing our mothers on our wedding days, and how we kept you busy all day so that you would not have time to miss yours. Well, I felt closer to my parents out here than I ever did in England. It brought back memories of the world I knew with them. The warmth of Turkey, the flicker of languages I did not understand but loved to listen to, the sense of our being a family bound tighter by isolation from the community around us. Perhaps I have always been destined to travel abroad? Married now and seeing my future in some 'other' place than England, I am deeply grateful to you for the friendship that has brought me to this wonderful place and to your brother.

Ted is well. Happy to be married. Very kind and attentive.

I think he has been lonely out here, and we feel connected by our love for you, for Riverdell, for all that we share. I hope it will be the basis of our sound relationship, which we both know has been a whirlwind.

He works long hours and there is little for me to do in the house. It's still the norm to have servants here, though he calls them house staff. Rose was livid, as you can imagine. Insisted on checking the contracts he had with them all, and their rate of pay. Demanded sick pay and more time off. My God, Ted was fuming with her meddling, but she won in the end. When does she not? She made friends with all of them and encouraged me to get to know them and their families. They are lovely... our housekeeper, Sayali, (Sai for short but only since Rose left!), the laundry and cleaning lady, Aarti, and Ted has a personal assistant, Arjun (poor Ted, he introduced him as his valet and Rose exploded, so we are using personal assistant – is this any better? I'm not sure, but don't ever tell her I said that). They all adored her, of course, and were even sadder to see her go than I. I have set up twice-weekly English lessons to help them improve their reading and writing skills. Rose says I am to begin with private lessons until I feel confident enough in my new skills to take a permanent position. The staff bring their friends and younger siblings, our kitchen is brim full, the twice-weekly sessions will soon grow I suspect.

But, marriage, I keep drifting away...

Before, I would have confided in you my thoughts about our 'relations', how strange it feels to be a wife. But as my husband is your brother, I shall save those thoughts for Kate and Rose, to spare you any discomfort. I hope you and Richard are enjoying your new home and married life, I cannot wait to hear happy news from you.

There is so much to see here. I feel lifted of the strain that has sat on me for the last few years. Bombay is magnificent in one breath and vile in another. You cannot imagine the size of it, the intensity, the noise, the joy, the misery. I am awash with this city. All my woes about health, the slog to finish my degree, they are washed away in the great current of this beautiful monstrosity. I hope this is the start of a fresh chapter in my life, where health will be better, and happiness takes the place of illness. Ted says we are to go to the mountains at the end of March. Kashmir, way up north in the tip of India. It is where he spent his final years in the army, and he has a villa there. He says the monsoon in Bombay is vile, and I will find it exhausting.

My teaching, with all its learning demands, keeps me busy and Rose has left me with a good sense of the city, and of the people who now make up my life. I haven't bonded yet with any of the wives of Ted's friends, there seems a strange reticence between us, but I hope that will change as they grow more used to me. It is only to be expected that they are concerned, as were you, about the swiftness of our romance.

And how swiftly life has changed, Elsa. Only six months ago we were celebrating your and Richard's wedding, now here I am – half a world away, an entire new life, work and marriage to understand. Sometimes I feel overwhelmed with it all and wish with all my heart Rose could have stayed longer, then I look out across the Arabian Sea with its breath-stealing sunsets and think, how lucky am I? To have found love, a home and a family of my own to make.

I will write often, and you must send news too. Much love to your father, please tell him we are happy and hope one day to have his blessing. I hope he is not too disappointed in me. He has been a second father to me for so long, I would hate to lose his kindness. I hope that grandchildren might ease the irritation of our actions and that, with time, we will be once more embraced as his dearest family.

MUCH LOVE,

BETH (THRELFALL!)

2

V igo was kind. His ride along the valley floor as it flowed down from the Pordoi Pass was a ride he would remember forever.

High on the achievement of punishing himself and surviving. Muscles stinging from exhaustion. Legs shaking with burnout. Moth cruised the road, floating into dusk as the villages ghosted past him. The bleak, soaring stone passes of the mountains giving way to a softer life. Birds flitting between spring green trees. Water rushing in thick streams across moss-rich stones. Houses, farms, villages.

You could live somewhere like this.

When the sun dipped towards the high walls he sped up, trying to catch the last shards of day as he rode west and south. The mountains were callous. They snatched the sun away, plunging the valleys into chill. Moth pushed on harder to stay warm. Pulling his head torch over his helmet and turning it on. He diverged from the main road, following the quieter routes through the villages. Gliding past the curves of a river. The noise a comforting challenge to the darkness.

The countryside was invisible by the time he rode into Vigo. He found a narrow road leading away from the river, followed its gentle incline, looking for a quiet space to pitch the tent.

You picked the wrong road. It's getting steeper.

He scanned the road both sides, squinting for a gate or field. Passed through a farmyard sprawled filthy and pungent across the road. A man hailed him in the dark. Moth slowed the bike to a halt, put one foot down. The call was a surprise. The voice firm, but not harsh.

'Buonasera.' He swivelled the light from his headlamp down onto the road.

'Buonasera,' the voice called, and stepped out from the doorway of the barn into the fading edges of Moth's circle of torchlight.

A slim man, with big hands. Moth sniffed the air. A hygienic tang mixed with rich muck. A dairy farmer, doing his last rounds before bed.

Don't make assumptions. Be careful.

'Lunga giornata?' Moth asked.

The farmer laughed at him, 'Sempre!'

Moth smiled and stretched. 'Anch'io.'

'Inglese?'

'Si, Inglese,' Moth confirmed.

The man looked at his bike, back at him. 'You early for the mountains.'

'I am, too early, but so...' Moth searched for the word, not wanting to give in to English, '... cosi alletante.'

The farmer laughed at him. It was something he had learned from James and Leon, farmers laughed more than they frowned, and they loved to laugh at the stupidity of others. Moth shrugged his shoulders.

'You look for hotel?' he asked Moth.

'Non, non,' Moth said, 'un posto dormire.' He patted the bag behind him. 'Tenda.'

'Aah,' the man said. He looked along the road, thinking it through for Moth, pursed his mouth and squinted in consideration.

'Vieni, vieni.' He beckoned Moth to follow him.

Moth gripped the handlebar in doubt. He was tired enough to take anything on offer. He dismounted, pushing the bike along behind. The farmer walked along the road a way, stopping outside another barn. Opposite it were a field and a sagging wooden gate, tied with string where the hinges had dropped, the bolt missing its latch.

He gestured broadly, 'here is good.'

'Si?' asked Moth.

'Si, si,' he responded, 'maybe...'

'Qui e buono,' Moth interjected before he could change his mind, pushing his bike toward the gate. 'Thank you.'

'No, no,' the farmer protested. He pointed at the barn they stood outside, 'intendevo, you sleep here.'

'Qui?'

'Si, qui... is dry, warm,' and he shrugged at the skies beyond their vision in the darkness. The global concern of the farmer.

'Sono molto grato,' Moth told him with feeling. The man smiled at him again. Showing lines full of hard work and long years, crinkling and rippling in the high barn lights.

'Prego, amico, prego.'

Moth stood beside the bike as the guy pushed open one of the large doors. The barn was filled to the brim with straw and hay. It smelled musty and comforting. He wheeled his bike in, propped it against the wall and let the man show him where he could make a soft place and sleep.

'Come un re!' Moth told him. 'Grazie.'

'Controllalo,' he replied as he walked away, 'e il mio mondo.' He waved a hand to indicate the vastness of the barn that could not be seen. Moth understood.

It's his world, you must look after it.

He knew how that felt. The bike might not be much. But it was everything to him. The farmer pulled the door to and left, walking with a spring in his step. Good people liked helping others but were careful with it. They stood out from the manipulative arses of the world.

The ones that give too much and ask too little in return.

So, Vigo was kind. He had a free roof and a soft bed for the night. He was hungry, with not much food to choose from and no chance to use the stove. He emptied his panniers and laid all his kit out, checking it to take his mind off hunger. He was unwrapping the tent to air when the door opened again. He turned, tension creeping into his shoulders. A woman stepped through. Her arms laden with a covered tray. She stared at him in silence, mutiny in her face.

The farmer has a wife.

Moth stayed holding the tent, waiting for her to break the silence. Leon's wife had taught him how to handle a farmer's wife.

In silence. With a whole load of respect and not an ounce of bullshit.

It worked. After a long minute of considering her husband's stupidity, she lowered her chest from its fighting stance and held out the tray in offering. Moth walked over, took the tray from her hands. She lifted the cloth and chattered away at him in fast Italian that Moth had no chance of grasping. She showed him where there was a water tap, found a bucket for him for the night. She beamed at him and patted his cheek before skipping back out the door, a load lighter than she'd walked in. He'd done enough to spare her husband a roasting all night.

Moth sat cross-legged on a pile of loose straw and drooled over the tray. Every mouthful needed attention. Warm porridge made with milk so thick it was cream. Topped with homemade jam that soured and sweetened his tongue at the same time. He licked the bowl clean, adoring its curves. Turned to the bread and cheese that lay next to it. The strong flavours mixing with crisp fluffy lightness. Overwhelming his mouth all at once, sharpened by the crush of ripe, sable grapes.

You jammy git. What did you do to deserve this?

He'd cycled over a mountain. Outwitted a snowstorm. Found free harbour. He deserved it.

A steaming mug of milky chocolate, sugar thick on the bottom of the cup. There was a plump furry peach, he left it for the morning. Feeling its flesh prickle beneath his fingers. Lay back on the straw surrounded by his unpacked bags and let the sugar rush over him, his body rocking.

His mind whirled to the roof. He longed for the open sky and the stars. Burrowed into the straw and his sleeping bag. Curling up in its warmth like a calf.

You could spend a week in here.

He was warm, dry and full. He was living as he wanted.

You're invincible.

He could not be touched. Opening the notebook, flipping the reducing stub of pencil over, he rubbed the former entry out. Nine days ago, he'd called home. Written down the meeting with Kit. Knowing he wouldn't go. He wrote across the faint imprint left on the page. Day 266. 24th March 2013. Vigo di Fassa.

About time.

He closed it with satisfaction and settled down.

It was a good way to go to sleep. The distant smell of cattle floating to him between the musty straw and dull rat droppings of the barn. But the caffeine and sugar made for interesting dreams and one farm merged into another, taking him all too easily back to France and Ventoux.

He'd ridden up the long farm drive in trepidation. It was the only one he'd passed with a sign outside, travailleurs necessaires. A sign that looked weary, left out too long in the sun.

Moth wasn't sure they still needed workers, but he went anyway. Worn out by the long ride south. Stripped clean as the empty plants. Numb, from trying to get away from the memories. Quiet, when Leon came out of the house and told him he was too late, the harvest was done.

That finished you good and proper.

Moth looked at Leon in mute exhaustion, stared down at the bike beneath his hand, unable to climb back on. He wheeled it about and paused, trying to start that walk back down the drive. Leon sighed and called him back in English. They had a stilted conversation. What could he do, what experience did he have? Moth's French unconvincing but persistent. Leon addressing him in English.

It was a farce.

Moth kept trying. Perhaps that was why Leon gave him a bed in the bunkhouse.

He took pity on you, who wouldn't have?

A shared bathroom and kitchen that felt a palace after two months on the bike and sleeping rough. The few other workers left on the farm mocked his cooking skills for the first week. When they realised that he could cook nothing other than porridge they stopped mocking and taught him how to cook. Sautéed vegetables and roasted chickens. Garlic and olive oil staining into his clumsy fingers.

He was set to work in the packing sheds. Overwhelmed with the abundance of the plant. Hands fumbling in ignorance and the sudden shock of a new life. The intense scent sweet, hypnotic, verging on the repellent. His bike-callused hands nervous of the tough stems, the tiny hairs, the soft swells of the buds. Exhausting hours of drying, sorting, packing while he tried to put the past few months behind him. To forget England, his parents, the trip that brought him here.

Borts.

Outside, in the intense brightness, trying to convince Leon that his tractor skills were up to the job. Working for James had given him some experience, but it was back to front in France. He hit two walls before he got the knack of the gears and went forward. Leon swore at him in bad English and kicked a broken brick across the yard in disgust.

Off the bike, he'd felt reduced. Everything he did, had done, would ever do, wrong. Futility swelling up between the broken walls and the empty plants of the fields. Worry gnawing at him inside.

What are you going to do next?

Box by box the flowers were packed up and despatched. One by one the rest of the crew moved on. To harvest other crops. On other farms.

Where are you going to go next?

The noise in the bunkhouse dwindled with the cheerful farewells, until he was alone. Adjusting to silence again as he cooked in the too big kitchen. By the end of two weeks, he was sweeping the barns out, and Leon was avoiding him. The couple in the bungalow at the end of the drive ignoring him. It was their full-time job.

It's time to go. It's time to go.

But he didn't know where. He didn't know why. Lost, useless, he stood at the end of the curving field. Holding a sprig of lavender in his hands. Pulling it through his finger and thumb in a repetitive, soothing motion. Looking out across the silent plants.

What did you think you were going to find here?

Perhaps his mother had done this as a child, somewhere not far from where he stood. What might his life have been if she'd not gone to England, not met his father, not stayed there?

Died there.

Trying to bring her back from the flowerless plants. Thinking how Isabelle had set him on the path of that memory. The Mont leering down on him in barren white indifference. The huge mountain daunting him. The empty bushes mocking him. He walked back to the bunkhouse. The jobs he could pretend to do, done past perfection. Leon nowhere to be seen. He found the bike in the bunkhouse shed, untouched since he'd arrived. He'd been glad to leave the trip behind.

Leave Borts behind.

It smelled of dry cat piss. Old but catching the back of his throat. He grabbed a handful of bread and cheese, a bottle of water and wheeled the bike out of the farmyard.

This feels weird.

The bike unsettled without the panniers. He played with the road, with the pedals, with the brakes. Feeling the wind

on his face again. Traffic passing by at tourist speed. The
Mont rising in front of him, growing larger as he travelled
towards it. His muscles aching with the forgotten effort. He
felt awry in the saddle. The once familiar discomfort of hard
leather beneath his buttocks. The long saddle nose beneath
his balls. Legs weak. Back aching. Muscles slackened and
loose.

Do you really want to do this again?

It had felt good. Not to be that person. He'd been peaceful
in the work.

The bike reconnected him to the ride. Asking with each
rotation, what could have been different? The pain in his legs
and the thoughts in his head. Tussling together and taking
hold. He wanted to give up.

Go back to the farm, try to be useful.

But he couldn't. The work was done. The bunkhouse
would be closed until next season. He had to go. Somewhere.

Even if it's only up the Mont for now.

The road took him away from the fields, rising through
trees. He lost the view. Life reduced again. To his heart
pounding. His body sweating. His mind churning. Breathing.
Motion. Pain.

He focused on the motion. One leg smooth after the
other. Sweeping round the turns in the road. Digging into the
next uphill. The straights getting shorter. The bends getting
sharper. The road sweeping into curves and arcs that
bounded the gradients. The thin grass fading to limestone
chalk. The sun getting stronger, the breeze increasing to fight
it. Heat against chill.

Mind over matter. You've got this.

His legs screaming at him. The road turning away from
the north, heading back south-west, into the late afternoon

sun. His pace slowed. Cars flew past him, enjoying the views on their way up, racing towards the tower on the summit. The great red and white mast. He resisted the view expanding at his side. Denying it. Slowing to a crawl round the last bends. To a breathless dead-legged wobbling halt on the final turn.

You can't get this close and walk the final few metres.

He had nothing left to cycle on. His legs shaking and useless. His foot touched the tarmac. He stumbled off the frame, walking past the buildings, the cars, their drivers. All staring at him. Refusing to look back.

Do not give them the satisfaction.

On up to the far end of the road where it started down the other side. Until he was above the old chapel, looking out over its roof. Only away from prying eyes did he set the bike down, sit on the coarse ground and look in exhaustion at the view.

The great distance stretching out from the summit. The late afternoon sun full and vivid on the fields and hills. His body waves of moisture and heat. He drank, savouring the warm water, tasting the salt from his lips as he swallowed. Eyes drinking in the scale he'd earned the pleasure of.

One agonising mile at a time. He'd forgotten the reward. The ownership. He watched the drivers getting out of their cars, wandering along the paths that wound across the summit, their phones raised to take in the views. Looking at themselves. Look, I did this. Photo snapped, climbing back in their cars, moving on to the next achievement. Moth savoured his moment.

You did this. Yourself. Alone.

He watched the view stretch out, an arc of choices. Where to go next?

You can't go north.

He'd come that way and would never go back. He'd done it, arrived, not found what he'd wanted.

Lost more on the way.

Now all he had was the vast space before him.

You can't go south, you're practically at the sea.

He wanted the land to tell him what to do. He wanted an answer. He looked at the chapel, asked God for inspiration and saw the flash of tourists' selfies. His plan redundant. Knowing he had to get back on the bike and go somewhere. Or nowhere.

East or west. Pick either. Anywhere is better than nowhere.

It was a long ride back to the farm. Shadows hugging the bottom of the hill. Dull after the high of the vista. Hands tired from squeezing the brakes. The inky sky infused with the scent of the sun-warmed fields. He wheeled up the drive, wondering if he'd been missed. The bunkhouse rearing up, charred dark against the sky.

The lights were on in the farmhouse and he headed that way to explain. Paused outside the window to the farm office, saw Leon and Leanne, the pc in front of them. Images scrolling down, face after face in a long list. Leanne's worried hand squeezing Leon's shoulder. They were looking for someone.

Don't wait around to find out if it's you.

He left in darkness. Packing with swift frightened hands. Tidying up with a guilty conscience. Scribbled a note. Thank you without goodbyes. Before he'd left, risking the extra moment, he'd gone to the packing shed and found a solitary sprig lost beneath the packing tables, squeezing it into the cigarette case.

He had pedalled away into the night, heading left at the

bottom of the drive because he'd gone right on the trip up the Mont. Going on instinct when there wasn't time to build a plan. Hoping a new plan would grow on the way.

West was good enough.

Deep asleep in the barn in Vigo, Moth was too exhausted to resist the memories. Wrapped up in his sleeping bag and a false cocoon of hot food. Oblivious to the chill seeping into his exhausted body as his heat rose to the high ceiling, missing the warm cocoon of the tent.

ISABELLE FOUND herself hijacked by Riverdell. By a dusty curve of the banister, a soft joint in the windowpanes, a painful crease of the curtains.

All of them astounded at her sudden importance. A clamouring call for consequence reaching towards the reeling emptiness inside. Asking her what she was going to do? With the banister, the windows, the curtains. She, Isabelle, their new owner. Until the sound of feet approaching pulled her back and set her free, dazed and blinking away the bemusement.

Feet seemed purposeful wherever she lingered, so she found herself retreating ever more to her workroom. The unfamiliarity of life made bearable by a needle between her fingers. The lack of proper work overlaid with pretence. Pushing away discomfort in opening the pages of her dusty old needlework books to chase down what was needed to hold two fraying pieces of fabric together. Reordering her thoughts in the details of stitches she had not practiced for many years.

She had picked apart one of the silk curtains with great intentions in the hollow, echoing days after Elsa's announcement. When her desperate wish to be busy collided with her apparent lack of usefulness. They had lain ever since, their guts opened out, the old fabric twisted this way and that with the hope that a resolution might be lying on one side or the other of the disintegrating fabric and the dirt encrusted lining.

Their absence from the French window, along with the increased emptiness of the room, let more light in than she had known for years. As the summer expanded into longer days the windows stayed open and she found herself wandering out into the garden, away to the river. Even the river seemed to be watching her with intense curiosity.

'Isabelle?'

She turned away from the river toward the house, calling, 'here.'

Kate appeared from the other side of the willow tree.

'Lunchtime,' she said. 'Elsa needs you.'

'Again?'

'Yep, happens every day about this time.'

'I didn't mean lunch.'

'Neither did I, dullard.' Kate took her arm. 'Come on, I know how onerous this vast inheritance is. Sorry to be dragging you back to it.'

'I didn't mean it like that,' Isabelle said.

Kate guided them to the tall windows, squeezing her arm in kindness. 'I know,' she said. 'Just trying to make light of it.'

'I'm sorry,' Isabelle said. 'I'm trying to help, honestly, but whatever I touch seems to unravel to useless pieces I can't make any sense of.'

'Life can do that sometimes,' Kate consoled her. 'In my experience, if you wait it out, it will eventually stop stalling.'

'I never thought of you as the patient sort.' Isabelle felt

the house rearing over them as they entered it. 'I thought you were more, grab the raging bull by the horns and pull it on track.'

'By choice, yes, but sometimes a bull refuses to budge. You have to outwait it.'

'Elsa seems to be enjoying herself anyway,' Isabelle suggested, trying to encompass the sweeping changes that had taken place in the past fortnight since Elsa had dropped her bombshell. The closing of the B&B, the absence of guests, Moth's return to school, Kit and Hester's despatch to Swansea.

'Yes, she seems most invigorated by it all.' Kate's voice was neutral. Isabelle could sense a tone of avoidance in it. She stepped into the workroom.

'I suppose Nat's enthusiasm is carrying her along.' Isabelle prodded a little harder. If Elsa had hoped for approval from Nat, she had not been prepared for the over-whelming joy that had erupted when Nat was made aware of the developments.

'Sheer energy is carrying it along,' Kate said. 'I hope they don't all fall flat on their faces when they finally sit down.'

Isabelle leant across her table, placing the scattered scraps she had been toying with into a tidy pile. Trying to look purposeful in front of Kate.

'Moth's due back tonight,' she said. Kate raised her eyebrows but remained silent.

Kate was avoiding engaging, with either the room, her activity there, or the talk about Elsa. Isabelle knew she was hiding something. It had been the same since the morning Elsa had announced her plans. The same morning Elsa had spent an hour in the sitting room talking to Kit and Kate, leaving Isabelle to sign documents in the library. The same day that Kit, tight-lipped, had disappeared to Swansea, taking Hester and her fury with him. The same day that Kate had attached herself to Isabelle's side with a deeply disturbing dose of reserved opinion.

'It'll be good to see him, make a nice break from all this packing up,' Kate demanded her attention.

'Hmm.' Isabelle fussed with the scraps some more. Moth's return to school had been in the dazed part of her reaction, when the world had seemed to speed up, and she slowed down. He'd left without a word to her, as Kit had, and though he'd been home for the weekends he spent all his time with Nat. 'It will be good for Nat to see him.'

'She's barely noticed he's been gone,' Kate said. 'Honestly, I'm sure she thinks this move is going to be one long holiday.'

'I think she's missed him. We all have.'

'Yes, the little sod,' Kate said. 'Running out on me just as I'd got him trained up a bit.'

'Still bitter? He is supposed to be at school, remember.' Isabelle folded a ragged-edged piece of velvet into a reluctant square, the nap sliding off itself.

'I can remember he's a schoolboy. Problem is no one else seems to.' Kate tapped her fingers on the calico top, nudging her to greater speed. 'Elsa seems to think he has the right to tell her what he wants to do now, regardless of her own opinion.'

'She's respecting his wishes.' Isabelle tidied her scissors, pincushion and tape measure up, coiling its smooth worn yellow ribbon round her fingers.

'She's given up on him,' Kate said. 'And is justifying it by trying to be the perfect grandmother to Nat.'

'Shall we go for lunch?'

'Oh, now you're hungry?' Kate peered across the room. 'When all this is done, you might want to rethink this space.'

'What do you mean?'

'You're rattling around in it now, and you'll have a whole house to play with. You might put it to better use. I never realised how much rubbish you were storing down here.'

'It isn't rubbish.' Isabelle tried to make it a statement not a protest but, even to her, the room looked dejected. The sunlight lighting up the walls in desperate need of a coat of paint. 'Besides, I thought you wanted me to think about doing something else in my life.'

Kate went to respond, grimaced and, as Isabelle watched, composed her thoughts, 'I did and, apparently, I was right. You made a start on thinking about other opportunities and wham, along comes this massive change with any number of opportunities.'

Isabelle wasn't convinced. Kate seemed to be saying one thing and encouraging her to do another daily, but she managed to accompany it with a strangled tone that suggested she was being immensely patient with her. That she understood Isabelle was in a brain fog. Which, as she did indeed feel brain-fogged, seemed hard to argue with.

'I don't want to think about it all,' Isabelle said. 'When I try and think about what's happening, I get freaked out.'

'Which is as I say,' Kate said, moving towards the door. 'Best to wait it out. Come on, let's go eat and see what useless artefacts of her life Elsa is struggling to justify packing up.'

Isabelle followed her, pausing as she turned to pull the door to. The room did look sorry for itself, perhaps there was something else to be done with it. But where would she move all her sewing stuff? The machines she could never part with, or the table, or the worn old stool she had perched on all these years. It caught her attention with its curved wooden seat.

'Isabelle!' Kate called from the stairs. 'Come on.'

Isabelle closed the door and turned down the corridor. 'Coming.'

THE HOURS between lunch and when Elsa left to collect Nat had become a steady routine of sorting. It was a huge house to pack up and not so huge a house to move to, and Elsa seemed unable to pack anything without her approval. Which was emotionally withering, as Isabelle hadn't realised how much stuff she was attached to without believing she had any right to claim it. Kate mediated, trailing behind them with a large notebook in hand, pen poised over the page, making it evident to both that her patience with the task was running out.

'I really don't mind,' Isabelle protested, for what felt the thousandth time. 'It's all yours to choose Elsa, you don't have to ask my permission.'

'It goes.' Kate scratched a note on her pad. 'Next?'

They were in the dining room, going through the small items of furniture, and the china and glassware in the cupboards. Elsa wanted to leave the largest bulk of furniture and take the details. Isabelle kept trying to persuade her to take the larger furniture too, not to have to buy new furniture. When they couldn't decide it meant a phone call to Kit, which Kate fielded. Elsa had tried a few and couldn't face the brutality of his opinion. Having been put in a position of power he was using it to the extreme.

'What about this?' Elsa asked, a hand upon the back of the slipper chair that sat in the window.

Isabelle's heart jerked. She opened her mouth to try and say yes.

'That stays,' Kate said.

'No, please,' Isabelle said, feeling awful. 'Take it if you want it, of course!'

'No, not if it means something to you,' Elsa said.

'It stays,' Kate repeated.

'I really don't mind,' Isabelle protested again.

Elsa looked at Kate, she held the pen over her inventory and looked back with raised eyebrows.

'No, I think we'll leave it here,' Elsa said.

'It stays,' Kate said for the final time and marked it on her pad. 'Next.'

The ordeal ended when Elsa looked at her watch, gasped in horror and fled for the school gates, Kate collapsed on the sofa in the guest sitting room in relief saying, 'tea, I need tea,' and Isabelle went to put the kettle on.

If the preceding few hours had been intolerable this had become her salve. For a little under an hour the house was theirs. It carried the faintest scent of what was to come. Not enough to taste or satisfy, a mere fragrance on the air that she could breathe in but not catch, before it evaporated for the next twenty-four hours.

She took a tea tray back and put it down on the table between the two sofas. Her time in here with Moth had left a different memory to enjoy. Although they all still called it the guest dining room, it was now defunct, for there were no guests. Yet neither was it part of the family home they had grown to know. Devoid of any solid purpose it had become the new timid heart of the house in disarray. It had become her and Kate's favourite place to relax.

'As she's not taking it, I think you should burn this.' Kate slapped the deep plum sofa beside her, scowling at the dust it caused. 'It's the most pompous looking, bloody uncomfortable sofa in the house.'

'That's what it was chosen for.' Isabelle poured them both a cup of tea and sat down, pulling a leg up beneath her.

'It's got to go,' Kate said. 'You should tell Kit to sell it, to give it away even. This is a wonderful room. You should empty it and start afresh.'

Isabelle drank her tea. It would take a few moments for Kate to stop thinking about the house, to relax from the afternoon's cataloguing.

'I think Kit's got enough to do without adding any more to his plate.'

'Kit's never got enough to do,' Kate said. 'He's horrible if he's bored.'

'He's not the only one,' Isabelle said to her cup.

'Fat chance of that,' Kate scowled at her.

'How are the staff disputes going?

'Oh don't!' Kate said. 'I would bash all their heads together if Mike hadn't banned me from interceding.'

'Well, you put him in command. Seems fair to let him sort it.'

'He's very different to me. The staff aren't used to this new touchy-feely team approach, building resilience or whatever. They want to be told what to do.'

'They're used to being told what to do,' Isabelle said. 'It doesn't mean it won't work just because it's different.'

'If you're trying to say I'm outdated,' Kate told her with feeling. 'You should know I find that mildly offensive.'

'As long as it's mildly, I can live with that.'

Kate snorted at her, kicked her shoes off and pulled both legs up on the sofa, trying to wriggle herself into a more comfortable position and giving up. Kate's painted toes gleaming at her from the sofa. Their bold magenta a flamboyant harmony with the sofa. The mules abandoned on the floor a well-worn moulded cover to the contents. Kate's shoes had always fascinated her. When she was growing up, when she and Hester used to play dressing up, Elsa's courts had always been Hester's choice. Isabelle would run downstairs and beg Kate to borrow her shoes, struggling to get back up the stairs in their slip sliding hugeness.

'Well, he seems happy to deal with the distress he's causing,' Kate was talking about her manager again, Isabelle tried to focus, 'and I suppose it needs to work his way, if I'm going to step back.'

'And are you?' Isabelle asked. 'I mean, you've talked about doing this before but never done it.'

'I haven't got much choice.' Kate thumped the sofa beside her again, waved the cloud of dust away. 'There's all this mess to sort, and I'll never see Elsa if I can't free up more time to get away. Plus, I want to have enough spare to keep an eye on you too.'

'Maybe not having much choice is something we both need.'

Kate's eyes peeped over the rim of her cup, her mouth hidden. Isabelle could see the muscles at the side of her face tightening.

'You might enjoy the change.' Isabelle tried to keep the vindictive smug tone out of her voice. 'Once you get used to it, whatever it brings.'

'Maybe you will too,' Kate retorted.

'I enjoy this,' Isabelle said.

'What?'

'Sitting here with you, knowing there's no one else in the

house,' Isabelle told her. 'Not wondering who's lurking round a corner or going to walk through the door.' Kate watched her with quiet eyes. Isabelle couldn't fathom what was going on behind them. 'I know it's selfish, but I hope you don't spend too much time in Swansea, not right at the beginning. I don't know how it's going to feel when they've all gone. I don't want the house to be empty all the time. I like having you here with me.'

Kate dropped the cup to her lap, her shoulders notching down a level with the tea.

'This place is going to feel monstrous when it's empty.' Kate let her eyes follow the filigree plaster ceiling architrave. 'It's too big. I mean, I know why Elsa stopped the business, you couldn't have guests here with all this going on. Elsa ravaging the house piecemeal, it's a bloody mess, but I'm not sure it was wise. You're going to need to fill the place somehow.'

'I'm sure Kit will make sense of it all,' Isabelle said. 'When he gets here.'

'Don't you have any idea what you want to do with it?' Kate's voice had that uncomfortable tone to it again, the one where Isabelle knew she was saying the opposite of what she wanted to say. 'If you let Kit start telling you what to do, you'll never shut him up.'

Isabelle considered the enormous room. She knew she wanted to do something different with it and thoughts lurked like sketches in her head. Beyond the open door, it overwhelmed her. The hugeness of the house. What to move out, what to move in, how to use it. How to make money, how to keep a house this big, how to... she shook her head, trying to push the expanding thoughts away. She had to keep bringing it back to something she could manage, one detail at a time.

'We should get rid of this.' Her hand stroked across the ornate bloodied pattern of the floral velvet sofa. 'You're right, it's horrible.'

Kate picked up her phone.

'What are you doing?' Isabelle asked her.

'Calling Kit,' Kate said. 'I'm not going to let you go back on that decision.'

Isabelle smiled, watching Kate's face when Kit answered the call. Blue eyes dancing, her spare hand flying up to emphasise her point, her voice returning to its normal tone. The afternoon sun coming through the window, warming Isabelle's back.

She left Kate talking and went to look at the river through the window. Moth would be back tonight, on the train. One more week of school and he'd be back for the summer, at least until he left for Swansea. Three more weeks, four at tops and the house would be empty. She would be looking out the windows at the river alone. Her reflection in the window was drowned out by the strong sun pouring through it. She liked the evening when the windows were dark in the house. She found herself walking past them late at night, wondering if the windows were watching her back. Assessing the potential of their new owner passing across the panes.

'He says about bloody time,' Kate's words impinged on her reverie.

'What?'

'About the furniture,' Kate said. 'We're to take photos and send them to him, he'll get it sorted.'

'Of course he will.' Isabelle blinked away the bright sunshine, looking back at Kate, who was wobbling in her vision. 'Poor man, he has to sort everything.'

'He's loving it.' Kate brushed away her concern. 'He'll be insufferable for a few months. The power will go to his head.'

'He's working incredibly hard,' Isabelle protested.

'Which is what he loves most,' Kate reminded her. 'Worry about yourself, not him. He's got Hester to keep an eye on him.'

'That's just weird,' Isabelle said. 'I can't get used to those two working together.'

'It keeps them away from us. Elsa is a stealth genius sometimes.'

'Yes,' Isabelle said, squinting across the distance, trying to see her. 'I think you went to the same school, didn't you?'

'I don't know what you're talking about,' Kate said, standing up, picking up her notepad, and flicking through it. 'Right, come on, clear those tea things away, let's take some photos of this stuff before Elsa gets back. I reckon Kit will have it sold by the end of the day. Now, how about those curtains too?'

'What?'

'Well, you can't tell me you like them,' Kate said. 'There's next to nothing in here to your taste. You should go for a clean slate, start one room at time.'

'I can't sell it all, what will Elsa say?'

'Elsa has listed what she wants.' Kate looked at her list. 'It will take about three boxes, everything else is yours to choose what you do with. This is the perfect room to start with, most of it was only here for the guests anyway. Admit it, you hate those curtains. Move out of the way, come on, I want a good photo for Kit.'

Isabelle moved away from the window, cleared the tea things, and went back to the kitchen. She looked out of the window to see Elsa and Nat pull up on the driveway.

Her moment of pleasure had gone.

'Hi.'

Isabelle jumped. She had been lost in the intricacy of her stitches. She looked up to find Moth stood in the open window from the garden.

'Hi,' she said, the needle quivering between her finger and thumb.

'You busy?'

'Avoiding busy.'

'Not easy,' he said, walking into the room and over to the table.

'You've been out early.' She threaded the needle twice into her top and sat back on the stool, away from the book spread in front of her. He looked as fresh as the morning, damp with a warm glowing hue rising in his face.

'Yeah,' he said. 'I figured I better get up early to get any peace from Nat.'

'She's missed you.'

'You reckon?' he asked. 'I don't think she's had time to miss me.'

'She's missed being able to talk to you.'

'She certainly has a lot to say.'

'How was the hill?' she asked, glancing back out the window.

'Dewy,' Moth said, looking down at his damp trouser legs. 'But amazing.' He leaned against the table, picking at the flustered edge.

'How's school going?' Isabelle asked. He grimaced at her, shrugged his shoulders. He didn't want to be there, it was obvious.

'You'll go to Swansea for the summer?' she asked.

'That's what Elsa wants.' Moth couldn't have sounded more unconvinced. 'How's the big change going? You getting any more used to it yet?'

'No.'

'It must get easier though, right?'

'No.' She was tired of people asking her the same question, in tones that dripped with the assumption that she was feigning humility. She was sick of pretending to be adjusting. Coping. 'It just gets weirder.'

'Yeah, I bet,' he said, grinning at her. 'You don't look the landowner type to me.'

'Don't mock me, Moth,' she said. 'Please, I can't bear it.'

He grinned even more. 'Hard not to, I can't think of anyone less suited to take this on.'

'Yes, I know. But people keep pretending it's the best thing that ever happened to me, and I just need to realise that.'

'I can sympathise with that,' Moth told her. 'People keep acting like losing my parents was the worst thing that ever happened to me.'

She was stunned into silence.

'I guess people don't want to hear the truth though?' He stared down her discomfort, holding her eyes. 'You're supposed to feel a certain way, right? Which makes it harder to say how you do feel.'

She felt brittle, knowing there were many ways she could respond to that statement and crushed by the options. 'I guess that's the difference between people and friends,' she said. 'You can tell friends the truth.'

He looked away. She'd disappointed him. Isabelle felt the draughts of the room on her neck, wishing she'd spoken with more confidence. She had no way of knowing how to return to the place they had known. When the house had belonged to them and they had belonged to it and nothing had seemed out of place. Elsa's bombshell had pushed them even further apart than Kit's arrival. To a place where Isabelle thought she must have imagined the sense that she and Moth had... had what? Had something in common? Could craft their own lives? Understood the glory of freedom. Of travel. Of belonging outside the family. But not alone. She lowered her head, ashamed of her own stupidity. Wondering if Kit might have been right, that whatever she'd thought she and Moth understood of each other was something altogether wrong in fact. The comfort she had felt in his company, the sense that she was not a failure, the ease of sharing space together, had all gone. Leaving only the emptying distance between them. Her, the owner of Riverdell. Him, a boy going back to school.

'This place looks bare,' he said.

'You wouldn't be the first to mention it,' Isabelle said. 'I feel redundant down here, but not sure what to do up there.'

'Stuck in the hallway?'

'A little bit, perhaps.'

'I wanted to ask a favour,' he said, shifting tack. 'I need somewhere to keep my stuff, and I don't want to take it all to Swansea. I wondered if I could keep it here for a bit, until I know what's happening? The bike, you know, and the tent and stuff.'

'Of course!' Isabelle felt the same lump of dread in her stomach when Elsa started treating her as the one in charge. 'You can leave it for as long as you want, you're always welcome here. You don't need to ask.'

'You haven't got your head round it all yet, huh?' Moth asked.

'I hate people asking me stuff like this.' Isabelle took the needle out of her jumper, stabbed it into the pincushion. 'As though I'm supposed to instantly become this person they want me to be. To become Elsa.'

'You are this person, in one way. I've got to ask whoever owns the place to keep some stuff here, right? But that doesn't make you anyone else, it doesn't mean you have to be like Elsa.' His hand was rubbing the calico along an old cut, fluffing up the loose threads. 'You're still you. You'll get that once they all leave.'

She felt small inside. Moth was half her age, and seemed to have found all his conviction, where she had none.

'All I'm saying is,' his hand stilled, smoothing the surface of the cut over, 'you don't have to be or do anything unless you want to. You can't see that now, but you will.'

'I wish I had your confidence.'

'I didn't have it either, he said. 'I needed to get away from Nat, and all this, to work it out.'

'And now you know what you want to do?'

'No, not entirely,' he said. 'But I know it's my choice and, even if I have to wait for other people to realise it, I'm not going to be the person they want me to be. Some devastated kid whose parents died in a drink-driving accident.'

'I never wanted you to be that.' Isabelle crossed her arms over her stomach, feeling the fluttering inside return that had disappeared as Moth walked out the study on that Monday morning, crushed by the signature she had put on the documents to assume ownership of Riverdell. A tingling sense that you could be who you wanted to be, as Moth said.

'Not you, I know,' he said. 'But the world at large.' He pulled himself up on a deep breath and stood back from the table. Pushed himself away from it, as though he'd strayed into deeper waters than he'd meant to. 'I have to go find Nat. I'll see you later.'

She watched the heavy door swinging shut behind him.

IF ISABELLE HAD HOPED Moth would bring a reprieve to the house packing, she was wrong. If anything, he seemed determined to prove himself invaluable to both Elsa and Kate. Between them and Nat's enthusiasm, Isabelle seemed to spend most of the weekend watching him from a distance. Feeling like her last thread had cut itself while she wasn't looking and taken with it any normal grasp on time she had ever had. Returning to the workroom to find it bare and cavernous.

'We need you to come and pack the curtains up,' he told her, sticking his head in round the doorway an hour after lunch on Sunday. Clinging onto the door without coming inside.

'What?' she looked up from the silk curtains in confusion, letting their crisped hem fall to the table.

'Kit's sold all the furniture and the curtains, and they need to go this afternoon.'

'All of it?'

'From the guest sitting-room,' Moth told her, laughing at her horror. 'Kate said you knew about this, but she's stuck at the bistro and can't come. She said to tell you to help. Sorry, ask you.'

'You mean tell me,' Isabelle said. 'I'm coming.' She went to find the roll of plastic to bag them in, her scissors and wide tape. 'Moth?' He'd already gone.

She made her way upstairs, carrying the heavy slippery roll of packing plastic herself. The guest sitting room was in mayhem, Elsa and Nat were wrapping the china and glasses up in paper and boxing them. Moth pulling the contents out and spreading them on the floor faster than they could pack.

'Kit's sold the lot to someone opening up a bed and breakfast.' Elsa was in breathless agitation. 'What a fantastic opportunity for them.' Moth stood up and went to spread the stepladders ready at the window, waiting for her. 'Moth will help you pack the curtains. The van is coming to collect in about an hour.'

'An hour!' Isabelle wailed.

They all grinned at her and kept on packing.

'It's a good job Kit's not here,' she complained. 'And Kate, for that.'

'Best stop moaning and get on with it,' Moth told her. 'You going up or am I?'

'I'll take them down,' Isabelle said. 'You take the weight when I unhitch.'

'Oh, I must vacuum the furniture,' Elsa announced, springing up from the floor.

'I don't think it's critical,' Isabelle said from the top of the ladder.

'Nonsense,' Elsa said. 'I can't have them going to a new owner with bits of dirt under the cushions. Nat, keep packing, mind you don't cut yourself on anything.'

Isabelle worked her way down the ladder, dressing and tying the curtains. She unhitched them, dropped them down to Moth and between them they wrestled them into plastic and wrapped them up. She moved the ladder across, climbed up and started the next curtain. She'd moved down three rungs when the front doorbell rang.

'Aah!' Elsa cried. 'They can't be here already.'

'I'll go,' Moth said.

Isabelle tried to speed up even more, and Elsa ran to see if Nat had much left to finish.

Moth walked back in with Lou, Fred and Ed cramming the doorway behind her.

'Hi all,' Lou called. 'We're early.'

'Oh, Lou!' Elsa cried in gratitude. She went over and gave the woman a hug. 'Thank God it's you, we had no idea who was turning up.'

'Well, I'm glad Kit's giving you a hard time too,' Lou told her. 'He's a sodding nightmare, oops, sorry,' she added, seeing Nat in the corner. 'To be frank, it's nice to get away from him for an afternoon. Hi, Izz,' she said, looking up the ladder. 'Hey, Moth.'

'Mmph,' Isabelle mumbled past the tie in her mouth.

'Right,' Lou looked at the room, weighing it all up. 'Ed, you help pack with Nat. Fred, you get those tables and chairs loaded up first. Moth, you help Isabelle. Elsa, I'll finish that job.'

'What do I do?' Elsa asked, stepping back from the vacuum with relief.

'Make tea, of course,' Lou said. 'It's been a shitty... sorry... long drive from Swansea.'

'He's sent you up from Swansea?' Isabelle asked, taking the tie out of her mouth and passing it behind the wadded folds of fabric her hands were struggling to hold against her chest.

Lou nodded. 'Two hired vans. Fred and I are taking some of the other furniture back down there. Ed's taking this lot on up to Yorkshire, he got the short straw.'

'I don't mind,' Ed said, handing wrapped glasses to Nat to box. 'Saves being back down there with Flash.'

'Flash?' Moth asked from the floor, where he was taping curtains in plastic.

'Flash Gordon,' Lou said.

'Ah-ah!' both Fred and Ed called out together in voices that rang through the echoing room, 'King of the Universe!'

Moth looked bemused. Isabelle grinned, she'd heard it before.

'It's an old TV thing,' Lou said. 'Kit's nickname. As in Flash Gordon, kitchen spray. No? Ok, now we feel ancient. Keep packing.'

'Is Kit being vile?' Isabelle asked.

'No, just very, very focused,' Lou said. 'Honestly, I don't think he's slept much this last fortnight, and he gets more productive with each day. You might want to avoid him for a few weeks.'

'Poor you,' Isabelle said.

'Yes, indeed.' Lou seemed to value the sympathy. 'Though Hester's taking the brunt of it. She's a star.'

Isabelle blinked at Lou's enthusiasm.

'Is he coming up soon?' Moth asked.

'Shouldn't think so, Moth,' Lou said. 'He's got kitchen fitters, plumbers, sparkies, decorators and a plasterer there on double time. He's all over them like a rash.'

'You forgot the two landscape gardeners,' Fred said between chairs.

'And the roofers,' Ed added.

'But it's all in hand, and Hester is making it easier,' Lou reassured the room.

'That girl is a gem,' Ed added.

'She deserves a medal for putting up with Flash,' Fred agreed.

Isabelle found herself floating by the ceiling, trying to work out the Hester who was being described.

'Hey, Izz,' Lou mocked from the floor. 'Penny for your thoughts?'

'Sorry,' she said, and went back to what she was doing. 'Miles away.'

'Which is where we need to be, and soon.'

Elsa walked back in with a tray of tea, and all the new arrivals murmured and grabbed a cup. They didn't stop for more than a few slurps though.

Moth helped her take down the final curtains and they packed them together. Ed and Fred grunting as they carried the heavy ornate furniture out. She and Moth grinned at each other as they went past, remembering their weight.

Lou emptied the room with relentless authority. With each flurry in and out, the light from the window reached further and closer towards the door. Isabelle could feel the room growing, breathing a sigh of relief as it was emptied. She watched as the last curtains were taken, the red and gold rug rolled up and heaved out, leaving a sun-stained rim to the room and a dark oak expanse of floorboard in the middle. The paintwork was chipped and stained in places previously hidden and the window frames had huge cobwebs hanging from the corners where she'd removed the curtains. Elsa went and opened the windows to clear the dust and Moth and Nat went out onto the balcony and peered over the edge, drinking in the view and the sunlight bouncing off the river.

'This is some room,' Lou said, coming in for the last time, dusting the task off on her thighs with satisfaction. 'What's Flash got lined up for this?'

'This one's not up to Kit,' Elsa said as she walked back

from the windows. 'It's up to Isabelle, but she's got plenty of time to figure it out, no rush.'

'Going to take some painting, mind,' Lou said. 'Stunning views, whatever you do, it will be gorgeous. You lucky girl.'

She said it with warmth, and not a hint of jealousy. Lou got to see some amazing properties working with Kit, it made Isabelle realise that for some people this responsibility that was overwhelming her was quite normal.

'Now.' Lou was straight back to business. 'I have another list of stuff to go back to Swansea. Can we go through that, get it loaded, then Ed can get on his way?'

'Of course,' Elsa said. 'Nat, can you come and help please.'

'Coming,' Nat called from the balcony and went running across the room.

As they filed out and dispersed about the house Isabelle felt the quietness of the empty room settle upon her. Moth came in from the balcony, leaning against the window surround, watching her wheel round, taking in the room.

'Pretty big place to fill,' he said.

'Mmm,' she walked over to him, looking back at the void. 'I have no idea what to do with it now.'

'It looks a lot better,' he said. 'You should make this your... oops, sorry, we're not supposed to do that.'

'Do what?'

'Tell you what to do.' He sent a guilty glance to the door. 'Elsa has banned us all from influencing you. That's why she sent Kit to Swansea. Much as she needs him there, it was to get him away from telling you what to do.'

Isabelle digested the dropped bomb, Kate's behaviour appearing in a light as different and clear as that streaming through the windows. She couldn't help but smile. 'Poor Kate.'

'Yeah, must be driving her nuts,' Moth said. 'Sorry, I shouldn't have said, hope you're not mad.'

'It helps.' Isabelle leaned against the wall next to him. 'I was feeling abandoned with it all, now I understand why.'

'Yeah, well, I still feel bad.'

'Well then,' Isabelle nudged him in the ribs with her elbow, 'how about you salve your conscience by helping me out. What would you do with this room?'

'I'd turn it into a hang-out den,' he said. 'With a massive television, a computer, a gaming console and a 'Do Not Disturb' sign on the door. Oh, and I'd set my bike up on a stand in the corner, plus, it's nice and close to the kitchen too, great for snacks.'

'That's not helpful.'

'Well, you did ask.'

'Ok, what do you think I should do with this room?'

'I think you should decide for yourself,' Moth said and jumped back from her elbow. 'At least if Elsa asks, that's what I said. Though, personally, I'd move your workroom up here. Seems to me it's time to move out of the basement. Plus, it's nice and close to the kitchen, great for snacks.'

'Move the workroom?' That seemed far too ambitious a project.

'Yeah,' Moth said. 'I like this room. It feels good to me, like it wants to be used. Not have the door shut on it or turned into some sort of fancy posh drawing room. Used once a year at Christmas or for parties.' He paused, moving away from the window and her, speaking to the room without looking at her. 'I have good memories of this room.'

She looked at his turned back, it seemed light years away from the time they'd last stood in here.

'I do too,' she told his shoulders. 'I liked it best as a hang-out den.'

'Remember that,' Moth said, moving away, flipping a grin at her as he headed for the door. 'Don't let me down and turn it into a funeral parlour. I should help Nat. See you later.'

Before she could protest, he'd gone. Leaving her abandoned again. Except now she realised there was a reason for it. Moth's slip about Elsa explained Kit's forced absence, and Kate's conflicting reticence and patience. Isabelle walked down the side of the room, her fingers trailing along the walls. Its huge high ceiling and wide marble fireplace felt tranquil, basking in their new emptiness and the warm sunshine. It would be colder in the winter. She turned at the door and looked back towards the windows. At the place where she and Moth had set up their holiday den. She could remember the feel of those few days, their peaceful, undisturbed luxury.

'Here,' Moth said behind her. She jumped out of her skin, clutching her arms about her waist. 'I thought this might help.'

She turned to see him standing in the doorway, her favourite chair from the dining room in his hands.

'I asked Elsa,' he said, moving through the room, putting it down in front of the window. 'She said you were keeping the chair.'

'I don't want to sit on my own,' she said, hating how lost it looked.

'Yeah, I figured that too.' He flicked his eyes behind her.

Isabelle turned to see Fred walking down the hallway from the study, the chair that Moth had chosen perched on his shoulder.

'Where's it going?'

'Over here,' Moth said.

'What about this one?' Ed called from the hallway, coming down the stairs. On his shoulder was a large armchair from one of the guest bedrooms.

'Elsa said she fancied one too, while you were thinking the options through,' Moth said, grinning. 'If you don't mind that is?'

'Of course I don't mind,' Isabelle felt a lump form in her throat. 'It's nice to have some input.'

'It's temporary,' Moth said, his hand lingering on the back of the slipper chair. 'Until you decide for yourself.'

'Of course,' she said.

'Gotta go. I'll...'

'See me later, I know.'

The chairs looked comforting in the window, the three of them arranged to best take in the view. It would be nice to have somewhere to sit that was different. They even looked as though they belonged there.

She looked away. The hallway was an ant line of moving furniture, heading for the vans on the drive, no one looking to her for help.

She retreated to the kitchen and from there, to the workroom.

MONDAY MORNING CAME with a swiftness fuelled by happiness. For all that the hours had been swamped with the discomfort of packing and the oddity of a house in uproar there had been a lot of laughter with it.

Isabelle was waiting in the kitchen for Moth. He was catching the mid-morning train back, taking full advantage of the school's sympathy. She thought how his coming home had been good for them all, but that it seemed to be Nat who had needed him least. She sipped a coffee and recalled her brief conversation with Kit that morning. He'd rung her at six, woken her in fact, to talk about everything under the sun. Asking her what she was doing, how were things going, how did the empty room look, what was she going to do with it. When she protested that she didn't know, he'd needled her with more questions.

'Elsa told Moth not to speak to me about what I should do,' Isabelle retaliated, enjoying the pause before Kit spoke, his enquiring tone turned cautious.

'He told you that?'

'Yes,' Isabelle said. 'He said she told you all the same.'

'She never told me the same,' Kit said in a high tone that echoed down the line. 'She packed me off to Swansea with Hester as fast as she could and gave me an impossible task to keep me busy.'

'I suppose it amounts to the same thing,' Isabelle said. 'But Kit, what am I going to do? Kate won't talk to me about anything but china and being patient.'

'Kate's advising patience?'

'Exactly!' Isabelle complained. 'It's driving me nuts.'

'I wish I could be there to hear that,' Kit said. 'It must be irritating her a lot more than you.'

'That's not helpful.' Isabelle, realising that sleep had gone, dragged herself up against the pillows. 'When are you coming back?'

'Not for a fortnight, earliest.' She could hear the frustration in his voice, truth puffed out through irritation. 'I've got the mother of all weeks ahead and it's going to be another week before I'm back up to help Elsa move. I know it's a long time, but it'll be fine. When everything is quieter, we'll work out what we want to, I mean, what you want to do.'

Isabelle heard the slip. 'She did say something to you,' she accused him.

'You're getting freaked out,' he protested. 'How's Moth doing anyway? Has he said much about school?'

Isabelle knew he was lying. Hiding under interest in Moth to cover it. 'Not much, apart from hating it,' she replied. 'Lou said Hester's been a great support. I didn't realise you two were so close.'

'It's not like I had much choice in it.'

The conversation had stalled after that, drifting in mundane queries that neither of them found interesting.

Moth walked into the kitchen, snatching at her thoughts. A rucksack hooked across one shoulder, dressed in grey school trousers, his shirt tucked in at the waist but open-necked. Trainers looking incongruous on his feet. Her coffee cup froze on its way to her mouth. He looked fresh, straight from the shower, his hair damp, scraped back away from his face with an indifferent hand. Isabelle was used to seeing him in casual clothes, he looked about five years older.

'You look smart,' she said, taking a final slug, putting the cup down.

'I look like a schoolboy.' He scuffed his feet against the floor, hitched his bag.

'No. You definitely don't look like a schoolboy.'

'I feel like one, anyway,' he complained. 'People are going to wander what I'm doing on the train mid-morning.'

'People will assume you're on your way to a business meeting,' she said.

'Well, I'm ready anyway.' He glanced out of the windows

at the magnolia tree, looked back at her. 'You sure you want to come? You don't need to. I know where the train station is.'

'I know,' she said. 'I want to. I think Nat would have happily skipped school to come see you off too.'

'Yeah,' Moth flashed a stricken look at her, hid it with tugging on his rucksack strap, eyes flitting away from her. She should have known he'd find it hard to leave her. 'It's tough still going to a school she knows she's going to leave.'

'It will be over soon enough.' Isabelle moved to the sink, tipping her unfinished coffee away, swilling the cup out. 'Have you got everything?'

Moth hitched his bag on his shoulder again. 'Yep, I'm good.'

She picked up the scarf she'd draped over the back of a chair. It was a cloudy morning, not cold but not warm, the first Monday in July. She'd woken feeling rough, sluggish, knowing her period was building. She walked toward the kitchen door, saw him staring at the room again before he moved to follow. She took the stairs down to the basement and out into the garden, holding the door open, waiting for him as he paused again, looking down the corridor towards her workroom. He'd spent a quick ten minutes the evening before packing away his bike and panniers, making her promise not to lose them.

'You sure you haven't forgotten something?'

'Yeah, pretty sure.' He moved forward, took the door from her hand, and followed her down the steps.

They left the garden by the gate to the road and walked along the lower curve of the castle walls, passing behind the back of the town. Cars came with intermittent curiosity, making them squeeze tight to the wall on the narrow pavement. The sun stayed a rising globe behind the hazy cloud cover, determined to delay the promise to lift and fill the day with bright sunshine. Light glowing on the cobbled pavement of Upper Linney as they walked past its lower entrance.

'Last week,' Isabelle said. 'You'll be back before you know it.' Their legs found the same distance, and the same speed, gliding over the space in companionable formation. 'You'll go down to Swansea soon though.'

'Guess so.'

'I hope you're planning to come back at least a little over the summer,' she said. 'Kit should be here a lot once he's finished the new house for Elsa.'

'That sounds reason enough to stay in Swansea.'

'I don't want to be totally abandoned. It would be nice to think the whole family hasn't decamped and left me to rattle about the place all alone.'

'You'll have Kate,' he said. 'I can't see her spending much time in Swansea over the summer, she'll be too busy at the bistro'

'That's evasion,' she said. 'I want to see you, and Kit.'

'Perhaps James might stop in a little too.'

'I shouldn't think so, I've barely seen him since I...' she paused.

'Since you became his landlady?' Moth added.

She scowled at him.

'Well?' Moth said. 'You are, after all.'

'I didn't ask to be.'

'No, neither did he,' Moth said. 'One of you might want to try talking about it though. This habit of ignoring the obvious is hilarious to watch, but I can't see it's going to help you get on.'

'Why does it have to be up to me to start it?'

'How mature,' he told her.

The road narrowed and Moth took the lead. Isabelle fell in behind him as they passed an overhanging viburnum tree, its yellow petals littering the floor where other people had brushed into it. His trousers were fitted against his legs, emphasising the way his legs moved, clinging to the muscles at the back of his thighs. They had gained definition. All the cycling was paying off.

'You will be back. At least for the bike if nothing else. You look as though you've got well into the cycling.'

Moth turned and looked at her, walking backwards for two steps. She raised her eyes from his legs, startled by their turning, meeting his clear gaze and quirked lips. She blushed, feeling a rush of guilt flood her face.

'Yes,' he said. 'I feel fitter.'

He turned again and kept on walking. She found herself struggling not to look at his leg muscles again, at the way his trousers were too tight, how they creased where they met his buttocks.

'You look stronger.'

'I'll be back for the bike, sometime,' he said. 'I'm not sure when. I guess there'll be a lot to do over summer. I'm hoping Nat will let me get away for a while.'

'You have anywhere in particular you want to go?'

'Loads of places,' his voice expanded into the air, full of enthusiasm. 'Scotland, Wales, Ireland, Norway, Europe, Alaska, Siberia.'

'Siberia?'

'It's one of the last great wildernesses in the world. I want to see if I can do it. All the way from Canada, through Alaska, over the Bering Straits to Siberia, and home.'

'On a bike?'

'Why not, it will keep me warm.' His voice was talking to the pavement ahead.

'I suppose that's one theory,' she said, her eyes battling the habit of looking downwards. At the pavement.

The path widened again, and she caught him up. They walked past Mrs Staines' house, eyes veering towards the front door with its damp curled paintwork.

'Pray she doesn't decide to look out the window,' Isabelle murmured. 'You don't want to miss your train.'

'I wouldn't mind,' he said. 'I like her, Marge more so.'

'We all like Marge more.'

They walked through the old graveyard, past the former church converted to a printing press. The gravestones were immaculate along the path edge, crumbling further back where the yews were unkempt and bushy, the ivy encroaching. The high walls that surrounded the place pushed back the noise of the town, making it feel hushed, reverent. Empty benches awaiting lunchtime escapees. They walked out of the high arch and back onto the main road, engulfed by the resurgence of noise, turning up the road to the train station.

It was a different route to the one she'd taken the day she came home, back in the spring, when she hadn't yet known Moth. When she was on her way to meet him, and Nat. Walking this way with Moth now, made her realise how far away that homecoming journey was. How much had shifted beyond recognition in those few fraught months. How much remained to sift into some final pattern that would make sense.

They sat on the platform beside the stairs that took passengers over the footbridge and to the south platform. Moth was travelling north, before changing to travel east. The place was quiet, a few elderly people sitting on the benches, planning a day trip out. Most travellers already on their way or arrived. The digital clock on the wall told them they had five minutes to wait, their train was next in. They sat in silence, watching other people.

'I wanted to thank you,' Moth said the words in a rush, catching her thoughts from straying about the platform.

'Oh, what for?'

'When I came here, I had no time for Elsa.' He stared at his hand hovering between his stretched open knees, the bag on the floor by his feet. 'I thought this was something we, Nat and I, had to do. It was never going to be a place we wanted to be. I was always thinking about what else I could do for us. I didn't want anything to do with Elsa. You changed that. You made me,' he paused, 'no, you didn't make me, you encouraged me to see her differently, to give her a chance.'

'That was an easy thing to do,' Isabelle said. 'I've known her a lot longer than you.'

'Well, I'm glad,' he said, glancing up at her, back at his hands. 'I feel happier about leaving Nat here, now I feel happier about her, Elsa, I mean. And you helped change that for me.'

'What about you?' Isabelle asked. 'Don't you feel happier about being here too?'

'I guess,' he said, picking at one of his thumb nails. 'I'm not sure, but I feel Nat has a home now, somewhere people will look after her. Good people. I find it's easier, going away, back to school I mean, knowing she's safe and happy.'

'You're an awesome big brother,' Isabelle said. 'I hope she knows that one day.'

'I make sure she knows it now,' he joked, adding in a quiet voice that trailed away, 'It's like someone lifted a weight, knowing Elsa will look after her.'

'Make sure you don't float away entirely,' Isabelle mocked him, with a gentle knee tap to his thigh. 'Next thing you'll be telling me you enjoy being back at school.'

'I can't say I miss working for Kate.' He sat back, away from his knees, settling onto the bench, their arms brushing together. 'But I wouldn't say that either.'

They heard the train approaching, tooting as it came in through the tunnel, under the town.

'It's time to go.' Moth stood up in a rush, grasping his bag. She felt the flutters in her stomach, looking up at him. He reached a hand down to her, pulled her up. They were stood close together, his hand in hers, not letting go and she felt the urgency of the moment, the peaceful morning disturbed in the rush of the train.

'Thank you for doing that,' he told her. 'For helping me with Elsa. I needed that.'

'You're welcome.' She was startled by his serious tone, unnerved by his closeness. She could smell him, fresh from the shower, warm from the walk. Something earthy, as though he'd been digging in the garden or mowing grass. A scent that confused her, making nonsense of the moment.

'And thank you for the walks, and the talks, and the swimming, and the porridge,' he told her. 'Take care, Isabelle.'

'See you soon,' she said, their faces close enough that the train was a blur behind his head, the platform blocked by the fringes of his hair. She gripped his hand tighter. 'Make sure you plan some time for me over the summer. I don't want to be alone.'

He turned her hand over, put something on her palm, closing her fingers over it before she could look.

'You won't be.' He kissed her on the cheek, startling her with the suddenness of it. As though he'd found the courage at the last minute, retreating while she was registering it. A soft and chaste physical closeness that hovered between them, like the memory of their fingers touching across the space between their mattresses. 'You'll never be alone. Kit won't let you!'

He pulled away, stepped toward the train, waved at her as he opened the door and got on. She took a step after him, watching as he moved down the length of the carriage, looking for a seat. Finding one on the far side so that he was already gone, out of sight, out of reach and her step towards him faltered. She could feel something rough folded in her hand but watched the train as the last passengers boarded and it glided away out of the station. She couldn't see Moth through the distance and her unfocused eyes. The train was a rural express, travelling light with only two carriages. Swiftly arrived, even sooner gone.

She was left alone on the platform, as the few people who'd disembarked dispersed. She looked down at her hand, opened the fingers. Saw a piece of fabric, springing open on her palm, cut to the exact size of the scraps she collected. A coarse, grey, woollen herringbone. Streaked through with red stripes, coarse and practical. Marked with a crease where her hand had folded it, crushed by his. Trying to make sense of why he would give her such a thing.

She looked back up to see the train had disappeared. She turned and began the walk home, slow steps that had lost purpose.

MANY MILES AWAY IN SWANSEA, Kit looked mutinously at the water erupting from the broken tap, listening to the plumber running for the mains connection, calculating how long it would take for him to turn it off and how much water was going to drip through the ceiling into the newly plastered kitchen below.

'Smegging scum sucking...' he began.

His phone buzzed. Henri.

'Hey boss,' Henri said. 'How's it going?'

'It's a nightmare!' Kit watched the water spreading fast, knowing he could do nothing. Waiting for it to end, retreating backward in fury. 'The plumber's flooded the first-floor bathroom, I'm watching it cascade through the floor, where the plasterer is stood beneath him, that's how fresh the ceiling is. How the fuck is your day going?'

'Better than yours it seems.'

'Marvellous, bloody marvellous.'

'Brace yourself,' Henri said. 'Yours is about to get worse. I need you for a day this week.'

'Not possible.' As in. Not. Happening. Where was that sodding plumber? He held the phone against his chest. 'Turn it OFF!' he screamed down the corridor. Why did the whole world want him? He felt as pressured as the flooding water. The only place he wanted to be was Riverdell, and it was the one place he couldn't get.

'Not not possible,' Henri told him. 'The D'Arby's are freaking out they haven't seen you and the Churchill's are getting a quote from Reynaud's. It's a big job, boss.'

Kit shut his eyes and held back the curses. 'I know.'

He needed it too. Elsa's job was killing his cash flow. The Churchill's deposit was essential.

'Set up a date, book me in for both lots, and anyone else you need me to see. One day, make sure you know what I need to know. Not tomorrow, the plumbers and sparkies are due back.'

'Can't be any later than Thursday,' Henri told him. 'Mr Churchill is away on business for a week from Friday.'

'Make it Thursday if possible, Wednesday if you have to. Book it up, let me know the times.' Kit watched the flooding tap lessen, sputter and dribble to a halt. 'Can you do Churchill's first. I'll have the night at home. Could you make sure there's food in the house.'

'Sure thing, boss. Thank you,' Henri said. Kit could tell he'd been worried.

'You're doing great Henri. Three more weeks, four tops, and we're back to normal.' Kit stood in the doorway, willing the spreading water to stop, daring it to seep over the threshold onto the underlay that had been fitted that morning in the hallway. That was his limit, right here, right now. The damn water had to stay that side of the bathroom door. He had carpet fitters looking at him in horror from either end of the corridor.

'Three more weeks and you're going to have to work triple time to catch up on what's going on here,' Henri countered. 'Four and you're in deep shit.'

Kit grimaced. It wasn't what he wanted to hear. It didn't give him any time to be at Riverdell. He might end up losing one of those jobs yet, to give Isabelle the time she needed.

'Boss?'

'I hear you,' Kit said. 'I hear you. Set it up, let me know. Get as much ready as possible for the visits.'

'Will do, boss. See you.'

'Yeah, bye.' Kit hung up, staring at the phone in his hand, trying to make sense of it all.

Churchills. Interior modelling of their new extension. Downstairs kitchen, upstairs master bed and en-suite. He'd managed to convince them to add the former master bed, now second guest bedroom, to the equation. D'Arby's. Total overhaul of their 17th Century moated manor. Library, drawing room, dining room, ballroom, and that was only the tip of that particular cash iceberg.

The plumber came back up the stairs, ignoring his look as he squeezed past him in the doorway and waded across the sodden floor. Downstairs he could hear shouts starting to come from the plasterer. Kit didn't know whether to stay where he was and dish out abuse or go downstairs and see the damage.

'Kit!' Hester called from downstairs.

He turned and walked towards the stairs.

'I'm coming, get buckets, it's coming your...,' a crash from downstairs followed by screams and shouts made him close his eyes and dream up ravaging, never-before-uttered curses, '... way.' The fresh-plastered ceiling had collapsed in the kitchen.

He clattered down the stairs and into the cloud of dust rising towards him. Yelling behind him, 'shut all the doors up here.' Hester, Lou, the plasterers and kitchen fitters appeared, coughing and shaking plaster out of their hair.

They waited for the dust to settle and looked at the damage. The floor was a rubble filled disaster. The ceiling was a dripping mass of timbers, hanging wires and collapsing plaster. The un-topped kitchen units were full of debris.

It was just another day in Swansea.

There was nothing right about the speed of the job. Constant crisis management with everyone looking at him to put it right. They'd been at it non-stop for two weeks, throwing money up the walls, and the house was trashed. He wanted order, completion, room after room done, doors closed, ready for its new inhabitants. Instead, he had mutinous workmen, missing light fittings, sub-quality plumbing fittings, delayed vans, boarded up holes on the ground floor where the new windows were due, ignored clients busting his balls, Lou tearing her hair out, Jamie ignoring him, and Henri cursing him in French under the workload.

He'd resorted to getting another phone to manage it all. If it wasn't for the endless intensity of his work calls, he would have been on the line to Isabelle daily, hourly. He was bursting with the need to talk to her, to be at Riverdell, to be part of the process. When he did ring, in brief moments of calm, like this morning, he felt castrated by Elsa's command to leave her alone. It hadn't started his day well to find out that Moth had let slip about that. Let slip like hell. Manipulative git, trying to drop him in it.

'What are we going to do!' Lou screamed in a rage.

'We're going to clear it up and put it right,' Hester told her in a calm tone, shaking muck out of her hair. 'It's a setback. It's not the end of the world. Go get Ed and Fred and tell them to bring wheelbarrows and shovels.' Kit watched as she took charge of the workmen. 'You lot, take a tea break, and make me a coffee. Give us thirty and we'll be back at it. Kit, go find Jamie. She's downstairs, tell her I need her.'

Lou stalked past him, followed by the fitters. He took one more look at it, Hester staring at him with her hands on her hips, daring him to speak, and turned away. He went to find Jamie, clattering down the dusty stairs that led to the lower ground floor. Being down here irritated him. It should have been the kitchen in his opinion, no doubt about it. Hester had decided otherwise. She might even be right, which irritated him more. He'd made her choose, two weeks ago when they'd arrived in Swansea. When he'd marshalled the team and declared the house an emergency project. When he'd told Henri it was time to earn his wage and sent him back to Bristol to begin delaying his other projects.

'What do you think we should do?' Hester had asked him as they prepared to start.

'I've told you the options.'

'Why aren't you telling me what to do?' Hester looked at him with distrust, suspecting a trap. 'You're not normally shy about that.'

'This is different. You have to own this decision.'

'What do you mean?' She looked at the three different designs he'd given her, quick sketches on rough paper.

'You have to live with the result,' he explained, tapping the pages. 'I can tell you what you might do, you have to own the decision. Because, if you don't like the end result, you'll blame me. First rule of house management, customer has to own the decisions.'

'That sounds a bit docile for you,' she said with a long look.

He smiled back and, barely, swallowed his retort. Planning juicy and vile atrocities against Elsa for putting him in this position. Lou and Jamie looking with fascination at the floor. This "policy" of ownership only applied to family and friend jobs, normally he'd be telling his rich clients exactly what they should do, not encouraging their opinion.

'I think this is the way to go,' Hester decided, finger tapping her chosen option, chewing her bottom lip.

'And Elsa doesn't have a preference?'

'Again, for the umpteenth time,' Hester said, 'she wants us to make the decisions.'

Kit looked at the sketches. Three options. Move the kitchen downstairs, knocking the whole floor into a large open plan living space. Or knock the kitchen and dining

room together upstairs, leaving a small sitting room and a
study in the rooms at the front of the house. Or leave all the
rooms as they were and refurbish and decorate. She'd chosen
the middle option. It wouldn't have been his choice. But it
wasn't his money either. And worse, which he didn't want to
admit, it wasn't his priority. Riverdell was. Riverdell and
Isabelle. He couldn't have everything, he too had to choose.

'Let's do it then.'

Lou and Jamie breathed a sigh of relief and smiled at
Hester.

'Did I choose right?' she asked.

'You chose,' Lou replied. 'That's all we need, a choice, now
we can make a start.'

So, Hester had decided, and Hester never wavered. Which
was why she wouldn't be daunted by the sodden disaster
sitting in the middle of her new room.

Kit strode down the lower floor corridor and into the
large room at the end. The one he'd explored with Kate and
Elsa on the day of Miss Shorrock's funeral, when it had been
filled to the brim with books. It was bigger now they'd
emptied it. Isabelle would have liked it. Hester seemed to
have taken a shine to it too and he suspected that if the
money worked out, Hester might find a use for it herself.

Kit hadn't realised before how daunted she was by
Isabelle. By the vastness of the workroom that Isabelle
commanded with such diffidence. By the confidence Isabelle
had in her work. By the way Isabelle had held onto the
creative flair they had once shared. He hadn't realised how
life had diminished Hester, until he saw her under the pressure of the renovation job.

Saw her in small moments, thinking things through with
an uncertain frown that deepened to a smile as resolution

came. Saw how she took charge of his team with the lightest of touches. Saw how she managed the multiple threads of the conversion as though she were painting a canvas. Working through the unfolding, chaotic process to the finished image fixed in her mind, a skill so few people had. Saw her moving through the house with a hand touching the damp soft plaster of the walls, feeling the new life inside. Saw how Hester's arms unfolded from their habitual defensive position over her chest. Saw how here, away from the dead end her life had become, away from Isabelle, away from Riverdell, Hester re-found some part of what she had once been.

It made him wonder, what might Riverdell become, afterwards? What might Isabelle become? What might they become?

'You're needed upstairs,' he told Jamie. She was managing paperwork at the temporary command centre they'd set up down here.

'I didn't like the sound of it,' she swivelled to face him. 'Was hoping I could hide down here.'

'Hester wants your help.'

'On my way.' She stood up and left without another word, the chair swinging in her swift departure.

Kit scowled at her back. This over comfortable relationship between Hester and his team was something he would have liked to protest. But time to protest wasn't an option. He looked at the wall planners. Mood boards, colour charts, sketches, contact numbers, meticulous planning grids, deadlines, objectives. All he needed to mastermind a six-month project compacted into six weeks.

Choices dictated by timescale. Each decision pushed to the wire. In the rush of dealing with the structural overhaul the decorative details had been pared down to the minimum.

It would be painted, carpeted and plumbed in. It would be furnished and functional. Elsa would have to add beauty in her own time.

He looked at the diagrams. He needed to finish something today. One thing finished at the end of each day. That was his coping strategy. He ignored the upper ground floor, currently in chaos and plaster dust. The attic delegated to their temporary digs. The second floor being painted. The first floor being carpeted. He set his goal and left the room.

He would tidy out the four principal bedrooms on the first floor and shut the doors on them today. And the carpet fitters had better not have any illusions they were leaving until those rooms were done.

KIT AND HESTER were cleaning out from the carpet fitters, hoovering up the loose fibres, gathering up the piles of underlay, offcuts, gripper rods and spray glue cans and hauling it out one black bag at a time to the bulging skip on the front drive. It was late afternoon, Jamie and Lou had gone home to Bristol, and the boys were outside helping the landscape gardeners.

'You're working them too hard,' Hester told him, again. 'You know you have almost a month left.'

'It never goes that smoothly.' Kit cast an eye over the upper floor repainted windows. They had been brushed up to within an inch of their exhausted life. They needed replacing, the single glazing would take its toll on the heating costs, but Elsa was used to single glazed old properties. He'd ended up replacing only the ground floor windows, which had been rotten enough he could have pushed them out with a flaccid dick.

'Mother's not expecting a perfect finish.'

'That's good.'

She was digging for an explanation he didn't want to share.

He wanted to be with Isabelle. It was that simple. But he didn't want to tell Hester that. Elsa had been clever, sending them down here together. The only chance he had of countering her intentions to keep him away from Isabelle was to get finished sooner than she expected and back up there.

His phone rang. He took it out of his pocket, Hester went back to cleaning. She was used to his wandering away on the phone. Which was good. It was Kate. He moved towards the back of the house, dustbin bag trailing in his hand.

'Hi,' he said. 'How's the bistro?'

'Mike's torturing my staff out of their good habits. How's the house?'

'Hester's seducing my team out of their bad ones,' he sympathised. He found a quiet spot in the back bedroom, sat down on the fresh thick carpet under the window. 'I'm sitting in the room that will be your guest room.'

'That's supposing I'll be a guest.'

'I've made it as tempting as possible,' he said. 'I'm optimistic you'll meet a wealthy retiree down here.'

'You've been working too hard. Your mind's going soft.'

'It's always soft where you're concerned,' Kit told her. It was a pleasure to sit down, to stop for a moment. He heard a gentle tut of irritation in her voice. She changed the subject.

'How's Hester getting on?'

'It's like watching a cactus flower.'

'Are you being sarcastic?'

'Not at all,' Kit said. 'Don't get me wrong, I thought Elsa was mental, sending me down here with her. Not to mention manipulative, getting me away from Riverdell, but it's been a revelation. I think she might be right. What everyone needs is a change.' He checked through the door, made sure Hester wasn't close enough to hear.

'You sound as though you're enjoying it.'

'I am, I genuinely am. She's been a star. The team adore her. I think they'd sack me if they could.'

'What, you're being less adorable than Hester?' Kate asked. 'Something is strange.'

'Yes, it is,' Kit lowered his voice. 'When are you going to come and visit?'

'I have my hands full too,' she protested. 'Between Mike retraining the staff, Elsa acting like a giddy schoolgirl, and Isabelle disappearing into the woodwork, you're not the only one juggling you know.'

'You should take a break,' he told her. 'Come and visit the beach, I have the tent in the van.'

'My bones are too old for the beach.'

'I'll cushion them for you.'

'Stop it. That's not why I called.'

'Why did you call?'

'What?'

'Well?'

'Oh, stop it,' she said. 'I called to see how you are.'

'So, you are missing me?'

'Of course, we miss you,' Kate said with flippant sweetness. 'The house is in complete uproar, you've disappeared to Swansea, and Elsa's driving me mad with this "nobody talks to Isabelle" policy. We don't miss you; we bloody need you.'

'I'm thrilled to be wanted.' Kit hadn't realised how tired he was. 'Trust me, I'd love to be there, but I've got the hardest yet to come. If the final fix plumb and electrics don't go sweet,

I've got workmen about to mutiny without dragging them back to make alterations.'

'Well, as soon as you're done there you better prepare to come and make sense of the mess Elsa leaves here.'

'Did you know Moth told Isabelle about Elsa's policy?'

'You are joking!'

'No.' Kit enjoyed the level of outrage in her voice. It expressed exactly how he'd felt. 'She told me this morning, said he'd "let it slip". Demanded to know if it was true.'

'What did you tell her?'

Kit wriggled on the carpet, despite its thick underlay. 'I told her I didn't know what he was talking about.'

'Oh.' Kate kept her silence, trying to figure out how to handle the same accusation herself no doubt. 'I wonder why he did that, perhaps it was a slip of the tongue? I can't say it's easy, tiptoeing round Isabelle.'

'It doesn't sound like Moth to me.' Kit thought about Moth standing in the bay window of the sitting room when he'd turned up to find their love nest, how hard it had been to better him. 'How was he, anyway? Isabelle said he was hating school.'

'Seemed content enough to me,' Kate said. 'He was charming, in fact. Couldn't have been more adorable. I'd say school was suiting him fine.'

'Adorable?' Kit wouldn't have used that word for Moth. He frowned at the open doorway. He hadn't spoken to Moth since he'd gone back to school, hadn't had time. A twinge in his neck told him he should feel guilty about this. Kit flicked at his knees again. New carpet dust, it would take three or four hooverings to get the worst up. He needed to get back to work. He didn't have time for guilt.

'We need you back here.'

'I can't come back for at least a fortnight.' Kit knew that was optimistic. Henri would quit if he disappeared to Riverdell. He pushed away the uncomfortable truth. 'And when I do come back, I don't want the first thing we talk about to be houses. I want you to tell me how adorable I am, what a wonderful job I've been doing, and how much you've missed me.'

'You're adorable, you're doing a wonderful job, and I miss you soooo much,' Kate told him with a voice that would have soured lemons. 'Better now?'

'No,' Kit said. 'I think I'll try Isabelle instead.'

'Good luck.'

They paused, silent on the phone. Kit could hear Hester tidying her way out of the bedroom and into the corridor.

'I wish you were here.' He longed for her, for the comfort of her smiling eyes softening her hard voice. 'It's a brand-new carpet, I'd convince you your bones are young enough.'

'Really?' she didn't sound convinced.

'Really,' he lowered his voice even more. 'I miss you, even if you don't miss me. I keep thinking about you in this house. I can practically smell your youthful self in the hallways.'

'When I think about that house all I can smell is cabbage,' Kate told him. 'Damp and cabbage. You'll have to have transformed it for my juices to get flowing.'

'But I have!' he protested. 'Well, I am. I'm working on it.'

'We'll see,' Kate said. 'I'm sure Elsa will drag me down there at some point. Though I still can't believe she's doing it.'

'You're going to have to forgive her at some point.'

Kate tutted down the phone. 'We'll see about that too.'

'You will, you always do.' Kit told her. 'Besides, if she changes her mind now, I'll strangle her for you.' He could see

Hester coming towards the door, looking for him. 'I have to go.'

'Try and get home soon.'

'Home?' he asked. 'Where's that?'

'Right now? Who knows?'

Hester was outside the door. 'Missing you,' he said in a firmer voice. 'Can't wait to get back and make up for lost time.' Hester walked in. 'Yes, you too,' he said in syrup drenched tones to Kate's vicious response. 'Bye, yes bye.' He hung up.

'Isabelle?' Hester asked.

'Uh-huh,' he said, and rolled to his feet, stretching his back. 'My God, I shouldn't have stopped. I'm whacked.'

'Everyone's whacked.' She walked back out the room. 'Come on, let's finish this, and order some dinner.'

Kit held the phone in his hand. Take out dinner, they were living on it, like Moth and Isabelle had. Moth. Something about Moth was troubling him. He found his mobile number and rang it. It diverted to answer phone, he should have been back at school by now. Maybe he was stuck in classes. 'Hi, it's Kit, sorry I've not been in touch, give me a call.' He left the message, knowing it was inadequate, and walked out. Hester was at the far end of the hall, heading for the last bedroom. One more room and his target was hit. He'd try Moth again later, if not, tomorrow.

HE ROLLED out of bed first thing on Tuesday when he heard Jamie pull up on the drive. His hand reaching for his phone, to find the battery dead from a night almost, but not quite, plugged in to the charger. Moth's number wasn't in his new phone. By the time he stopped swearing, plugged in the phone and got downstairs, the day was already ahead of him.

Two sparkies, two plumbers, Ed, Fred, Lou, Jamie, the plasterers, decorators, carpet-fitters and chippies came at them in a quick-fire round that left even Hester with her head against the wall at one point. By the time he got upstairs to the recharged phone, Henri had left thirteen messages in increasing tones of desperation. Kit called time out from all the demands at midday and locked himself away downstairs for an hour to resolve the queries.

'Right,' he said after answering detailed questions on other projects, draining cold coffee from a chipped mug. 'What's left?'

'Your times for those appointments, boss. Thursday. You have the Churchills at nine, we leave at twelve. Hopefully at the D'Arby's by three, you have until seven with them. That gets you back to Bristol late Thursday evening. I'll drive, you'll have to catch up on the way. You need to be back here Wednesday night to prepare for Churchills.'

Kit wrote the details down. 'I feel tired already.'

'I'll make you breakfast, you can listen while you run,' Henri said. 'Think of it as a mini power break to recharge you.'

'That's a stretch,' Kit said. 'Well done, see you Wednesday night.'

'See you Thursday morning,' Henri corrected. 'I'm not waiting up for you to arrive at midnight.'

Kit drew reassuring lines under his final notes. Henri sounded relieved. 'Did you take any time off this weekend?'

'Did you?' Henri retorted.

'That's not the point. How much overtime are you doing?'

'Same as all the rest,' Henri said. 'But don't worry, you'll make someone else pay.'

'Absolutely.'

'Did I mention Reynaud's offered me a ten percent pay rise to return.'

'Cheeky bastards,' Kit said. 'Again? They don't know when to take no for an answer.'

'What makes you sure I said no?'

Kit could feel discomfort in his back from sitting down. A run in the gym would be bliss. 'Did you?'

'Did I what?'

'Say no?' Kit circled the last words, one at a time.

'I said I'd take it under consideration.'

'That's spiteful, you know they think you're being serious.'

'I wanted to see if they'd go up to 15% again.'

'You know I'm not giving you a raise, right?' Kit asked.

'Yeah, I know,' Henri told him.

'Piss off and keep dreaming,' Kit said. 'You can tell me all about it on Thursday.'

'Look forward to it.'

'Yeah, can't wait either.'

Putting the phone down, he savoured the quiet in the basement. Trying to think through what task he stood the best chance of finishing that day. He remembered his promise to call Moth and tried again, to no avail, tapping his fingers on the desk in irritation when the answer phone kicked in. Moth was ignoring him. He rang Henri back.

'Boss?'

'The D'Arby's. It's about 30 minutes from Rugby school isn't it?'

'Eh, I think so. Hang on, let me check.'

Kit could hear the computer going.

'Yes, ish,' Henri confirmed.

'Leave me some time at the end of the day,' Kit said. 'I want to call in on Moth.'

'Ehm.'

Kit recognised the tone of French disagreement. It always worked wonders on clients. Suggesting, rather than telling them outright, that what they were asking was either impossible, ridiculous or, worse, tasteless.

'Even 20 minutes?' Kit asked.

'I got it, boss.'

Kit hung up. He rang Moth again, to the same effect. Kit frowned. He didn't have time to wait. He rang the school. An upper-class accent answered, 'Rugby School.'

'Hi, can I speak with Moth, sorry, Timothy Threlfall,' Kit asked.

'May I ask who's calling?'

Kit grimaced, his mouth twitching at the tone. No pleases here.

'Kit de Lavelle,' he answered, trying hard not to alter the tone of his own accent to intimidate the speaker.

'One moment, Mr de Lavelle.' The line went onto hold. Kit stood up and pushed the swivel chair back, looking at the wall charts. Shelving, he would get the shelving on the first floor done, the wardrobes in the two front rooms and the laundry room at the back.

'Mr de Lavelle?' another voice asked. Female. Pin sharp, calm and controlled.

Kit felt his spine ripple. 'Indeed.'

'I'm afraid Timothy is away with the cricket team until tomorrow,' she said. 'Can I be of any assistance?'

'I want to arrange a visit with Moth. I'm part of the family.'

'Yes, of course, we're aware of that.'

Kit couldn't tell if he was irritated or intrigued by the careful choice of words, did they care he was part of the family or not? 'I shall be calling in on Thursday evening, please make a note of it. I shall speak with Moth later.'

'Of course, Mr de Lavelle. We shall look forward to your visit.'

'I'm sure,' Kit said. He hung up, shuddering at bad memories. Arsehole places. He tried Moth's number again. How had he even got on the cricket team? He hadn't been at school for more than a few weeks.

'Hey, Flash,' Fred called from upstairs. 'Get up here and make sense of this for us.'

Kit sighed. It would have to wait until later. They would have the wrong boards in the wrong room and screw holes everywhere before he could stop them.

HE GOT SO sick of trying to call Moth and getting ignored he was cursing at the phone by the time they locked up the house on Wednesday evening and walked down to the beachfront for an evening meal. He growled at the sound of Moth's answer phone again.

'Everyone ignoring you?' Hester asked, grinning at Ed and Fred.

'Imagine that?' Ed said, tucking an arm into hers.

'Who'd have thought?' Fred added, taking her other arm.

Kit watched them walk away down the street. 'You're getting the first round in,' he called after them.

'You're getting the rest,' Hester called back. They were taking full advantage of his absence for an evening.

Kit looked at his phone. Moth's number was on permanent redial. His texts were being ignored too. It was infuriating. Modern day technology gave no one the excuse to be out of touch.

He turned from watching his team bounce downhill, looked back up at the house, eyes scanning. Windows that needed cleaning, paintwork that needed patching up, the front yard a dusty rubbled mess, the garden access full of dried mud. He wanted flowerpots on the wide steps leading up to the door before he left. It was that clear to him. Deep blue porcelain pots with silvery fronds and spiky grasses waving out of them, softening the lines of the steps up.

He turned away, feeling the sea breeze cut across his cheek. Hester and the crew had disappeared. The silence of a midsummer evening settled on him, the steady purr of occasional traffic, the wind ruffling his hair, the glistening light dancing on the water, the calls of lazy gulls gliding over it. Kit stopped in his tracks. It was good to stop, take it in. Remember there was more to life.

The door of the house he'd stopped beside opened and a man came out with a ream of papers tucked beneath his arm. Bent down to put them in a green waste bin. Noticed Kit, below him on the pavement.

'You've been busy,' the guy said, cocking his head uphill.

'Indeed.'

'When are you moving in?'

'It's not for me,' Kit turned to look back at the house. 'I'm managing it for a friend.'

'When's he moving in?'

'She,' Kit emphasised, 'will be moving in when we're done.'

'Looks a lot left to do.'

'Yes, a fair bit.'

They both stood looking back at the house, Kit feeling the judgement of the stranger in his aching bones. If the outside looked a mess, it was nothing compared to the inside.

'Strangest thing,' the guy said. 'Old girl lived her whole life there, never even knew her name. Turned round and she was gone. Never noticed for a month.'

'Indeed,' Kit answered again. The conversation was unnerving him.

The guy raised his hand in polite dismissal and turned to go inwards. Kit walked the rest of the way down the hill. The evening seemed to have embedded weariness into his shoulders, the conversation sitting leaden in his gut. He would have dinner, give out last instructions and head off. A night at home would put him right.

UNABLE TO RESIST GOING BACK to check last niggles, plastering the house in post-it notes, he'd made it home by one in the morning, rolled into bed in a daze and was bawled out of it by Henri at 6.20am, with savage comments about his time keeping.

Henri talked at him non-stop until they left for the Churchills' on the luxurious Clifton Road, where he ended up in deep argument about the shade of paint for the master bedroom and the layout of the awkward shaped en-suite. The Churchills taking more energy than he thought they deserved or realised he hadn't got. When they'd spent an entire twenty minutes discussing the intricacies of one cushion for the guest bedroom, he suggested they reconvene after Mr Churchill returned and felt more geared to deal with domestic issues. Henri glared at him. Kit scowled back. It wasn't his fault the only time this couple spent

together was deciding on housewares. He wasn't bloody
Relate.

They left later than planned and Henri swore in French at
the hold-ups on the M4 before they turned onto the A-roads
that took them towards Cambridge. Kit fell asleep somewhere past Swindon, buried under a heap of sample and
paint books. Just after three o'clock, Henri pulled into a dirt
ditch lay-by not far from the end of the D'Arby's drive and
woke him up.

'You've spittled on your cheek,' he told Kit as he tried to
right the crumpled fabric squares of the sample books.

'How delightful.' Kit gave a massive yawn and tried the
best effort at a stretch that the Bentley would allow. Henri
handed him a pack of wet wipes. 'Don't people use these
things to wipe kids' arses with?'

'Once you've had a kid you never live without them,'
Henri said. 'They deal with all sorts of crap, not merely the
juvenile kind.'

'Oh God, this tastes disgusting,' Kit complained.

'You're not supposed to eat it.'

'I need some water.' Henri offered him a bottle. He drank,
pulled down the sun visor and checked his reflection in the
mirror. 'How do I look?'

Henri looked at him with a frown. 'Rakish?'

'That's never good.' Kit fluffed his hair up, pushed it back
to the side. 'Now?'

'Windswept?'

'You're sacked as a personal assistant,' Kit told him, slapping his cheeks and trying to get some colour in his face. He
felt the stubble starting on his chin with an irritated hand,
found a tin of lip gloss in the dash, put some on as consola-
tion. With more water and a good stretch of his legs outside

the Bentley he began to feel the blood flowing. He felt the phone in his trouser pocket, remembered again about ringing Moth, and reached for it.

'Boss, we gotta go, we're late,' Henri called from the car, sensing distraction.

He put it away again, got back in, focused hard on the books in front of him. Something was wrong, and he needed to pinpoint it. He needed to get the colours to harmonise in a more energetic way. They were bordering on dull. The size of the rooms would diminish them even more and the ballroom was a monster that would dwarf Isabelle's workroom. He pursed his lips, flicking through the samples.

'We don't have time to change it,' Henri said, not for the first time.

'We don't have a choice, it's not right,' Kit argued. 'Did you bring the Colefax, and the Bennett silks?' Henri nodded. 'We'll take them in. I need to see it in the room, then it will come.'

'Lot of money to spend on a whim.'

'It's always a whim,' Kit told him. 'Just look awestruck when I suggest it, as though you've never heard anything as bold and daring.'

'Awestruck?'

'Overwhelmed by my brilliance.'

'I'm not sure what that's supposed to look like,' Henri said.

They pulled up in front of the house. It was lush, even by his standards.

'I forget how gorgeous this place is,' Kit said. They watched as Mrs D'Arby came out of the house, her shorts cut upwards across the top of her muscled thighs, her cropped top hovering away from her ribs, welcoming the eyes upwards. Waving at them, a huge grin sitting beneath enormous dark glasses.

'That's weird,' Henri murmured. 'I never struggle to remember.'

They both smiled at her and waved back, watching her impossibly long, shiny, bouncing brown hair swirl about as she called into the hallway of the moated house.

'How does she see anything inside, wearing those?' Kit asked.

They watched as Mr D'Arby came out of the house. In rough slippers and a shirt that flowed loosely over his bulging waist. They had a wager that the age gap was about thirty-five years. He wasn't old, not yet, but she was no more than twenty-five. Mr D'Arby had found his third wife, Arianna, in Budapest, at an art exhibition. She was the happiest woman on the planet, in Kit's opinion, and Mr D'Arby looked like he was supping on Viagra and fucked senseless for pudding.

'There might be advantages to diminished eyesight,' Henri said as they got out of the Bentley.

'Kit!' Arianna gushed, coming down and swamping him in a warm pressing hug that emphasised her pertness and dusky scent, reminding him that he was a human being, not a crumpled, exhausted to-do list. 'At last, at last, I'm so excited. Oh, Henri, you're such a star.'

Kit noticed that Henri took a lingering hug in his stride as he walked over to Mr D'Arby and shook his hand, keeping it in his and admiring the long driveway and the stripe pressed lawn in fastidious detail until he felt the man warm up. 'Henri, get all the stuff out, lay it out for me. I need to have a grand tour first.'

Arianna bounced up the steps. He offered his arm to her and they walked into the house.

'Now, it's been too much of a delay,' Kit patted her arm, 'and you've been the most wonderful patient darling. I need to refresh my senses. Walk me through it all. I have something tickling at the back of my mind and I need to grasp the aura of the building again. And your paintings of course, they've been inspiring me, I need to commune with them.' He heard a sigh from Mr D'Arby behind him.

'I'll see to the refreshments,' he said in his faint American accent and trailed away from them toward the west wing, where the kitchen lay.

Kit smoothed the hand clutching his arm. 'We're going to have such fun,' he told Arianna.

She was delightful. As a client it was blissful for a change. Youth loaded with beauty and intent on outrage, armed with a fortune and supported by a doting husband who had no interest. What could be better?

They left Henri emptying the Bentley of sample books and headed down the grand hallway toward the picture gallery filled with her enormous canvases of over-sized nudes. It always got his creative juices flowing, looking up at the gaping vulvas, and vein-ridged penises, glistening with moisture. The huge round breasts that wobbled beneath armpits, their vast array of pinks and browns, the tempting pertness of the nipples hovering within mouth reach. She was in love with the shades of human skin. It was an orgy of the senses. Colour overriding scale, toying with vision. He wondered what the children from the other two marriages made of it. Most of them were older than the third bride. What fun. What immense fucking fun she was having.

By the time they left, Arianna had all but orgasmed in the ballroom. She was dragging Mr D'Arby back in there as they pulled away.

'My God, she'll kill him by the end of the year,' Henri said.

'I think I need a minute,' Kit said. 'That woman makes me want to rut.'

'Enough boss, I'm not clearing your rut off the windscreen,' Henri laughed at him.

'You did an awesome version of awestruck, by the way.'

'It wasn't hard,' Henri told him. 'You sold them the idea of painting a 70 foot ballroom the colour of a throbbing penis, with curtains the shade of menstruation trimmed in afterbirth, and called it a glory of the intimate.'

'I told you, I was inspired.'

'Yeah, but what the hell by?' Henri asked. 'That's what I want to know.'

'Other than the thought of an orgy in that ballroom?' Kit asked. 'Right now, not much.'

'I'm not sure you're in the best frame of mind to visit a boarding school,' Henri mused. 'I feel a moral responsibility to take you elsewhere. Perhaps a brothel?'

'Oh hell! The sodding school, I've been trying to ring Moth for two days.'

'Well, you'll be there in...,' Henri checked the Satnav, '... 24 minutes. Seems pointless now.'

AN HOUR later Kit wished even harder that he'd found the time to make that phone call.

He and the Headmaster of Rugby School were sat either side of a large mahogany desk looking at one another in a mix of guilt, consternation, anger and dread which reminded Kit all too much of his own school days. He decided to focus on anger.

'How the hell have you not noticed his absence for four days?'

'Timothy's behaviour has been trying, Mr de Lavelle,' the man explained. 'As a school we have had to develop strategies for handling his anger.'

'Anger? What anger?' Kit asked. 'Anger at being back in this shit hole I should say.'

The man smiled back at him with a benevolent toleration that could only be fuelled by long service to the filthy rich. Kit knew all about that.

'What about his friends? Have you asked them?' Kit asked.

'I'm not at liberty to discuss the other pupils at the school. School policy.'

'Are you serious?' There was something about this room that brought out the unpleasant in him. Holding onto his language was getting harder by the minute. 'He disappears, you don't know about it, you haven't contacted the family and now you want to withhold information about the conniving little bastards who've helped him? Don't you think the police will want to know?'

'Yes, of course, but that will be police business when it gets to that stage.'

'When it gets to that stage?' Kit yelled, standing up and putting both his hands on the wood, where their warmth felt clammy and uncomfortable. 'What stage is it at now? How long do you allow your fee-paying students to disappear for before you contact the family? Let alone the police? What's the school policy on that?'

'Please calm yourself, Mr de Lavelle,' the man protested, leaning back in his chair and raising both hands in a manner that resembled a clipped duck. 'I understand that you are concerned...'

'I'm more concerned by your lack of concern!' Kit bellowed.

He wanted his voice to extend beyond the walls. This man needed to sweat if he was going to get what he wanted, which was access to some of Moth's friends who might know how to contact him. He watched the man slip lower in his chair, cringing as Kit's voice filled the room.

Kit had arrived over an hour ago. An hour that had been, at first, a bemusing justification of his contempt for public schools. An hour that had reminded him of why he'd left at such a young age. An hour when he'd been pampered with coffee and a tour of the latest technology block while the school attempted to produce Moth.

His mild arousal from the hours with Arianna dispersing in cold contemplation of the scuff marks of many feet on floors, walls and stairs. His distaste for uniform coming to the fore as he watched the young students being scoured clean of identity in their blazers and ties. The time wasting made bearable by the Deputy Head who'd escorted him.

Until he was escorted into the Headmaster's office, which brought back such starkly clear memories of former retaliation as to leave him stunned. Remembering Kate turning up to collect him when he was expelled. She had been gorgeous, haughty and dismissive, sitting on his own Headmaster's desk with indifference. In one breath reminding him of and making him long for his mother. Kit was struggling to separate the images between past and present when the Head informed him that they seemed to have mislaid Moth.

A cold clammy weight had bloomed in his gut. A silent blinking awareness growing in his head. Moth was missing.

What had they missed? What had he, Kit, missed? Kit recalled his strange decision to come back to school, a decision that had seemed, at the time, to come from nowhere. But now seemed to have stemmed from Kit's arrival at Riverdell, from the moment he walked into the guest dining room and bawled Moth and Isabelle out. A moment that returned to Kit with crisp lucidity, making him feel sick, breathless and the room too warm for his day-long, travel-crumpled suit. Which was right about when he chose to focus on anger.

'I am concerned, of course, but I do feel calmness is the best way to handle this situation,' the Head protested.

Kit's hands were balling into fists. 'Yeah, sure let's do calm,' he replied. 'I'm calmly considering whether to ring the police first and get you suspended for negligence, or the other parents I know at this school and advise them to take their children home. I'm calmly considering which idiot put you in charge. I'm calmly considering how you will tell Mrs Threlfall you have lost her orphan grandson. I'm calmly,' by this time his voice was a roar, 'considering whether to punch you myself or have my chauffeur do it for me. I'm calmly...'

'Mr de Lavelle.'

A voice behind him interrupted his tirade. He looked round in irritation. The Deputy Head was stood in the open doorway. Her pristine white blouse and navy pencil skirt tight enough to get attention from any man in the building. It had worked on him.

'What the fuck do you want?' he yelled.

She stepped through, closed the door and smiled at him with a calmness that made him itch.

'I think you've made your point.' She walked behind the desk to stand beside the Head.

Well, well, thought Kit. A career opportunist if ever he

saw one. Perfect. Now this he could use.

'Really?' he asked, straightening his shirt as he stood back from the desk. 'I thought I was just getting started.'

She smiled again. A rearranging of the lips and tightening of her elegant jaw that bestowed such a glacial tolerance and profound contempt that he was distracted anew. Her green eyes flecked with an amber light that matched the lightest tints hiding amongst her russet hair. Eyes that suggested, like a fine French finish, that there were deep layers beneath the polished surface.

'No. I think we're done,' she disagreed. 'I have taken the liberty of calling the police, Sir. We've searched the grounds and it's abundantly clear that Timothy is missing. I think it wise you speak with Timothy's grandmother. I have spoken with Timothy's friends and may be able to offer some light on the situation. But we should inform his guardian.' She placed a hand on the Head's shoulder, keeping her sharp green eyes on Kit the entire time.

'Well at last,' Kit sat down in his chair. 'Someone with a set of balls.'

'Perhaps you should use my office to call Mrs Threlfall, Sir? I can wait here with Mr de Lavelle.'

'Of course, Susan,' the Head said and got out of his chair.

Susan? Kit had noticed the door to her office earlier as he waited outside it, DEPUTY HEAD, and underneath it the smaller letters of her name, Ms Suzanne Harper. The idiot Head couldn't even pronounce her name. Suzanne, not Susan. Far more elegant.

'I've spoken with Moth's closest friends,' her voice changed as the Head left. Lowering, becoming more concerned, more engaged. 'He seems to have been both sly and thorough in his preparations. He told a different story to each of them and used them against one another to cover his absence. He's also taken advantage of the busiest week of the school year to confuse us.'

'He can't think much of them as friends,' Kit said.

'He's been careful enough to make all of them appear innocent in the matter.' She moved from behind the table, coming closer to him, leaning back against the hard edge, her legs crossing at the ankles beside his feet. 'None of them will suffer the consequences of any help they've given him.'

'Any idea where's he gone?' The scent of her perfume was a distraction, subtle but dark. He couldn't pinpoint it, couldn't ignore it.

'Not much that makes sense. Possibly London, possibly Dover.'

'Little bastard.'

'Moth's always kept himself to himself,' she said. 'He chose his friends... carefully, but not always wisely it seemed. Now, though, I begin to wonder.'

'Wonder what?'

'If he hasn't been planning this for some time. It takes an unusual array of circumstances for him to have disappeared without notice. For enough people to expect him in enough places without his being missed for several days. Without questions being raised.'

'Seems like a pretty basic flaw in your system,' Kit countered.

'Mr de Lavelle,' she murmured. 'Kit...'

Kit felt the hairs on the back of his neck curl. With that one word, his name, and the way she spoke it, Kit felt his attention focus. Her hands leaning on the table, supporting herself, were fine, slim fingered, manicured. Her whole frame was all held in, polished, restrained. Captured in her hair, a masterfully loose chignon. The highlights tamed, pulled up and held with a single clip that would undo all the bracing.

'Kit, I think you're missing some of the picture,' she said, soft enough that he leant closer before realising she'd reeled him in. 'Not knowing Moth perhaps as well as we do, not knowing some of the friends he chose to keep.'

Her voice was low, concerned, deepening, drawing him in, pulling him closer. Kit pushed himself out of the chair, stood up opposite her. Planting his feet apart, his toes pinioning hers, peering down onto her more relaxed pose, trying to regain control. Finding instead a position where he couldn't help but focus on the unbuttoned top of her blouse, the disappearing diamond of her throat. Damn, she was good.

'I've spoken to everyone at the school who might be able to help, to no avail,' she told him, smiling at his closeness like he'd shown her some trust, not tried to intimidate her. 'But there is someone who, well... formerly a pupil, who left the school, that Moth was always close to.' Her eyes glanced away in discomfort.

More pennies dropped.

'Ben,' he said. 'Moth told me about a friend called Ben, said he used to be a school friend.'

'Precisely,' she murmured to the corner of the desk, making him lean forward. 'Of course, I can't say anything about current pupils, but...'

She cocked her head, her green eyes narrowed, a flash of white teeth tugging at the inner edge of her top lip. Kit felt his attention focus even more. On the curve of her hip, how it folded the uncreasing fabric of her skirt against her hidden form. The light from the tall windows behind her creating a glowing halo that nibbled at her white shirt, the curve of her neck. The high walls of glass fronted bookcases funnelling his vision toward her, giving him no escape. There was something in the moment reminiscent of being in trouble, making his head thick with the desire to undo the topmost button of her shirt.

'No?' he tried to focus.

She shook her head. Kit felt his gut muscles clench, his buttocks tense. His hands were twitching with the urge to explore that revealing neckline and the last thing he needed was to mess the moment up with a sexual harassment charge.

'A swap?' he suggested, his voice thicker than he would have liked.

'A swap?' she asked, her voice masterful, naïve, offended.

'Hmm,' he mused, 'perhaps a favour, from me? In return for the contact number, of a former pupil?'

'A favour?'

'Parents, family, tend to talk to one another, about school issues,' he said. 'To one another, to the press.'

She considered, as though the thought was a surprise. Reaching into her blouse, her folded elbow grazing his chest in the tiny space between them and sending slivers of cotton rubbing sound into the air, she pulled out a slip of paper, tucked inside the shoulder strap of her bra. Kit's breath took his resistance away on a soft sigh. This woman was amazing. He wanted to kneel at her feet and adore her. She held the paper up between two delectable fingers. He tried to think about Isabelle, swamped the thought with his concerns for Moth and felt liberated again. Swam back into the pool of her eyes, where piranhas lurked.

'You're a fascinating person,' she murmured. She put the piece of paper between her teeth, straight as a cricket fence, reached behind her and took the pen from its holder beside the Head's jotter, took his hand and wrote on it. Kit was dazzled by the temptation of moist lips held back from the white paper and the scratching of the pen on the surface of his hand. Moth, and all concerns for him, effaced in the growing awareness that he needed to get out of this office. She took the paper out of her mouth and offered it to him. Kit took it, stepping back, one step, another, fumbling for the door handle. Unused to retreat.

'Pleasure doing business with you, Suzanne.'

Henri was waiting for him in the warm evening car park, stood by the Bentley.

'How'd it go?' he asked. 'How's Moth?'

'Done a runner,' Kit growled at him. 'Used all the turmoil as cover and buggered off.'

Henri stared at him, speechless, mouth agape trying to catch up.

'Get in the car, Henri, we need to drive.' Kit pulled open the passenger seat and got in.

Henri reversed the car out on the gravel and headed for the exit. Kit felt relief to see the school slipping away and the strange desire to see which room she slept in. It appeared in his thoughts, a door chinked open, at the end of a long corridor of closed dormitory doors. Good God, how many boys wanked themselves to sleep at night thinking about her hair clip. Or her cleavage. Or the colour of her underwear.

'Boss?'

'Hmm?' Kit looked away from the school.

'Where next?'

'Home. Bristol.'

He looked down at the slip of paper in his hand. Saw his pen-scrawled skin. He shivered, focused again on the number on the paper, on the name. He had no leverage here. What he needed was knowledge. Knowledge was power.

3

KASHMIR, INDIA. 13TH JULY 1966

Darling Rose,

You're pregnant!?

But how? When? I can't even imagine you being with a man, let alone long enough to conceive! Has my own defection changed your heart at long last? Or was it a whim you needed to test?

I am stunned. Horrified. Overjoyed. Worried. Too far away from you. And oh, how I wish I was with you, could talk to you. Your letter reached me over two months late and you must think I have no feelings to have not called. But you know me, I can't stand the phone at the easiest of times, let alone with such news to discuss. The letter was sent on (tardily) from Bombay and arrived after we left for the mountains, your momentous news has sat here kicking its heels in my absence.

We have been travelling. Ted took me to Ladakh, in the Himalayas, for my birthday. It was gruelling. Long weeks of travelling and, with such visions of natural beauty at every turn in the road, I lost all track of time and thought. We returned to Kashmir a week ago and I have not had a chance to reply to you since. Ted has returned to Bombay but insists I remain here until the monsoon is over. He suggests the hot months of October and November will be trial enough for me in Bombay without the misery of the rain to deal with first.

I wish you could be here. Over two months on my own and you would love this wild place. It is vast and cosmic as no place I have ever seen. The nearby city, Srinagar, lies strung out on lakes and parks cradled in the lap of the mountains, filled with tulips and almond trees. In the spring they say the blossom display is the beauty of Kashmir, I cannot wait to see it. The valley is wide and lush, with mountains towering in the background. It takes us three days to get here from Bombay and none of easy travelling, but it is rewarded. Ted has a villa in the east of the Srinagar valley, in the foothills. A low-slung bungalow type place surrounded by a vast garden, acres and acres run wild with neglect. Behind us rears the massive Kolahoi and the road that leads to the Himalayas. The sun sets on our verandah behind the Pir Panjal Mountains, a natural barrier between Indian Kashmir and Pakistan. Ted was posted here in the first days of partition, before he left the India Army. He will not speak of those times but grows more distant with the memories. He lives in near solitude, a respite I think from his endless work amidst the melee of Bombay.

The villa is badly furnished, ill-repaired and far too large. Yet I love it! It is laid out in three wings round a large court-yard with a now-redundant fountain in the middle. A low wall creates a fourth side to the courtyard and holds back the garden, barely. Empty rooms lie dusty and mouldy behind closed doors. Ted says many such places were abandoned by the British in the last days of the Raj. In the quiet evening shadows, it reminds me of Riverdell, and I wonder if that is what tempted him to buy it. He plans to retire here but, when I see him lost in thought and crushed with sadness, I wonder if that would be a good thing for him. Arguing with his father and insisting on staying in India cost him everything and I suspect what he stayed behind to help with has scarred him in hideous ways. None of which, of course, he would ever admit to his father, any more than he discusses it with me. They are as proud as each other.

This must be some of the most disputed land in India, strung as it is between Pakistan and the insatiable greed of China. From the moment the British left, Kashmir has been the pawn of national, political and religious parties. I can understand their longing. The valley is precious, sublime and stirs in me a desire never to leave. I am peaceful as I have not been since you left. We have one member of staff, Kishori, who we call Kish. She is perhaps in her fifties, I think, but cannot decide. Her face is strangely contorted down one side, and she avoids looking directly at people and speaks only Kashmiri, which Ted began teaching me before he left. I would be worried about the language barrier but as she ignores everything we say anyway, it seems irrelevant. Ted adores her and I shall make a good effort to befriend her in the months ahead, as I try to make this place feel like home. So, I am busy, excited and here, now, your news. Pregnant. Six months pregnant too.

You say nothing about how you are finding pregnancy, but I imagine it is a breeze to you as all else is. You will make a wonderful mother, I am sure. Though doing this all alone, well... both no more and no less than any of us should have predicted. I can only imagine William's response, though I struggle to decide if he would have been more upset you are not returning to academic studies or are an unwed mother-to-be? I bet Elsa was shocked and terrified for you, and no doubt Kate entirely supportive. You shall be the first of us to be a mother! Leading us on in life as always.

Why do you hope so much for a daughter? A boy will not, as you say, be one more useless man in the world. My adorable wild Rose, whatever child comes, you shall raise it with the same determination and freedom that lives in you, and this child of yours will be as strong as you are yourself. If you have a son, you will raise him to be remarkable, not useless. You do not mention the father, and I shall not ask for, as you say, this child will be yours alone and yours entirely. Though I suspect those long nights on the ocean liner that took you home were not all lonely, from the timing of the pregnancy. I am glad Grandma is with you to help and loves you as much as she ever has, to support your every choice.

Ted and I are trying for a child too.

I feel that this is the whole purpose of our intimate relations. Being with Ted is nothing like I have known. And though you did everything you could to prepare me for it on our trip to India, I fear you have spoiled me for any man. Ted is somehow shy and brusque in the same kiss. Determined to please me by pleasing himself. Half-dressed and in the dark. Though our pleasure in each other's company remains strong, it seems our pleasure in the bedroom is to be less successful.

At least my body seems to prefer India to England. My periods have become bearable, and the pain that once lasted almost a month is now only about two weeks. Ted won't come anywhere near me when I bleed. Making me feel even more like a baby-making machine, rather than his lover. Should I talk to him about all the many ways we can be together? It seems impossible to begin, but we are new to each other, and time will make me more confident. But now... two blissful months alone. I return to Bombay at the end of September. You must send news there as soon as the baby is born. I wish I could be there with you for the birth. I cannot wait to hear what you will call your child. And when you will visit.

Forgive me again for the long delay in responding, and for not phoning. I prefer the intimacy of these letters between my dearest friends, which I can hold close and read and reread to my heart's content. When we speak on the phone it is often a very public affair and I am crushed with loneliness in the absence of your voices afterwards and the great distance between us is torture.

I miss you, Rose. Was I naïve to think it would ever be otherwise?

ALL MY LOVE,

BETH.

4

M oth woke in the barn to the sounds lurking in his dreams. The barn huge and bone cold. Cows lulling in the morning air, swollen and full too.

He wanked hard and quick. The smell of their muck drifting fresh through the walls. Mixing with the spunk in his hand. Fog inside him thick enough to drown in. He crawled out of his bag, fingers stiff with cold. Threw water from the tap over his face. Pushed the naked memories into his clothes. Left the barn and went to find the cows.

Watching at first. The dawdling haunches, the spurting milk, the singing machinery. The farmer working, talking to his cows, calling, soothing. Strong hands, soft voice. The normality bleeding into the morning. Draining away his tension.

Watch until you see something you won't mess up.

Open this gate, that way, at that time. Five cows to a line. He offered a hand, got a shrug in return, and a watchful silence until he did it right. When they were all done, he helped hose the dairy down, and they walked the cows back out together. Somewhere in the mix the bad dreams faded.

Cows sound like cows in the meadow.

He'd earned his breakfast. A warm affair in the farmhouse kitchen. When he went back to pack up, the barn was full of straw.

Not ghosts.

Standing in its quiet vaulted space, breathing in the musty fumes, he decided, when he went home, he would work with farmers. Not farming. But doing something with farmers. Farmers gave him confidence in life. The way they got up and applied themselves to an endless task without despair. Believing they could do it. But he wouldn't milk cows.

Twice a day, every day? Not you.

He couldn't do it. He'd watched James long enough, and Leon, to know he couldn't live that life. Hitched to a freight train. Waking to the same worries. But still, being with them made him feel a better person.

You get back on the bike every day.

But that wasn't the same at all. The effort it took to get back on the bike had taught him he was more like Isabelle. It wasn't the journey, it was the destination that got him back on the bike. Wanting to know what came next. Needing the unknown ahead.

That sounds more like Kit.

They'd had that in common, Isabelle and Kit. Shying away from being put into a place, set to a task, other than the one they wanted.

That was pretty much all they had in common.

And perhaps he hadn't been ready to admit he was more like them. There was something comforting in his time with James, with Kate too. A solidity. Decency.

You liked that.

He'd liked the idea of building his own life, making his own way through the world. Making the world his own. But the world hadn't been in agreement with him on that score.

He left by mid-morning. Riding casually through the valleys. Watching the road dip in and out of shadows cast by the clefts between the mountains on his right. By lunchtime, the sun was warm on his back. The night soothed away. The rhythm of the road strong and quiet, taunting him with its emptiness. Pulling at his muscles with an ache that hit too hard for the level route. The tarmac stretching out for long moments. Empty. His mind foggy from the night. The lines tempting him to weave through the gaps.

That's a quick way to get dead. Dick. Stay straight.

He hit Bolzano in a blare of traffic after lunchtime. A big ass town stuck in the pit of the mountains like belly button fluff. The aggression of the city hitting him in waves of sound and life. Punching him out of the haunting stillness of Vigo.

Moth slowed down and tried to adjust.

Focus on traffic.

Find the route.

Bleed out the noise.

He pulled away from the town and up onto the steady incline the other side. The waves of noise reaching out, dragging him back. His legs leaden, his shoulders twisting with discomfort. He stopped early afternoon for a late lunch in a barren field, lying down out of sight from the road behind a hedge.

You should keep moving.

The Mendola was next. Another long hard climb and he resisted thinking about it. The bad night eating at his energy. His back tight from the soft straw. He stretched out from eating and closed his eyes. Tiredness pulling him in. The passing cars soothing him into a doze. Pulling him out and sending him back. Each car a wave he couldn't resist.

It was late afternoon when he came to. Hot, nauseous, panting. His body sweating as he tried to focus. His mind recoiling from the images. The dark cold water. The beach. Borts.

He rolled onto his knees, looking outwards, trying to focus on where he was going. Saw the mountain rising ahead. Swaying over him with contempt.

You don't need to do it. Take the valley road.

Venice was south. On a clear road. With no mountains.

You don't need to do this. You've done the mountains.

Kit was on the other side of that last mountain.

In theory. If he's still there.

His dead legs counted the height. He ached inside and out. Hot sweats of stress rushing over him. Trying to calm the panic.

What's the bloody point.

You're too tired.

You're too slow.

He won't be there.

You don't need to do this.

He'd told himself that before. He did need to do this. It didn't matter when he got there, it wasn't about being on time for Kit. There wasn't a rush. He did need to do this. He couldn't ride on, wondering again what he'd left undone behind him.

That was different.

It's the same. Same as Borts. He wouldn't run away again. He'd decided to go see Kit. Even if he got there late. He wasn't going to let one more mountain make the difference. Then the mountain would have decided, not him.

He would ride for one more hour and stop. Set up camp before it got dark for a change.

Get a decent night's sleep.

It would be better to do the pass tomorrow. He checked the map. An incline, sharp bends, a space of fields before the real slog. He got to his feet, head groggy and spinning, forcing the bike back onto the road. The hour was a long one, the incline relentless. It dragged out and out and his legs grew heavier, his pace slower. The day was giving up on him when he arrived, took one look at the fields and his hopes crumpled. The fields on the map were tree plantations.

Shit. Impossible to camp in there.

He rode a bit further, the road getting tougher.

You'll be stuck going up the mountain if you keep going.

He turned back. The release of going downhill sweet in his muscles. He would have to camp here. On the curve of the road as it headed downhill, he stopped, leaning against the barriers. He was high enough up to have a view of the mountains he'd come through. Curving away in ridges from the valleys and up to the tinted clouds. The light was bleeding fast, plunging into the pass above him. He could see the houses that guarded the nest of fields. Tried to guess his best option. The fields highest up, right in front of him, least planted near the steepening sides. He could see it better coming downhill.

He chucked the bike over the barriers, leapt over with one hand holding it, lifted it up and took trembling steps down the rocky sides. He passed through rows of trees, budding and thin in the high air. The next field over was empty.

Visible to the houses.

Beyond it stood another one. He stared at the distance, counting the tired steps between him and it. He'd be safer there.

Is it worth it?

He took them. Made it. Put the bike down against the fence and looked behind him.

Please let no one have seen.

He waited long minutes. Anyone who'd seen him would have had time to get there. He wasn't going to put the tent up to be told to take it down again.

They can do it themselves.

They'd have to pick him up and carry him out of the field. He was flat out tired. Scared of sleep. Of what he couldn't fight, asleep. The weight of his dreams crushing him. Seeping into the real world as the light seeped away down the back of the mountain.

He threw the tent over the bike and looked at the ends that needed pegging. Sat down. Flat on his butt in the field.

Watching life fade through orange clouds and the mountains turn graphite, burning at their tips. Sitting there when the blue hour came, the tent flapping unrigid in the mild breeze that stirred the young trees. Grey turning indigo and taking the other colours with it. A blotched, ink-wash, snakeskin sky. A seeping poison he couldn't out-ride.

He hurt. His body hurt. Legs, butt, back. Muscles, ribs, mind. His gut hurt. Even something inside, right in the middle hurt. His diaphragm perhaps. Aching, winded.

That's the mountains coming out.

Biting back only now, when he was done. He could die like this.

Sat in this field, too tired to put up the bloody tent.

Watching life ebb into some castrated shade of blue.

Lying down and closing his eyes as the last drop of flame lifted to the stars. Moth waited it out. Not sure if he was waiting for pain to pass, or death to come.

It's not a bad place to wait.

Part way up a mountain, the view stretched out before him. He wouldn't mind, dying here. Away from them all. Alone. Himself. Whoever he was. Waiting with near pleasure. Life at a distance and gorgeous.

Massive and fading. The high stars making it all part of something connected. Him fading into the same. Each breath long and clinging.

Perhaps this was what it came down to.

A quiet end in a quiet place.

Too worn out to protest.

Thinking about Nat, Elsa, Kit, James. All of them as distant as the stars. Far away.

Except, her. You'd want to see her again.

He'd want Isabelle to know. She'd given him the courage. In soft drops, here and there, seeing him as a person. Making him anew through new eyes. That was what he'd wanted to say, that last day, as the train pulled in. He'd wanted her to know. She'd made the difference in his life.

He closed his eyes to the dusk and mountains. Saw her again. The last time he'd seen her.

Perched on the stool at her worktable, stitching life back into some neglected scrap. Her attention absorbed. Nothing but the sound of the popping fire in the huge room. He'd waited there for hours. He'd had no choice. She walked in when he wasn't expecting her, freezing him in a panic on his knees. The pannier bags pulled out from the boxes they'd packed them in.

She mustn't see you. It will ruin the whole plan.

She was quiet. Buried in her work, oblivious to all else. Searing a memory into him that wouldn't fade. That overrode everything he'd decided. That she was best with Kit. That she and Kit were right together. That she would be happier if he left. Free to do her own thing. She was only there baby-sitting him. She unbecame all those things he'd convinced himself. She was alone. Hunched over and nursing her focus. Hiding everything inside.

Like you.

Her back curled over. Her hair falling forwards. Her fingers holding and moving fabric. He dared to move, to fragmentally rearrange his screaming muscles until he could lie down on the floor. Praying she wouldn't come his way, find him in the diminished mess of the room.

Ruin everything.

The near two weeks of careful effort. Hiking cross-country from the next train station. Hiding out in the old coal shed in Mrs Staines' overgrown garden. Watching the house from the scrubby slopes of the castle until he was certain the police had dismissed the bike, not taken it away. Taken the bait of misleading information. Given up interest.

What does she think about it?

Did she think at all, or push it away with the needle? He wanted to know. Lying in the dimness, watching the curve of her back. He wanted to stand up, go to her, ask her.

If she cares about you? Is that what you want to know.

Ask her to keep his secret. Ask her to help him. He wished she wasn't there. It was so hard, not to stand up, not to walk towards her, not to ask one more question. Not to tell her...

... tell her what?

He didn't move. Rigid with the thought. Tell her. Before you go. All of it.

You don't need to tell anyone.

What would be the point?

It won't change anything for you.

He couldn't change his pain, but he could prevent theirs. Nat's. Isabelle's.

Think of the plan.

The plan was his future. Hers had been chosen for her. He'd chosen his own.

He stayed on the floor, watching her intent back, until she left. Stretching and sticking the needle into her pin cushion, turning off the lights as she pulled the door to. Waiting longer to be sure she was gone. Knowing she would have woven the needle into her clothes if she were coming back.

She might be up, making porridge. Be careful.

Moth pulled the pannier bags out, the tent. Checking all the pegs and lines were with it. He uncovered the bike against the back wall, strapped the pannier bags on. They would feel odd, the tent on one side and nothing on the other.

Not for long. Tonight's the night.

His hoard of kit was in the tin storage locker in Mrs Staines' shed. The waiting was over. He was leaving. He rolled it out through the door, down the corridor and out of the garden back door. Swapping it for the replacement, rusty, old and bought cheap from a charity shop. Chosen for its likeness in size and shape, not its usability. He carried it back into her workroom, wary of drips on the floor to suggest he might have been this way. Each step cautious of trainer squeaks. Handling the heavy door with confidence, knowing exactly when it might catch and echo.

He draped the cover over the impostor and tweaked it.

It fits a treat.

He headed for the doorway, got tempted passing the

table. Drawn in by the sight of what she'd been stitching. Some old scrap of fabric she was piecing back together, forming into something new. He could make nothing of it, but the colours called him. His fingers reaching, feeling the texture, the strength in the stitches that held it together. Discarded beside the emerging work were smaller patches. He picked one up, wanting to pin it to the table. To let her know. To say good-bye.

That's a really dumb idea.

Instead, he pulled a needle out of her pin cushion. Wove it into a scrap as he'd seen her do, twice in and out to keep it secure. In the old dresser he found a silver cigarette case he'd seen when searching for a penknife to steal. He laid the scrap and the needle inside it, musty vapours rising, weighing it in his hand.

No more than a few ounces. You can cope with that.

It was hard to leave. When it came, when all the creeping and planning was done, down to that last moment in her workroom. He'd spent so much time there, beside the dying fire, on the sofa, watching her work at the table. It was harder to leave that silent room than anything else, even to say false goodbyes to Nat. Beyond that room Moth wasn't sure who he was.

First step is the hardest.

The first step to finding out was the step he took to leave that room. Leaving behind the strange bubble she had made for them in it. A bubble he didn't fully understand. Leaving meant letting go of making sense of it. The moments when his body leaned towards her. The moments when all he felt was calm and a strange rising joy inside. A sense of invincibility. Leaving meant finding out what he was capable of on his own. It took him longer than he wanted. That first step. His hand touching the hard surface of the silver case in his pocket.

You can always come back. Later. If you want to.

That idea took him out the door. That, and the plan. In his head the plan was the shining light at the end of the tunnel. An idea he'd been growing for years.

There's a way out. You can get out.

It had grown brighter and stronger with each piece of the track that he put in place. Those last few months, when his dad derailed the whole thing, had been hard. But he'd been careful, working his way around the hiccups. His parents, Riverdell, leaving Nat alone. Took the bonuses. Working for James, the bike, Mrs Staines, Elsa. He'd watched, waited, plotted, made it happen.

The money gathered. The bank account sorted. The contact system. The happiness he showed at Riverdell. Going back to school. The passport from Ben given to his younger brother, passed to Moth. The teachers he'd riled, the bad vibes he spread, the confusion that would cover his disappearance. The false hints he left, the train tickets, the web links, the passing comments. It gave him time, time to get to Riverdell, time to collect his stuff.

It had all hung on the bike. The one thing he couldn't control. His greatest hope hanging on Isabelle's determination to look after it for him. It was a weak link. And nothing could make it stronger. He'd thrown some part of his future to the Gods, hoping for luck, knowing it would be harder to try again if he was caught that first time.

And the Gods listened.

All those weeks coming together.

Weeks of waiting and planning. He made it into the house. From the house to the bike. From the bike to the boat.

All by yourself.

Alone. Truly alone. Watching himself. Listening to himself. Without words outside him.

No one telling you who you are.

Orphan, brother, nephew, grandson. Child, youth, schoolboy. Rebel, troublemaker, loser. Little Timmy.

Words, words, words. Each one a label. All belonging to others.

Like Kit had told him, all an expression of other people's discomfort.

He wanted to hear what he was for himself. He wanted to leave all the other masks behind and become that person.

The ride to Holyhead was his first taste of freedom. The traffic stress contrasting with the eerie moments of road silence. The sound of the wind rushing past. The road gliding between mountains and past the coast. Snowdonia opening out before him. Something rugged in the land.

Something rugged inside.

Nights sleeping wild in the tent. Arriving beside the sea as the sun dropped into it. He slept high on the beach at Criccieth. The tall grasses whispering against the taut fabric. The sound of the sea against the pebbles echoing inside him. Moved on the next day washed clean inside.

The ferry to Ireland easy and quick. No questions, no stares. Himself, watchful, nervous on the inside. The world oblivious on the outside.

You're disappearing.

Learning how to seem distant. Focused, confident, relaxed. A young man, travelling alone, exploring life.

Nobody's business.

Passing from Wales to Ireland, down the eastern side and onto the ferry to Roscoff without a mutter. It was a long ferry trip, an overnighter on seas, rocking back and forth, hoping for success, dreading failure. Thoughts and current making him sick. Being returned. A runaway. Watched. Mistrusted.

A failure.

Wheeling onto the European continent without a question, without a look at his false passport from Ben. Three weeks after leaving Isabelle at the train station he was in France and heading south.

It was hot. August in France made him sweat all day long. Following the coast road as much as possible. Some days it was only a glimpse from a distance, some days, hours at a time with the sea breeze cooling his wet back.

It was hard. Riding busy roads and strange customs. Slogging down the middle of France. Long days in the saddle. Short nights in the fields. Copses, riverbanks, fields. The first few clear as a bell, but soon merging into glimpsed pitches in semi-darkness. Etching place names in his notebook.

It was intense. Days when he woke in treacle. A mental sludge lying over him that he fought his way through to stand up. When it took most of the day to cycle the fog away. Pushing hard to banish the thoughts, be tired enough that he could sleep that night. Exhausted but peaceful, clinging onto his new sense of self by a thread.

But though the days were hot, hard, or intense, and the difficulty of getting back on the bike grew with the distance he put behind, they added up to something greater. Him plus the bike plus the plan.

Self-propulsion. Self-creation.

Riding in the power of the sun alone, full of a life that was his to define, one day at a time.

Pushing back the frustrations. The limitations of age. The guilt of leaving. The memories.

A long, straight sun-gilded trajectory he was passing through, to a wide-open place where other people had no bearing.

Before he'd learnt that the plan wasn't enough.

Before Bort-les-Orgues, where he found the limit of courage.

Before Ventoux, where he found the fields empty.

Before Guethary, where he crawled into Beau's restaurant.

Moth felt her memory like a needle of pain. He longed to pull her postcard out, to see her handwriting. He squeezed his eyes shut against the tears, huddled over his stinging chest.

Why is it your kindest memories hurt the most?

He'd tried to pay her for the meal, but she'd laughed at him, mocking him in quick fire French. He was exhausted, battered with misery and gratitude at such unexpected kindness that he struggled to keep back the tears. Gulping and blinking and sweating with a surge of emotions. Humiliated, fumbling. She pushed his money away, holding onto his hand, frowning at his face.

Those eyes see right through you.

She pushed him back down at the table, gave him another drink and left him to sleep, propped up against the wall, while the wet stormy day drenched the streets outside. She braved the showers, wheeled his bike into the shelter of the slapping canopy and threw a plastic tablecloth over it. When he woke, she made him wash the dishes. Fed him again and left him at a quiet back table for the evening while her customers came and went in small groups. When the last had left she wheeled his bike in, propping it against the counter, looked at him long and hard, and locked the door behind her as she left. When she came back in the morning, he was sweeping the floor, rested and brighter, expecting to leave.

But Beau hadn't let him leave, not for two more months. Not until she could squeeze the extra flesh on his cheek again with a satisfied smile.

Moth opened his damp eyes, sat on the hard, cold ground below the Mendola. Swamped with memory, the tent flapping at his attention, his eyes trying to focus outwards. The lighter patches of sky behind the clouds fading into an all-consuming darkness.

It was a choice. That was all it came down to. When the plan failed. Because it did fail, at times.

And you must choose. To give up, or to get up.

It was his choice. It was personal.

Like faith.

It wasn't about what made sense. It was about his choice.

Give up or get the hell up.

Your choice, Little Timmy.

He rolled onto his knees, crabbed onto his feet and forced himself to finish the tent.

So much for an early night.

He was too tired to cook porridge. He ate what was left of lunch. Drank a load of water to fill himself up. Ten minutes later he pissed. Crawled into his tent with the bag for his pillow. The pain was going. Leaving tiredness.

His choice. It was all he had. Even at Borts, he'd had a choice.

Do something.

Stick to the plan.

Or do nothing.

You must stick to the plan.

The plan had won.

He got to Ventoux. Cycled all the way there. *A* Without getting caught. When he got there, he was messed up in the head. Empty fields greeting his hope, and always the mountain rising out of them. Alone. Like it had been for her. Like it had been for him. Alone, when he left again, without a plan.

Moth lay in the tent and felt its thinness crushed from outside by the dark sky. He reached inside the bag beneath his head, found the notebook. Opening it, he saw the echo of former plans underneath the entry for Vigo. The rubbing out showing in the harsh narrow light.

If only it was that easy to rub out the past.

You do what you can about what you can.

Some things didn't get etched in pencil. The ones he needed to rub out had been written indelibly.

Tattooed on your bones.

Out of sight. Where no one could see them. There whenever he undressed. Lurking in the darkness at the end of each day.

He wrote with chilled, numb fingers, *Day 267. 25th March 2013. Bolzano.* Shut the notebook and tucked it away.

He pulled the cigarette case out. Inhaled the aroma of lavender in the darkness. Let his finger travel up and down the soothing length of the needle.

He hadn't liked cycling without a plan. Left at the bottom of the drive was not a plan. Southwest was not a plan. It was a direction. The next few months taught him that much. Taught him hard. Until he found Beau. Who taught him better. When he left, he made sure he had a plan. Vienna. Because Beau had plastered pictures of it all over her restaurant. And it was east, away from the ocean.

Towards cheaper countries.

Same as now. It might have changed. But he'd changed it. The new plan was still his.

Divert. Meet Kit. Leave again.

Head southeast. Away from central Europe. Turkey. Beyond, to Asia if he could make it. To cheaper living.

Warmer weather for the winter. When the night came down, when that inky stain spread over him, Moth always made sure of the plan. Fixed it in his mind to ward away the dreams, and the memories. The plan was what got him through the night.

Past the memories of the beach at Bort.

When the light was fading but enough to see her lying on the sand.

When the door closed behind his mother's disappointed face.

Moth curled into a padded ball, the cigarette case wrapped into the protective centre. When he shut his eyes, he hoped the dreams would stay away.

The plan a light fixed in his mind. Him, standing between what he couldn't change and moving toward what he might yet stand a chance of achieving.

ISABELLE FELT PUSHED out by the silence. Riverdell a frosty, echoing accusation, unspoken guilt stalking her shadow across the windows.

She opened doors hoping for sense, but the stark rooms presented more questions she didn't understand, let alone dare to answer. One by one she propped them open, nervous of what might grow behind them. Making fabric bags from scraps with big grab handles, filling them with dried beans and rice from the kitchen. Taken from the huge storage jars that mocked her solitary presence.

She pushed away thought. Found comfort in the familiar workroom. A cushion she could fix.

Re-purposed with careful stitches and supportive scraps for borders. Her hand sewing a trim along the edge to cover the fraying where the piping cord was showing through. It was laborious work, sewing one side down to the piping, folding a piece of bias-cut olive silk to the back and teasing the new trim to attach to it. The corners took longest, working out the bunching of the trim and the ruching of the bias silk. It soothed her one difficult stitch at a time. It was late, the night still outside the open windows. The river lazy and thin with summer quiet, trickling over the weir and through the mill race in the background. Thoughts pausing her fingers. Wondering where he was. Wondering how. Wondering why.

It was the why that kept her moving. A thought she had to keep walking away from. Keep herself busy. She resumed stitching. It was the why which no one wanted to talk about.

Even Kate, never one to shy from a subject, turned her concerns away with a vexed huff. Kit avoided the subject altogether, claiming loyalty to Moth's choice. And Elsa, well, after her first few days of shock, stilled apathy in her chair in the study, pale as the unread pages of her book open on her lap, she'd set her lips in a tight line, put away the letter he'd sent her and returned to her focus on Nat and Swansea. Moth's disappearance was added to their refusal to talk to her about Riverdell.

Nat had been the first to receive communication. A letter telling her he was fed up with school, had gone on holiday with a friend and would be back later in the summer to see her in Swansea. With strict instructions to get his bedroom ready for him. Nat hadn't seemed surprised at all. And her total lack of concern encouraged the idea it was but a holiday, and the words 'run away' disappeared from their vocabulary.

Kit had been complicit in this, encouraging it. Moth was travelling with a friend. Moth wanted time to himself. Stop being a bunch of old women. He was a young man, not a little boy. No news was good news. Moth was fine. Everything was fine.

Five weeks after the news had come, ten days after Elsa and Nat had left, Isabelle came to the realisation that while everyone else was "fine", she was not. Absolutely, terrifyingly, not fine. Her fine was haunted by the why of Moth's absence.

She gave up coercing the bias silk to smooth fraying corners. The cushion had defeated her for now. She would try again tomorrow. She trailed a finger across the completed section, felt the ragged edges of the fibre underneath. The silk was not strong enough for the task. She hadn't chosen well, it would not last long. She sank the needle up to its eye in the pincushion, feeling the hard table resist its point underneath. It was late, she left the workroom, made her way up to her bedroom.

Between those two spaces she was held together, like the pieces of fabric she reworked. Glad that she could retreat between rooms that made sense. All thoughts lost in a sleep that was tired enough to keep the why at bay.

IF SHE WAS LOST, Kate was tired.

Isabelle watched her from the table. Making coffee and toasting bread, talking about the bistro. Talking about the managers, the customers, the menu. Talking about anything to cover over her tiredness. Trying to tell Kate that she was supposed to be doing less, that was the point of handing over management, had been as helpful as telling the rain to go back to the cloud.

'What are you doing today?' Kate came to join her at the table.

Isabelle was tired of the question. What was she doing? Today, tomorrow, ever? How did she know? The days evolved, from one moment to the next while she waited for inspiration to tell her what to do.

'I have no idea.' Isabelle had run out of options for pretence. 'I really have no idea what I'm doing. Everything I've known has up and left. Which is not what I'm used to. I'm used to being the one that up and leaves. I keep thinking I still should.'

'Well,' Kate said, blinking at her in surprise. 'Well, I suppose that's a step in the right direction. At least you acknowledge you're not doing anything.'

'Well,' Isabelle could hear the defensive tone of her own voice. Shine it back, that was what Kate did. It was her meanest trick to win an argument. 'What would you do, if all your life turned upside down while you blinked, without so much as a please or thank you? No one there to tell you your options?'

Kate opened her mouth to reply. A prim reply, no doubt, Isabelle thought. Full of how she made sure no one could do such a thing to her. Life was hers to control, and hers alone. Isabelle waited for her to speak but she stayed silent, a slight frown between her eyes. Not the normal frown of irritation or contempt, but a line of consternation. Her own trick working against her.

'I don't know.' Kate looked up with a weak smile. 'I think I might need a bit of time to figure it out too.'

'That's what I'm doing. Waiting for time to figure it out for me.'

'I would maybe be a bit more proactive than that,' Kate said. 'I don't like the idea of anyone deciding for me, not least time. It's a slippery bastard when you leave it in charge. One day becomes a week, a month, a year. Before you know it ten years have passed by and you realise you never chose the decision you ended up with.'

'I think I'm waiting for Kit,' Isabelle confessed. 'I need him to help me decide what's best.'

'Kit thinks he knows what's best for everyone.' Kate picked up a piece of toast, took a bite, held it aloft in the air. 'He's a lot like his mother in that. I wouldn't let Kit tell you what to do, you'll end up with a life that's a fair shade of what he wants, not you.'

'But I don't know what I want,' Isabelle complained. 'I don't have this big-picture, blue-sky, ultimate-goal plan. I never have.'

'I think that's always been clear.' Kate bit into the toast again, Isabelle watching the crumbs fall to the floor as Kate used it to punctuate her point. 'But surely, along the way you've worked out what you enjoy in life, and what you don't? How about concentrating on those? I always felt life sort of pieced itself together, an inch at a time. Until you knew what you wanted to keep and protect.'

'Like a patchwork quilt?'

'A good metaphor,' Kate said. 'One that suits you.'

Isabelle stayed quiet, thinking. Listening to the slow turning of her coffee cup, its rough base tugging at the smooth china of the saucer.

'You can always remake it, after all,' Kate added. 'What's that thing you always told me about fabric? You can unstitch it, move it, try it another way. It's... what do you call it?'

'Non-resistant,' Isabelle murmured.

'Exactly, that's what you need to be. Malleable, but purposeful. Purpose keeps you going, through the bad times. Which is when we need it most.'

In Kate's words she found a flicker of excitement, a hope to catch hold of. But as soon as Kate left, the drift would set in. Leaving her in some desecrated room clutching a protective cushion or curtain to her chest, worrying about its trailing threads.

'You have all this space to command,' Kate said. 'You can do anything with it. But if you do nothing, it won't take long at all before it all crumbles around you.'

'No pressure there then,' Isabelle muttered, feeling the flicker drown in the dregs of her morning coffee.

'Pressure is necessary, Isabelle.' Kate stood up. 'Pressure is the essence of life. If you don't cope with it, there's something you need to build into your decisions, how to reduce it. Now, fascinating as this conversation is, I must go to work. Will you come and see me today? Or shall I come down later?'

'I'll come and see you, this afternoon.' A flicker of guilt ran through her as Kate arched her eyebrows in response. 'I know, I know, this time, I promise. After the lunch run. We'll have a cup of tea together.'

'Three-thirty,' Kate told her in a no-nonsense tone. 'I shall boil the kettle and pour it over you if you let me down again.'

'I promise.'

'Right, I'm off. Good luck with out-waiting time.'

'Thanks, much appreciated.'

Kate came and kissed her on the cheek, a warm arm around her shoulders before she left through the hallway.

Isabelle heard her open the front door, and exclaim, 'Oh, hello, no, of course, come in, come in,' followed by footsteps in the hall. Multiple footsteps. Kate backed into the kitchen, her arm coming last, left out in supplication to someone in the hall. Isabelle stood up to see who it was.

'Isabelle, it's Asha to see you.'

Isabelle walked forwards, saw Asha behind Kate.

'Hello.'

'I can come another time,' Asha said. 'If it's bad now?'

'No, not at all,' Isabelle reassured her. 'It's fine, please come in.'

'I, though, must go,' Kate told them. 'You two have fun. Come and see me again soon with James. Come for supper one evening at the bistro.'

Kate walked out and they heard the front door shut behind her.

'Coffee?' Isabelle asked.

'That would be nice, thank you.'

'Are you happy in here, or do you want to go outside, enjoy the sunshine?'

'Here is fine,' Asha moved to take a seat at the table, putting her bag down at her side. It was a large bag, bulging outwards as she released the handles. 'I'm between appointments in town, I mustn't stop too long. I was hoping to speak with you.'

'Oh, of course.' Isabelle started up the coffee machine, her hands feeling clammy. 'How do you have your coffee?'

'Black, please, and strong.' Asha folded her hands on the table before her, looking about the room. Observant, taking in the details, as though she was at work, not here on pleasure. Frowning at the dresser full of china. 'I thought Elsa would have taken that precious stuff with her. Poor you.'

'I know, and now I don't know what to do with it.' Isabelle's anxiety increased in the presence of Asha's matter-of-fact calm. She sat down, small talk punctuating the air as they kept an uncomfortable silence at bay.

'So,' Asha said, with a tight smile, taking a polite sip from her coffee. 'I hope you won't mind my coming to see you. I asked James to speak with you, but he said he couldn't. I haven't told him that I'm coming.'

'It sounds serious. I'm sure James will understand.'

'Perhaps, men can be funny like that,' Asha said. 'They have pride in ways that are stupid. I don't know if he has told you, but James has asked me to marry him.'

Isabelle blinked. The news a stone hitting water. Ripples on the surface as the great weight dropped beneath. Willing happiness to appear on her face.

'No,' she heard herself say. 'He hadn't told me. I'm happy for you, for you both.'

'I love James.' Asha raised her chin as she spoke. 'I feel I have known him much longer than the months we have been together.'

'That's wonderful.'

'But,' Asha twisted her hands together on the table, squaring her shoulders, 'I feel bad saying this, it will make you think badly of me. James has told me he will never leave the farm.'

'And you don't want to live there?'

'No, I am happy to think about living there,' Asha looked straight down the long table, directly at her. 'But I do not want to marry a man who does not own his own home. Or for it to not be our home if we are married.'

Isabelle sat back, blinking some more. Tiny pebbles following the first rock. James' farm belonged to her. His ex-girlfriend. She was his landlady, and would be theirs, if they married. She cringed. It seemed hideous to her. And James would never speak to her about it, she could see that clearer than the table between her and Asha.

'I don't want to tell him I can't marry him because of this,' Asha said. 'He will think I don't love him. He will think it is because of money that I say no. That is what people will think. But I don't want my married home to always feel like it is your home. I want it to be ours.'

Isabelle watched Asha's calm face, her steady voice explaining the painful truth as though she were outlining the particulars of a house. Isabelle was withering inside, feeling awful and useless and guilty.

'It is not easy, living in another country, and people think nothing of you to start with. Simply because you are not one of them. I want James' family and friends to think well of me. That I love him for the right reasons.' Asha drained the strong bitter remnants of her cup, put it down on the saucer with a firm clink.

'I don't think any of us doubt that,' Isabelle said. 'We're all delighted for James. I know I am. That he has found you, that he is happy. That his feelings are returned.'

'I think it will make him miserable if I say no,' Asha paused, savouring her words. 'It will me, too.'

'But you don't feel you can say yes?'

'No,' Asha said. 'I worry I would always be dissatisfied, and that would make our life, how do you say it, soured?'

'Tainted, I think.' If Elsa were here, she would know the right word. If Elsa were here, she would know what to do. But she wasn't. Elsa had left them to make their own decisions. Left her in charge. 'What do you want me to do?' Isabelle asked. 'I mean, is there anything I can do?'

'Sell the farm to James.' Asha ran on in a rush of words. 'I mean, not all the farm. I know enough about land value that we could never afford it. But the farmhouse, and the yard itself. Something that was ours. I have a good job, I think we can get a mortgage, we could manage. I know it's much to ask and I don't think you will do it, or even that you should, but... I have to ask, to try.'

Sell the farmhouse. Isabelle hadn't thought about selling anything. In fact, she hadn't thought about doing anything with anything. She wasn't yet in a place where any of it seemed hers to think about doing anything with. Asha had thought a lot more than her, there was no doubt about that.

'Is this what you asked James to ask me?'

'I asked him to ask if you could change anything,' Asha lifted her head, and straightened her back. 'He said it wasn't his place to tell you what to do about the estate. His pride comes first.' She looked at Isabelle, looked away. 'I have less pride, more love.'

Isabelle was bemused. She hadn't thought about how it would impact on other people in real details.

'I wish I had even one tenth of your courage. I can see why James wants to marry you.'

Asha smiled at her, a cautious smile, with a wobble at its edges. 'I have nothing to lose by asking you. It seems a simple thing to me, if you want change, you must seek out how to get there. To say, "I cannot, because..." is such a British way of doing things. I find it all the time. It's ridiculous.'

'I'll bet. Still, I admire you,' Isabelle said. 'You make anything seem possible. You make the whole weight of this,' and she indicated the house around them, 'feel less heavy. Kate has that skill too.'

'But it shouldn't feel like a weight,' Asha protested. 'Life shouldn't be ugly china stuck on a shelf, that you're too scared to get rid of because of your family. It's your life, you decide what matters.'

Isabelle watched her, her arms rising from the table and expanding outwards in a gesture that held possibility, courage, even impatience. She felt small in its shadow, and yet, a tiny bit hopeful too. Braver, in that fleeting instance.

Asha stood up, went and put her cup down in the sink. 'I have to remind myself all the time to stay Polish, not to end up British. You're all so reticent. I have to go in a minute, to my appointment.'

'You make it sound simple.'

'It is. I could tell you in ten minutes five different things you could do that would make life easier.'

'Really?'

'Of course. That is just work.'

'Will you?' Isabelle asked. 'I mean, would you? Tell me? Help me?'

'Will you?' Asha asked, standing in front of the sink and looking across the table at her. 'Help me?'

'If it can be done, yes.' Isabelle stood up, put her hands on the table and tried to be convincing. 'I want to do what's best for this family. For Elsa, for Moth and Nat. And James. If I can help you, one hundred million percent, yes, I will do it.'

Asha moved to get her bag, took her diary out, flicking through the pages, pen point poised, 'I can do tomorrow, at 10am. Is this too soon?'

'No! Tomorrow, really? Brilliant, yes.'

'Yes,' Asha agreed. 'It is best to be swift, I think. If we cannot make resolution, I must tell James no, and sooner would be kinder.'

'Don't you dare tell him no,' Isabelle said. 'There has to be a way we can sort this.'

'Well, let's see.' Asha shut her diary. 'We will start with a meeting tomorrow, it will be a business advice meeting, to give you ideas.' She made a move towards the door.

'Thank you,' Isabelle walked behind her, out into the hallway.

Asha opened the front door, turned in the doorway and looked past her, at the large hall, the spreading stairwell, the coloured glass window. 'You know, Elsa made this a beautiful home. Now it's your turn to decide how to do that, for you. Don't be afraid of it, enjoy it.' She offered her hand and Isabelle reached to take it. 'Be ready for tomorrow, make sure you have all the information about the estate.'

'I will.'

Isabelle closed the door, turned and looked at the hall. It seemed less daunting, lingering in Asha's glance, a challenge to be put in order. Isabelle walked towards the study, taking her phone out of her pocket, selecting a contact as she walked down the east corridor. The doors to the morning room, dining room, sitting room and study were propped open with their new doorstops, casting skewed shapes of light onto the hall floorboards that it wasn't used to. Arguing over which way to send her shadow. Sending a glimmer of sparkling dust-filled morning sunshine across the mirror that hung on the end wall. A mirror that had all too often been lost in the shadows of the long hallway, with the doors carefully closed against it. She walked into the study as the phone was picked up at the other end.

'Good morning, Isabelle.'

'Rob, hi, how are you?'

There was a pause before he answered, 'Fine, thank you. And you?'

'Fine, yes.' Isabelle wondered how much truth was hidden behind his own fine and took a deep breath to rush on. 'I wanted to see if you can come over, sometime today, possibly. I know it's short notice.'

'Is everything alright?'

'Yes, fine, fine. I wanted to clarify some bits and bobs, I'm a bit confused.'

'I'm going to struggle, I'm sorry.' Isabelle could hear him rummaging papers in the background. 'I can try and cancel an appointment maybe, but...'

'No, don't do that,' she said, looking round the room, deflated and overwhelmed. 'Perhaps first thing in the morning?'

'I'm in a meeting all morning,' he said, his voice showing the strain of trying to help her. 'Look, I'll try and squeeze the afternoon up and come over later, at the end of the day? If you can see me then?'

'I'm not doing anything,' she said, hating the truth hanging in the air. 'Free all evening. If you can, that would be brilliant. I'd appreciate it.'

'I'll get there as soon as I can at the end of the day.'

'Thank you, I'll do some food,' she said. 'One less thing for you to fit in if you're helping me.'

'Thank you, Isabelle, that would be kind.'

She ended the call, put the phone down on the desk that sat squarely in front of the window, looking towards the door. Old, heavy, dark wood, with a padded leather inlay and an aperture at the back between the drawers on either side. It pulled you in, held you fixed where you sat. Giving the impression to anyone who walked into the room that they had no choice but to sit opposite, and somehow beneath, the person that commanded it. It was a desk that needed to be commanded, by a single strong person. As Elsa had, that day she threw all their lives into disarray.

It was not her desk. She needed a desk that reminded her of herself. Not even a desk. A high table, with a stool to perch on. Like the table in her workroom. Where people could lean or perch wherever they felt comfortable. The sort of space that had made Moth feel comfortable.

Isabelle scanned her memory of the house. There was no other such table, she was sure, and only the stools in her workroom to perch on. She needed to find a replacement, and she needed help to move the current desk out.

She went and opened the drawers, frowned at the packed contents. Elsa must have left it all here thinking she would need it. She rifled through it, bemused at the contents. She could pack them all away and be none the wiser. But Elsa had used all the boxes in the house for her own packing. Isabelle pulled the entire drawer out and smiled at the simplicity of the answer, wondering where she was going to put the contents. And the drawer. And the desk.

She looked at the rest of the room. It was filled with things she didn't want or didn't know what to do with. She was drowning under all this stuff. She carried the drawer out into the corridor. Looked at the open door of the sitting room, down the corridor towards the morning room, the dining room. Titles that gave designated purpose to those rooms. When they were used. How they were used. The doors stood open on rooms adrift, contents pulled apart, purpose unpicked. She placed the drawer on the floor of the morning room, went back, took another, repeated the process. An array of ornaments, lamps, side tables and chairs following her down the corridor as the sun crept round the house and tried to peek in at her from another angle.

The study looked bigger when she'd finished. Lighter. She dragged the unused Chesterfield sofa from behind the door to the fireplace, placed it at right angles, put two chairs opposite, a low coffee table in between. The carpet showing signs of sunken distress despite her best efforts at vacuuming. She hefted the reduced weight of the desk again and grunted. No chance, it weighed a tonne. It had to be gone by the evening. She wanted Rob to see that she was moving on, that she was determined. She didn't want him throwing water on the fire Asha had built.

Isabelle checked her phone, less than an hour before she was due at Kate's. She would go by way of the charity shop and see if there were any desks that suited her. She walked out of the study, saw the door of the morning room open, the messy contents visible. She kicked the fabric weight aside, let the door fall shut and walked away. She didn't need to see it all at once.

SHE ARRIVED ten minutes late at Kate's, who opened the door to her flat with a glare and a steaming kettle in her hand.

'Don't scald me!' Isabelle begged, panting from having run flat out through town.

'Give me one good reason?'

'I've been busy, I promise.'

'Really?' Kate lowered the kettle.

'Yes, yes, yes, yes,' Isabelle chanted and danced past her while she had a chance, dropping a light kiss on her surprised cheek. 'I've been moving furniture, and I've arranged to see Rob, and I've got a meeting tomorrow morning, and I've bought a new desk for the study, in reclaimed scaffold boards on iron builders trestles.'

'It sounds awful,' Kate said. 'What was wrong with the old one?'

'It was awful. A headmaster's desk, or an accountant's.' It was Isabelle's turn to be surprised. 'I thought you'd be pleased.'

'Well, I'm pleased you're doing something, but it's not perhaps what I expected.' Kate let the door fall to behind her, following Isabelle into the flat. 'Where did you buy the desk from?'

'I went and looked in the charity shops, but they had nothing,' Isabelle said. 'And I was walking back up here and saw this reclaimed furniture shop. It was in the window, I loved it.'

'How much did that cost?'

'Not as much as it should, which is why I'm late. The guy was telling me about where he gets his stuff to reclaim from, and I said I might be getting rid of some furniture, and he said...'

'Are you?' interrupted Kate.

'What?'

'Getting rid of furniture?'

'I might be, anyway, he said...'

'What furniture?'

'Will you listen?' Isabelle said. 'He said he would be interested in looking at more stuff to repurpose, and I offered him first refusal in exchange for a reduction on the desk.'

'How much did it cost? Tea or coffee?'

'Tea, please. £85.' Isabelle's stomach began wobbling as she faced Kate's queries. The frantic pace of her day stilled in the light of Kate's kitchen with the steam rising from the kettle spout between them. Kate holding it aloft in the intense silence.

'I know, it's a lot of money,' Isabelle said. 'But I needed a fresh start. Right? That's what you said.'

'I didn't say spend money to get it.'

'You're worried, I understand. But I've made a start.'

'Why is Rob coming to see you?' Kate asked instead, moving towards the work surface.

'I want to make sure I'm clear about the estate, for tomorrow.'

'What's your meeting tomorrow?' Kate asked.

'With a property agent.' Isabelle watched Kate turn and frown at her again, spoon held in her hand.

'A property agent?'

'Uh-huh.' Isabelle looked away. She hadn't checked with Asha how much she was free to talk about.

'This wouldn't have anything to do with Asha by any chance?' Kate asked slowly.

'Asha?'

'Isabelle, I was not born yesterday,' Kate told her, turning back to the cups and talking over her shoulder. 'I left you flat as a pancake with Asha this morning, now here you are brim full of optimism and a new desk to boot. It doesn't take a genius to put those two together.'

'Ok,' Isabelle sighed in defeat. 'Genius. Yes, I have a meeting with Asha tomorrow. She has offered to help me with some professional advice on what my options might be.'

'And why would she do that?' Kate asked in a neutral voice.

Isabelle opened her mouth to respond and shut it again, looking for an answer that wasn't a lie, but wasn't the truth either. She opened her mouth again.

'You know what,' Kate interrupted, raising a hand to silence her, back remaining turned. 'I don't need to know. I trust you two to work it out.' She stirred the cups, left the teabags to brew, turned and looked at Isabelle. 'I like that girl. She's exactly what this family needs. A fresh attitude, and some guts to go with it. Whatever you're up to, tell me when you need to, if you need to. And if Elsa asks, I know nothing.'

Isabelle smiled limply.

'That's what I thought. Now, as for this desk, what are you doing with the old one?'

'About that,' Isabelle started. Kate sighed in dramatic anticipation. 'I was wondering if you could lend me a few muscles for half an hour.'

'When?'

'Now... ish... possibly,' Isabelle asked.

'Now? Really?' Kate shook her head. 'You do nothing for weeks, now it has to happen instantly?'

'Just this one thing, and I promise it won't take long.'

'Just this one thing, *now*,' Kate said. 'I have a feeling it might expand if Asha has any influence over things. Oh, alright. Go and see if you can find Tom and Bert, I think they're in the cellars. Ask them, no, tell them I said they can help you for fifteen minutes, no longer. Tell them not to ask Mike first, either.'

'Do I get tea first?'

'No, I need them back as soon as possible, you'd better do it now. You can come tomorrow and tell me what you're up to.'

'Thank you,' Isabelle said, fleeting across the kitchen to drop another kiss on her cheek.

'Tomorrow,' Kate warned.

'Promise.'

Kate rolled her eyes at her and muttered as Isabelle left.

'DOES IT ALL MAKE SENSE NOW?' Rob asked, sitting back on the sofa opposite her in the study.

Isabelle looked at the paperwork spread out before them on the low table. Her head ached from it all. The enthusiasm and burst of energy that Asha had given her that morning all fizzled out. Not even the excitement of her new desk, positioned to face the fireplace rather than the door, with a neat array of pots of pens, pads, papers and a pincushion, had outlasted Rob's steady neutral rendition of the extraordinary position Elsa had left her in.

'It's too much,' she grimaced at the papers.

The house itself was only the starting point. James' farmhouse was one of three, and the land he farmed less than half of the entirety. Aside from James she had eight other tenants. The two other tenanted farms, three tenanted houses in town, the two bungalows at the end of the drive to James' farm and Mrs Staines' house, which she had financial responsibility for yet no income from. Across the narrow road from Riverdell was the isolated empty barn that sat beside the old guests' car park, set in five acres of riverside meadow. Plus, there were pockets of land lying further afield, let out on long-term peppercorn rents, shares in funds she couldn't even begin to understand and trust fund accounts.

'It's an awful lot to take in,' Rob admitted.

'I wish Elsa were here to tell me what to do with it all,' Isabelle said, sitting back in her chair. 'I feel she's dumped it all on me and run for the hills.'

'You need to see it more positively,' Rob told her in a firm voice tempered with a kind smile. 'She's given you complete freedom to deal with it as you see fit. She trusts you.'

'But what about her income,' Isabelle said. 'Explain it to me again.'

'You explain it to me,' he said. 'I think it will help you understand better.'

She frowned, but he was right. She kept pushing away her comprehension by asking him to repeat the details. She sat forwards again, shuffled some of the papers around.

'Right, let's see. The house in Swansea she owns outright, with no debts on it.'

'Correct.'

'The two bungalows she has a lifetime interest to 50 percent of the income or value if sold.'

'Correct.'

'Plus, she has a lifetime interest in 50 percent of the income from Mrs Staines' house, of which there is none, or the value if sold.'

'Brilliant, see, you do understand,' Rob paused and looked at her. 'I understand why you're struggling. When the boss told me the score, I wanted nothing to do with it either. But, after the initial shock, I think she did the right thing. She wants to look after Nat, and she's stopped trying to do all this, to do that one thing to the best of her ability.'

'I never understood before why David was so angry with her.' Isabelle twirled a pen above the papers. 'I thought he was unreasonable, asking her to sell, and refusing to speak with her when she said no. It makes me feel like it's my fault. That perhaps something could have been done earlier, and the whole family would have been happier.'

'You weren't involved in those decisions,' Rob said. 'You

cannot take responsibility for what you weren't given the chance to change.'

'But I can now?'

'You're in charge now, yes.'

'What would you do?'

'Not a chance! I can advise you on the legal ramifications of your decisions. I cannot, and will not, tell you what to do.'

'You're as bad as the rest of them,' she said in frustration. Isabelle looked at the table again, thinking it through, trying to make sense of it all.

'I like the new look,' he said in a conciliatory tone.

'Hmm?' She glanced up. Rob was looking past her, at the new desk.

'The change of furniture, moving the rooms about. It's a good start.'

'Oh, thanks,' Isabelle felt a flush of contentment. 'I'm not looking forward to Kate seeing it, I think she feels I'm procrastinating. Again.' Isabelle was trying not to think about how many weeks she'd spent clearing out the basement hoping to find a purpose, only to find an emptier room to kick her lost heels in.

'You're making a start,' Rob said, 'in your own way. Which is what you need to do.'

He picked his glass up and took another sip of the wine. Picked up a straggling crostini from the plate of snacks.

'What I struggle to grasp is how it all fits together,' Isabelle said. 'How the finances of it work.'

'Elsa did a great job of it, but she had guidance from Kit. I'm surprised he hasn't been here more to help you.' There was a hint of criticism in his careful tone.

'Elsa nabbed him first,' Isabelle explained. 'He's been flat out getting the house ready for her and now I think he has clients screaming at him. He calls most days, and he's due up next week, hopefully.'

'Hmm,' Rob finished off the crostini. 'Well, until he does get here, try thinking of it as a complete asset. If you look at the big picture the bottom line should balance out. If you start looking at it in isolation it gets difficult to make sense of.'

'I can't cope with it when I try to see it altogether,' Isabelle complained. 'I feel this need to break down each aspect, deal with it one segment at a time.'

Rob looked at her as though at a child, waiting for her to catch up, accept the whole package and move on with it as Elsa had.

'I mean, it's already changed, right?' she pushed on. 'Without the B&B, the bottom line has changed, right?'

'Maybe not,' Rob said. 'Elsa ran that business for her own income, and she kept it, for the majority, out of the estate. There were some years when a large problem needed an injection of cash, but otherwise she's been wise. She saved a good deal of money over the years, and Richard was just as careful. I know you're concerned about Elsa and her finances, but she has an adequate retirement fund and enough savings to manage the development of the property in Swansea.'

Isabelle kept staring at the table, chewing on the end of her pencil.

'All I'm saying is, you don't need to worry about selling everything and giving it away to the family.' Rob sounded kind even when he was trying to be tough with her. 'Your grandfather built wisely on what he inherited and held it together with careful management and reinvestment, as has Elsa. All you need to do is follow their lead and enjoy it.'

'But I don't want it.' She sat forward in her chair, her hands reaching out over the table, desperate for someone to understand. 'That's what no one will listen to. I don't want all of this. It's too much for one person. And I have no one to share it with.'

'You will have, one day,' Rob said.

'What, like Kit?'

'I'm sure he'll be a great support. As soon as he gets here.'

'Kate thinks Kit will manage it for me, same as he did for Elsa.'

'Elsa was always in charge.' He leant across and began straightening the sprawling papers from the table, pulling official documents out from under her lists. Her writing looping and creative, trying to capture the details in a sketch that made sense to her but looked out of place against the formal documents spilling from Rob's folders. 'Don't be mistaken about that.'

'Whatever the future, this isn't what I want.' Isabelle remembered Hester's contempt in the study that day when Elsa had revealed the inheritance, when Isabelle had voiced the sense of overwhelming horror she felt. Hester telling her that what she felt seemed the epitome of selfishness. 'I understand how other people feel, but it isn't how I feel. Responsible for all this, not having the freedom to choose my own life.'

'Life rarely is about what we want, in my experience,' Rob told her with a weary, weighted look. 'You have to make the best of the hand you're dealt, and you've been dealt a generous hand, Isabelle. Don't throw away the Royal Flush because you were hoping for a Jack.'

'I won't throw it away.' Isabelle thought about Asha. 'But I grew up with this family, and I'm not going to forget them, or keep it all for myself.'

He downed his glass of wine and reloaded papers into his briefcase.

'I have to go.' He stood up, checking the table for anything left behind. 'I'll do all I can to support you. Or, if it helps, I understand if you want to appoint a different solicitor to handle your affairs.'

'Why would I want to do that? Isabelle looked up from her chair in surprise.

'Elsa has asked me to remain her solicitor but, under the circumstances, I asked to be excused. Kit is sourcing her a new legal advisor in Swansea. I understand if you take the same option.'

'Don't you want to be my solicitor?' Isabelle felt breathless thinking about the idea of trying to find a new one. She wouldn't know where to start, she'd have to ask Kit to help too.

'It will always be a pleasure to help, Isabelle, but I understand if the change in our personal circumstances as a family mean you wish to make other changes.'

Isabelle remembered the courage she'd tried to summon to say something similar to Elsa, in this same room, not too many months earlier. It had worked out mighty different in the outcome.

'You've been family for so long, Rob,' Isabelle said. 'It feels the same to me. I don't want to change solicitor.' She stood up as he finished gathering his things. 'In fact, I desperately don't want anyone new, to add to the massive changes already.'

'As long as you're sure. It's always open to reconsideration.' Rob stood and looked back at her with a relieved smile.

Isabelle held her hand out to him, squeezed his. 'I'm sure, and don't ask again, please. If I want to reconsider, I'll tell you. Deal?'

'You promise?' he asked.

'Promise.'

He squeezed her hand back with a small smile and said, 'Deal.'

She watched as he climbed into the Audi estate car on the drive and inched his way out over the gravel, unlike Kit, who came and went in an aggressive spurt of wheel spinning glory. It would take him nearly an hour to get home to the flat he now had in Shrewsbury. The house he'd shared with Hester was empty, abandoned by them both, waiting for Hester to resolve. Rob had walked away from the house and the marriage without a penny. She could understand that he might find her reluctance to celebrate her newfound wealth a bit churlish.

As she locked the front door behind her and went back to the study, Isabelle felt that, understandable or not, Rob had not judged her thoughts. Despite his own feelings, he had stuck with the role of advising her. Perhaps that was the consequence of being a solicitor but, professional impartiality or not, it had been a relief to give voice to her feelings and not have them hurled back down her throat with a dose of venom.

She curled up on the sofa where Rob had sat and looked through one list after another. The estate reduced to single line statements she could visualise. The words rising from the page and taking shape. Not unlike a costume developing in her mind. It never came as a complete image, but sections, details that rose within her and needed to be pieced together.

What tonight had shown her, pulled out from the mass, was the singular fact that all the profit from the other assets linked together about paid for the upkeep of Riverdell, a huge house with bills to match.

It didn't provide an income to live on, which is why Elsa had kept guests. It wouldn't provide for the future. If she sold some of those assets to help the family, she would have to figure out a way of making some of that capital value reinvest to look after the house. Or find a new income stream for herself. It was like an old job she had started, left and returned to after too long a break. None of the pieces matched, or made sense, her brain was struggling to add it all up.

At the end, she found herself lacking a reason. Costumes all linked to the main thread of the film's story. Furnishings always led towards the person at the heart of the home. But with Elsa gone, with Nat and Moth gone, with her own solitary life the only thing left in the house, she found herself wondering if Riverdell was worth it.

Looking at the papers and lists scattered about the desk had given her a headache. Working on a low table did not suit her. She glanced over at the new desk, thrilled with its solidity and size. The desk was perfect, whatever Kate might think of it. Familiar without being too big. All it needed were the stools to suit it. She would do it tonight, ready for Asha's visit. Show her how determined she was to make it work.

Down in the workroom she grabbed her heavy work worn stool, and the other, lighter stool on the far side of the table, the one Moth had often perched on. She couldn't carry them both together but, by stages, from the workroom to the kitchen, the kitchen to the corridor, and into the study she got the stools in place. Running her hand over the surface of her old perch in this new place gave her a thrill of comfort.

She wandered back down to the workroom where she'd left the lights on. It was looking emptier, there was no doubt about it, and the absence of her favourite stool made the table look strange. She glanced round once more and was about to head for the door when her eye swept over Moth's bike, under its dust cloth. She went over, laid her hand on its handlebars, feeling the frame under the fabric. It was a reason for him to come back. Which was ridiculous, because she knew Nat was a much bigger reason, but at some point, he would come back. It meant too much to him to not come and get it. Of all the things she didn't understand, she knew at least that much. James had made him earn the bike, through hard work, and it had been the best decision. She thought about James, about his working to keep a farm that belonged to her. About Asha, if she married him, feeling the same way. She couldn't give the farm to James. A guilty gift or an act of charity. That wouldn't make it theirs. Whatever Asha suggested tomorrow she must remember that.

KIT FELT ODD. Wriggling to find relief but unable to get comfortable whichever way he twisted on the car seat, waiting for the temporary traffic lights to turn.

Perhaps it was his pants, too snug in the hot summer weather. He knew all the noise about wearing looser boxers but couldn't stand how they looked. But that made no sense, the air con was on full blast. Still, he couldn't stop twisting on the seat. The roads weren't helping. They felt as strangled as his privates, gorged by the summer holidays and afternoon rush hour.

It wasn't the best-timed journey, but it was the only window he had in the next three weeks. One he had sneaked away in feeling guilty. The rest of the team were at breaking point, even Ed and Fred had lost their usual sense of godly joy. Jamie had taken two days off with an asthma attack and

Lou had fallen out with Henri so often he suspected they were either shagging or falling in love, and he couldn't decide which would be worst for the business.

He'd been on his way to the D'Arby's that morning and realised he was about as close to a night at Riverdell as he was likely to get. When he rang Isabelle to suggest he might call in, she'd been delighted, then surprised, then, well, then... he couldn't decide. Ambiguous was the best stab. Working hard at thrilled by the end of the conversation. Leaving him with the beginnings of the itch in his pants that was driving him to distraction now. Not the comfortable itch of anticipation he was used to either.

Kit felt out of control.

On the fine edge of it, anyway.

Henri had done a stellar job of holding the waters back while they worked on Swansea, but he hadn't prepared Kit for the full extent of the work that had been developing in his absence. Kit had dragged himself away from Swansea ready for a break and got hit by a tsunami instead. While all the time he knew Isabelle was alone at Riverdell. In a decisive void, which he wanted to fill. The weeks rolling on with repeated broken promises to get there.

But his weren't the sort of clients you said no to. Not unless it was about their choice of furnishings or colour scheme when contemptuous denial was obligatory. But not the work itself. That bred all sorts of discontent that tended to spread. He'd seen competitors get above themselves, saying no with spectacular lack of understanding to the nuances of social networks, then complaining about the Chernobyl taint to their names, ending up working for Laura Ashley, or Debenhams. It was now the end of August, and the first chance he'd had to get to Riverdell since he'd

escorted Elsa away from it, a month ago. August 30th. Barely
August.

Kit turned the music up, tapped his hands on the wheel,
hated the track and flicked it on to the next one. By the time
he'd made it through the traffic lights he turned the music off.

There had been a chance he might have made it to see
Kate before getting to Riverdell. A chance that had disappeared in the hold ups on the motorway. Not that Kate was
one to be rushed. But it had been long enough since he saw
her to assume some degree of mutual urgency. Though she
gave away no hint of it on the phone. In fact, between her and
Isabelle, Kit was beginning to feel more uncomfortable than
even the stress of his workload offered. They had taken to
talking in riddles.

In Kate's defence, the summer onslaught of visitors to the
town always reduced her to near incoherence. Of the salty
variety that didn't have patience to finish listening to other
people's conversations, or to offer sympathy for their plights,
especially not his. Releasing control to her manager seemed
more stressful than doing it all herself, she had no time for
helping Kit. Or rather, she now only had time for Isabelle,
beyond herself, and was plain annoyed that he wasn't there
taking that role. They found themselves verging on an argument about Riverdell, or Isabelle, and retreating from it in
equal measure, breaking away in ragged tangents.

Putting down the phone in dissatisfaction, he would call
Isabelle instead, who would murmur at him. No salt, no
impatience, no sense. Droplets of information that didn't
hold together as a picture he could put on a mood board. He
knew she'd moved a lamp, swapped two pictures, even
bought a new desk. She talked a lot about cushions, curtains,
furniture. She asked him infinite details about work, until he

realised that he was talking about himself, in a rush of over-whelmed thoughts. When he pulled up short and turned the conversation back onto her, they went wandering down the disarrayed halls of Riverdell again.

From Kate all he could get was shortness and work. From Isabelle all he got was procrastination and inconse-quence. Kit wanted to know what was going on, and he wanted to know nothing was going on without him, and he was worn out by not being able to get there, and he was frac-tious with the process of getting there. His pants itched again. He scratched hard. He needed a shower. He needed to get out of these clothes and be wet, soaked through, and he wanted to hold someone in his arms. He didn't mind too much who.

Since June he'd been working on projects he would normally give a limb to take on, while the one project he wanted to sink his teeth into remained impossible to get to. Now here he was, on his way. Driving back to Riverdell. To Isabelle and Kate. And there was no Moth to contend with.

This brought a smile of victory to his face which guilt removed. He wasn't proud of how glad he was that Moth was out of the scene. More permanently out of the scene than anyone realised. Kit spurred the Bentley on for a glorious stretch of open dual carriageway that ended too soon in a final junction onto the winding A-roads. A-roads. What a joke. A-hole roads, more like.

Chasing down Moth had taken longer than he imagined. Ben had been a slippery little sucker to find and a brick wall to get any sense out of. When Kit had tracked him down, through a steady unpicking of contacts that had some mutu-ality, via an older brother who didn't appreciate being asked about him, he'd found Ben in a bar in London. Less than happy to be disturbed in his 'work', which Kit had come to understand was less than 'official'.

'Who's asking?' Ben had retorted, in a curt but unmistakeable upper-class accent.

Kit had taken in the too bright, up-market bar in distaste. It was full of city workers, suits abounded. Ben's casual open shirt and jeans were a mockery.

'A friend of Moth Threlfall's,' Kit responded, taking the stool next to him at the bar.

'Really?' Ben asked. 'What's a friend of Moth's doing, talking to me?'

'I was wondering if you replaced your passport yet?' Kit shook his head at the bartender looking his way. He had no intention of stopping long. 'I heard from your brother you lost it, about the time we lost Moth.'

'Friends, brothers, you seem to know a lot about me.' Ben put away his phone.

'Indeed,' Kit said. 'I've been trying to contact Moth. Seems he doesn't want to be contacted.'

'Perhaps you should take the hint.'

'Perhaps you should take the hint, you jumped up little prick,' Kit kept his tone neutral, hardening his words. 'Word is he decided to go travelling with a mate. Except that mate doesn't appear to exist. I don't buy that bullshit and I'm pretty sure someone else knows more than they're saying. Here's the thing, you wet nurse runt. Those contacts you have in the city, the ones you supply, the ones who told me I'd find you here, I put them in contact with their contacts when you were sucking on tits and playing with your winky. And if you want to keep in their good books, you'll tell me a thing or two.'

Ben remained quiet, looking at the far wall of the bar with its array of shining bottles and seductive names. Kit pulled a pen out of his jacket, took a napkin from the bar and wrote a name on it. Ben looked away in discomfort. It took a few more nudges, but eventually, giving him no information about Moth, Ben had conceded, 'Look, I'll tell him to get in touch, if he calls. Let's leave it at that.'

Ben was nineteen, and he had confidence Kit had to admire. This was no petty criminal. This was a career arsehole in the making. He'd moved on from drugs at school, into embezzlement and money laundering, amongst other things Kit preferred not to explore. People made money different ways, he'd learned that over the years from his clients. However they made it, they came to him ready to spend it. Kit tried not to judge.

'One phone call, and I'll leave it alone.' Kit stood up to go. 'No phone call and you and I will be getting to know each other better. A lot better than you might like.'

'He isn't coming back you know,' Ben said. 'He's been setting this up for years. His parents dying, that was a glitch. Only stayed for his sister. Said she had someone better to look after her now.'

'One call.'

'I can't promise anything.'

'No, but give it your best shot, there's a darling.' Kit had picked up the serviette and tucked it away in his jacket pocket as he left.

Kit itched in his seat again. Thinking about Ben made him uncomfortable. That had been weeks ago, and nothing, no contact. Kit was making sure that Ben knew he wasn't going away. Enough that if, when, Moth got in touch, he felt Ben would pass the message on.

It irritated Kit not to be able to find him, but there was a comfort in the fact that no one else could either. A deeper comfort in knowing this would be the first time he went to Riverdell and Moth wouldn't be there. He tried to look forward with anticipation but still the discomfort niggled him.

KIT WAS BEGINNING to feel like the proverbial princess and the pea. No matter which way he tossed or turned something kept digging him in the ribs.

'I think he's speechless,' Kate said with amusement.

Kit grimaced at her, and turned back to Isabelle to speak, but couldn't. There didn't seem to be a point at which he could start to make sense of what she'd said.

He sat in the echoing, barren guest sitting room, between the two of them looking like a pair of giggling schoolgirls. Kate was looking at him with a smug sense of delight in his discomfort, nestled into one of the armchairs with a wine glass hovering in front of her amused chin. Isabelle sat on the floor in front of the chairs. Her grand schemes spread out in front of them on the floor.

'So, I thought, forgive me if I missed something,' Kit emphasised each word, treating them as the children they were acting, 'that you promised Elsa you would make changes slowly, after careful deliberation.'

'Yes, I did,' Isabelle said. 'I know it's a bit different to what I said.'

'A bit?'

'But I have good reasons.'

'Which she won't share with us,' Kate added.

'Have you spoken to Elsa yet?' Kit ignored Kate's comment. He would find out what the reason was later, after Kate left. He refused to get hung up on that issue.

'Not in detail,' Isabelle said.

'What did you say?'

'That I was looking at making some changes.'

'That's a bloody big understatement.' Kit liked the way his language made her blink.

He leaned back in his chair and looked at them. Their faces were flushed with the triumph of their discussion. An evening that had felt like a car crash to him. Arriving to find them both there, to find the house in disarray, to find Isabelle had put the direst new desk in the study, to find her plan for the estate laid out in front of him during the course of supper. A supper he had fast lost the appetite to eat. A swiftly downed bottle of wine was not helping his cause.

He felt tired. Even more in need of a shower. A dull ache wallowing between his shoulder blades that he knew came from not enough time in the gym and which was threatening to explode into back pain. He was wrung out, while they both looked radiant. Full of the pleasure of revealing secrets they had been conspiring together over.

'And you're really going to give up the bistro?' he asked Kate, unable to keep the scepticism out of his tone.

'I'm seeing it in a more appealing light now.'

'Even though you hate giving control to Mike?' Kit pressed home. 'While you're still there.'

'It will be easier if I'm not there, watching it all change.'

'And you two think you can live together?' he asked Isabelle.

'Well, it's not exactly together,' Isabelle explained, infuriating him. 'We'd be neighbours.'

Kate's eyes were sparkling as she looked at him.

'And remind me again where the inspiration for all this came from?' Kit asked.

'From too much time alone, in all these empty rooms,' Isabelle said. 'And Rob has been a huge help too. He's made me take lots of advice.'

Rob needed to shove his advice right up there next to the rod he couldn't pull out.

'Rob agrees with it all?'

'Not exactly.' Isabelle's hands began straightening the papers in a protective way that made him frown. 'But he says it's not up to him to tell me what to do, only how to do what I want to do.'

'How careful of him,' Kit said.

'I was hoping you'd be a bit happier,' Isabelle said. 'I didn't want you getting away from work to have to do more work here.'

'What's up?' Kate asked, sinking further into her chair. 'Jealous she doesn't need you as Knight Protector?'

'A little.'

'Not even a bit relieved she doesn't?' Kate added.

'A little,' he admitted, resisting the urge to soften. 'I guess I'm used to the role. I don't appreciate having it taken away from me.'

'Isabelle said something similar to me.' Kate curled her hand across her ankle, smoothing it over the bridge of her bare foot, where it was tucked on the chair.

'Did I?'

'Yes, remember, about how would I deal with change if it was forced upon me,' Kate said. 'It made me think about what I might want to change for myself.'

'Oh.'

Isabelle looked shocked that Kate might have listened to her. Not as shocked as he was. He looked again at the various plans spread out on the floor in front of them. Isabelle's eyes larger than normal on the other side of them. Bloody puppy dog eyes. If she had a tail, she would be wagging it right now. Full of the bone she'd found and fetched. He wanted to growl at her.

It wasn't because she'd done a lot of work without him, either. She'd grasped the package of the estate, not just in essence, but in detail. Details like the life interests, the condition and value of the properties, their development capabilities. Details which there was no way she could have worked out alone. Because they were good, sound ideas. Sound ideas he wanted to refute but couldn't. Sell some of the less well-maintained property, reinvest in seeking planning and sell the prime development land. She would make money if she followed it all through, serious money. It was the potential success of the ideas that was the most insulting. Because she hadn't needed his help, and he knew she couldn't have done it alone.

'Well, you've had some help,' he mused. 'In my absence.'

Isabelle looked down at the papers. 'Rob has been really helpful.'

Rob had never seemed that bright to Kit.

'But you must proceed with more caution,' he argued. 'Elsa was always cautious. I can't say we always saw eye to eye, but at least I understand now why she did what she did. She was caretaking it all, to hand over.'

'Yes, and she might have done it differently if it had been hers to control.' Isabelle had used that statement enough times in the last hour that he was sick of hearing it.

'Maybe.' Kit looked at Kate, who beamed at him. He would slap her arse for that look later. 'But it's all too fresh, Isabelle, it doesn't feel yours yet. You might regret later throwing something away.'

'I'm not throwing anything away.' She sat up straighter on her knees. 'I'm releasing and reinvesting, to secure the estate in the current climate.'

'Christ, where did you hear that from?' He saw Kate and Isabelle exchange a glance, a tiny fraction of a glance anyway. If a glance could stretch around corners and bounce off wine glasses. Two cagey bitches they were, hiding something from him. 'You aren't wrong, I understand what you're doing, but don't do it wholesale. Sell one piece at a time, word will get out, you'll generate more interest and get a better price that way too. And it will give you time to think.'

He looked down again at the papers, sat forwards in his seat, and pushed one of the maps aside. It was hard not to get dragged in.

'Look, this barn here.' He pointed at the map, to the barn opposite the house gates, where they had created a parking area for the guests. 'You might be able to get planning for ten houses on the land, but do you want ten more neighbours? With the construction traffic that will entail. Sell the other properties first, get planning for four or five executive homes, real individual character ones, and sell the plots individually. As the land is developed it will become more desirable, more valuable.'

'See, I told you he would have useful ideas,' Kate said.

He glared at her, wanted to sit back, couldn't resist continuing.

'Plus, if you want to go this route, Mrs Staines' house sits in over two acres of overgrown garden. Separate the house from the garden before you sell it. Seek planning on the land, again, individual plots. Generate your buyers' market over time.'

'I didn't know that.' Isabelle pulled the map back towards her. 'I thought it was all part of the graveyard.'

'So did the church wardens,' Kit said. 'But we had a threat of Japanese knotweed in the graveyard about ten years ago, we had to do a survey for insurance. The guy could barely get into the garden. When he did, we found out how big it is, and it sits in the heart of prime development land. There's a huge stone wall that separates it from the church yard. The church-wardens were devastated. It's got to be one of the most lucra-tive aspects, if you can get her out, and get planning on it.'

'Should have turfed them out years ago,' Kate said. 'I never understood why Elsa kept her on.'

'Something to do with her father.'

'Good heavens, was he shagging Mrs Staines too?' Kate asked.

'Only explanation I could ever figure out made sense,' Kit said.

'What about Marge?' Kate asked.

'Oh, please,' Kit grimaced. 'The thought of Marge in a carnal position, enough.'

'What's wrong with that?' Kate asked from behind her wine glass. 'Older women do have sex.'

'Yes, I know.' He glared at her, aware she was enjoying the return of a conversation he'd started at Miss Shorrock's funeral. 'But I don't think Marge ever had sex, even when she was young and irresistible.'

'What, old can't be irresistible?' Kate asked.

'Dig yourself out of that one,' Isabelle muttered.

'Yes, go ahead, start digging,' Kate taunted.

'You have to ask yourself what your priority is.' Kit turned back to Isabelle. 'If you want to stabilise your portfolio, Mrs Staines' house is a liability. Although you don't have any legal obligation to sustain the tenancy, there is the obligation of precedent to overcome.'

'That's why I was thinking about moving them into one of the bungalows,' Isabelle pointed at the maps. 'Even if we write off the income from one of the bungalows, Elsa will have her share of the income from the sale of the house to compensate against it.'

'Plus, the development of the land. First thing you have to do is give notice to the tenants in one of the bungalows.' Kit paused, trying to recall the details about those tenancies. They were both standard, short-term six month lets, neither of them long-standing tenants. 'If you drag Elsa into it too much, she'll resist moving Mrs Staines and Marge out. If you push it through, she'll probably be relieved. It will give her capital she can reinvest for her own lifetime, and for Nat and Moth, as she wants to. I think she will see the sense in that.'

'Which is all the more reason to get on with it,' Isabelle agreed. 'I don't want to sit on it and get too stricken with anxiety to do anything.'

'As for the rest, I don't get it,' Kit said, trying to reel her back in. 'Selling the big house and developing the barn land is enough Isabelle. I don't understand why you want to sell the farms too.'

'Only the farmhouses and buildings, not the farmland,' Isabelle explained in a tone that made him want to snarl. 'They have capital value, and I want to pour that into the development here at Riverdell.'

'That's bollocks,' Kit snapped. 'The value of the farmhouses is nothing compared to the value of the land. Agricultural land in this county has gone through the roof in the last decade, and the income from it is negligible. The houses and yards won't make you as much money, and their income is higher.'

'But I don't want to sell the land,' Isabelle said. 'It's impossible for the farmers to buy. It could be sold for huge developments that would impact on the landscape, and I don't want to be responsible for that.'

'Says she who is developing a riverside meadow!' Kit leaned back, taking a swig of wine, they were both looking back at him with wide eyes. 'You two are holding out on me. Something doesn't add up. If you need to sell a farm for finance, sell one, why all of them? And, if it must be more, again, piecemeal, one at a time, build expectation, maximise the potential income. If you don't do it that way, you have to have a good reason.'

'Just because it's not reasonable to you, doesn't mean there's no reason to it,' Kate told him with delight.

'If I sell only one farm, it will upset the other tenant farmers,' Isabelle tried to ease Kate's teasing. 'Surely they all deserve the equal right to bid for their own properties. And while the properties bring in a decent income, they're in less than perfect condition. Nothing has been invested in them for years.'

'They?' asked Kit, peering at her. 'Have you spoken with all of them? Or just James?'

'I haven't spoken to James about it yet,' Isabelle looked back at the floor. He wondered if he could distract Kate long enough to kick Isabelle and get away with it.

'How do you know he'll appreciate you making him buy it?' Kit asked. 'He might think you're being greedy. Be prepared that he may not thank you for it.'

Isabelle didn't reply, chewing on her lip and looking at

the papers on the floor. He felt a total shit but at least she'd stopped looking like she needed a tail to wag.

'You're not being very encouraging,' Kate told him. 'And you've said nothing about the developments here.'

'I've been working flat out for months,' Kit snapped at her. 'When I finally get back for a break, you two have birthed the bloody Enterprise in my absence and I'm trying not to slip on the placenta.'

'That's disgusting,' Kate told him.

'A bit grim,' Isabelle agreed.

'All I'm saying is, give me a chance,' Kit complained. 'It's a lot to catch up on when I've had Elsa telling me "no, no, no" for the last twenty years.'

'Fine,' said Kate, slipping her feet to the floor, brushing down her trousers, and standing up. 'I'll leave you two to argue over it, you can tell me what you think tomorrow.'

'I have to leave first thing,' Kit retorted.

'What?' Isabelle asked. 'I thought you were stopping for the day?'

'I can't,' he said, twisting the watch on his wrist. 'I have to be in Bristol for an 11am appointment.'

'I thought you were running your own business,' Kate said. 'Seems to me it's running you.'

'People in glasshouses,' he told her, 'shouldn't throw...'

'Alright, alright,' she cut him short. 'Let me know what he thinks,' she said to Isabelle.

'I'll walk you back,' he countered, standing up.

'I'm quite capable of walking myself home.'

'I know that,' he told her.

'I'll clear up,' Isabelle said, shuffling papers together.

She wasn't looking at him, Kit felt like he'd kicked a puppy.

'I'll be right back,' he told her, offering her a hand to help her up from the floor. Kate walked out of the room. 'Run me a bath, will you? I need to soak my bad mood away.'

He left the house a few steps behind Kate, who seemed in a rush to get away, caught her at the gate and turned her away from the hill that led up to the town, heading along the lane that ran behind the castle.

'Why are we going this way?' she demanded.

'I need a longer walk. Five extra minutes with you.'

'I'm not sure I want five extra minutes with you,' she told him. 'You've been absolutely vile.'

He took her elbow and nudged her along the road anyway.

'I don't need assistance just yet,' she told him, pulling her arm away.

She walked ahead of him, turning up the pathway that led in a long slope toward the foundations of the castle and would bring them into the town square.

Kit could have growled. He knew she was right, but she was pretending ignorance of the bloody good reasons for his being such a dick. It stung, that she seemed to be missing the obvious. Or didn't care. He let her walk away for a few paces, wondering whether to leave her to go home alone, then stalked after her, into the dark evening shadows of the trees that edged the narrow pathway. He caught her elbow again and, when she tried to snatch it away, pulled her close beside him. She resisted, trying to bat him away, glaring at him in fury. Her face full of shadows in the late summer evening beneath the trees.

'Why are you mad at me?' he demanded. 'You took such delight back there. How am I supposed to react? How the hell am I going to see you if you move into a bloody flat at Riverdell?'

'You mean how are you going to see both of us?' she retorted. 'I thought this is what you wanted. A life with Isabelle, no more us.'

'I thought it was what I wanted,' he said. 'I don't even know what she wants. Let alone you. I'm tired and confused.'

'You're hedging your bets,' she countered, resisting his arms as they held her elbows, pulling her closer. 'You wanted out until you realised she might not want you, like I warned you. Now, suddenly, I'm not so redundant.'

'You've never been redundant,' he told her. 'Why now? This sudden decision to retire, to move down there?'

'We all have to make choices. Maybe I can see my choices diminishing as I get less irresistible.'

Kit pulled her closer. 'I never said that about you. Ever. You flaunt that bullshit at me, when you know I can't fight back, in front of Isabelle. I want you now, as much as the day you first picked me up from that bloody school. Stop pretending it's me who's scared about your age. I'm trying to do what's right by Isabelle.'

'And I'm doing what's right by myself.' He was shocked to see tears coming in her eyes. Tears of rage she shook her head to get away from. 'I want to take this chance while it's there, not miss it, waiting for something else to come along. If I can't have you, at least I can still mean something to her.'

She was shaking with anger, her hair swishing as she shook the tears away, the falling anger pooling in the lines below her eyes. Kit leaned closer and kissed her. He couldn't say anything, didn't know what to say to make it better.

'Get off,' she told him. 'You can't ignore this and kiss it better.'

He kissed her even more. His mouth remembering her face, hungry kisses that fluttered over her skin, closing her eyes, easing the frown from her lips. He felt her slacken in his arms, the fight going out of her frame.

'You selfish bastard,' she said, her arms reaching for him.

'You stubborn bitch,' he told her, bending his neck to kiss her throat.

'You play me like a fool,' she complained. 'Here one minute, gone the next.'

'You play me like a secret,' he countered. 'Something you're ashamed of.'

She hung her head on his chest. He'd stung her now. Crushed a fighting dog this time, not a puppy. The castle looming above them, the trees softening the sound of the river below.

'I've never been ashamed of you,' she said in a strangled voice. 'I always thought you were ashamed of me.'

'I asked you to marry me, for fuck's sake, woman.'

'You were seventeen,' she protested. 'You'd have done anything for sex.'

'I still would. With you.'

She beat him on the chest, 'You never asked again.'

He lifted her head, looked at her. 'No, I didn't. By the time I plucked up the courage, I realised it wasn't right for either of us. Remember that night on the beach in Swansea? I had the ring there to ask you with,' he told her, touching a finger to her tears, wiping them away.

'I don't believe you,' she told him. 'You'd say anything to win an argument.'

'That's your choice,' he told her. 'But don't blame me for all the bad choices we made.'

She hung her head on his chest again. 'I don't know what's happening anymore,' she mumbled from his shirt.

'Me neither,' he told her. 'But I still want you, and that's the truth. Never changed.'

She reached up and put her arms round his neck.

'Even now?'

'Right now.' He pulled her close. 'Right bloody now.'

Kate's body moved into his, muscle to muscle, a glove upon his skin. He kissed her, and her kisses came back. His stress melting in the taste of wine on her tongue, salt on her cheeks. He pulled her into the trees along the path, holding her steady as her mules stumbled on the roots.

They felt their way back towards each other. Fumbling on the buttons of her blouse. Pushing aside the lace of her bra, finding the weight of her breast in his hand. She unzipped his trousers, pulled his dick out the front of his underwear. He felt the sharpness of her nails as they trailed underneath his testicles, making him gasp. She bent down and took him in her mouth and the warmth of it, the molten cushion of her tongue against him, took his breath away, making him arch back against the tree, tension from the past months focused on the slit of his dick as she flicked her tongue over it, tautening his skin downwards with her hand.

He pulled her up, pushed open her blouse, slid his mouth across her nipples while she played with his erection. They grew ragged, their eyes glimmers of white in the night, pushing away the distance as their tongues caressed. He undid the button of her trouser, slid the zipper down. Pushed aside the light cotton of her pants, probing his fingers inside her until she murmured in his mouth. She pulled back, turning away, shimmying her trousers down. He lifted a hand to grasp her breast as she bent forwards, pulled her close by her hip. She reached behind, held his dick and guided herself back onto it, pinning him between the hard tree and her dimpled buttocks, his pants cleaving round his hard on as she pulled him past the ruched crotch of hers and inside her. The urgency slipped away into pleasure, into breathing, into the curve of her back as her blouse rode up. He came, swamped with a need that had waited too long, unable to hold back, gripping her by the waist and pulling her onto him as he closed his eyes and floated away on the moment. Knowing she wasn't done, knowing he could do better, unable to hold back any longer. His dick withering inside her as she straightened, slipping loose as she pulled forward.

She pulled her trousers up, leaned back into him, letting him wrap his arms around her. His hands tucked upon her breasts, fondling them. Sank her head backwards against his shoulder. He reached a hand down to her pants, but she nudged him away with a hip. He understood. She'd wanted him, the reassurance of him, not the pleasure. Kate could look after herself.

'I'm sorry,' he muttered into her hair. 'I'm not at my best.'

She pulled away from him, turned, stroked his cheek.

'What have you done to my hair?' she asked, reaching a hand to tidy it up.

'Never looked better.' He reached out to rearrange it.

Kit pulled up his trousers, straightened his shirt. Helping her straighten her clothes, running his fingers through her hair to tidy it. They air was thick with the smell of them. His need for a bath, her scent lingering on his drying fingers, rising with the woody earth beneath them in the cool darkness. He pulled her close, vision narrowing to the ease between them, the return of what they knew best. An intimacy that pushed the world away.

Kit kissed her lips playfully, followed the curve of her cheekbone, found the hollow at the side of her eye with his mouth.

'You better get back,' she said, her eyes turning away, looking down the path.

'I said I'd walk you home.' He looked past her, up the path to the castle. 'Come on.'

He pulled her back onto the path, kept hold of her hand and walked on. She laced her fingers through his. They remained silent as they wound uphill beside the castle walls, emerging into the high open square. He kept hold of her hand all the way to the bistro, open and full of customers. Stood outside the back entrance, not letting go. She pulled her hand away, raised it to leave a lingering touch on his cheek, walked away from him and inside.

Kit watched her shut the door behind her, saw her turn into that perfect hostess, a word here, a laugh there, as she wound her way towards the stairs that led to her flat. Her hair was messy, and her trousers creased. Her pants would be damp with him. He felt emptied, unfulfilled, wanting to go in with her, to walk through the busy brightly lit room and follow her up the stairs. Make a better job of it. Pull that deep and contented smile from her only he knew. He turned and walked away from the shadows beside the door.

ISABELLE WAS LEANING against the window frame in the guest sitting room when he got back.

As he walked into the room she said, without turning, 'Your bath will be cold. You took longer than I thought.'

'She gave me a right bollocking.'

'What for?' Isabelle asked, turning now.

'Not supporting you.' He stayed where he was. 'Which I suppose I deserved.'

She didn't reply.

'I'll go bathe,' he said. 'Won't be long.'

He turned and walked into the hallway, counting the steps on the way up to her bedroom. Fifteen bedrooms empty and she had to keep the one furthest away.

The bath was lukewarm. He let out some of the water, turned the hot tap to refill and threw off his clothes with relief. He sank into the water and slid beneath the surface with closed eyes and a deep breath, letting it out and sinking down to the bottom of the tub as he grew heavier.

He was sick of coming here filled with anticipation and finding disappointment. The water was hot and comforting, and his frustration had gone, spent in the moment with Kate. The weight of her thighs pinning him to the tree, their needs matched. For once, he had no desire. Not for Isabelle, not even for touch, or closeness. He put a hand down to caress his dick, floating in the warm water, soft and content. Snuggling into his rising balls as he floated up to the surface and opened his eyes. Isabelle was stood in the doorway, a bottle of wine in her hand, two fresh glasses.

'You looked like you needed another drink.' She held the bottle up. 'I can go if you want some peace.'

'Pour yourself a glass,' he said. 'Pass me the bottle.'

'Seems a bit drastic,' she quipped.

'Drastic times, sweetheart.'

'It's not so bad, is it?' she handed him the bottle, sipping from her own glass as she perched on the toilet seat. 'I'm sorry if you're disappointed. I wanted you to relax, not have to come back and sort me out.'

'I know.' He leant back in the bath, the bottle of wine

hanging from his hand over the side of the bath. 'I don't understand why you can't leave it alone for longer. Give us time to adjust.'

'It's easier this way.' She was evading him, he could feel it in his clenching stomach, sat up in the bath and swigged from the bottle. 'The sooner the better, for everyone's sake.'

'That's the bit I don't get,' he said. 'Who are you making these changes for? It's all yours, Isabelle. You don't need to do any of this for anyone else.'

'Any changes I make will upset someone. Better make them sooner, while we're all reeling, and get the whole process done. Otherwise, it's like putting on a plaster, then ripping it off again.'

'In one breath you say you're doing it for the good of the family, in the next doing it to minimise their pain. You'll have to forgive me if I seem less than enthusiastic. And in all this, I'm unclear where we come, or me, for that.' He'd done it, said it. The thing he couldn't say in front of Kate.

'I'm not doing it for me,' she defended herself. 'Well, a bit, obviously, but for the family. I want to help Elsa, Hester and James, and Nat.'

Kit couldn't believe she'd side-stepped it, blanked the whole issue that was sitting between them.

'How's it going to help Hester?' He picked on the most useless point of her evasion.

'Because it will be over, whatever changes I make. She can be upset, get over it, move on.'

'And James?'

'Similar.'

'And you're going to give some of this to Nat?' Kit asked.

'I'm going to encourage Elsa to put it in trust for Nat,' Isabelle said.

'And Moth?' Kit asked.

She drank from her wine, looking into the mirror opposite her. From where he lay in the cooling water, Kit couldn't see her reflection.

'Not exactly.'

'Not exactly how?' he asked, taking a pull from the bottle. There was an acidity to drinking red wine from the bottle, unaired, compressed and brutal, that just suited the bitter moment unwinding in the steam.

'I wanted to give Moth a chance to do more,' she said. 'When he comes back, I thought he might want the other flat. I don't know if he wants to go to Swansea. I wanted to give him the choice, or the income from it, to do something else if he wants. And it will be less financial pressure on Elsa.'

'What?' Kit felt anger sour in his stomach. Too much wine hitting the tiredness and lack of decent food. Moth. Again. It always came back to Moth.

'You know Moth,' Isabelle protested. 'He's unhappy, he wants his own life. I want to help give him some choices. maybe, if he feels he has more choice, he might come home. I thought you'd understand that.'

The mood between them was chilling faster than the bath water. All she'd unveiled to him that evening, the monstrous changes to an established estate, and Kit knew exactly why she was struggling to tell him this part. For one flicker of a second, he held out that he might be mistaken. That this, her concern for Moth, was not the instigator of the whole lot. That flicker died with her defensive last statement. Kit knew evasion when he heard it.

'I do understand.' He slugged from the bottle, flaming the irritation rising from the knotted pit in his gut. He understood that she was covering her tracks. 'Better than many. But

I was hoping to see some consideration of our choices in all this. It seems you've thought about everyone but us.'

'If I get all this sorted, I'll feel I can make choices again.' Her voice had that crushed tone in it again. He hated it. He hated how she cowered, before him, before Hester, before the world. Kate would never have lost an argument with such little effort.

'I don't see how throwing yourself into these changes gives us any choice, you'll be tied up for months.'

'It won't be that bad,' she said, putting her drained glass down on the floor, standing up and wrapping her arms against her waist.

'Not that bad?' He laughed at her, watching her wince, trying not to enjoy it. Trying to keep his anger stemmed beneath the water, drowned out by the wine. 'Isabelle, you don't have a clue what you're taking on. Multiple sales, the legals, planning, development. Get real, it's going to take years, let alone months.'

'Well, you can help me,' she said, resisting his dose of reality. 'And maybe Moth will too. He might want to work on it with me, with us, when he gets back.'

'Moth isn't coming back,' Kit told her. Her crumpled face a slap in return.

'Of course he is,' she said. 'He'll be back at the end of the summer.'

Kit stayed silent. Resisting the urge to tell her categorically otherwise.

'I know he's being difficult, but he'll be back. We need to leave him alone for a bit. He wants some space, that's all.' Her face was full of concern and faith, full of conviction.

'He doesn't want space,' Kit sat up in the bath, sluicing the water from his hair. 'Face it, he might not come back.'

'Yes, he will.'

'Christ, why are you so sure?'

'He'll come back because of Nat.'

'He's already in touch with Nat,' Kit disagreed. She was lying, that wasn't what she thought. She wanted to believe Moth would come back because of her, and she couldn't say it, hiding it behind Nat. 'Unless you've heard from him too?'

'No, I haven't.'

'And yet, you're so confident he's coming back you're prepared to offload your inheritance to impress him?' He took the soap and sat up on his knees in the bath, soaping himself. His pits, his balls, his arse. Angry with her for being this naïve. Angry with himself for being such an idiot. The only thing that had felt right about this visit was Kate. Her breasts in his hand, his pants cushioning his dick as he slid into her warmth, her waist curving in front of him, her arms clinging onto his neck.

'He'll come back for the bike.'

'What?' Kit stood up from the bath, water deluging the floor. He stepped over the edge, dripping wet and naked. Wanting her to see him. Wanting her to want him. She looked away. 'The bike?'

'The one he bought from James. It means the world to him. He won't leave it here, he said he'd be coming back.'

'Said, when?'

'When he left for school.'

'And what else did he say?' Kit asked. He grabbed a towel and threw it over his shoulders, walking away from her in to the bedroom, bottle in hand. As she followed him, he began to roughly dry his hair, juggling the towel and the bottle.

'He said...' Isabelle said, struggling to recall, '... he said, I helped him feel better about Elsa.'

'What about Elsa?'

'About trusting her, about...' Isabelle paused, and a frown appeared over her eyes, '... about leaving Nat with her.'

'Really? He thanked you for helping him to feel better about leaving Nat behind?' Kit pressed the point home. 'Anything else?'

Kit finished towelling himself dry, stood, swigging from the bottle, naked and enjoying her discomfort. His nudity was making her crumble. He could tell. Nakedness wasn't something people were comfortable with, especially when they were lying.

'No. I can't remember anything else, anyway,' she said. 'You should put some clothes on.'

'Why?' he asked. 'I haven't seen you for weeks, months, and now you want me to get dressed? Don't you want me anymore?'

'I don't like you this angry.' Isabelle moved away from him towards the door.

'I'm not angry with you,' he said. 'I'm angry. There's a difference.'

'Well, you're taking it out on me.'

'You're the only one here,' he said. 'The entire house is empty. *Your* empty house. We could do anything we want, and you're telling me to put my clothes on. How civilised, Isabelle, how very civilised.'

'It doesn't always have to be about sex, Kit.'

'Which means what, you don't want sex with me?'

'No, I didn't say that,' she protested.

'Well, what do you want?' He knew it was a shout. He wanted to pull it back, but it was too late, reverberating in the increasing space between them, making her wince. Kate would have shouted right back at him.

'You're drunk. And tired. And angry.' Isabelle walked backwards from him.

'And you're obsessed with Moth,' he yelled, her reasonableness pushing him over the edge. 'It's always Moth this, Moth that, even when he isn't here.'

'Why are you mad at him?' Her voice withered as his rose. 'I don't even know why we're arguing over him. It's got nothing to do with him.'

'Because you can't even see it,' he roared. 'Why else are you doing all this? It must be for him, and you won't even admit it.'

'It's not for him!' She burst into tears in shock at her own temper.

Two crying bitches. All because of him. Kit swigged from the bottle, roared in frustration and threw it as far as he could. It hit the far wall and didn't even break, rebounding and oozing its bloody dregs on the carpet while Isabelle cried. Christ, he couldn't even break a bottle properly.

'Well it's not for me, that much is clear,' he told her in a cold, harsh voice. 'Whatever you're doing, and why, it's got nothing to do with us.'

Isabelle walked out of the room. He followed her.

'Why don't you admit it, you don't want us, do you?' he demanded, following her down the corridor, catching her at the top of the stairs by her elbow.

'I don't know what I want,' she sobbed. 'I have everything I didn't ask for and now I don't know what I want.'

'Including me?'

'I don't know!' she shouted, trying to pull away from him, trying to go downstairs. 'I need time to figure out what I want. Why can't anyone understand that?'

Kit stood back, reeling, letting go of her arm. She took

advantage and started down the stairs away from him. He went to follow. Stood on the brink of the first step and watched her fleeing. Saw the shadow of truth in the landing window as she passed it. Did he follow her, sort it out, make it better? Or let her go? He hadn't had to think about following Kate. He'd known what to do. Now, as change seemed to be sweeping through the cold halls, he realised he didn't know any more than her.

He stood at the top of the stairs. Heard her steps echoing through the empty house. He went back to the bedroom, found his keys and phone where he'd dropped them on the bed. Walked downstairs naked, the evening air catching the last of his damp skin in a blissful chill, got in the car, the cold leather cleaving to his skin and drove away.

It was the first time he'd felt comfortable all day.

5

Dear Kate,

Such news! How I love these letters that come for me, full of the details of your lives. How all our dreamy expectations are turning into a lively reality.

Married! I never expected to hear such news this quickly. You sound full of love and joy. What bliss to hear your happiness. And how sweet of you to tell me that I missed nothing as you and Patrick eloped to London and it was but the two of you at the ceremony. It makes me feel less guilty that you and Elsa missed our wedding.

I would never have thought you would marry an Irish Catholic, though as you say, Pat's Catholicism is lax enough to ignore the church wedding. Does this mean perhaps you will return more often to Ireland and your family now? Does Patrick have a large family? How I envy you such a future. Ted and I have a small circle of friends here and no family. When children come, they will be smothered in love by the staff of the house, but perhaps will always long for that special bond with grandparents. And I long for when we can return to Riverdell with a grandchild for William. Though, it appears not to be on the immediate horizon. We had hope at the end of last year, my first pregnancy was confirmed in December and we were giddy with joy at the news. How odd to celebrate Christmas here, but the hope of a child made it wonderful. Sadly, my body declined the adventure. I miscarried in early January. Our fresh risen hopes crumpled in the aftermath that my body inflicted on me for daring. These are the best months in Bombay, and I missed it all. Spending nearly two months in bed recovering the disaster. Ted is now too anxious to even kiss me.

But... you are not only married but moved to London. How wild for you. I loved it the one week I spent there with my course and I am sure you will adore living in the city. It will suit you down to the ground. AND – how much news your letter contains when I reread it, I can barely keep pace – you have abandoned history for haute cuisine. But you did so well in your studies. A Master of History, and now you are apprenticed as a chef? How on earth did that come about? You were so passionate about history, especially colonial history. Ted will be astounded to hear of it. He always admired the extent of your knowledge on India. But I shall tell him, as I realise now, even while I write, you are doing what your quick and passionate heart catches hold of. For when have you done otherwise? If Rose is our fierce and fearless leader, then you are our poet, Kate. Immersing yourself with joy into what life gives rather than lamenting what it takes. Striding forward, never looking back. I remember the suppers and midnight treats you used to whizz up for us at old Shorrock's, after her vile cooking had made us retch. Perhaps the seed of your future was always there, on the back burner. I think you will make a great chef. You have the perfect sort of passion for it. I cannot wait until you visit us. Bombay is a feast for the senses, you will adore it. It is aggressive and delirious, even contained outside the closed windows and the darkened room. The staff have been wonderful, looking after me no matter how late Ted is at work. Next month we go to the villa in Kashmir again, I cannot wait and hope to be there in time to see the almond blossom. It gives us such quiet, contented time together, away from his demanding work schedule here. Though I adore Bombay I don't think I could live here all the time. It is as exhausting as it is stimulating.

Have you seen Rose? How is she? And the baby? She writes such fleeting letters and I long for news of him. Christopher. She told me she named him for the patron saint of travellers as that is how she was blessed with him. And now calls him Kitty. Poor boy, I hope she grows out of that. He will be tormented at school if his mother still calls him Kitty by then. What does he look like now? The photo I have is all dark hair and closed eyes, scrunched face and curled fists. He looks like a fighter about to go into a boxing match! Will you and Patrick start a family soon? Elsa writes that she and Richard are waiting, to give themselves time alone together before they start. I long for a child as soon as possible. To hold such a precious new life in my arms, filled with endless possibility and hope. Elsa was the first to marry, Rose the first to motherhood and you the first (and only, now Rose has decided not to return to her studies) to academic success. I long to be the first at something, and perhaps I can hold onto the hope of being the first to give William a grandchild for a few more years in Elsa's tardiness?

What other news have I for you? Its value withers rather, in the momentousness of yours. My teaching work, which I returned to Bombay in September hoping to immerse myself in, has floundered. Firstly, in the heat. You cannot imagine the intensity of this city in October and November. It roasted me alive. I was useless and felt pathetic. Living in the shade and only darting out at night to feel the ocean breeze. I managed to set up some small evening classes here at home with older children, their middle-class parents desperately trying to improve their English for jobs and universities. And I taught freely to the local kids who can afford nothing, though Sai was most unhappy to have their bare feet and rag-dressed bodies in her house. Then, the miscarriage. It rather ruined everything. Ted banished all visitors out of fear of infection, silly man. How is my wasted womb going to get infected through teaching English to poor kids? The wives of his friends, those few I was trying to build a friendship with, have not returned yet. I fear they were only trying out of appearances, much as myself, and were eager for any reason to stop.

How I miss Kish, our housekeeper in Kashmir. We had grown close in our quiet ways and would read to each other in the evenings. We couldn't understand much of our two languages, but how soothing to be read to and wonder what was written. Though Sai is amazing she has no time to pamper me and Ted is too tired to read to me when he returns home at night. There was a great financial crash here in India last year. The rupee value was slashed, and Ted's workload has become overwhelming. I don't know the ins and outs of it, you will be disgusted by my ignorance no doubt, but I suspect he is having to restructure his business to cope with it. Indira Gandhi is reviled for it and the people panicking about work. Ted mooted that he might have to sell the villa in Kashmir but, and I am selfishly glad, the value of it is negligible now and those willing to buy such a large, remote property, few and far between. My health has maybe swayed him too, he is anxious for me to return and recuperate. I dread the journey there, but the destination will be worth it.

Ted asked me to remember him to you, as he always does. He shall enjoy hearing your news no doubt when I read it to him, as soon as he is free, and be as ecstatic as I that you have found love and security in your new adventures. My love to Patrick, he sounds adorable, how did you put it, 'ruddy and huge and bright as Elsa's silverware'. I can't wait to meet him and look forward to your letters telling me more.

MY LOVE TO YOU BOTH,

BETH x

6

He crawled out onto the flat edge of the Mendola Pass in the dull middle hours of the morning. Squeezed flat between the mountains. The deep sleep he'd woken from feeling shallow. Pain twisting through him, growing in intensity as his strength ebbed.

He thought he'd left it behind. In the sapling lined field that floated above morning mist hiding the valley floor. He'd wanted out before anyone came pushing him on. Away from the last few days. Away from that crushing inward tiredness he couldn't pinpoint that had left him sitting on his arse in a field the night before. Hours later, his numb legs forcing the pedals around, nothing should have stopped the feeling of jubilation that he'd made it through his last pass.

Nothing except the pain in your chest.

Moth faced it down. Forcing through it with strong deep breaths that took all his focus and made his head swirl with oxygen.

Look at what you've achieved.

Giving himself credit. Trying to talk the weariness away.

Trying to ignore the memories. He thought about the long downhill into the valleys ahead. The easy days of riding through the hills, down into the Lake basins.

You can relax, enjoy the miles.

Some time with Kit at the end, rest time.

Maybe even fun time.

He told himself all this. But waves of tiredness came back at him and made his legs shake. The bike wobbled with the pathetic pace.

Limping over the crest of the pass he pulled off the main road into a small village. Stopped under trees and put his foot down. Feeling the tightness in his chest. Deep inside, crossing through his ribs and reaching stiff fingers into the muscles of his neck and down into the back of his shoulders. Shooting into his hips as he dismounted.

You could have pulled a muscle.

Carrying the bike about was never easy and the last few weeks he'd done it too often. He fought the urge to stop. Trying to breathe away the discomfort and regain his energy. The weight of the bike dragging it towards a tree. Leaning despite his best efforts, pedal clanging out the way. He dismounted, sank to his haunches beside the bike, onto his knees, onto his arse. Propped up against the tree, hearing cars slow down and pass by him.

You need to get up. Someone will stop.

He avoided eye contact. Watched their black wheels churn past him. Trying to look as normal as possible.

You should get back on the bike and get away.

It was soothing to sit there. Ignoring the urgency twisting his chest. The minutes trickling away. He could see them, outside his reach, where he couldn't grab hold of them.

Whizzing down the mountain while you sit on your arse.

Moth struggled to focus, to keep himself together. Ideas arguing it out from each side of the plan. Pain twisting sense apart down the middle.

You need to get to Iseo.

He shouldn't go see Kit.

You should get back on the bike.

He should never get back on the bike.

What the hell else are you going to do.

He should go home and see Nat.

You know better than that.

He should stop thinking he knew anything. The confusion dissolving the little energy he had left. He shut it all out with his eyelids. Focusing on the pattern of his breathing. Trying to use it to snare the pain in his body. Frustrated by how the pain chased itself in playful patterns instead. It was fine, he would get up in a minute. He knew he would. Get back on with the plan.

Without a plan you're the same as anyone else.

Pinned to the moment by the weight of life. Wrapped up in thoughts and emotions, not knowing what he was doing. Where he was going.

It's no better than drifting like rubbish in the breeze.

Waste product chucked out by someone else, waiting to be picked up by the next person. The ride west after leaving the farm at Ventoux had been like that. Deciding from one day to the next which road to take. Stopping at random times. Ending up sleeping anywhere with no access to food. Waiting for another evening like the one in Bort.

Scared of every sound, wary at every stop.

Bort. He tried to get up. But the images were stronger. Moth shuddered against the tree.

You need to get up now.

There was no energy left for the fight. His hands curled into fists, shaking. Useless.

You're not useless.

Useless as he'd been then.

Flying high on his flight away from Riverdell, heading for the lavender fields of his mother's memory in Ventoux. Outside Bort-les-Orgues where the Dordogne marked the district line. In the height of the tourist season. People everywhere.

You should have kept moving.

Moth closed his eyes against the tree. He'd been fighting it all morning. Fighting it since the night at Vigo. He was too tired. The pain inside his chest picking at the tight nugget of the memory. Peeling back the careful layers he'd wrapped around it. Pulling him in.

He had found the beach by accident. A dirt track leading down through dark trees. Ending in a small car park. Empty as the night. Ahead, through thinning trees the lights dotted around the shore reflecting off the lake.

He'd left the bike hidden in the trees, walked down to the water. Sat on the soft, unexpected sand of the beach and watched the surface darken and the distant lights brighten. Sound travelled far and he could hear... holiday laughter.

Fun. Happiness. Good times.

Moth felt it echo inside him. Full of self-belief and achievement. He stripped to his pants, swum out into the lake. The top layer of water warm, cooler depths soothing his leg muscles as he trod water. The beach hovering, a slim line of brightness flickering as the clouds passed over the darkening sky. Lost somewhere between night and day.

He lay back, floating in the ambient water. The sound of people surrendering to the lapping of water against his ears.

He closed his eyes. Lost sense of where he began and ended. Not sure which part of him was skin, which part water. He felt himself clean inside and out. He would step out of the lake and be wholly himself.

Your new self.

The past a door shut tight and locked.

He heard the car before he saw the lights. His eyes opened. He curled into motion, legs dropping back into the depths, looking back to the beach. Watched the slow passage down the rough track.

One car.

He started to swim back to shore. But the voices were quicker. Out of the car. Laughing, shouting. A burble of drink and fun.

Male. Female. Many male. Two, maybe three. Only one female.

Moth stopped swimming.

It's too late to get back to shore.

He swam back out. Keeping his movements small, hushed. His body submerged. Edging his way through the water, across the small peak of the bay and away. He'd left his clothes hidden by the edge of the beach, he might be able to grab them without being seen.

If you can get out the water without being heard.

Lights strobed over the surface, he took a breath and lowered himself to his eyes, hating his hair all over again. Reduced his movements, treading water. They were using the lights from their phones to get to the beach. Stumbling and laughing at the tree roots. The chill from the lower water touched his legs and fear snaked up his spine. They sounded senseless.

Full of drink. Full of shit. Full of dick.

Moth hated them all. He hated being there. He hated that they'd ruined his moment. The first stone hit the water and he froze. Another landed to his right, splashing his face. Lights flashed across him. Laughter broke out. Weak and useless with distance and alcohol.

They're too drunk to see you.

Moth stayed treading water, getting tired, trying to find the floor. Shivering with cold and too fearful to move. Picking up the sounds. Five of them. Four blokes. One girl. They were local. She wasn't. Speaking poor French. Trying to act older than she was.

What is she doing there? Alone. With four guys.

Drinking from bottles. Smoking. Red glows in the dark, lighting up the curve of the bottles. Chucking stones in the lake without looking where they fell. He shouldn't have worried about being seen.

They're not looking at the view.

The girl fell over in the dark. Laughing at herself. Moth watched it happen. Sickness spreading through him as understanding sunk in. The four guys laughing at her, kicking sand at her efforts to get up. One went to help her. Held out a hand and pulled her up. Laughed as he let go and she fell again. The other three laughing. Watching. Her, still laughing.

Stop laughing, stop laughing.

Moth frozen in the lake. Water lapping at his face, his nostrils, his fear coming fast in short breaths. Stiff with understanding. Saw it come to her too. Her laughter stopped. She was trying to talk. A babble of sound drifting out to him. Confusion. Fright. Drunken protest.

She's too scared to scream.

The weight of the guy pushing her back onto the sand.

His cigarette chucked aside, winking in the sand as it extinguished. Three phones lighting it all up for him. Recording the moment. Her summer clothes pulled away. Her skin a smudge against the sand. Hands scrabbling, batted away. Her mouth covered by her skimpy top. The guy grunting. His buttocks out of his trousers winking in the moonlight with a short fuse and fast breath. Slowing, savouring, kicked away by the next guy with a curse. A brief breath for her to sob. Wretched anguish lifting into the sky. Reaching out to his.

Don't cry. Don't make a sound.

Stifled by another hand. She was silent by the third. Limp by the fourth. A crooked castle in the sand, backlit by the wobbling phone lights. Moth watched it all. Too scared to move. To make a sound. Too scared of what they might do to him.

Watched it all. Heard it all.

Got the hard-on to prove it.

Fighting dead legs in the freezing water. Hating them. Hating himself more. Blood pumping in his dick, heart pumping in his chest.

He remembered the night with Isabelle in the river, a sudden curiosity to know what a woman looked like naked. A feeling he'd never had before that night. Never had since.

He watched them, lying spent on the sand with their dicks waving at the phones. Laughing at each other as they grew limp. Spunk shining back. The castle abandoned. Moth grew exhausted. Paddling, trying not to splash. If they saw him out there, at the end, what would they do?

Fuck you. Kill you. Kill you both.

They went quiet in the end. Running out of drink, out of fun. Stood and straightened their clothes up. Moth watched. Stomach knotted. Knowing he could do nothing.

Feeling ten again.

What are you going to do?

Confused, frightened, unable to stop it.

Then they left. Back to the car. Back to the town. Easy as that.

It's over.

For them. It would never end for her. It would go on and on, forever repeating itself. Moth crawled toward the shore, legs dead, shaking. He found the bottom with numb toes and walked through the quiet laps of water to the far end of the beach. Climbed out where the water met the stones, avoiding the sand. He found his clothes, held them against him, looking out at the lights across the lake. Camp sites, hotels, marinas.

Which one should she be at?

He looked at her. A hump on the dark beach. Passed out drunk and distressed. Her skin streaked with moonlight. Her small breasts with the dark circled nipples, her legs thrust apart. The sand churned and ragged by the small hollow they'd taken turns to bang her into.

Now you know what naked looks like.

Now he might never be able to forget it.

Moth walked away. Back to the bike, shaking and cold. He dressed, turned the bike and rode away. His dick throbbing on the saddle. Rode until the hard on gave up. Found a rough field as the sun came up and slept behind a hedge. Telling himself over and over.

Nothing you could have done.

Follow the plan.

Nothing you could have done.

He never knew what happened to her. If she'd lived, with the memory of the night to wake to. If she'd died, drunk, cold and cast off on the beach. He tried not to think about it. To put it in the box with the other thoughts, the ones he couldn't do anything about. The things he could do something about were the ones that got him up.

You can do something about today.

He would do something about Nat. Not now, but later, when no one could tell him what to do, he'd go back. He'd make sure nothing happened to her.

He leant against the tree on the Mendola Pass, picking himself back up from the rock bottom at Bort. Wishing it would stop coming back to him. Fighting the questions that came with the memory.

Which part of him was wrong? Which part was his fault? Wondering what if. What if his life had been different? What if his mother hadn't died?

What if you'd seen it differently, that first time?

What if it had been what it should be with a girl. If it had been what he was hoping it would be. What he'd felt that strange, unexpected moment beside the chestnut tree at Riverdell. Lightness, hope.

Would you be different?

What if it wasn't the sound of rape that came first in his head in the mornings. If his dick didn't seem to wake him from bad dreams to worse memories.

Who would you be?

He'd clung to his determination to find his mother in Ventoux and tried to outride the questions.

Except Ventoux had been empty. Of all the beautiful flowers she'd longed to see. And he rode away from there with nothing left. Anxious about the future.

Anxiety that attracted trouble. Those nights when the bike moved beneath his hand and he lashed out. Swearing and punches coming back at him until he roared louder from his own fear. Chasing the foothills of the Pyrennes, too nervous to tackle the mountains. Going where the road seemed easier. Taking a route that seemed quieter than the next. Trying to get away from his own head as much as other people. Moth had stopped looking at the map. Packed up and got back in the saddle and navigated somewhere between the compass and the mountains to his left.

Until he ran smack into the Ocean on the seafront at Guethary.

You're out of road.

Shocked at having nowhere else to go. The dark sky endless and full of hate. A cliff face rearing up, the boundaries between sea and sky lost in a storm. A wall he couldn't ride round that hit the emptiness in his head and crumpled him in the chest.

You've failed. You're lost.

The memory of those tears rushed in shame through his body again, leaking out through his hard-pressing fingers below the Mendola.

You didn't help her.

He'd failed. What was the use of running away if he let this stuff happen to others? It had crushed him, that ocean. He'd wept and wept.

Stop crying. People are going to see you.

Moth fought the pain in his chest. Tried to stop it from breaking him. He couldn't do that again. He couldn't bear the pain.

You didn't deserve it.

The memory of Beau coming afterwards. Comforting him. How she picked him up, dropped him down in her world without a question. Beau.

Holding the ocean back. You didn't deserve it.

But she'd helped him anyway. Piecing him back together one bowl of food at a time.

Moth's breath was ragged as he grasped the image and opened his eyes, the village road bleary in front of him. His stomach growling at him, stabbing with hunger. He wrapped his arms round his waist, nursing a pain he could understand.

Food, you need food.

He hadn't had his refuel day since meeting Mila.

Mila.

He clung to her name.

That's why you helped her.

To put it right, to pay back what he'd done wrong.

She'll have had the package by now.

Had she taken the tickets and gone? Had she trusted him enough from one small meeting to head into a world she knew nothing about?

You wouldn't.

It would come into the category of 'too much given for too little reason' to him. He shouldn't have risked so much, his precious postcard thrown in a bin with the ticket. But she'd pulled at the part of him that hurt, that remembered. The part that woke him with guilt.

Moth sat forward onto folded knees and put his head in his hands. Thinking of that line in Nat's email, 'Isabelle said to tell you Happy Birthday'. That one line attached to a hook.

Reeling you backwards.

Now, here he was cycling through the mountains as a result.

That wasn't part of the plan.

The glaring error seemed pitiful to him now. He'd left Guethary, stronger and wiser. Set his course to Vienna.

Enjoyed the ride there, fuelled by new confidence. Found it as beautiful as Beau had described. But afterwards he'd wobbled. Gone south knowing only he was going south. Working at the map daily, feeling the gaps in his plan.

That's how Kit had snuck in.

Through Lost. Through Lonely.

Looking for comfort from Nat on his birthday. Seven words and he'd crumpled. Rung Kit.

That's how Mila had snuck in.

Through Guilt. Through Memory.

Twisted the new plan further. Doubt washed over him. He tried to stem it behind his fingers. He was heart sick of doubt and questions.

You can carve the next target into the damn handlebars.

He'd repeat it to himself and drown out Lost and Lonely. Shout down Guilt and Memory. He focused on it now.

Venice. Venice. Venice.

He'd finish this stupid side trip and go to Venice. And he'd choose the next place there. Set that before him. He wouldn't let another Mila in.

Why would she ever give up what she had to try something sent by a stranger.

She'll have more sense.

He hoped she took them and left the dump she was stuck in. Waiting to see which one of the arseholes around her tried it on first. Moth wished he could call her. Tell her he wanted nothing back. It was safe. Safer than what she had. He thrust the wishing away.

You did what you could.

The rest was up to her. He sat upright, looking down the road.

Whatever happened he would never see her again.

Venice, Venice, Venice.

Meet Kit, prove his self-sufficiency, get some rest. Move back on with the plan.

Venice, Venice, Venice.

Vienna had been a plan. For no reason other than a postcard in Beau's shop. It had taken up two months of his life in well-controlled fashion. Northeast. Back through France and across the top corner of Switzerland. Fast and hard, each day plotted out on the map. Rest days planned in. Adhered to. Two months growing stronger, quicker, sharper. Believing again. He needed to remember that time.

You need to get back into that state.

Him, the bike, the plan.

It needs to be tighter than that.

The plan needed to be growing ahead of him, ready to reach out and grasp, target after target.

Moth pulled the map out of the bag. His stomach aching, his chest tight as he twisted. If he couldn't get rid of the pain, he would focus on the plan instead. He got the map out, went through the day's ride ahead. The steady downhill first, zigzagging through the foothills as they melted into the longer valleys ahead. Heading for Male for the evening's stop. There it was, on the page in front of him. Lines and symbols marking out the route. Calling him onwards. Drowning out the doubts and regrets. From Iseo, east to Venice. The boat to Greece.

It was his best option. He had to have it solid in his head before he saw Kit.

Or you'll end up wavering again.

He might get talked out of it. It was his life now. He made it. He chose the plan.

Asia. Cheaper. Warmer.

His finger reached across the Adriatic Sea, tracing ferry lines. Igoumenitsa. Northern Greece. He would follow the northern border and find a way into Turkey.

Venice. Igoumenitsa.

The names comforted him. Silencing the journey past.

He rolled to the side and onto his feet. His chest curled over its pain and bit into the movement. His stomach growled and clenched. He checked the bike, trying to get his breathing steady. Swung on and headed through the village back to the main road.

Three hot meals. That will set you right.

He would start in Male with breakfast. He created a café in his plan. That would be the start. A café. Somewhere local. A long breakfast, hot food, a mug of coffee to fuel inject his system. He saw the table. Square and wiped clean. The plate of food. Steam rising from it. His mouth filled with moisture as he thought of the smell. He would set off on a full stomach, easy riding until lunchtime.

But no, first, the overnight stop.

Before breakfast in Male. He would camp on the outskirts this side of the town.

Get a sound night's sleep.

Thoughts fell in place with the pace of the bike. Tiredness lingered, shadowed by the weight of memories. The pain in his chest a discomfort he hunkered over. Fixing it somewhere between the handlebars and his pumping legs.

March was coming to an end and promising spring, but the weather was volatile. Testing him as he rode down the last declines of the Mendola. The wind picked up, trying its best to shove him right back up the mountain. The clouds thickening, racing across him backwards as he swept forwards. Morphing his sense of speed. Making him question which way he was riding. Spots of rain came from nowhere and threatened with enough force to make him think of stopping, before disappearing in a fickle rush of sunshine. The road changed too.

Wider and faster. Watch your sides.

The wind pushing him one way conflicted with the rush of traffic coming from behind him. He took as many diversions as he could through the villages, but the road was inescapable. Pushing the world one way, down through the valley floor. Racing the river that ran there.

Carrying you with it.

He struggled with it. The sense of control. The wide tarmac laid with purpose in mind. Moth felt tight after the cavorting freedom of the Dolomites. The roads had lent themselves to the bike. To him. This was different. This push of purpose and destination. It mocked him with its confidence.

It was bordering evening when he got to Male. The light refusing to wane. Wallowing on the hills, deepening on the road. The day dragging itself out. He was going over a flyover, battered by wind, lorries roaring past. Lights brightening on the cars coming the other way as darkness increased. Male appearing as a stain spread across the disappearing valley floor.

That's a big tunnel up ahead.

A dark pit with traffic rushing into its bottle neck and him being swept towards it. Down beneath the flyover he could see the river. The water churning white and frothy over its wide, ragged bed. Gleaming in the shadows, pulling him away from the tunnel. At the end of the flyover a track went down to the river. He felt the hairs on his neck prickle as he left the road.

You're too visible. A lone tourist calling it a day.

He didn't stop to look confused. Pedalling with false confidence, sweeping into a huge parking area and carrying on to the far end of it. A narrow road ran parallel to the river and he followed it. When the sound of the road faded beneath the rush of water he slowed and scanned for a place shallow enough to cross, the last thing he wanted was to sleep on this side of the river. The hope eluded him. It was deep and full, sluicing round big boulders he would slip on. The weight of the bike daunting him. The narrow road curved under a high pipe wrapped in metal security guards and barbed wire, leading to a bridge. The buildings on the far side didn't look tempting or quiet. High security lights flooding across the concrete, trucks turning in the yards. Away on up the road he could see the tops of buildings peeping above the trees.

Moth cycled back towards the pipe, slipped off the bike, and pulled it into the trees away from the river. The mossy floor and thick peeling trunks of pines dimming the water noise. Stopping, listening, weighing up the odds, he felt his muscles start to shake, the cold biting into the exhaustion. He'd pushed himself to emptiness and his body was fighting back.

You need to sleep, and soon, and safely.

He pushed on further into the tress, found a space big enough, put up the tent. He crawled inside and pooled his food reserves on his lap, eating the tired leftovers with the zip open. Listening to the river hissing beyond the road. In the dipping light of the head torch, he found the notebook, opened it. The lines in front of him empty again. He'd wanted to rub out that date with Kit so much, now the lines seemed to underline the emptiness of his future.

Only twelve days ago.

Twelve days of wondering and Kit had changed his whole mind. He'd been desperate enough to rub it out, write his own day across it. Now that he'd ridden over the top of it, he could only think if Kit would still be there. If Iseo would prove as empty as the lines in the diary. Moth filled in the next line. Day 268. 26th March 2013. Male. A few isolated cars went by while he looked at it. Another nowhere stop. He shut the cover, tucked it away.

It was darker beneath the trees. The lingering light obscured. He dozed into a food tiredness that deepened into sleep.

'I TOLD JAMES.'

Isabelle was filling the jug with water for the coffee machine. Her stomach lurched as Asha, walking into the kitchen, began their conversation with her usual indifference for niceties. Running water hit the top of the kettle and splashed all over her.

'It's alright, don't panic,' Asha said, grinning as Isabelle tried to avoid the water.

'What did you tell him? What did he say?'

'I told him that I was helping you.' She set her heavy bag down on the table. 'That Rob had put you in touch with me, that you were struggling and needed help. I told him that you and Rob were planning changes to the estate and that I couldn't tell him what they were, because it would be unfair on you as a client.'

'Did you tell him about, you know?' Isabelle stumbled over her words. She poured the water into the tank, wiped her wet top with a tea towel and went to grab cups.

'I didn't tell him that I came to see you, no.' Asha frowned, fingering the handle of her solid bag. 'I feel bad about that, if I'm honest. But I did admit that I have been to see you several times already, and that I didn't want to tell him because I wanted to see if I could help you first.'

'How did he take that?'

'Quietly.' Asha pushed the bag away across the table, took off her three-quarter length coat and draped it over the chair, her business jacket and trousers looking smart in Isabelle's relaxed kitchen. 'But he took it. He asked how you were coping. I think he's glad to know people are helping you. He didn't say as much, but I think he felt relieved.'

'He never did say enough,' Isabelle said, and regretted it. She shouldn't have shared that bit of knowledge about him.

'He's getting better. It's been good for him, not being here, and Elsa moving away. And Hester. He seems sharper, more focused on the farm.'

'Have you told him about my plans?' Isabelle asked.

She and Rob were putting the final touches to the letters to the tenant farmers, offering them the chance to bid for their houses, yards and twenty acres of nearest land. The details of it were much more complicated than she had imagined. It was early October already, and the letters wouldn't go out until at least the end of next week.

'No, of course not. Are you going to make coffee or keep asking questions?' Asha liked to stay focused. She was always short on time, and patience, Isabelle was learning.

Isabelle turned back to the cupboards, looking for spoons, struggling to bring it all together, like her mind. Elsa's habits of years were mellowing as Isabelle relocated one item at a time closer to where she used it, inching the kitchen toward that of a single person, not the catering hub of a guest house.

'I also told him I would marry him.'

Isabelle dropped the spoon and whooped at Asha's quiet statement. She danced across the room and wrapped Asha in a hug, who hugged her back in surprise. Isabelle felt tears starting and held on for grim life.

'Oh my God,' she pulled back, brushing them aside.

'Why are you crying?' Asha asked as tears sprang into her own eyes.

'Really? You said yes? But we haven't done the letters yet, it may not work yet.'

'I know,' Asha admitted, and Isabelle could feel the fragility of her confidence through her business suit. 'I'm praying nothing goes wrong. But I wanted him to know I loved him. I couldn't bear the unanswered question. That's why I told him, about working for you. I said I couldn't keep a secret from the man I wanted to marry.'

'What did he say?' Isabelle asked. 'Oh no, sorry, you don't need to tell me.'

Asha held onto her arms as she pulled away. 'He didn't say anything. He just kept grinning, stupid English man, and holding me.'

'Oh my God.' Isabelle squeezed her hands and danced back across the room. 'I am thrilled for you, for both of you. This is amazing. Oh, do tell me you've told Elsa, she is going to be ecstatic. And Hester.'

'He is going to tell them today,' she said. 'I asked if I could be the one to tell you.'

Isabelle pulled her cupboards open, rummaged in the back, found a bottle of champagne left in Elsa's store for such unexpected announcements by guests, and held it aloft in victory.

'It's three in the afternoon,' Asha complained. 'I have to

go back to work.'

'I don't care.' Isabelle fetched large glasses, filled them with ice and popped the cork. 'We need to celebrate.'

They took the glasses, clinked them together, and drank, grinning at each other over the top. A rush of alcohol and bubbles hit her stomach.

'What about Kate? And Kit?' Isabelle asked. 'Who's telling them?'

'James suggested we go and see Kate tonight at the bistro,' Asha said. 'He's going to ask Elsa not to say anything.'

'I'll keep shtum too.'

'He didn't mention Kit.' Asha looked straight and hard at Isabelle.

'I'm sure Kate will tell him.' Isabelle returned to the cups. 'Coffee?'

'Definitely no more champagne,' Asha said, putting down her glass. 'But it was lovely, thank you.'

'I am buzzed,' Isabelle told her, heating milk. 'And stressed. Now I fell more pressure to get this right.'

'I hope it will help James when the letters go out. That he won't feel on his own making the decision.'

'But it still has to work.' Isabelle took the coffee over to the table. 'Thank God we decided to do all the farms, this will make it easier for him to accept.'

'Will you call Kit?' Asha pursed her lips at Isabelle. 'I want someone to tell him.'

'Oh, Kate will, or Elsa. They talk to him most days.' Isabelle pushed on past the conversation. 'Now, where are we at? The Staines house, right?'

'Particulars are in.' Asha pulled them out of her bag and waved the glossy folder in the air. 'Though, as your friend, I'm telling you, you need to call Kit.'

'Wow,' Isabelle ignored her, holding her hand out for the brochure. 'Let me see!'

Asha held them to her chest and scowled at her. 'You're ignoring me.'

'You're such a bright woman.'

'Yes, stubborn too, according to many others.' Asha refused to hand them over.

Isabelle sighed. She didn't want to talk about Kit. They hadn't spoken in over a month. Not since the night he'd left. 'He doesn't want to talk to me.'

'You don't know that if you don't ask him.'

'If he wanted to talk, he would call.'

'You're both as bad as each other.'

'Then we deserve what we get,' Isabelle concluded. 'Now, please may I see the particulars for the Staines House?'

'No.' Asha resisted, but she'd put a lot of work into this and she was as excited as Isabelle. 'You may see the particulars for 'Peel Villa'. You need to stop calling it the Staines House, it sounds awful. Goes on the market tomorrow unless you say otherwise today.' She handed over the details.

'Wow, it looks amazing,' Isabelle said, flipping through the pages. 'How did you manage this?'

'I was quite pacific with the photographer.'

Isabelle ignored her slip. She liked Asha's occasional slips of language, it made her more human. There was much about Asha that Isabelle could have been intimidated by, but which her kindness kept at bay.

'You make this sound amazing.' Isabelle read the details. 'Fantastic opportunity, first time on the market in over half a century, commanding presence, fine period details, enviable location. How can you be so vague, yet so alluring?'

'Practice.' Asha waved the compliment away with her

hand. 'We have to get them through the front door, to see past the damage. It's a big restoration project.'

'POA, that's tempting,' Isabelle said.

'Kit suggested it.'

'What?' Isabelle looked up in confusion.

'Look, don't kill the messenger, alright?'

'What do you mean?'

'Elsa asked me to get in touch with Kit.' Asha tossed her guilt aside with a hand wave. Isabelle was glad again she was in Asha's good books, the woman took no prisoners. 'After your conversation with her, about making changes.'

'She told me she trusted my decisions, especially if I was working with Rob.'

'Yes, except she rang me and asked me to get in touch with Kit, to keep him updated. She said it was her way of supporting you.'

Isabelle looked at Asha with a scowl. 'Is this a day for dropping secrets?'

'It does feel that way,' Asha admitted without a drop of penitence. 'I wish you would all start talking to each other. I've never known a family as bad at communicating.'

'You're about to join it,' Isabelle told her with a sly grin. 'You better get on board or you'll upset the apple cart.'

Asha shrugged in derision. 'Can't make an omelette without breaking eggs.'

'Why keep telling me to call Kit if you're already talking to him?' Isabelle wanted to be upset, but there was a drop of comfort in knowing he already knew what she wanted to tell him, rising like champagne bubbles through the bitter coffee as she swallowed.

'Because I'm sick of being the middle woman,' Asha

complained. 'He's been nothing but helpful. I wish you could believe he cares about you.'

'He walked out and hasn't called since,' Isabelle protested. 'Drove away, when he was drunk. He must have been pretty desperate to get away from me. What else am I supposed to think?'

'I give up.' Asha threw her hands up. 'When I speak to you, I tell you to call him. When I speak to him, I tell him to call you. Perhaps if I stop speaking to both of you, you will have to talk to each other.'

'You wouldn't?' Isabelle asked. Asha was her strongest ally, and she had an answer for all the queries that Rob raised.

'Don't test me,' Asha threatened.

'Did he help with these?' Isabelle asked, waving the particulars in the air.

'He saw the drafts,' Asha said. 'Tweaked some details. He is Elsa's way of keeping in touch with it all but leaving you to do as you want.'

'Doesn't she trust me?'

'Of course she trusts you, else she would be speaking to you herself,' Asha sounded impatient again.

'Am I being thick?'

'No, just typically Threlfall.' Asha smirked at her. 'Kit suggested the POA policy, and that not to be revealed unless serious interest was expressed. He also suggested we block book viewings and arrange for the tenants to be out during those viewings. And that we conceal the seller's identity.'

'And what was the final price that we settled on?' Isabelle asked.

'The final price that you settled on was £475,000,' Asha told her.

'God that sounds a huge amount of money,' Isabelle said. 'Did Kit agree with it?'

'He wanted to push for more,' Asha said. 'But I argued that you wanted a quick sale. He agreed in the end.'

Isabelle returned to looking through the brochure. Retreating into an unsettled silence as the pictures and plans outlined the first real evidence of her changes.

Selling the Staines house, or rather, Peel Villa, had been easier than expected. Mrs Staines and Marge had clung to each other and wept for joy when she went to see them with Rob and explained what she wanted to do. Isabelle had been speechless. They had been worrying about it for years and not wanted to say anything to Elsa. Asha had rolled her eyes and snorted something about "British communication" when she heard.

The tenant in the larger of the two bungalows had complained about the situation, but Rob hadn't given him much room for manoeuvre. The contracts had been watertight, and they gave way over the necessary notice of two months. Not that the tenant hadn't had his revenge. They'd moved out in under two weeks and left six years' worth of rubbish in the garage, and three dogs' worth of shit filling the back garden. When she went to view it, she had been shocked at the state of the kitchen, at the abandoned broken furniture and the stained carpets. It had convinced her she didn't want to be a landlady at all if possible. Asha had arranged for someone to go and clear it out, and they'd not let Mrs Staines or Marge anywhere near it until afterwards. An uncomfortable thought nudged her.

'Asha, who sorted out the mess at the bungalow?'

'Hmm?' Asha could do a mean impression of linguistic incomprehension when it was convenient.

'You know what I mean. Did you get Kit involved on that too?'

'All you need to know is that your family are helping, they are supporting you. Even if you are too stubborn to speak to them.'

Isabelle frowned at her and got a saccharine sweet smile in response. She wondered what else she didn't know about. Apart from what she was beginning to realise she didn't know about.

Such as Mrs Staines and Marge. Who'd held hands in girlish excitement when they walked inside the bungalow while she explained what they were going to do to update it. A mobility bathroom, removing steps to the garden, under-floor heating in the revamped kitchen, opening the lounge and dining area to create a more open-plan, accessible and well-lit property. All funded from the sale of the big house. Isabelle had thought it might be Marge persuading Mrs Staines to move, but Mrs Staines had been full of how much easier life would be for Marge. How much Marge would love the gentle garden, and the lack of stairs, and having neighbours to talk to.

Anxiety about moving out of the old house had never existed, they were vacating it like rats a sinking ship.

'Well, happy to go ahead?' Asha interrupted her thoughts.

'Do it.' Isabelle had no doubts. 'Get it on the market. What's next?'

'We have plans.' Asha pulled yet another large envelope from her bag.

'Have you got any more to share with me today?' Isabelle asked. 'Or are you going to keep drip feeding me?'

Asha ignored her and laid out a large sheet of white paper on the kitchen table, smoothing out the creases with careful hands. Isabelle stood up and went to look at them. The plans for the conversion at Riverdell.

'Oh God, it looks so official.'

'Getting cold feet?' Asha asked.

'Hot sweats.'

The sharp lines revealed the footprint of the house, repeated four times; basement, ground, first and second floors laid out with their innards exposed. She'd seen drafts and had grown used to reading them. What signified a door, a window, where steps were, which way they ran. Riverdell was becoming a project even to her eyes.

Her eyes picked out the changes, three lines that made such an impact. Two humble walls erected, no wider than the corridor, that would separate the two new flats from the remainder of the house. And one wall removed, curving stairs descending from beside the main stairwell in the hall down into the garden room.

This had been a revelation from the architect who had found old plans of the house to back up his theory and came, one day, tapping against the panelling that ran between the stairwell and the guest dining room, his eyes lighting up with excitement as he listened to the hollow reverberations. He'd gone downstairs into the garden room and knocked holes in the dead space between it and the workroom. Came out covered in dust and crowing in delight. The original staircase remained. It was damaged where the walls had been put in but salvageable. The new plans showed the staircase reinstated.

Isabelle had her doubts about this. She could have made another flat from the basement, accessed from the same back entrance. But she'd been outvoted. She'd insisted on the upstairs flats having a room that looked out over the river and gardens. She felt that, without that view, they were too pokey. The thought of Kate taking one of the flats gave her a focus she found helpful. She wanted to make it feel special, to give the flats some of the grace that the old house had, not shoehorn two financially sound flats in. Even with the loss of those rooms she would have a seven-bedroom house to rattle about in. But Asha and the architect, and Kit she wondered now, told her she was taking too much from the main house. She compromised by agreeing to keep the basement and reinstate the stairs. She wasn't sure what she would do with the basement, but Kate had thrown her penny's worth in, backing Asha, as had Rob, as had the architect.

Here was the result, laid out in front of her.

'You're very quiet.'

'Sorry,' Isabelle said, looking up. 'It's a lot to take in.'

'Not happy?'

'Not not happy. Stunned. I can't believe this is going to happen.'

'Only if you want it to.' Asha stressed, laying a concerned hand over hers.

'I do,' Isabelle said. 'I really do. It looks amazing. I can't wait to show Kate. I hope she doesn't change her mind.'

'She doesn't seem the sort to change her mind.'

'How long will it all take?' Isabelle straightened up. Looking at the plans from a wobbly distance. 'I mean, what comes next? I don't know where to start. Which builder do I get?'

'Hmm, it is a lot to consider. Shame there isn't a friend you could ask to help,' Asha mused.

'Oh, enough already.'

'You know I'm right. There's no way you can manage all this without it taking over your life.'

'I could give it a go.' Isabelle felt how weakly it came out. 'You must know a good builder, or I could ask the architect to manage it.'

'Yes, that's true.'

Asha gave her no more assistance, looking at the plans with the same refusal to help etched on her face. Isabelle shifted on her feet in the silence.

'James told me you and Kit have fallen out before,' Asha prodded. 'He said you always make it up.'

Isabelle didn't reply. The thought of calling Kit filled her with dread. She missed him. She missed him more than she could believe. She wanted to share this with him, and she was scared. Scared of how angry he'd been. Scared of his anger at Moth. Scared at what she was doing without him. Scared of him taking over if he did help. With Rob, Asha and Kate's support life was beginning to make a little more sense. She didn't want Kit to take that away from her. To swamp her with the confusion she had felt when they argued.

'Talk to Kate about it,' Asha suggested. 'She knows him better than me.'

'When are you going to get married?' Isabelle asked.

'What?'

'I was wondering, are you going to have a long engagement?' Isabelle turned away from the plans. 'We've hardly talked about it. I mean, come on, this is exciting stuff. What are your plans?'

'I don't have plans yet, we only decided last night,' Asha said, trying to catch up with the change of conversation. 'We need to think about it.'

'Will you get married here? Or in Poland?'

'I don't know, probably here. I don't have a big family, and this is home.'

'And when?'

'Stop evading me,' Asha said.

'Stop evading me,' Isabelle returned. She folded up the plans.

'Not for a year or two, I think. It is nice to have time to anticipate it, not to rush. And we need time to sort all this.' She pointed at the paperwork on the table. 'We need to think about what we can afford, if we do manage to get our bid on the farm accepted.'

'Good plan,' Isabelle said. 'But you two getting married, that will be the icing on the cake. Elsa is going to be overjoyed with this. Prepare yourself for that.'

'Do you think she will want us to get married here?' Asha asked, and Isabelle heard a hint of anxiety in it.

'She'll want you to do what you want, not to feel pressured by anyone. That seems to have been her response in recent months, from my own experience.'

'Strange to think about being part of a new family,' Asha said, her voice weaker as she began to think about it, her own huge decisions coming to the fore.

'Sure you want to join it?'

'Revolution from within,' Asha said, grinning at her. 'Besides, who wouldn't want to marry James?'

They looked at each other and burst out laughing.

'Oh no, that was awful,' Asha said.

'It was hilarious,' Isabelle told her.

'I'm sorry.'

'Good, now you have no right to nag me,' Isabelle taunted her.

'I'm going back to work, before I say anything else stupid.'

They hugged goodbye. It had become the most natural thing. To hug this woman who was marrying James. Somewhere in the closeness growing between them the distance between her and James grew greater, more comfortable. Isabelle even felt excited about the wedding. Asha's wedding.

'WELL, how long's it going to take?' Kate asked.

'I don't know,' Isabelle admitted.

'And when can you start?'

'I don't know. I think we need to sell the Stain...Peel Villa, first.'

'Peel Villa?' Kate asked. 'God, I didn't know that was its name, how awful.'

'Well, that's its name.' It was odd how defensive she already felt about the property. She'd always been the first to criticise it before... before she became owner.

'Sort of appropriate I suppose. After all, most of the wallpaper is peeling off the walls!'

'Oh dear, I hadn't thought about that.' Isabelle had noticed that none of the peeling wallpaper was in the pictures. 'Well, I can't change it now. It goes on the market today. It's now a matter of finance, everything that comes in goes back into the redevelopment. But there's no income now from B&B, and we've got to refresh the bungalow before they move in. This house is only being funded from rental income, I'm living on savings, and Rob is running up bills I don't want to even think about. I guess we have to wait and see.'

'The thing is you mustn't worry about it.' Kate was always practical about the money. 'At the end of the day you go to the bank with all your plans and ask for an overdraft to see you through. Which will incur costs, I know, but you calculate those into the loan.'

'I don't know enough about this stuff,' Isabelle admitted.

'I've only ever had to earn and save before, not do finance.'

'Well, at least you've been sensible enough to save,' Kate told her.

'Only because you and Elsa beat it into me from before I could draw or sew!'

'Weren't we right?'

'Aren't you always?'

'It is comforting, I must admit.'

Kate looked at the plans on Isabelle's new desk. Isabelle leant against the window, watching her. There was something comforting about the height of the window now she'd moved the furniture round. It suited her, the right position to lean and think, before moving on again. It was mid-morning. Kate had popped down to see how she was coping with the news of James' impending marriage. Isabelle had been prepared for her, moving them on from the wedding news to the conversion plans. It had worked in reverse with Asha and it worked with Kate. Her winter mules were kicking their heels out from under the fringe of her trousers as she leaned over the desk. A thick, dark blue cardigan showing the waist where it rode over her shoulders, a fine silk blouse peeping out below. Kate looked chic, even the windy day had added to her look.

'Are you excited?' Isabelle asked.

'Excited, nervous, anxious,' Kate said, looking up. 'Part of me is wondering what on earth we are doing, part of me thinks it's genius. What about you?'

'Excited about all the changes. Nervous about the money management,' Isabelle said. 'You know, if you change your mind, I can let the flats out to someone else. I won't be upset.'

'I'm not going to change my mind.' Kate walked over to her by the window. 'Though thank you for the thought. I've already begun arrangements with Mike and Dee. I shall hand over after New Year. It's the dullest possible time of year, and perfect for letting them find their feet. I'll be on hand for any problems, and as soon as the flat's ready, I shall move.'

'And they're definitely going to take the lease?'

'They're overjoyed,' Kate waved the concern away. 'When I told them I was going to lease the business out I didn't realise they would be interested, I thought they would stay on as managers under the new landlord.' She paused, tilted her head slightly and added, 'It's odd how people react differently to how you expect.'

'Like Mrs Staines and Marge?'

'I was thinking more about Kit.' Kate took another step towards her, her blue eyes pinning her against the window frame, glasses held in her hand. 'He behaved awfully, I know, but we didn't consider how hurt he'd be that we'd made plans without him.'

Isabelle didn't reply but folded her arms together, stacking resistance between her and Kate.

'We might have to admit we're out of our depth,' Kate said. 'Even with Rob and Asha onboard, we need him. He is the expert at all this, after all.'

'If he was upset before, he won't be any happier now.'

'Nonsense,' Kate said. 'You know Kit, he gets over an upset even faster than he can clean it up. He cares about what's happening here, and for you, for us, for all the family. He calls me daily, and Elsa, even though he's swamped with work. He's had time to adjust to what's happening. We need to ask him to help, Isabelle, and I know that's a difficult thing to do.'

Isabelle stayed against the window.

'Well, that's the quietest no I ever heard.' Kate folded up

her glasses, tucking them into her cleavage.

Isabelle tried not to smile. It always surprised her, seeing Kate with glasses on. There weren't many occasions when she needed them, and she hated admitting it. Only Kate, at sixty-eight, would consider using her bra as a glass case. She claimed the only advantage of her breasts shrinking were that she could hide her weaknesses there instead. For that is what glasses were to her, a weakness, a sign of ageing. Not for her the vile string round the neck, or the annoyance of losing her glasses. They were always safe where she needed them. Out of sight, easy to hand, cushioned against damage.

'What exactly did you two argue about?' Kate nudged the conversation on.

'I don't know,' Isabelle replied. 'He was angry. Angry that I'd made plans, angry that I hadn't waited for him. Angry that... about Moth.'

'Perhaps he was plain angry?' Kate suggested. 'He always has had a temper. My God, you should have seen him at fifteen when he got expelled. The Headmaster was cowering behind his desk when I got there. The problem with Kit is that he has such a strong handle on life, he rarely has occasion to be angered, so when he does show it, it can seem, well, a bit overwhelming.'

'I've never seen him that angry before.' Isabelle looked at her toes, dressed in socks against the cold that was beginning to seep through the house, as Kate had predicted. She was resisting closing the doors though.

'Perhaps he's never been that confused before?' Kate offered. 'He doesn't like being out of control. Or, more to the point, he can't stand anyone else being in control, especially of him.'

'I'm not in control of him,' Isabelle protested.

'You know, he waited a long time for you to not be with James,' Kate stood closer to her, placing a gentle hand on her folded arms. 'I don't think he ever thought it would happen and, when it did, he wasn't even sure what it meant. Then all this,' she used her free hand expressively to encompass the study, the house, the estate, 'happened. And, when he gets back from managing a mammoth task in Swansea, finds that we'd conspired together without him.'

'That's not what happened,' Isabelle protested.

'Not for us, I know. But for him, perhaps a little bit?'

Isabelle looked down at Kate's hand. It was slender, the knuckles bony, the skin spotted, loose, moisturised. An elegance and energy captured in the poised fingers.

'Why did you argue about Moth?' Kate kept her hand with a soothing presence on her skin, keeping them connected.

She looked up at Kate. That was the hardest thing to explain, because in her emotional memory of that awful night, she couldn't remember what they had been arguing about. Except that Moth had seemed the issue it all hung on.

'I said that maybe, when Moth came back, he might want one of the flats. Or perhaps to use the income from one, to help him choose what to do.' Isabelle saw Kate tilt her head, trying to understand, narrowing in on her discomfort. She pushed on. 'It was an idea, nothing major, and he freaked out about it. Said I was behaving like an idiot, and it was all Moth's fault. Went on a rant about my not wanting him, not wanting us. I didn't understand any of it. I walked away, because he was so mad, and the next thing I knew he'd driven off. He was drunk too, and I called him, he never answered. I mean, he just walked out, left all his clothes here. That's how much he wanted to get away from me.'

'And that's why you won't call him?' Kate tugged at her reluctant arms and took both of Isabelle's hands in hers, refusing to let her hide. 'Because he drove away drunk and naked to get away from you?'

Isabelle didn't reply. That had hurt, that and the things he'd said about Moth. Somehow, they had hurt more. The suggestion that there was something awry, unpleasant in her wish to help Moth. But she didn't want to talk about it. Not to Kit. Not to anyone.

'Or because he yelled at you about Moth?'

'I'm not sure,' Isabelle said. 'Both, I think.

'You know, he didn't drive far,' Kate rubbed her hands between strong fingers. 'He spent the night in a lay-by on the bypass. Feeling a right idiot, I should imagine.'

'Did he?'

'Umm, stupid man,' Kate said with amusement. 'Drove home the next morning when he'd sobered up, bursting for the toilet and unable to stop because he had no clothes. Horrified his neighbours too.'

'Not that he'd care about that.'

'The thing about Moth,' Kate said in a gentle tone, peering closer at her. 'None of us like looking in a mirror.'

'What do you mean?'

'Kit and Moth. Has it never struck you how alike they are? Perhaps because you didn't know him at Moth's age. Kit couldn't stand restriction. He always had this sense of outrage that he should have to do things he didn't want to do. I'm not surprised that Moth has gone off the radar. I don't think he felt he had any choice. Moth won't come back until he wants to or needs to.' Kate let that sink in. 'And when he does, he won't accept help from any of us, darling, no matter how much we might want to give it to him.'

Isabelle didn't mention the bike. Kit's reaction to that had been ample enough to persuade her against sharing that information again.

'But I don't think that's why he was unreasonable,' Kate continued, curling her fingers round Isabelle's hands, putting them on top of each other, soothing the top. 'I think Kit saw Moth as a rival for your affections...' she held up her hand and stalled Isabelle's attempt to protest, '... I know, it seems ridiculous, and I'm not saying he had cause to suspect you,' she paused and looked askance at Isabelle, 'but he might have reason to suspect a young man like Moth. You forget they spent a lot of time together.'

'I'm nearly twice Moth's age,' Isabelle protested, removing her hands in agitation and shoving them in her pockets, crossing one foot over the other on the wooden border of the room where it slid out from beneath the rug. 'And he's family.' The thought of James and how close they'd grown, for family, made her tension clench into fists inside her pockets. Kate tried and failed to control the quirk in her lips. Isabelle grew warm with Kate watching with amusement as she tried to hold onto her sense of outrage. That was different. Totally different. 'How could he think I would get involved with Moth, in that... way... like, like... what does he think of me? Why does caring for someone always have to be about... about...'

'About sex?' Kate stepped away from her, back to the desk, standing between her and the plans, looking at her, knowing she had pushed it as far as she could.

Isabelle watched her in confusion, not knowing how to respond. Wanting the awkward conversation to end. Aware that there had been a moment, a single moment between her and Moth that had pushed that boundary. A moment that had never been discussed, never been repeated. While instead, the trust between them, the happiness they had shared and the sense of closeness that had built, that was a thing she could neither explain nor label.

'I can understand how you feel,' Kate said. 'But, trust me, it's not as preposterous as you think. Plus, Kit is, let's say, liberal enough to be aware of that, and much, much more aware of how Moth might see it than perhaps you, or I.'

Kate put a hand on the plans and traced the outline of the flat that she would be moving into. It gave Isabelle a thrill, to see how much she had connected to the idea. To think about the day when she would be here, at Riverdell, where she had always seemed integral.

'I think he knows he messed up,' Kate told the plans, giving her space. 'He would be able to help us achieve this not only quicker, but better. I think he understands that whatever happens between you two is only going to unfold at the end of all this.'

'I don't know how to talk to him.' Isabelle dropped her chin, focused on the carpet.

'You pick up the phone and start,' Kate told her. 'It's up to you. I understand if you can't do it, I know how much you hate conflict.' She walked over to Isabelle and raised her chin from her chest. 'Poor girl, always had to walk away from a fight, even as a child. I never met anyone who could run so fast from raised voices.'

'I don't remember that many raised voices.'

'Everybody argues and most of us raise our voices in temper, but not you. You always walk away. Such an irritating habit.' Kate smiled at her. 'If you'd heard the arguments I've had with Kit at times. He can drive me insane and then make me want to... anyway, think about it. He's abject, always a good time to take advantage.'

She turned to go, pausing at the door and looking back.

'I'll see you tomorrow, have fun.'

Isabelle listened to her humming as she walked out of the house. She moved away, not wanting Kate to see her back at the window. She picked up the plans and walked out to the hall, lying them out on the flattened top of the piano lid. She had to move the photo frame to avoid knocking it, putting her mother and the other three girls on a side table by the corridor that led to the study. She smoothed over the plans, trying to conjure up how the hall would feel, opened again to the bowels of the house below.

There was something comforting in the hallway as it was. It felt expansive, opening to the bright window on the landings and calling the onlooker upwards, or outwards, down the tempting corridor, through the many doors. She couldn't get beyond seeing the new staircase as something that would be a gaping hole, yawning downwards into the darkness of the lower floor. It would create another route for the draughts that were already beginning to chill the house. Making it bigger, as she was trying to make it smaller. Echoing. The flats upstairs, with Kate in one of them, fighting back against the hugeness of the silence, and its frightening responsibility.

Isabelle could see the house, rising from the plans. The same way she could see a dress rising from a sketch. Her mind filling it in. Standing in the hall, worrying over the hole in her floor, imagining Kate moving in to the first floor, she let her visualisation rise to the top floor. Seeing what she didn't want to admit to Kate, or Asha, or anyone. That the ring fencing didn't stop with Kate's flat. It was echoed above, in Moth's.

She traced its outline, seeing him in it. It would need someone young and fit to live there, on the second floor. And it was humble, with the lower ceilings of the attic floor adding to its charm, and the great views from the southern bedroom over the river and out, round the curve of the Bread-walk cliffs, tempting the eye towards the distant hills of Wales. She couldn't help but think of it as his, had insisted those bedrooms go with the flats because she knew he loved that view. A thought that Kit had tossed aside, with the same disdain as unwanted lettuce from a bun.

Moth. The silence of the house seemed to speak his name. Waiting.

She was waiting. Waiting for the Staines house to sell, waiting for things to start, waiting for Kit to call, waiting for Moth to come back. Even the house was waiting.

Isabelle looked hard about the room, grasping for purpose. The mess was beginning to bother even her. There was no sense anywhere, bar the kitchen and the study. And it would all get worse in the development. More rooms would need emptying, more of it would need to go. She left the plans on the piano and began to walk back to the study. The picture frame caught her eye as she entered the corridor and she swept it up, taking it with her to the new desk. There was a layer of dust on the glass, which she wiped away with the hem of her long top. There was a layer of dust on the whole house. Elsa had cancelled the cleaning contract with a grimace of guilt towards Isabelle.

She entered the study, seeking a new space for the photo. The mantel over the fireplace was empty, facing the new desk. She placed it there, retreated to the desk, went back and replaced it on the other side, returned once more to the desk, smiled. She could see them all now, though it was more from memory than clear sight. The three women she remembered, and the one she didn't, Rose. It comforted her, the thought that they could watch over her decisions. It was a step closer to Kate being there with her. She looked at her mother, wondered what she would have made of all this if she were alive. The thought led to her father, and what he would have said about the inheritance that had landed in her lap, forever forbidden to his. She stared at the photo for a long time, and thoughts of Moth slipped back into her head. What connected her to them, connected her to him. Even if no one could understand that. Least of all her.

She shook the thoughts away. Kate's words had made her think too much. Certainly, more than she normally did about Moth.

There was too much she couldn't do. Things she had to wait for others on. A host of tasks to achieve before she could think about what she would do afterwards. She thought about the flats. The rooms would need emptying. They were waiting, to be altered, repurposed. The house had to be picked apart before it could be remade. She never had liked unpicking. But at least she had practice at it. And patience in bucket loads. She would begin with the unravelling of space. She would start at the top and work down. The same as she would tackle a pair of curtains. Unpicking it backwards from how it was made.

ISABELLE FOUND it a more daunting task than she imagined. Furniture, ornaments, pictures, mirrors, books. The house was weighed down with history. Emotional dust scattered across every heirloom. It didn't help that starting in the first room on the top floor, the southern room which would become the sitting room for the second flat, had necessitated removal into the next room. That had been Moth's. Where there was no memory of Moth. She picked up and put down books and ornaments, looking for it. Struck by how easily he had removed all memory of himself.

She was walking back along the corridor, down the flights of stairs toward the kitchen and a cup of conviction, when her hand paused on the banister that led to the ground floor. The family portraits stared back. Watching her pathetic efforts to take apart decades' worth of accumulation. They berated her with their dead eyes, as they had intimidated guests for many years. Kit had always said that was the desired effect.

Isabelle had no idea what to do with them all. The new flats would demand some were moved. She had no desire to hang them anywhere else. Elsa hadn't taken a single portrait. The pictures she'd chosen had been from her bedroom, or the study, or the sitting room. Elsa hadn't wanted the weight of all those eyes on her any longer either. She walked downstairs trying to hold on to the thought, feeling even more alone.

Passing through the kitchen unseeing, on through the boot room, pausing there. The pegs that lined the walls above the two-tier rack of shoe holes stared back like a summer-abandoned school cloakroom. Scuffed walls, dark marks, dirty wood. Her whole collection of five coats sat on individual pegs nearest the far door. She'd tried to move her shoes downstairs from her bedroom to fill the holes, but they'd crept back up out of habit, or discomfort. She moved on, more uncomfortable under the gaze of those hooks than the eyes of her ancestors.

The workroom was suffering from her absence. It felt both unfamiliar and comfortable when she walked in. As though time had stayed its course and she was coming down to work, leaving the world above to its own devices, but the moment she arrived she felt lost. She had no work to do and the demands upstairs seemed to press down through the floorboards, reproaching her.

Moth's bike was leaning against the far wall, shrouded in its sheet. She moved across to touch it. Her hand feeling the metal end of the handlebar softened in its cotton sheath.

If just one thing would change, just one of all the things she was waiting for, she might be able to gather that thread up and pull it towards her. Grasp the future that seemed to be sitting out of reach. Moth hadn't waited. He'd decided to go and find it for himself. Elsa hadn't waited, she'd assessed, decided, acted. Kit, Kate, Asha, all of them. Yet here she was, waiting. Clinging to the only reason she had that he was coming back. Why was she even here, she should have been in the kitchen?

Isabelle turned away. She would start again, not in Moth's room. She would do one room today. Another room tomorrow. She moved to leave, her foot caught in the sheet, she stumbled, putting her hand out to steady herself, watching as the sheet wafted toward her. Understanding hitting her with the metal frame as the handlebars whipped round on her, gasping as the weight and awkwardness caught against the stretched sheet and the bike tumbled towards her.

She tried to catch it, tried to get out of the way, tumbled and sprawled across it. Catching her leg on the chain, her right hand squashed by the twisted shank of the handlebars. Shaken and horrified she might have damaged Moth's pride and joy. She prised herself to her feet, pushing herself up from the frame.

Stood looking at the bike that had revealed itself.

Stood trying to take in what she was seeing. Or rather not seeing.

For she was not seeing Moth's bike.

Not seeing in a way that couldn't reach her brain.

Stood, waiting for comprehension.

HIS PHONE RANG. The tone that told him it was Isabelle.

Kit froze mid-stride. The ring tone impinging upon the delicacy of the moment. He tried to resume but he'd paused for too long a second.

'Do you need to get that?'

He looked towards his trousers. They were hanging on the chair on the other side of the room. Trying to hold back the urge to lunge for the phone. The second ring ended.

'Kind of.' His effort at nonchalance came out as a squeak masquerading as a cough.

Legs released him, muscles slackening from his dick, nails sliding across his back with irritation. The third ring started. It would cut to answer phone after that. He would have to call her back. He'd waited forever for her to call. He tripped over the bed sheets on the floor. Grabbed the trousers with shaking hands. The condom beginning to slip down his withering shaft, smearing against the pristine linen in the process. He found the phone as the third ring ended, swiped the screen across, threw it to his ear.

'I'm here.' Please don't let it have rung off. Silence. Silence so deep he could hear his heart in his throat.

'You were right.' Her voice leaping into the abyss and stopping his breath.

He'd never heard her so deflated. His heart booming at

the sound of her voice. God he'd missed her voice. It shouldn't sound this sad and broken. He withered in guilt.

'I was?'

'Yes.'

'About anything in particular?' He tried to catch her mood.

Hands slithered across his back, slid downward past his hips. Fondling him, pulling the condom off with a twang, bringing the erection back with deft touches. Her head nestled on his shoulder. He switched the phone to his other ear. She pulled his foreskin down the shaft, tightening her hold as he tried to concentrate. Two impeccable manicured fingers entered his anus and, as he tensed in reaction, paused, letting his muscles relax. Moving again, widening the path with another finger, punishing him for abandoning her, fingers slick with lube. He knew what came next. She knew how much it turned him on. Oh Christ, he was on a knife edge.

'About Moth,' she said. 'He's taken the bike.'

Kit was struggling to concentrate.

'Bike?' he asked, trying to keep his voice normal.

The grip on his dick became even stronger as the three fingers became four and pushed aside his muscles. He took a deep breath, tried to relax. Tried to focus. She decreased the pressure on his dick, relief slipping into intensified pleasure as her duck-billed hand probed deeper, increasing the movement with her front hand to bring him to an orgasm he couldn't stop. She made him come, swift pulsating strokes of his dick, balling her other hand into a steady fist as it started, just like he'd taught her. Her teeth tugging at his ear lobe. He closed his eyes, gritted his jaw and strangled the groan rising in his throat.

'I don't know how,' Isabelle carried on, oblivious to his conflict. 'When he went missing, I checked, and the bike was here and now it's not. It's a different bike. He switched it. He's already taken it.'

'He switched the bike?' Kit gasped as she directed the eager spurts of spunk over his trousers. She unballed her fist, began to pull her hand out. He coughed, habit of a lifetime. Felt the muscle close as her fingers slid out, trailing a damp line up his spine and into his hair with gripping fingers. She twisted his head to face her and forced his lips aside, sucked his tongue between her teeth and nipped before releasing him. He held the phone away, turned and watched as she walked away, naked, to the bathroom. Put the phone back to his ear and took a deep breath.

'Is it a bad time?' Isabelle asked. 'You sound out of breath.'

'Just finished a gym session,' he lied.

She turned at the bathroom door and smiled at him, her lips curving, her eyes grim. She would make him pay for that. He turned away, trying to gather his thoughts. Weeks and weeks of waiting for a phone call and it had to come now. He felt as guilty a sinner as ever lived. Guilty both ways. Dammit, he needed to concentrate.

'Give me a minute, I'll catch my breath.'

'You don't normally do gym in the afternoon,' she said.

'Have to grab it when I can.'

She snorted from the bathroom. She'd heard that one too. He held his breath, whatever he said now could wreck the balance. At both ends of the phone.

'He's not coming back, is he?' Isabelle asked, her voice hollow, flat, deadened out by more than the phone line.

'No.' Kit wanted to lie, to make it better, but he couldn't. 'I don't think he is.'

Silence lay on both ends of the fragile connection. He looked in irritation at his soiled trousers.

'Are you?' she asked.

'Do you want me to?'

'Do you want to?'

He had to think fast. The wrong words, the right words, which way he put them. Who took most umbrage? What could he salvage? What would it cost him? Too many thoughts, too little time to resolve them. The habit of years winning over the lust of recent months.

'Just say when.' He heard the bathroom door swing to behind him and click into place. She'd heard. He shut his eyes. It had been such bliss.

'Come as soon as you can,' her voice full of tears and distress.

The phone went dead. He looked at it in his hand. Bloody phones. He hated them. He went and sat down on the bed. Waiting for her. It would be a long apology. A short farewell. That was the best he could hope for. He picked up the crumpled bedsheet from the floor, wiped his limp dick on it.

It had been a long wait since he'd left Riverdell. He'd thrust accusations of middle age in Henri's face with a vengeance. Working all day, shagging all night, pushing thoughts away while he waited. Wondering if Isabelle would call, shaken by how much he wanted her to. Calling Kate in longing, staying away in guilt. The upset between him and Isabelle a greater barrier to them than his rash decision to brazen out a relationship had ever caused.

The bathroom door opened. She came out, dressed in a thin bathrobe. Her face washed, her auburn hair damp and curling against her throat, her green eyes flashing amusement at him.

Ms Suzanne Harper.

'Who was that?'

'An old friend,' he told her.

'An old fuck friend?'

'Yes.'

She stood before him, opened her robe, letting it slip from her shoulders. She should be running a convent, nothing more. Looking at her made him feel guilty and horny in the same breath. It was intoxicating.

'You're leaving,' she stated.

He didn't respond, put his hands on either side of her hips. Hips as full as Isabelle's were slender. Hips that let your hands sit on them, comfortable in their own weight, needing no grip. Her stomach a firm, rising warmth, the diadem jewel of her navel a perfect glory. Weight and muscle balanced enough to make him feel young again. Young like he'd felt when Kate first stood naked in front of him. His every muscle harpooned in his dick.

He wasn't sure if Isabelle was in need of him or rescuing him. Ms Suzanne Harper would unman him in the end. She would turn him into one of her prefects, sitting outside her door, purring for a crumb of her attention.

'You owe me an orgasm.' She lifted his chin from the contemplation of her navel. 'A great big endless orgasm.'

His hands travelled over her belly, caressed their way down her thighs, across the back of her legs, up to grasp her buttocks.

'Make it worth it,' she told him, moving closer, leaning back into his cupping hands, straddling his feet, pinioning them between hers. 'Or I'll make you do it again, and you'll be later than she wants.'

Kit looked at the russet curls of her pubic hair. He wanted

to grab some dignity from the moment, not to be some boy ordered to do his duty. But those fine short curls were more than he could resist. He put his mouth down and parted their sweetness with his tongue. Her hands snaked into his hair and took hold. She would have his hide if he disappointed her.

Ms Suzanne Harper. Kryptonite, it turned out.

He slithered his tongue across the nub of her clitoris, throbbing with what he'd left unfinished. Tucked his probing tip inside her lips, felt her hands pulling him closer. She pushed his head back until he was lying on the bed pinned beneath her, drowning in her. Her hand was cradling his tired dick, caressing his balls. She wouldn't let him leave that easily. She ruled him. With an iron fist.

It was two hours before she let him leave.

A protracted apology.

She withheld her orgasm like a benediction he didn't deserve, making him work for it. Sweat for it. Afterwards, she gathered his clothes up, put them in his arms and showed him the door. Giving him time to hop into his pants, putting his shoes on top of his crumpled arm full of clothes, throwing his bag on the floor beside his toes.

A perfunctory farewell.

Nearly naked, stinking from the rut, layered in her odour and refused a shower. That was how she wanted him to go to Isabelle.

He watched the door as she shut it in his face. Her stunning body retreating behind its closing thud, the turn of her hair and the flash of her eyes his final image. Kit glanced down the corridor. It was a five-star hotel. They wouldn't appreciate his pants shocking the patrons. He pulled his trousers on in the corridor, slipped the phone and keys in a pocket, grabbed his bag and walked away from the closed door to the lift, shrugging into his shirt.

He emerged, rumpled and stained, into the unkind light of a stormy afternoon in the foyer of the hotel. The décor made him jealous. Someone was making a lot of money doing up this old hall on a regular basis. That Osborne and Little paper was from the latest collection, and the curtains were hand blocked to an archive design. It was her preferred hotel, out of the many they'd tried. Leaving at 4am to be back at school, shimmying into her pencil skirts with the same ease she threw them off, getting out her diary and scheduling their next shag.

'Was everything satisfactory with your stay, Mr de Lavelle?' the receptionist asked.

'Yes, perfect,' he lied. 'My partner will be staying on. I've been called away on work. Please send her up a bottle of wine. With an afternoon's treatment in the spa, perhaps a massage, whatever you have available. Something special to make up for my abrupt departure.'

'Of course, Mr de Lavelle.' She smiled perfect understanding. She picked up the phone and arranged to have his car brought to the front. 'Is there anything else I can do for you?'

'No, thanks.'

'Good afternoon, Mr de Lavelle.'

He walked out and stood on the stone steps overlooking the sweeping gravel driveway that approached with a wide curve. A lowered lawn ran away from the old house on the opposite side of the drive, filled with calligraphic knot gardens, roses and fountains. Hidden behind a belt of enormous Douglas firs the new three-floor extension to the original manor house looked out over a golf course and a lake, endless acres of lawn as impeccable as her nails. It was exuberant, restrained, confident, elegant. It was exquisite.

She was exquisite. Wrapped up in the wound of a painful divorce. On a career mission that outshone any romance. Generous, giving, demanding, reticent. Sumptuous. Addictive. Ms Suzanne Harper. He came adrift in the gaze of her disdain. He wondered how long it would have gone on if Isabelle hadn't called. His car pulled up in front of him and a young, annoyingly fit valet jumped out.

'Any more bags, Sir?' the driver asked glancing at the small travel bag he chucked on the passenger seat.

'Only the ones under my eyes.'

'You'll have to carry those yourself, Sir.'

'Bloody typical.'

He lowered himself with care into the seat, trying not to show it as the valet closed the door on him. His butt stung, though he tried to ignore it, and his balls ached. He'd outdone himself, even by his standards. It hurt to drive away. He knew she wouldn't let him back. She was not the sharing type. One at a time, a clean bill of health and safety rules established. He liked a lover with rules. It set clear guidelines to the game.

He drove away towards a woman who had no rules. No guidelines, no goals, no mission. Kit had known where he stood with Ms Suzanne Harper. Where he stood, when he sat, how he lay. Certainty left behind in the rumpled despoiled bed. He felt desiccated, he couldn't go and see Isabelle in this state.

He fired up the Satnav, found the nearest Travelodge, headed for it. He made the journey back to Riverdell in stages. Stopping to shower, changing into clean clothes, even succumbing to food at a service station, texting Isabelle his arrival time. He rang Henri, chided him on details, called Lou, soothed her irritation. He spoke to two clients, rang and chivvied a supplier to the point of harassment and began to feel he'd removed himself from the hotel bedroom. Kit was back in charge.

IT WAS early evening when he pulled up in the courtyard at Riverdell. The magnolia tree was subdued, its spring glory faded to a heavy indifference. Leaves drooping towards the earth, dramatically taking it in turns to fall, dejected in the flash of his headlights. The porch as small and humble as the hotel had been preening. Kit felt superior in its shade, relief flooding through him at the way he grew stronger in the weak cast of its fly-riddled light.

He looked at the front door. His hand reaching out and hovering over the handle. He glanced back at the Bentley. It hadn't gone well last time he was here, walking out with nothing more than his phone and his keys. Freezing in a lay-by while he waited out the night and the wine. He pushed the door handle down and walked in. The house lay silent. The hallway bedraggled, confused, dusty. He called out, 'Isabelle,' took two steps in and let the door swing shut behind him. No response. He walked towards the stairs, letting his voice reach down the halls.

'Helloooo?' Nothing.

All the doors stood open, propped back. He walked into the kitchen. Empty. Back in the hallway he stuck his head into the guest dining room. Chairs grouped in the window same as the last time he was there. Empty. Headed for the corridor leading to the sitting room and study. He felt his feet catch, falter, seeing the plans laid out on the piano. He couldn't resist. He retraced his steps and looked over them. It was a shock, seeing the final printed details. There was something tangible in them that hadn't come across on the emails he'd received. He put his hand out to touch them, retreated it, headed for the study.

The new desk looked more bedded in than he remembered, filled with papers. The sofa looked well used, its cushions in need of plumping. It wasn't the Riverdell he'd helped look after with Elsa anymore. It was a whole new place. Isabelle's place. He walked out, uncomfortable. Peeking in the other open doorways, seeing more disturbance.

Kit lost momentum in the hallway, settling on the second step of the stairs. He didn't have the conviction to go looking any further. Idle hands tapping his knee in discomfort, the soft pat-pat-pat reverberating into the stairwell above him. It had the same quality as her voice on the phone. An empty echo falling back down on him like the dust that dulled the furniture. Above him the house yawned. A ruin recriminating him with its empty bedrooms, long corridors and gaping doors.

The house had shone before. Every small surface, each little corner. It was too much to manage, alone. And they had left her alone. Overwhelmed by the huge change and unsure where to settle in the aftermath. No more cherished than the furniture adrift in the rooms. He swallowed discomfort away. Guilt was an oil slick. A rare disaster, but inescapable. Kit stopped tapping his knee, twisted his watch and flattened his palms on his knees. The dust glared back at him, hiding the sheen of the veneers beneath.

He'd run away from a situation that threatened to expose

him. Their renovation plans had rebuilt more than the house, restructured more than the estate. It had shown him that the past was being shed, the edifice restructured from the basement to the attic. To secure the future, that was what she'd said, releasing, and reinvesting. The words had pared his civilised conveniences away.

She'd had to choose. Kate had chosen. In those choices he'd had to face he couldn't have them both. In retaliation, he'd chosen Ms Suzanne Harper instead. And lost himself.

The mess in the house was brazen. A cluttered, distressed, expression of the mess his life had unravelled into. The mess he hadn't got the balls to tackle. Kit sat upright, straightening his jacket around him.

There was a lot that needed clearing up. It couldn't go back to where it had been. Too much had been taken away. It had to be rethought from the ground up. He needed to catch up. The girls in his life were moving on through the chaos, with no clearer vision of the end than he had. But they'd had the guts to get on with it. He'd run away. The sour taste of guilt rose in his throat again. He swallowed it as the front door opened.

Isabelle stood on the threshold, her face lit up with the knowledge that he was there, her hands full of shopping bags.

'You're here.'

Kit stood up, held out his hands, saying, 'No less.'

Isabelle dropped the bags and walked across to him, the door catching on the shopping as the plastic bags collapsed. She threw herself into his arms and buried her head on his chest. Kit pulled her close and clung on. The smell of coconut wafting through her hair, her bones hard beneath the layers of clothes, his body relaxing into the familiar.

'About bloody time.' Kate walked in after Isabelle and added another bag to the floor.

Kit looked up in surprise. She walked across and joined the moment, hugging both him and Isabelle. The blue scarf against her throat tickling his neck where it found his skin.

'Well, it's nice to be missed,' he mumbled to both their heads.

'Good, you can cook.' Kate pulled away and went to pick up the shopping. 'Isabelle has dragged me away from work on the promise you were coming and made me shop.'

'She's been working too hard anyway.' Isabelle left him to go and help. 'I told her I'd rung and apologised, and you said you would come.'

'Better late than not at all. I can't cope with you disappearing precisely when I decide to rearrange my life.' Kate walked into the kitchen and left them standing in the hallway.

Kit walked forwards and picked up the final bags, asking, 'What's for dinner?'

'Humble pie, I fear.'

'Not the first portion I've had,' Kit said.

He walked into the kitchen ahead of her, saw Kate pulling stuff out of the bag. She held up a bottle of wine and asked in a mighty tone, 'Are you drinking or driving tonight? Or doing both again, like a dick?'

'Let's all have a drink,' he said, 'then we'll work out where I'm sleeping. Ok?'

SIX WEEKS LATER, like a magician having stacked a house of cards with nimble fingers to watch them all be blown over before the final reveal, Kit was trying hard to consider how Isabelle must be feeling.

He wanted to have the most gargantuan strop.

The silence in the kitchen was tempting him to break it. A perfect crisp sheet of ice he wanted to skate over first. Kate's eyes bored into him with hawkish intensity. He tweaked his mouth muscle to see what she would do. Her eyes narrowed to arrow slits without changing a single other feature of her face. Spectacular, but if Isabelle didn't respond soon, he would jump into the abyss feet first.

The past six weeks, from his return in early October to now, the seventeenth of November, with only five working weeks left until Christmas, had passed like Vin Diesel. Fast and furious. He'd come to the conclusion he had reached supersonic speed and told Lou to inform the team his nickname was no longer Flash. It was to be Concorde.

'It's not yours to decide.' Lou waved aside his demand with a hand swat designed for an irritating fly.

He and the Bentley had become attached to the point that he was beginning to think their love affair was coming to an end. Handling a workload on the run up to Christmas that could have justified turning him into a foul-mouthed bastard of an employer but which he consumed, like the Bentley, as fuel to the fusion of his charming efficiency. Racing onwards to tick off the next task, with only vivid details lingering in the rear-view mirror.

The D'Arby's alterations, tick.

The ballroom had received its reincarnation and been as gorgeous and unbearable as ice cream on sensitive teeth. Arianna all but panted herself to orgasm when he unveiled it, Mr D'Arby's sex life went into the stratosphere, and his chequebook loosened with his pant elastic.

Christmas in Swansea, tick.

Kate had declined her invite, refusing to leave Isabelle alone, irked with Elsa for asking her and frosty at the disappointment expressed at her prompt decline. Kit handled his invite with smooth compromise, as he knew how to do at Christmas, when all people became unreasonable. He figured he was travelling north to Riverdell anyway and agreed to spend Christmas Eve in Swansea, leaving before Santa arrived on the actual morning.

Christmas stealth marketing, tick.

He turned down 57 requests from friends of clients based in London who'd begged him to do their festive decorations this year. It was his all-time high. The total potential profit he turned away made him wince.

'I'd pay a bonus, Mr de Lavelle,' they wheedled.

'Oh, it's not about the money,' he demurred, flipping screens on his phone to his newly cleared out notes. 'It's loyalty, I have to think about my regular clients first. Perhaps next year. Try calling me in the New Year, we should get to know one another.'

'Well, I suppose the dining room does need a refresh.'

'Call me, let's chat, I'll see if I can squeeze you in.' Kit hung up.

He found the new meta-plans he'd started making, the long-term goals that the team didn't need to know about. At the top, in capital letters, after turning down said number 57 request, he wrote, 2013 OWN CHRISTMAS.

Team management, tick.

In Bristol huge boards of post-it notes in organised colours had taken over the kitchen. Lou had likened him to a general planning a battle, which he liked so much he went and bought an antique swagger stick. Kit had no idea how generals had managed before the arrival of post-it notes but he developed a good opinion of their management strategies based on the comfort to be obtained from his swagger stick.

He even started writing little messages on the back of the notes, inspirational quotes, personal favours, suggestions for family happiness or marital sex. Not all the messages were equally well received. Jamie reported back that her husband liked the new suggestions and requested more. Lou told him to stay the hell out of her sex life, but she liked the inspirational quotes.

Mishaps in communication had occurred.

Like when he wrote a note for Ed and it ended up being Fred who did the job, and Fred's girlfriend was not as appreciative of free advice as Ed's and hadn't valued the suggestion that she wear wide-legged trousers rather than leggings to make the least of her figure. Of course, Ed would have known that was a message that needed translating, not passing on verbatim, as Fred had. Fred's girlfriend was now trying to persuade Fred to leave and get another job. She hadn't yet realised that Fred never went anywhere without Ed and Ed wasn't going anywhere fast because Kit was financing his mortgage. Fred's girlfriend had lit the fuse that would end the relationship, but it wasn't his fault. Fred's relationships were as abortive as Ed's was longstanding. Life had casualties after all, and they all loved the new Monday morning routine. Kit roared away to the next task.

Preparing Kate to move out, tick.

Kate had made it clear that if he and Isabelle fell out again, she would reassign his gender. To the eunuch tradition of old. While it had been fun watching her say that round the mouthful of his dick, her teeth had been sharp enough to convince him.

He buried the frustration of Isabelle's retreat from him into the cocoon of Kate's affections. Their efforts to unravel the cluttered mess that was her sprawling flat over the bistro, haphazard depository of all the years of devotion she had poured into her business, unearthed a lot of memories, an equal amount of embalmed wildlife and a disproportionate level of insecurity.

'Oh God, am I doing the right thing?' she'd ask, looking at an ornament as though her life depended on it.

'Yes, you are,' he kissed her ears, sucking the lobe to distract her.

'What if I hate it?'

'You'll love it,' he progressed to her neck, easing the item of distress from her hand.

'I don't know what to take.'

'Take it all,' he eased her rumpled blouse aside, slipped his hand inside her bra, pulling her towards the kitchen table.

Packing Kate's life up amounted to murmuring reassurances while he made love to her on the nearest available flat surface and the new managers coped with the Sunday lunch rush down below. Even his love life had developed an aspect of routine that was beginning to chafe around the crotch.

Watching stunned bemusement spread across Isabelle and Kate's faces, waiting for them to catch up, he tried to remind himself it was only six weeks. That his manic capacity had not, in fact, been going on since the start of all time. But, when he tried to reason like this, he realised it couldn't be. It had to have been longer than that. Even he, Concorde, a name in need of some bold fluorescent highlight on the side of the grey van, could not have achieved everything that had been done in those six weeks.

Move out Mrs Staines and Marge, tick.

Having frowned over Isabelle's ambitious plans for the refurbishment of the bungalow, he sent in the decorators, tripped down to see Mrs Staines and Marge and, with bucket loads of charm, threats, sherry and the promise of a three-day sojourn of Ed and Fred themselves, hastened their moving to the next week. They decided they couldn't wait for the alterations. The great teapot unpacking began.

While Mrs Staines was muttering about robbers, Marge counted out the thousands they could find into neat piles on the kitchen table. The piles expanded, off the table, across the work surface, the dresser, and onto the floor. 637 piles of thousands. With 637 teapots abandoned and going nowhere, along with most of the furnishings.

When he asked Mrs Staines how much she thought was missing, she declared she'd found nine empty tea pots, and they never kept a tea pot empty.

'£9,000?'

'Exactly,' she said in increased consternation, 'and I'm quite sure I know where it went too.'

Marge farted at the table and said 'codswallop' under guise of a cough. Kit let Mrs Staines wander away before begging Marge for more information, topping up her sherry while they waited.

'Oh, don't mind her, she buys a teapot a month,' Marge told him. 'Even she can't keep track of how many teapots she has. No one's stolen the money. Now, as for the silverware, that's another matter.'

'Who stole the silverware?'

'Yon young fella you sent over,' Marge told him. 'I knew what he was up to, even caught him at it once.'

'Moth?' Kit was stunned. 'Moth was stealing? Why didn't you tell me? Or Elsa?'

'I asked him what he was up to,' Marge said, licking her big coarse thumb with a loud, wet slurp, leaving Kit with the image of her ancient tongue rasping itself against a thrusting upright fleshy digit stuck in his mind for days. 'He said he was Robin Hood.'

'He what!'

'Ay, you heard me, take from the rich to give to the poor. Said he took no more than wouldn't be missed and asked me if I'd miss it.'

'Cheeky little bastard, didn't you mind?'

'Mind?' She glanced at him over the money with a bemused frown. 'Lovely young lad like that keeping us company, seemed fair pay if you ask me. Besides,' she paused, leant back in her chair and checked the hallway was clear. 'It's not mine to keep anyway, is it? Nor hers either.' She jabbed an elbow towards the hall. 'Most of this stuff came to her family by way of marriage, the Staines never did anything much except make their bed where it best served their bank.'

'Jesus, Marge.' Kit reeled back in the chair. 'So, that's where he got some funding from.'

'Surprised with you,' Marge told him, leaning back from her counting job and taking a long sip from the brimming schooner. 'Always thought you were the bright one. Anyone with an eye in their head could see he was hailing out of here the first chance he had.'

Kit remained quiet. Not wanting to tell her she was right, to admit he hadn't seen it coming.

'Best thing for it. A lad such as Moth doesn't need a halter on him. He'll take to biting if he's stabled too long.'

'Marge?'

'Yes, dear?'

'Is there anything else you know that I might have missed?'

Marge looked at him, her hands crossed over her old belly, the schooner trapped by its stem on the rising flesh, her shoulders stooped over it like an old guard.

'No doubt about it, my lovely,' she'd said. With a look so direct and piercing, daring him to ask her more, that Kit had felt discomfort tickling his nose with the sherry fumes.

Sell the Staines house, tick.

The emptying house displayed unremitting evidence of decades worth of architectural neglect. He told Asha to put a hold on any more viewings, and to inform the interested parties that an offer was now on the table. Asha told him she couldn't ethically do that. He put a cash offer on the table and told her to work from that. She said that was even less ethical, at which point he asked her what did she know about what he could afford to buy or not? It had the desired effect. By the end of the day Asha called to say she had three far more substantial offers on the table, and he was a both a genius and immoral.

'Just call me God,' he suggested, wondering if the team would prefer that one.

Sell the unwanted contents of the Staines house, tick.

It brought in the tidy sum of £57,000. A sum which no one wanted to claim. Mrs Staines refused to accept it saying that the furniture and fittings had been sold with the house to Elsa's father. Elsa refused on the basis that she had no idea where they'd come from or who they belonged to, and Isabelle was too busy trying to get rid of her assets and looked horrified at the suggestion.

As he ranted to Kate, 'Only in this stupid backwater of an

existence can a house full of belongings not belong to anyone.'

Being blessed with fewer idiotic scruples Kit paid himself for all the time he'd spent on handling the house, and the relocation of its tenants. He gave Ed and Fred a bonus, got a full valet on the Bentley plus a new set of low profiles, and split the remainder into three. He donated a third each to the charities of Elsa and Mrs Staines' choice and put the final £10,000 away in a bank account. He knew where it would go, but not how to get it there. He gave the house keys to Asha and washed his hands of it.

Organise the conversion at Riverdell, tick.

He'd found and employed a building team who were booked to start on Boxing Day, when no one else wanted them. They had a four-week target that made Swansea look like a walk in the park. He'd hounded the local planning department to get final approval for the conversion to flats. Employed a decorator, at his own expense, to start tidying up the bare rooms and spent hours, seriously too many stupid hours, arguing with Isabelle over the contents of the house and where to rearrange them, and what shade to paint the emerging shape of her home.

The exact shade of this elusive blank canvas had taken uncountable arguments to settle and he wasn't sure they'd decided on, so much as defaulted to, the shade of non-existence, sorry, 'Ammonite', she'd selected. The single advantage to these wearisome arguments was that, with seven different paint range catalogues laid out on the floor in room after room, he was inspired to make another entry to his meta-notes. 2013 CREATE MY OWN PAINT RANGE. He rang Henri.

'Boss?'

'Don't sound so nervous,' Kit told him. 'Tell me, what do we know about creating paint?'

'Eh, nothing,' Henri told him.

'See what you can find out.'

'Why would I want to do... no, don't tell me,' Henri forestalled him. 'Don't tell me anything else at all until next year.'

Empty Riverdell for the conversion, sort of tick.

In the attempt to create order ready for the builders he and Isabelle had borderline fallen out. She couldn't decide what to do with the contents of the rooms that needed emptying and his patience has an urgent fuse. In the end they agreed to fill the unused rooms in her part of the house, shut the doors and wait until a better time to decide. It was a poor solution, but Kit was learning when it came to Isabelle to sidle into his goals, not belt them straight at the net.

Moving sideways at supersonic speed had become the norm. From the first day, all those weeks ago, when he came down from sleeping at the bistro, feeling replete, peaceful, ready to work through the plans for Riverdell and Isabelle had brought up Moth and the missing bike. She showed him the old un-roadworthy replacement and argued for telling Elsa and the police.

'Why would we do that?' Kit asked, choosing his words with care, wondering how to edge around the issue.

'It might help them find him,' she said. 'If they know he might be travelling on a bike, it might help.'

Kit worked hard at keeping a straight face. 'It would be easier to find the proverbial golden needle in your workroom. I mean, there are a lot of people who ride a bike, and to the best of my knowledge, they don't have number plates, or insurance or road tax requirements. I don't see how it's going to help at all.'

'But we ought to share anything we know if it helps find him.'

'Is that what Moth would want?' Kit asked her, pretending to think about it.

'Don't you think we ought to be trying to find him?'

'Yes, I do, but the police aren't interested, they've got better things to do.' Kit dropped her a morsel of comfort. 'I've been trying as well. I'm in contact with a friend of Moth's and made him promise to get Moth to contact me. But, if we send the police after him, or make it harder for him, he won't thank us for it, Isabelle.'

'What if he doesn't get in touch?'

'He will. When he's ready. And we need to be here for him when he does. Moth spent a lot of time preparing this, I think we should respect his determination.'

'I don't feel right, doing nothing.' Isabelle looked at the rusty old bike in front of her with a twist to her lips. 'It feels as though we don't care.'

'The fact that we can't prove it to him, doesn't mean we don't care.' Kit went and took her hands in his. 'Right now, I can't prove to you how I care in the way I want to, I'm having to do it the only way I can, by helping you.'

She blushed at that and ducked beneath her hair. Another evasion he added to the list.

'That's about all you can do for Moth.'

'Will you tell me? If he does ring?' she asked. 'You will tell me, right?'

'Let's wait until he rings to argue over that.' Kit edged his way out from a direct promise, wheeling the old bike out of the workroom and putting it for the rubbish.

All was set on course for a glorious rendezvous between plans, finance, and the eventual second chance to secure his

future domestic arrangements, whatever they were destined
to be. Things were in fact so satisfactory he couldn't kick off
about the fastidious Monday morning team meetings, the
predictable Sunday afternoon tumbles with Kate, or the relief
with which Isabelle had retreated from him sexually. Kit
knew he was being supportive of everyone's needs, that he
was tolerating a level of routine that suited them all while not
himself, that he was being civilised and well-adjusted on all
fronts.

Positively sodding domesticated in fact.

Until Asha and James walked into the house this Sunday
morning, while he was thinking he only had five weeks to go
until Christmas.

He, Isabelle and Kate were sharing a breakfast of scrambled eggs on bagels with coffee and juice. He'd even cut some
chives from Kate's rooftop garden before he walked down and
was feeling smug about the forethought. Which was why he
was battling the sudden urge to be ugly and unreasonable.
Throttling the need to say how thoughtless they were being,
while he stood there and watched Kate threaten him with
dire consequences if he spoke in response first.

'Someone say something,' Asha said with a small nervous
smile, her fingers laced through James.

'Wow,' Isabelle said, looking at them both in stunned
amazement, and, in floundering shock, finding more words. 'I
mean, wow, this is amazing. I mean it's all a bit sudden, but
you must be thrilled.'

'I'll say,' Kate added and stood up to go and give Asha a
hug. 'Do you have any idea how happy Elsa's going to be?
How far are you?'

'Not far at all,' Asha said. 'Seven weeks.'

'Happy?' Isabelle found her feet and followed Kate's lead

away from the table. 'She isn't going to be happy, she's going to be delirious. James, this is wonderful, I'm delighted for you.'

Kit watched her give James a hug. It was a spectacularly awkward moment for two people who'd spent years in an intimate relationship. He wondered with a frown if that might be him and Isabelle one day but forced the thought away. Only James could ever be that uncomfortable with a past lover, even if he had just informed her that he was about to be a father, at long last, with someone else.

'Not to be a sour puss,' he said, putting down his spatula and coming forwards. 'But is there any chance that we could stop adding to the list? Don't get me wrong, I love a challenge, but on top of everything else, a baby, really?'

'There's never a good time for a baby,' Kate told him with an indifferent wave of her hand. 'Stop being a sour puss.'

'Congratulations,' he told Asha. 'Though I think you have terrible taste in men. Let's hope the baby takes after you.'

'I'll take that as approval.'

Kit shook James' hand and grinned at him. 'Good plan, going with a Catholic, smart move.' James' eyes goggled in a most satisfying way.

'Go finish the eggs, before they ruin.' Kate stabbed a finger into the small of his back to move him away from James, making him wince. 'Don't mind him, he's been far too restrained and civilised for far too long. Darling, I'm so happy for you, you're going to be a wonderful father. It's fantastic news.'

Kate gave him a warm hug, even as Isabelle was hugging Asha in a long and emotional congratulation. Those two were getting far too close considering they'd shared body fluids with the same man. Looking at Kate he had to laugh. Talk about sharing body fluids.

'What's so funny, he will be a wonderful father,' Kate said.

'Oh, I know, I wasn't laughing at that,' Kit said. 'Though I'm intrigued, does this mean you're going to bring the wedding forwards?'

'We haven't decided yet.' Asha sat down at the table, pulling out the nearest chair, leaving James perplexed. Hopping on his oversized feet, trying to decide whether he should sit in his normal chair or next to her, deciding on the one beside her. Kit smirked into the eggs. 'We're a bit tight to fund a wedding, buying the house is more important. But I want to be married before the baby comes. It will probably be a small registry office wedding. We'll have a bigger celebration a few years down the line.'

'You won't do it.' Kit stirred the eggs with one last confident flip. 'No one ever does after the event, you won't have the time or money. You'll have a mortgage and a baby instead, and you won't be working full time.'

'Do you have anything positive to say this morning?' Kate asked him.

'The eggs are cooked,' he said, and laughed again, looking at Asha.

'Oh, you must have a wedding, not just get married.' Isabelle said. 'You can't let it get pushed aside.'

'This is a once in a lifetime opportunity, buying the farmhouse,' James rubbed his rough fingers together, stroked the palms down his jeans. Kit could hear the fibre screaming from the oven. An idle thought popped up, how such rough fingers must feel on skin. Kit batted it clean away. That was a step too far. That was the current routine pickling his brain. 'It's more than I ever dared dream of. We talked about it all night. It's the most important thing to both of us to get right. And marriage is more important than the wedding.'

'I know,' Isabelle managed to look contrite. 'But you don't want to look back and regret anything. This is a huge celebration. We've had enough bad luck as a family you must share some of this good stuff too. I'm sure Elsa will help. Kit, come on, you're the creative genius, come up with some suggestions.' She looked his way, followed by the rest of them.

'Crème fraiche on the eggs?'

Kate gave him a long silent look.

'Oh, alright,' he complained, picking up plates and taking them to the table. 'But I do think your timing is atrocious. Well, think about it, you could have a wedding at the farm, or at the bistro, if you do it before Kate leaves. She'll stand you an occasion, you can get a special licence. Or you can have a wedding here, the house is big enough after all.'

'We can't do it at the farm,' Asha said. 'I want to be married in the next few months and the farm will be wet and filthy. It would only be suitable for a summer wedding and I'd be bulging out of my dress by then.'

'Well, you're more than welcome to use the bistro,' Kate said. 'We can close it down for the day and have a special event. I'd be delighted to do it for you.'

'Same here,' Isabelle agreed. 'It's your home as much as mine, James. You grew up here, it would be wonderful to see you two married here.'

'It's kind of you both,' Asha looked at James with a timid smile as she spoke. 'But the house is the most important thing and, with financing that, it's not possible to spend money on a wedding too.'

Kit returned to the Aga, took the final plate from by its side. Isabelle and Kate were watching James, to see what he'd say, but he remained silent, holding Asha's hand. They both had a smile that was being brave but covering a painful disappointment. Kit resisted the urge to slap them both with the eggy spatula. The truth was the sale of the farmhouse had been agreed, and even with Isabelle's generous acceptance of a much lower offer than the other two tenants had put in for theirs, Kit knew James was scrabbling to get a mortgage. Even with Asha's earning potential Elsa had had to call in favours at the bank to help them out. It was going to be a brutal crawl to the finish line to raise the capital.

Honestly, if they could have worked on the family planning a bit, there wouldn't be this situation. They could have had a gorgeous vintage style wedding at the farm one summer. He couldn't fault them for not being able to keep their pants on, but there was a difference between the act and the conception. There were enough ways of controlling procreation these days. What on earth was James shooting out of his terribly polite dick? Even at Saga speed he was hitting ovaries left, right and centre. He threw the frying pan into the kitchen sink and went and sat down with his plate. It was time to weigh in.

'It seems a bit piss poor to me,' he told James, taking a mouthful of egg before it grew cold. He couldn't stand cold scrambled egg. 'You take this marvellous, intelligent, adorable woman, hitch her to the life of a poverty-stricken farmer's wife, get her knocked-up so she can't get out of it and, to cap it, deny her a wedding of any sort. Shame on you.'

All four of them looked at him in astonishment. He was done with long looks though.

'Stuff your prissy looks,' he said. 'Not to mention the fact that you have the audacity to turn down two brilliant and, more to the point free, offers of a wedding venue, from members of your own family, because you're too proud to accept their help without labelling it charity.'

'Kit,' Kate said in a warning tone. 'I think you're laying it on a bit thick.'

'I think I'm laying it on fine.' He looked at James, a forkful poised on the way to his mouth. 'Go on, deny a word of it.'

James glared at him, trying to work on a sense of justified anger. Kit put the egg in his mouth, picked up a bagel and tore a chunk out of it. James gave up, dropped his eyes and put his head in his hands. His fingers pushing back his receding hair most unflatteringly.

'It's all come at once,' his voice rumbled through his coarse fingers. 'And I want it all too.'

Asha put a hand on his shoulder. 'We're fine. We know what our priorities are, and that's what counts.'

'Yes, but what you need is not the same as what you want,' Kit rammed home. 'And what you *want* is a wedding to show the world how proud you are of each other, not a naff registry office marriage that looks like a shotgun affair to ease some visa extension pregnancy through.'

James groaned in his hands.

'Kit!' Isabelle protested. 'No one would think that.'

'Hester would,' Kit said. 'That's exactly what she'd think, and say, though not to your face, of course. But, hey, on the bright side, at least it will give Isabelle a break at Easter lunch next year.'

'Since when have you given a damn what Hester said?' Kate asked.

'I don't care what anyone says. That's not the point though, is it, James?'

James looked up from his hands in misery. Asha looked stung. Kit smiled happiness back at them from behind his bagel. All that tension from the routine of his current life was draining out of him in the glow of James' defeat. Kit finished his bagel and put his fork down with a clatter of heavy steel on fine china.

'And of all this, the hardest bit is knowing that this wonderful woman who wants to marry you, you are a bit crazy by the way, don't let it be said I didn't warn you,' Kit interjected to Asha. 'This gorgeous woman is being loyal and brave by telling you she doesn't want a wedding. I mean, come on man, what woman doesn't want a wedding?'

'I never wanted a wedding,' Kate said.

'Nor me,' Isabelle added.

'Neither of you are normal.' Kit leant back in his chair. Kate was looking enticing with her irritated glares at him and sympathetic frown at James. He felt back to himself again. He looked at Asha. 'Go on, tell me, honestly, you don't want a beautiful wedding.'

'I can't say that,' she admitted. 'Of course, under normal circumstances, I would have wanted a wedding. I want the whole world to see how happy I am. But these are not normal circumstances, and I'm happy with what we've decided.'

Kit, Isabelle, Kate and James looked at her. She had stuck her chin out a little with her final statement. She should do it more often, it made her face look leaner.

'Hmm, I'm not convinced,' Kate said. 'Sorry, I know you're being wonderfully loyal, but I think Kit's right.'

'I sort of have to agree,' Isabelle added.

'Oh God, I'm so stupid,' James groaned, planting his elbows on his knees and burying his head in his hands again.

'Finally, you see sense,' Kit told him. He laced his fingers behind his head and snared some of the thoughts that were flying round the ceiling. 'Head up numbskull, here's what we're going to do.' He waited for James to look up at him. 'You'll have the wedding here. This house needs a purpose, and a wedding is a good place to start if you ask me. Between us, Isabelle, Kate, Elsa, myself, we'll give you a wedding. It will be our wedding gift to you. Not some pissant affair either, but a ball-busting, tradition-farting, English wedding and, what's more, we'll be bloody grateful that you allow us to do so, rather than asking us all to fly out to Poland to watch you get married somewhere we can't interfere in the arrangements at all. It will be a surprise. We shall arrange the whole shebang, you provide the guest list.'

'You can't possibly do that,' Asha protested.

'Give me one, just one, really good reason why not?' Kit asked her. 'And it needs to be a good one mind.'

She sat and gaped at him, looked at James, who had half-risen from his slump to watch her.

'I think you might struggle,' Kate said, prodding encouragement. 'It's a great idea, I mean who wants any of those awful wedding presents anyway. Much more fun to let us plan the wedding.'

'But it's not...' Asha protested, and stalled. 'James, don't you think, I mean...'

'It's a great idea.' Isabelle reached out a hand to encourage her. 'Nat will be so excited, and I can make the dresses! Oh please, let me, that would be wonderful.'

'But we should do it for ourselves,' Asha complained.

'Why?' Kate asked. 'What's family for, if not to help you celebrate the good times and help in the bad times? No one can do everything for themselves and, even if you could, which you can't, not right now, why would you want to? Isn't it more fun to share?'

James picked Asha's hand up and looked at her. 'Please,

think about it. I want you to be happy, not to look back later and regret what we didn't do. I'd never forgive myself if that happened.'

Asha gasped in irritation, and started to protest, but something in his eyes, in his voice, in the dejection oozing from his slumped shoulders, stopped her. 'Really?' she asked. 'Do you really want to do this? I'm happy to be married, it's not the wedding that counts.'

'I don't want anyone, ever, to think I'm not proud of us.' James was too big a bloke to make his voice as small as he needed for that to have stayed between them.

Kit smiled to himself, casting a twinkling eye at Kate's frown, that sting about Hester had worked a treat. 'Well, do we have a deal?' he asked. 'Total control mind, you don't get a say in anything, except maybe the date, a little bit, and the guest list. Possibly some colours, we'll see. It'll depend on how I feel.'

Kate and Isabelle leaned forward over the kitchen table, Kit could feel the tension in the room. Asha and James gripped hands and looked at one another, sharing a different sort of smile. An anxious smile, but hopeful. A smile that was trying not to smile.

'Let's do it,' James begged her. 'Please.'

She gave it one more second of denial, gave in and smiled back at him. 'Ok,' she said, 'let's do it.'

Isabelle and Kate erupted from their seats and danced round the table squealing in delight. Kit grimaced. This was going to need a whole new column of post it notes on the control board. James' grin grew to a ridiculous level and Asha started crying. Well, of course she would, she was pregnant, there would be a lot more of that to come. He pulled his phone out and started looking at dates.

7

My adorable Rose,
     I am so glad for your long letter. I have read and reread it for days in the lingering light of the mountains, preparing myself to return to Bombay. I am glad it reached me here, where I always feel closest to you.

Thank God you have stopped using that awful moniker and reverted to Kit. Kit is a proper name for a boy, and I am glad for him. The photos are adorable. How big he looks, and walking already, he is going to be a force to be reckoned with. And his dark hair has grown so blonde and is adorable that length. Those sweet curls remind me of your own. There are not enough photos of you. I'm having to piece you together from an arm here, a leg there, a flash of curls between. Have you lost weight? You look slimmer and more athletic even than before. How on earth you are managing with mother-hood and work is beyond me. But I could never imagine you as 'just a mother', I think it would have driven you mad. To think, my Rose, a lobbyist in Parliament. How perfect for you. It must be such a buzz and you will be brilliant at it. And to be contributing to the huge milestone of the abortion debate, I hope it goes through and you can count that as a success in your life. Do you know yet? News is slow to reach me here. How quiet and unimportant my life seems by comparison. I hope this winter to be able to set into my teaching in Bombay with more vigour. The long months in Kashmir have restored my health.

It is seven months since I have been 'home' as Ted calls it, though I feel that this place is more home to me than Bombay. His work this year has been unbelievable, I fear he is keeping much from me out of concern. After we arrived in April, he stayed only a few weeks before having to return. He has been back, of course, once in July, though sadly only for another fortnight, and again in early October. He seemed in need of a good long rest, wrecked from work and the long trip here. My health having improved, we tried once more to rekindle our intimacy. He has been too terrified to come near me since the miscarriage, there was so much blood I think he thought I might die! How feeble men are sometimes. But here, with rest and quiet, we began to remember one another again, and he was perhaps gentler and more patient than when we were first married. I think we both enjoyed the closeness that we had before – long talks in the evening, late dinners where we read to one another, time out on the verandah where we watched the sun set. He was sad to leave, and I know begins to hope for a child again. Nothing yet, but I shall be home soon, and we will have the kind winter months in Bombay to try again. I wish we could live here. I never look forward to returning to Bombay, but financial necessity dictates it. I wish I had made it here in time to see the blossom beside the lakes in Srinagar, I so longed to take photos of it that I could take home with me to the city.

Thank you for the other pictures. How adorable to see a picture of Patrick and Kate. Well, of Patrick. And of Kate. Could you not get them to pose together for one shot? I wish we could have been there, images of Riverdell in the summer fill me with longing and the desire to be close to you. Patrick looks exactly as Kate described him, 'ruddy and huge and bright'. Ted was shocked when I told him of her marriage, I shall look forward to showing him the photos to reassure him that the whirlwind romance was not rash. And anyway, as I told him, who are we to stand and judge on that score. ~~I look back in amazement at how swift our own romance was and wonder if...~~

You say you are concerned for her. That he is stilted and loud, 'typically Catholic', and she looks irritated with him. You are not the best to judge affairs of the heart when it comes to men, my love! Perhaps be more positive. Kate was never going to have a 'quiet' relationship, let's face it. Perhaps she needs someone loud to stand a chance of balance in her marriage? Elsa and Richard look as content as two doves in a nest. How lucky they have been to find such joy in one another. And you? You do not mention anyone special? Will you not share your secrets with me now? I would be happy to know that you are with someone and full of love for more than your boy and your work. You have so much passion to give someone, do not hide it away from yourself, or me.

I sit writing in a lovely study that faces south east. It has the sun rising behind Kolahoi, and curves across my window through the morning. In the far east I can see the long shadow of the mountain plateau, it reminds me of the Mynd that we could see from the bird tower on Climbing Jack. I hope you will come here one day, that we might explore the mountains together. I had such dreams that this would be the start of a great adventure, my coming to India. I imagined myself travelling around the world. I did not think how much life would be shaped by marriage. Ted worries for my health and would not take us to the mountains this year. I think he feels he was in some way responsible for the miscarriage and has become overprotective. How I long to walk on those soaring horizons once again.

There is an enormous wall map in this room. It is woven from the finest cashmere and silk, as only the people of this valley could possibly do, and has hand painted on it a map of ancient India from before the Raj. When the country was not really a country, but a great sweep of separate princedoms and beliefs. India as we know it is a British construct and, in trying to force something together that had always coexisted apart, began the melting pot of fervour that India is now. Ted talks about it with passion, and Kate would understand, I am sure. It is all beyond me a little, but the map, I adore. I love to trace the lines of the states and sound the old names out. To imagine what it might be like, to travel through such a world. It inspires my old dreams in me, to travel and explore. I have asked Ted if we might bring it to Bombay and make a copy for the house there, and he has agreed. Though not quite yet, he says, money being tight.

Kish and I have been spending all our time working on the villa. We go slowly, tackling one room at a time. Much of it is rotten or broken so we have thrown it all out into the far end of the garden and are burning it slowly. The old walls are soft and rippled and absorb a coat of paint as if no one has loved them in centuries, let alone decades. I want the house to be simpler, to forget its past and embrace a sweeter future. We work on the garden too, which is overwhelming but beautiful, beneath all the years of neglect. I am learning Kashmiri slowly and this is helping me no end. When we go to the floating markets Kish makes me do all the talking. How they laugh at me and shake their heads, but they are all too scared of Kish to try and make a bad deal with me. I thought she was in her late 50's but now discover she is almost 70!

How remarkable a woman she is. She lost her whole family in the Partition massacres. I do not know the details, but Ted told me a little about her. She was Muslim, trying to cross into Pakistan with her children and grandchildren. Her husband, sons and sons-in-law murdered before her eyes, her daughters, well, Ted would not say, but I have heard rumours of what happened to the women. In speaking of it, that awful weight fell over him. He told me how he found her clinging onto the dead body of one of her grandchildren and brought her here. She had been beaten, the bones of one side of her face crushed where she tried to protect her grandchild. My heart constricts thinking about it again, I know Ted spared me the worst details. She renounced all religion and refuses to speak of any faith. In India, this is most unusual. How such a damaged heart could possibly love again is beyond me, but she has become the maternal figure I never knew. I shall miss her dreadfully when I leave, and though I have asked her to come with me, she refuses.

I absorb her loving ways as much as I can. The thought of becoming a mother seems even more daunting now. Do you think it is possible to be a good mother when you struggle to recall the love of one? You always had Grandma and Elsa was old enough to truly know her mother. ~~I guess perhaps I should talk to Kate about this, this weight that sits upon me. I long for a child and, though you write of motherhood as if it is easy, I am scared. What if I am not a good mother? What if I cannot conceive? Will Ted still love me?~~

Now, look, my thoughts have strayed and made a mess of the letter. I have crossed the nonsense out as much as possible. If my letters start to look shabby, I shall end up having to write them out again!

Take care, my love, a thousand kisses to your adorable boy. I ache with the need to hold him.

BETH x

8

H e was startled awake by thuds. Music booming.
Doors banging. Heart hammering.
Waking into groggy awareness in the dark,
fear opening his eyes but exhaustion struggling to focus
them.

It's distant but near.

Car doors. They were car doors.

His body tensed. His mind struggling to catch up.

Voices. Laughing.

Girls laughing. Moth covered his ears. The sound set him
on edge. Made him anxious.

It's just laughter.

It sounded like a wildlife call.

He reached out, felt the outer wall of the tent pinging
against his body, waiting for the slightest ripple. Muscles
primed to bolt. The laughter persisted. Music cutting in and
out through bodies and trees. The tent fabric rippling with
the impact of air. Moth succumbed to exhaustion, fear
leaking out of him, leaving his muscles weak.

It's laughter. People having fun. You should try it some time.

Unable to stay focused. Rocking with the music ebbing through the fabric. He fell asleep before they left, high girlish laughter ringing in his ears, seeping through his mind. Twitching his body

When he woke again it was early. The pre-dawn bird song and a train rush in the distance. He let sound waver in through the tent. 5am light reaching its way through darkness. Bad dreams and echoes tickling the back of his mind. He sat up, his head rising into a gargantuan headache that had no right to be loitering in the too small area at the top of the tent. Eyes stinging, neck rigid with pain. He pushed past the wave of discomfort and opened the tent zip. The cold morning air sucking the fetid night breath out, making his head spin. He lay back down, too tired to get up and pee. Cold and trying to find the night's warmth in his bag. Overwhelmed by the intense urge to not move.

To never move.

To never get out of the bag, the tent, the trees.

To stay there and let the bike rot into the ground.

You're going to be breakfast for rats.

He pushed the sludge back, focused on breakfast. Hot food. Meat, eggs, milk. A whole load of protein and fat rushing through his muscles and chasing the bone ache out. Coffee, he'd even try coffee today. He could almost smell it. Moth sniffed again.

Nope, that's you, not coffee.

He knew it was bad when he could smell his own dirt.

Shower first.

Then breakfast.

He latched onto these things. Seeking out a swimming

pool, a café. Claiming the morning piecemeal. The clouds retreating, light growing stronger in the tent. Hunger stirring him. Getting up and packing the tent away.

There was an oasis of quiet outside the tent. Nature chased back by his strangeness. He moved in a slow hush that fitted the uncertain greyness of the hour. Overhead, above the branches, the light growing stronger. Tendrils probing their way down to help him. Moth put his helmet on to free his hands up and wheeled the bike down to the road. Concentrating on the ground. Watching out for sharp sticks or stones. He was too tired to lift it. He wheeled the bike out of the shadows, the front wheel finding the tarmac, lifted his eyes with relief from the ground, and froze.

Straight ahead, on the other side of the road and reaching down to the river, was a mass of tents thrown about in haphazard abandon. An oversized campfire was smoking in the middle, struggling to rise into the clinging, damp air by the river, its smell hovering over the embers.

That's why you didn't smell it.

He broke out in a sweat. Heat and moistness pounding the headache against his skull. There were people down by the river, past the campfire. Cars jutting out amongst the trees.

Small, flash cars. Low wheels, shiny bonnets.

The sounds from the night came back. He tried to unfreeze, to look casual. His body refusing. Watching in a daze as the people looked up at him. They waved.

Don't wave back.

Reactions kicked in. He jerked his head at them and moved forward. He turned towards his right, trying to get the back wheel safely onto the road and a leg over the frame. Grateful his hands were busy, his head covered by the helmet.

He put a foot on the pedal and began to push his body forward into the swing that would take him away. His eyes sweeping over them.

Older than you, but not much.

Kids, bunking out by the river. He felt the bike gain momentum, let his other foot catch the arc of the second pedal. Feeling its solidity beneath his trainer. Heard the zip opening from the tent nearest him.

A girl crawled out, laughing at someone inside, straightening up as he caught level with her. She flinched in surprise, jumping back from the unexpected movement. He turned away to look at the road, hoping he hadn't made an impression, stuck with hers. Her brown eyes blinking through smudged make up. Her ruffled dark hair jerking in the flinch. The gasping perfect oval of her mouth. The pulsing flesh of her tongue. Her neck tanned all the way down to her cleavage. Her breasts swinging loose against the thin top she'd slept in. Her nipples pulling a line down the fabric as she jumped back, disappearing as she pulled the two sides of her sweatshirt close against her body.

Just like Mila.

No, she's different from Mila.

Yet the same. Young, beautiful, repelling.

Moth pushed into the pedals, pulled away, his head pounding. Knowing her eyes were watching him go, resisting the urge to turn back and see how many others had seen him. Hoping they'd forget him. Straining to hear cars starting up but the woods and the wind rushing past him swept all sounds away.

They're too hung-over to care.

As the adrenaline ebbed, the cold morning took its place and his muscles complained. His legs felt weak, pain creeping down his spine. He needed that shower and some food.

Painkillers.

He added to the day's list. He would pick up some ibuprofen, take a dose with each meal. By evening he would be back on the road and fired up again. He'd be fine.

You are fine.

He stood in the shower until his muscles stopped shaking, until his stomach unclenched. Trying to outwait the pain in his chest, pressing two fingers into the throb, willing it to go away. Giving up, doing a slow two lengths of the pool and getting back out to shower again. Dressing in the near deserted men's changing room. His hair a shaggy mess, his eyes sunk in shadows, skin dry and rough.

You look trashed.

He looked ill. Whatever was wrong with his chest was taking its toll.

Or a drug addict.

Thoughts crossing over in their effort to express his self-disgust. He was glad Nat couldn't see, he would scare her.

Or a tramp.

He scared himself. In a proud way. Battered, bruised, and clinging to victory.

You did the mountains.

On a bike, at the wrong time of year. He'd set off from Vienna doubting he had the capacity to get out of Europe, aiming for a flat border and an easy crossing. Stood there in front of the mirror, looking like a homeless loser, doubt took a left hook and went down on the cold, wet floor.

You can do it. You can make the plan work.

His stomach rumbled, focusing him. He stayed a moment longer. Because life was Ok. Tired, hungry, but focused again.

Pain burrowing inside his chest but he was standing tall, clean, and free. Not too tall, because it hurt.

But clean as a whistle, and free.

Life was his. Moth grabbed his bag and left.

Male was better than he'd expected, if confused. Not sure if it was a tourist spot or a sports buff destination. On the fine edge of the major mountains and determined to cash in on the fact. Large enough to attract tourists and boost its income, not quite large enough to stand on its own financial feet. Dominated by the busy road that ran through it.

Going somewhere. Unlike this place.

He lingered over breakfast at a café set on the corner of a plaza and making the most of its position. Not unlike the town. The plaza more of a crossroads than a centre of attention. Vibrant red painted doors, well-tended planters either side.

His breakfast platter contained a selection of cold meats he couldn't recognise, with sharp salted flavour that hit his stomach hard. Tamed by the warmed bread and sweet-scented olive oil. A selection of dried fruits punching sugar into his system. He lingered at the table after his plate was cleared, trying to let it settle. Feeling the food toying with the pain in his ribs. Worried he'd hurl if he moved. His heart was booming with the coffee, and the blood flowing through his veins combined with the queasy feeling in his stomach.

You needed this.

He gritted his teeth and tried to keep his feet steady. It felt more like sitting on a boat than at a table.

The town was worth watching, even over a queasy stom-ach. The Italian locals standing out from the tourists. Moving with intent, weaving in and out of the straggling tourists with disinterest. Sure-footed over the cobbles that wobbled the visitors. Looking right for the day, for the weather. The tourists kitted out for sports ambitions or loaded down with bags and cameras. Moth's attention drifting between identifying the customers, and back to watching the steaming spouts of the machine and quick hands of the baristas. They made it look effortless.

Kate would be impressed.

This, this elegant ease, was what she'd tried to teach him. The way the cups danced through the air. The twist and snap of the coffee filter head. The rush of air that gurgled in the belly of the milk jug. No more stress between them than the flurry of one set of customers to the next, their flirtatious banter in Italian clear as day.

He was hypnotised, his hand curling against the cooling cup. The rolling speech, the hair that flicked and sparkled, the long-fingered nimble hands, the tight clothes stretched across their hips, peeking from behind the aprons when they cleared the tables.

You're staring.

Moth forced his eyes back to the street, seeking refuge in the strangers outside. But they kept coming back to watch the baristas. Two guys and a girl. Not a hair between which of them was the more gorgeous.

The taller guy.

The shorter one's fitter but knows it.

No, the girl. The girl.

Moth's eyes went back to the start of the circle. The sparkling light of the café, the early sunshine streaming in, the steam rising and hissing.

He got what Kate had been saying. How it could all come down to this, a precise skill that had a place and time in life. That mattered for the moment's pleasure it gave to someone.

He wanted to be part of that moment. To belong. Right here and now. Grounded in their world like the coffee beans tapped into the filter head. Not fleeting through it.

Is that what you want?

He watched the taller guy, skated over the other guy, forced his eyes back to the girl.

You don't know what you want.

He took a tentative sip of his cold coffee. Torn between pushing away the teeth-jangling intensity, lingering in the moment. He knew they would clear it as soon as he emptied it. Kate had taught him that too.

Customers don't linger at an empty table.

Even though the place wasn't full they were too well trained to forego the habits. When he couldn't face leaving, he caught the eye of the passing waitress, ordered a pastry and a hot chocolate. Watching while they made it. Wondering which one of them would bring it across to him. Staggered by how much it mattered when the decision was made, the tray launched through the air towards him, taking the breath with it out of the room. His airless chest tightening around the nugget of pain.

The taller guy, slim.

Thin. Thinner than Isabelle.

Black jeans painted on to his skinny legs. A white shirt hung across shoulders too wide for the slim hips, the collar looming above his collarbones, cradling his neck. The sleeves were rolled up, showing strange tattoos that Moth had never seen. White grey against the darker, tanned skin. Trailing down his forearm, into the paler shades of his slender inner wrist and palms. The muscles on his forearms a bulging contrast, the rolled sleeves taut against them. His black apron bibbed over the shirt and strung low on his hips, swaying at the hem as he walked across the bright café floor towards him.

Moth had only ever seen a man strut. Kit, or the shorter guy, or his father.

Arrogance from the toes up.

This guy didn't strut. This guy glided. Across the floor towards him with a tray balanced on his hand. His feet sliding, the apron hem swishing. Relaxed confidence parting the airwaves in front of him. He presented the coffee to Moth. It was that smooth. Arranging the cup, turning the handle, laying down the pastry, tweaking the knife, serviette tucked under the rim. Everything exact. Without an ounce of fuss. A waft of something subtle hovering over the table as he lingered in his work. Something Moth couldn't put his finger on. Coffee. Warmed by steam. Sweetness. Sharpness. Salted meat. Tugging at him.

You smell of nothing.

Moth's stomach twisted.

You don't look your best.

His hair the worst possible combination of ginger and shaggy. His hands too big. His legs too exposed in his shorts. His plastic bag toiletries inadequate to his needs. He felt English and crass and ignorant in the face of this... this...

... Italian smooth bastard.

He looked up at the face. Olive skin, brown eyes, full lips, dark hair sweeping up and away with exuberance.

He should be in a shampoo advert.

He was talking to him, clarifying the order, voice deep and light-hearted at the same time. Moth hadn't heard a word.

'Grazie.' Moth mumbled, handing over the money. Looking down at the table.

'E il benvenuto, signore,' the guy said. 'Enjoy.'

The switch to fluent, relaxed English shocked him to silence. Not because most people didn't end up trying to speak English with him, recognising his Italian was faulty, but because...

... it normally takes more than a single bloody word.

The guy was stood in front of him, empty tray balanced on one upraised hand, twirling with an excess of energy, expecting a reply. Moth stared up at him. Bone tired and exposed.

It's time to go.

He regretted ordering the drink, dragging out the moment. The guy looking at him, waiting for a response.

'I will,' he managed.

'You're visiting the mountains?

Moth struggled to put speech and thought together. His body taking over. Warmed through by the engagement, the familiar language, the familiar environment. His brain trying to catch up.

Shit, it's time to go.

You've spent too much time alone.

Say something.

Shut it down, it's time to go.

'No, I'm passing through,' he said. 'I just did the mountains.'

'On that?' the guy asked, looking out the window at his bike parked across the road.

Moth looked with him. Saw the bike locked up, in clear sight, the panniers visible. All visible. Himself visible. The ache in his chest deepened. His brain was fuddled.

You shouldn't have left it there. Idiot.

He was such a fool.

With no smell. And what is this? Now? Here? What the...?

'Yes,' he grasped the handle of the cup, trying to encourage the guy to move away. Aware of pressure growing inside him.

'That's impressive.'

'So is your English.'

'Two years in London,' the guy said.

Moth looked up. He needed to kill this conversation.

Kill it dead, and fast.

He had to get out of this café.

Before you end up caring about someone else's life.

But Moth couldn't retreat. He looked up to encourage him away with a scowl and lost focus. The guy sparkled in a way that pushed other thoughts out. The café, the revealed bike, the other customers listening. Moth aware of his own body, the gross outfit he was wearing, chosen for the bike, for the life. The gangling length of his limbs sticking out from the table, the veined legs rising from his scruffy trainers, the coarse fingernails he curbed with his teeth. This guy, a smooth slender rod. Himself a fish, hooked on a too-strong line.

Get up. Walk away. Do it.

He couldn't. He didn't dare stand up. He was stuck. Between the table and the guy.

'What took you there?' he asked, aware of his curtness. Trying to stop a blush from rising. Remembering Kit telling him never to blush.

'Studying. I did my MSc at LSE.'

Moth dropped another notch in his own estimation. This guy had a masters, was drop dead gorgeous and could make coffee this well. Make an art form of presenting a pastry. The whole value of his life popped like a bubble in his head. The plan sliding down the back wall of the pristine cafe.

What are you doing with your life?

'What are you planning to do with that?' Moth asked.

More importantly, what are you going to do about *this*?

'I'm waiting for job applications to go through. The UN in Geneva, I've applied for fifteen jobs since last year.'

'That's persistent.'

Moth focused on his coffee, his head was spinning. MSc, LSE, UN. This guy spoke in acronyms. Now he didn't only feel inadequate, he felt young and dick ignorant.

'You have to know what you want,' the guy shrugged. Slow and laid back. Making the shirt ripple across his clavicles. Easing open the neckline to reveal a knotted leather thong tucked down inside. 'Or you lose focus, right?'

'Right.'

It's time to go. Right now. Out, away from this bloke.

Away from how low he felt about himself. He couldn't feel any worse. He couldn't sink any lower. But he couldn't move. If he did, the guy would see his hard on. Creased painfully in his lap below the table.

It's this café. This place. You, you weak schmuck.

He couldn't help it. The stunning baristas, the coffee, the food, the conversation. The act of being a real person. His shorts were too loose to help him, it would poke out like a handshake.

You would choose today to not wear cycle shorts.

He'd wanted a change at the pool. Not to put the same clothes back on. He lifted the cup, heard it rattle against the saucer. Pressure bursting inside him. His head swimming, his stomach roiling, his chest constricting everything, the pressure funnelled to his lap.

'Hey, I'm sorry, I'm disturbing you.' The guy tucked the tray beneath his arm, held his hands together in a sort of half prayer, took a step back from him. 'It's nice to try out my English.'

'It's good,' Moth told him.

The guy grinned and turned to leave, looking back.

'Your Italian is shocking, but keep trying, yes. It's always nice when you English make the effort.'

'Grazie,' Moth said, loaded with irritation, squeezed out between gritted teeth.

He watched the guy glide back to the counter and revert to Italian. His apron strings were tied above the point where his shirt was tucked into his jeans. The ends trailing down over his jeans. Moth looked away. His dick crushed, swollen and twisted. He needed to move, to rearrange himself. It hurt.

How long before you sort this?

How long before he had the chance to walk out without any of them seeing. He refused to look at the baristas again. Focused instead on his pastry, the street outside, the dregs of his cup, the perfect moment to escape that he needed. Fear fuelling the mental demand to shut his body down. Watching everything from under his hair until he got up and went in a sudden rush. The door pinging shut behind him as three other customers came in.

His hands were shaking as he unlocked the bike. Swamped in a rush of heat, food, coffee, arousal, panic. He put the front bag on the handlebars and went to shift the rucksack from his back onto the top of the panniers. It wasn't there. Moth froze in horror and the sweat rushed out. Swamping, damp at his armpits, heat paralysing him. His brain wouldn't respond.

Where is it. Where is it. Where is it.

'Hey,' the deep voice called from behind him.

Moth felt sickness rise through him. He couldn't turn.

'You forgot your bag.'

He couldn't hold it in. He rushed from the bike to the nearest side street and threw up against the wall, holding himself up with a shaking hand pressed against the bricks. Drenched in sweat. He felt a hand on his back and flinched.

'Hey, are you alright?'

He wanted to punch out at him, fling the bloke back but all he could do was puke again.

'This is not good for business you know,' the guy told him, laughing. 'Eat breakfast at Marno's and throw up outside.'

Moth tried to fumble an apology, was wracked by another wave of nausea. His stomach cramping him over. Feeling bad about himself sunk to another level. He heard the guy retreat. He couldn't see him. Curled over, wretched hurling gripping his centre in a vice, twisting him inside out.

Where's the bike? What's he doing? Get a grip you prick.

Another wave of stomach cramp collapsing him, one agonised vertebra at a time. Lowering him over his own sickening innards. He staggered back from the stench at his feet, leaning against the wall, trying to focus. The guy came back beside him. Moth glanced up. Saw the easy smile, the concerned eyes, the impossible whiteness of the shirt, the teeth, the sails in his eyes.

Why does he have to be so... so... perfect.

He handed Moth a damp steaming cloth, turning with a bucket of hot water to swill the sick towards a drain. Walked away, curving out of his stricken sight. Moth heard the cafe door ping, silence, ping again, he came back with another bucket. Swilled and left again.

Where's the bag?

He put the towel to his head, wiped the sweat away, tried to clean his mouth up. His hair stuck to his forehead.

You stink again.

The awareness wafting into his nostrils, the smell of vomit and sweat churning his guts. He sank down against the wall until he was sat on his haunches, doubled over a stomach that was heaving but empty.

The guy returned, wheeling his bike round the corner. Looking nervous with the weight and size of it. Leaning it against the wall and propping his bag on it. He turned and leaned back against the wall next to his bike, watching Moth with pity in his eyes and a grin on his face. If he'd had the strength, Moth would have walked the four feet and punched him.

If nothing else, at least your hard on has gone.

'You cycle through the mountains in this season you are going to pay the price,' the guy told him.

Moth grunted. His body telling him the same thing. Too tired, too hungry, too stressed.

Maybe it's altitude sickness.

That's all it was. This reaction, this surging overtaking of his body.

'Where are you staying? You should go and rest for a few days.'

'I told you, I'm passing through.'

The guy looked at his bike, back at him. 'Camping, huh? You know how to live in style.'

Moth didn't respond, hunkering over the pain inside. Longing for the bloke to leave him alone.

You'll be fine, take a few minutes. It will ease.

'You need to rest up, too much coffee and food. You need

to eat a little bit, plain food and water. Not coffee. Makes it worse.'

'Yeah, no shit,' Moth said.

The guy grinned back at him. Moth knew he was being rude, but it didn't seem to be affecting the guy's desire to help. Nothing he did seemed to be affecting him.

'There's a park in town, go down this road, past the big church on your right, and behind it. There's a park there, quiet, not many people use it in the morning. You can rest up for a few hours.'

'There's a lot of big churches in town.'

'This is the first one you come to on your right. And I mean big, huge. Ok?'

'Ok.' Moth rested his head against the wall behind him. The wall was solid, cold, rough. It focused him.

Not smooth and sweet. That's not your style.

It was familiar, hard, abrasive. Holding him up. He could deal with that. This... this kindness... that was the unpleasant bit.

The guy stared, shook his head at him, said, 'You don't want people helping you?'

You don't need help. Tell him. Tell him.

Moth trusted the wall behind him. Not his voice, not his thoughts, not the moment.

'Wait one more minute.' He glided back out of sight. Moth heard the café door ping.

'That's fine,' Moth told the walls, 'I'm not going anywhere yet.'

The door pinged again. He came back, put some bottles of water and some bread in a bag on the top of his rucksack.

'Not everyone is an asshole, you know,' he told Moth.

'That's not been my experience. And it's 'arsehole', not 'asshole'.'

'That's a shame, you spend too much time with *arse*holes, you'll end up becoming one. You should make better friends.' The guy smiled a broad wide grin when he repeated Moth's poke at his language. Moth feeling a blush start somewhere low down again.

'Chance would be nice,' Moth agreed.

'"One chance is all you need." Jesse Owens.'

'Seriously?' Moth complained. 'I'm stood here puking my guts up and you're going to quote my own language back at me.'

'I can quote it in Italian, Spanish, French or Chinese if you prefer?'

'One day you'll be in charge of the UN, you know that, right?' Moth told him.

'Really?' he said, his brown eyes lighting up. 'You think?'

Moth took it all in, the hope, the determination, the doubt, the hope. Light as vulnerable as March sunshine dancing in his eyes.

'The day they appoint you, I want you to remember me puking at your feet when you walk into that fancy office. And make sure you use that bloody quote, Every Sodding Day, to irritate someone else.'

'I'll call and let you know,' he retorted, grinning at Moth. 'You know, you look better when you scowl than when you smile. It suits you, that English nose of yours.'

They stayed silent, Moth looking anywhere between the sky and the ground and the walls, willing his body to take control of itself back. The guy looking at him, vision straight as a laser.

He sees right through you.

Moth not knowing what to say. Whether to tell him to get stuffed for what he thought about how he looked, or to tell him what he thought about how the guy looked. Which would involve making up a lie to create an insult.

'You look a little better. More human. You should try getting to the park,' he told Moth. 'Whatever made you throw up, it will come in waves, with little spaces in between when you think it's over.'

Moth wanted to argue, had a strong urge to argue, felt it morph into a stronger urge to retch again. Grimaced at the fact that he was arguing a losing battle. He stood up, his legs shaking at the effort, determined to show he was strong enough to move on. By the time he made it across to the bike he had a film of sweat all over him. He took hold of the handlebars and pulled the bike upright. The guy kept leaning against the wall, watching him.

'Good luck,' he said to Moth.

'Grazie,' Moth said, turning the bike out of the alley. Willing himself not to stumble.

'Grazie, Luca,' the guy suggested. 'Mi chiamo, Luca.'

'Grazie... Luca,' Moth said. The name rolling across his tongue, forming his mouth into a hollow, lingering on the vowels. Snapping shut as it left.

Luca, looking at him, expecting him to give his own name. Moth stayed silent.

'Ok, 'Sick Boy', have it your way,' Luca said.

Luca pushed himself off the wall and started walking away. Moth watched him go, holding onto the weight of the bike to stay upright. The café door pinging shut behind him, taking Luca's scent with it, leaving him with the faint odour of sick. Moth pushed the bike out of the alleyway and headed down the street, looking for the quickest way out of town. He could see mountains leering at his efforts over the tops of buildings. Looking wild and free and full of places he could hide.

Escape is but a street away.

But all those side streets lost focus in the sweat of his upset stomach. The street he thought might lead to the mountains turned into another twist in the guts of the town. He hated Male as much as he'd liked it an hour earlier.

Another dumb arse small town you can't get out of. Again.

Three side streets later he was retching to no effect. His legs shaking, his head pounding with the sounds coming from his throat. It was another twenty minutes and a bottle of water later before he got back on the bike. By the time he came level with Luca's 'big church', more of a cathedral, it wasn't optional to go past it. By fits and starts, fighting it all the way, Moth ended up in the park.

This is not a park.

It was not much more than a large square, bounded by trees. He'd hoped for acres of woody isolation. Found himself sitting on a bench resenting the thinness of spring trees, longing for a thicker canopy.

Who would call this dump a park?

He sat in the shaded square. Cold and shivering. The fireball of pain in his chest the only solid thing to hold onto. Wondering what was inside him.

No desire to join the UN that's for sure.

Or the persistence to put in fifteen job applications. Or work with brilliance and commitment at a job he didn't want to do to get where he wanted to go.

Luca's a schmuck.

Moth hated himself. He tried to turn it focus it on Luca. But the guy was too sorted.

Too good looking by far.

Too genuine with it. Too focused.

Too much in your head.

Moth shook his cloudy head and focused on the trees, sipping water determinedly until the bottle was empty. Clenching his teeth against the surges of his guts. After twenty minutes the heaving stopped. He took some oats from the bag in his pannier, mixed it with water and let it soak. Took tiny mouthfuls and let it slide down his throat. Ten minutes later he threw it all up again in the bin next to the bench. Advancing from the bench to the cold grass behind it to lie down, hoping no one had heard him. If a local policeman went by, he would be moved on. He could hear shoes entering the far gate.

Pull yourself together and out of here.

He struggled upwards into a seated position. Feet came towards him on the pavement, clicking in high shining heels. Looking up from the grass he saw slim legs, glistening with some sort of invisible coating, topped by a fitted skirt, stop in front of him. Moth tried to look calm and controlled, sitting cross-legged on the grass, his arms wrapped against the spreading pain in his chest and gut.

'Sei 'Sick Boy'?' the girl asked in Italian, struggling with the strange English words. He winced, nodded, remained silent. Now someone else knew him.

By a really stupid name.

She handed a package down to him in a brown paper bag. Moth didn't reach out a hand to take it. She put it down on the grass beside him, keeping outside of his reach.

'Luca li mando,' she said and walked away.

Moth watched the shoes, click-clickety-clicking down the path. He picked the bag up. Inside were some sachets. Rehydration powder was the best stab he could see. They looked well sealed, but he wasn't going to take the risk. More water, with sealed tops. He read the words on the side of the sachets. He would find a chemist, get some of the same. The water he took out of the bag and put with his bike. At the bottom of the bag was a small card. He reached in, pulled it out. Mando's written on one side. On the other, a phone number. Luca's name scrawled beside it.

You don't need it, put it in the bin.

He stared hard at it. The numbers merging into one another on the white crisp background, as pristine and glowing as the white shirt. Moth trying to think of any good reason to keep it. Looking at the long curls of the writing, the upward flick of the final tail. As confident as his hair, swept up with gel into the air.

Put it in the bin. You don't know shit about him, don't trust him.

He tucked the card into his notebook, marking the space where filled lines met empty. It was small, fitting a treat, tucking itself away inside the pages. The weight of the card marking his place. It was useful. He left the sachets and the bag in the bin, on top of the sick that stank, making him retch again. Ill or not ill, he needed to get out of here right now.

Luca might have told any number of people about you.

They might have told someone else. How long before any one of them got suspicious about him.

He struggled with the map, finger following the tracing lines. The road he'd come along the night before was too big, too fast. If he'd struggled with it yesterday, there was no way he'd cope with it today. He needed to go south, but direct south was the river. Taking him back to the campers who'd seen him that morning. North were roads that would take him back to the mountains. He had no choice but to ride the valley floor, taking the old road through the interlinked villages. Further along there were options he could consider. Wobbling on the bike and throwing up in side streets was the perfect way to get noticed in small towns like this. He pushed out of the square and southwest on the first street he came to.

He found a chemist and got some rehydration sachets. Which his stomach rejected again. Between stopping to puke, recovering from puking, getting back on the bike, and retracing his route to avoid the large southern road, he covered three kilometres in two hours, making it to the next small village. Exhausted. Fighting his body, the sweat, the cramps, the nausea. Panic closing him down.

You're fine, it's fine, keep going, a bit further.

He parked the bike up against a tree, open fields showing him the valley floor all the way down to the river and the main road, looking between it and the map. White capped mountains rearing up ahead and behind him. A small copse of trees sat in the road ahead. Above it three large lodges looked above the treetops toward the southern mountains. He wheeled the bike closer and kept his eyes peeled to see if any cars were coming.

You need to sleep. An hour or two. You'll feel better.

If he could rest, he would wait for night and cross the valley floor. There was another road south through the mountains. One ridgeline to make it over and it dropped to follow another valley floor all the way down to Iseo. It had to be a better option than this dodging of villages and towns when he was this sick. He pulled the sleeping bag out of the pannier, opened it and wrapped it around him. Lay down with the bike wedged under his leg. He plucked crumbs off the bread roll Luca had given him. Letting them melt away into his mouth. Making a pathetic hole in the bun before his stomach begged him to stop.

Luca's number played in his head. All he had to do was call, ask for help. He'd have to be in much worse trouble before he did that. Especially from someone whose life plan made his own resemble a fart at a firework show.

Kit's enough of a test for now.

One that had yet to play out. He wasn't going to run tests concurrently.

Keep it simple. Keep it tight.

Moth talked himself into a troubled doze, hoping no one was looking into the copse from the windows of the lodges. Hoping that the mountains were a more appealing view. Curling into his pain beneath the spiny trunks, the thin fresh canopy. Trying to be invisible.

It was a cold and filthy February. The garden grey and washed out, all colours dragged into the dark current of the river that crept higher with each week that passed. Isabelle sat in her study, nursing a cooling cup of coffee and listening to the strange silence of the house. Trying to figure out how it had become February?

The door to the study was open behind her and the long eastern hallway seemed to stretch in her mind, all the way past the closed doors of the rooms and into the empty heart of the house. She could sense it waiting, the high window looking down into the hallway and the gleaming new entrance. Its breath held as much as hers, wondering who all the work was for. Until it could hold no longer and came whispering into the fire-warmed comfort of her study, a soft draught chasing through the bright room and puffing at her ankles. Looking for company in the echoing empty house. She pulled her legs up to the chair seat and clutched tighter at the remainder of her drink.

If she had hoped for clarity when Kit came back, for some sense of order to be restored to life, for an anchor to pin her down in the unravelling which had begun with Elsa's announcement and pinned itself to the moment when she found Moth's not-bike, she had hoped in vain. Kit had seemed to rise over her as fast as the winter river had the garden, sweeping her from one year to the next.

There had been a false lull at Christmas when she thought perhaps, now, now we will get to what matters.

On Christmas Eve, she'd wandered through the house with a pygmy pop-up Christmas tree, the sort that erupted out if its box ready decorated and needing only to be plugged in, trying to decide where they should spend their Christmas day. She looked in at the guest sitting room, distraught beneath the wintery sky scowling through the huge windows. Stripped of its former glory and doused in 'Ammonite' paint, it seemed to have grown another three foot in every direction. There were curtains being made to soften it, though not in the workroom. Kit had evicted her from the basement.

They argued for days over where to relocate her to. He insisted on the guest sitting room, she refused. She would not give it up as her favourite room and, using the only power she had to sway him, claimed the wedding as reason.

'It's the perfect reception room,' she argued. 'And not just for the wedding, afterwards, if we do more.'

He stood in the middle of the room, scowling at her, watching as she circled away from him, gesturing at the details of the decor.

'It's the right size, it has the best view, it's in the best location,' she ticked off her arsenal. 'I can shut the east corridor off, keep the rest of the house out of bounds.'

Holding her fingers crossed behind her back, praying with a held breath, because Kit had gone into such a mega-drive following Asha's announcement that even trying to reason with him turned him into a diva. Kit screwed his eyes up at her, thinking in scowls and blinks, phone held to his ear all the while.

'With a neutral background I can add colour accents for different events, change it for the occasion.' She used her hands to exaggerate the plan. Making it a plan, denying it was anything but a plan, not a whim, with enthusiasm borrowed from Kate. Along with Kate's wind-milling, confidence inspiring arms.

'Fine, have it your way,' he said. 'The sitting room it is.'

And off he went, talking to the supplier on the phone, holding it against his chest, bellowing at Ed and Fred to follow him. While she snuck to the doorway, not daring to believe she'd won, nervous to leave the room exposed.

'But we're calling it the drawing room from now on,' Kit yelled at her from the far end of the corridor.

She detested it, loathing the pretension, thinking that Moth would hate it. 'That's fine,' she called. 'Whatever you think best.'

She liked having the workroom across the hall from the study, found herself comfortable with the connection between old and new parts of herself. Needles travelling across the corridor in her jumper, finding themselves stuck into the arm of the sofa, into the rough corner of her desk. And she liked the growing character of the guest si... drawing room.

On Christmas Eve, as she peered in with the overwhelmed tree in her hand, the room looked ragged and wild in its emerging plumage. The first wary curtains hung, judging her ideas, waiting for their mates. The wooden floor stripped and limed to a grey sheen that stretched to the horizon. The furniture sent to the upholsterers. It was holding its breath, waiting for the final image she was trying to bring forth. Whole rooms were far harder than single items, and keeping the ideas together in her head, out of Kit's hands, was daunting. She wasn't ready for any more of Kit's scathing opinions in here. She wandered on with the Christmas tree.

The morning room and dining room doors were shut, and she moved on past. She knew what was in those. Furniture. A lot of furniture. Another pending battle with Kit. Who thought that what you did with a house full of family memories was as easy as a house full of clients' memories. There were more rooms upstairs, stuffed from the emptying of the rooms for the flats. They would have to wait too. It was another thing placed into the unclear future. The future when the jobs that were being done were done and the job that needing doing was begun.

She walked down the corridor to the study, placed the tree on one of the mismatched side tables, dragged it closer to a plug and turned on the glory. It was cringe worthy. But it was her first very own Christmas tree. She felt protective of its haphazard arrangement of lights and baubles, tweaking them into alignment.

Having expressed their contempt for the tree, Kit and Kate relaxed into Christmas. Both too tired to complain with any conviction. Isabelle cooked a huge pot of spiced lamb stew, served it up with fragrant rice and naan bread, and poured them glass after glass of wine. They spent the day between the kitchen table and the study, where they dozed in front of the fire.

Isabelle left them dozing, proud to have managed a Christmas day of such little pomp and aggravation, wondering if she could set it as a new tradition. Retreating to her bedroom and leaving them to find their own way to bed. All the usable bedrooms on the first floor were made up, theirs to choose where they slept. On the chaotic top floor, only her room had a bed in it. For when it came to it and Kit turfed her out of her bedroom, she found she could not bring herself to move down an entire floor. Elsa's bedroom was sacrosanct. There was no way she could take it, and all the other rooms on that floor seemed too redolent of the house's impersonal, business past. She felt that if she abandoned the top floor no one would ever go there.

'So what?' Kit argued. 'Who cares? Take the best room, turn the top floor into an attic.'

But she couldn't and moved no further than the other end of the corridor. Taking the bedroom that felt most right to her, the one that had been Moth's for the four short months he lived there. Even though there was nothing there to remind her of Moth, except the view, which reached past the curve of the cliffs and towards the setting sun. Kit had taken it all in with tight-lipped silence, turned on his heel and walked away. She went to bed, gazing out at the dark night and the rippling thick surface of the river gleaming back at her, wondering where Moth might be on that night. If he'd shared Christmas with anyone. Sickness rising in her as she considered the edge of all those other possibilities that presented themselves whenever she thought about Moth's continued absence. Pushed back by the knowledge he was in touch with Nat. Still alive. Well enough to write. Holding onto the hope that the peace of their Christmas day heralded a new phase, when perhaps they might at last tackle this question. This only task that needed prioritising.

It was a hope that got slammed out of her thoughts with the arrival of the first builder's van on Boxing Day. She was too sleepy to recognise it and, knowing Kit was there to manage, turned over and went back to sleep. An hour later, Kate appeared with a tray of coffee. Tucking herself into Isabelle's bed with the papers, muttering over the noise she'd braved to get them hot drinks. The peace of Christmas ended, and it never returned.

Kit ripped into the destructive part of the conversion with equal parts vigour and hangover on Boxing Day morning. Armed with a sledgehammer and dressed in a top-to-toe white dust suit, while the builders looked on in bemusement. He sat down at lunchtime, the boiler suit peeled back to his waist, rings round his eyes from the dust mask and a grey tint to his hair, delighted with the shimmying cloud of dust and noise that was engulfing the house.

'A fortnight of this, and we rebuild,' he said. 'Don't bother to dust, or vac, it's worthless. Keep as many doors closed as you can and ignore it.'

Only Kit could have ignored the mayhem that he unleashed. Anyone else would have found it as violating as she did. There was nowhere she could go that she wasn't hailed with a question or a detail, presented with a mess, or assaulted by the sound of her house screaming. The demolition as intense as warfare, craters appearing in her wounded walls and floors. When the fortnight extended into three weeks, she was creeping timid as a mouse past the workers. Creating paths in the grey dust that covered everything, trailing lines between the kitchen, the new workroom and the study, scurrying past doors. Tentative, less visited pathways appeared as she ventured further in the evenings, soon swallowed back up the next day.

One day the noise changed, the dust stopped falling and emerging out of the grimness was a whole new shape to her life. One where habits imprinted on her brain over years came up against blocked passages. Where she set off to do a job and, after three steps, realised she was going in the wrong direction. Where she paused, in moments of blank confusion, turning left or right instead of going straight on.

Upstairs the builders evolved into chippies with large strong hands and quiet faces. Electricians with frowns and mutters deciphering the hieroglyphics of ancient wiring systems. Humming plumbers whose mechanical taps echoed down unexpected pipes. A plasterer with a face rearranged by a violent past soothed her walls into blissful contentment, pinking up the raw edges left by the builders. Kit evolved too, from his wall-busting, white-suited samurai into a ballerina, floating, twirling, ordering, calming, rearranging, challenging. His support act of Lou, Jamie and the boys descended the week before the wedding and took over her house in a maelstrom of noise that picked her apart one nerve at a time. Vacuuming away the impossible dust, revealing the new shape of life to her one timid room at a time.

The main hallway, stairwell, and guest... drawing room were glistening. The wooden floors oiled, with a light touch of lavender oil added to overcome the smell. The rugs cleaned and exhibiting subtle colours lost for years. Gone was the heavy sense of an old family home greeting honoured guests. It was lighter, cleaner, free of clutter and history, more welcoming and malleable. The house itself gleamed out. The wood, the glass, the silver. The lines, curves, corners and mouldings. All backed by the hushed shade of Ammonite.

In the drawing room, the final curtains had been hung with anxiety. Isabelle stepping back with a rush of pleasure to see some of her own, original work stamping its identity for all to see. The variegated shades of grey, dusted plums, iced blues, silvered limes and fragile lilacs, drawing the eye outwards, past them. The silk draped, gathered, dressed and stitched into folds, reminiscent of old statues. There was no symmetry to it, the formality and scale of the windows denied. The hems puddled on the floor, as though the window were too small for its dressings. The windows pulled down, dressed down, scaled down to something soft and indivisible from the room. Focusing the eye on the loveliness of the sky beyond, and the tempting curves of the landscape.

'You know,' Kit began to muse, rubbing his fingers together in excitement, eyes narrowing in a calculating professional way. 'You should do more of this.'

'I ought to make tea for the boys.' She backed away from him, towards the door. Anxious to leave him fingering the edges, inspecting the details, hoping he'd move on to another idea by the time she came back.

Sitting in her study on that cold February day, Isabelle felt the same momentary peace she had known on Christmas Day, the letting out of one breath before drawing the next. And though it was still not the breath she wished to draw in, she knew that she was getting closer. She had only this day left to herself. Elsa and Nat were due to arrive tomorrow, on Monday, the first day of Nat's half term. The wedding was on Thursday, Valentine's day. The days in between would be relentless. Kit more so.

Isabelle kicked her heels on the rung of her stool, poked

at the paperwork spread out on her desk, raised her head and listened to the empty, echoing halls of Riverdell.

Silence had become something she was unaccustomed to, something she had forgotten. Waking earlier to the absence of noise, she had been swamped with confusion. Unsure where she was or what she had woken to. Her eyes staring at the unfamiliar ceiling of her bedroom and waiting for her brain to piece it together. All through the quiet, slow hour that followed she walked through her house in wonder. Trying to remember how she'd arrived here, in this new and strange place that seemed to come from somewhere remembered. Wanting to share it with someone, relieved to be alone. Landing in her study with a cooling cup of coffee and facing the paperwork before her.

More contracts from Rob. Contracts had become normal. The ones selling the Staines House, the one selling the first parcel of land adjacent to the swiftly renamed Payle Villa. Apparently, Peel hadn't appealed to the new owner any more than it had to Kate. Kit hadn't cared what they renamed it, they'd paid £150,000 over the asking price in a final battle that had raged like World War Two, to the eleventh hour of the eleventh day of the eleventh month, as he described it. A battle which had covered her legal fees, Elsa's ability to help James and Asha put a down payment on the farm mortgage, and a commission for Asha that cinched their mortgage. Now, it was the contract selling the first of the farms. Looking at it she could feel a quiver of anxiety in her stomach at the thought of Elsa's arrival. She signed the documents and pushed them to one side. Rob was collecting them later, she'd invited him to dinner with Elsa, Nat and Kate. She leaned on her arms on the desk and scanned the room. There was not much to do bar wait for the evening.

After Lou and Jamie got the house spotless, wiping away all those weeks of workmen, dust, and the longer, more lingering months of her domestic neglect, Kit declared that she could afford a cleaner now, and that he'd arranged one for her. She tried to protest.

'It's not a bloody request, Isabelle,' he swore down the phone. 'You need a weekly.'

'I can manage,' she said, hating the word.

'You're not putting all my hard work to waste because you're too tight to pay someone a wage,' he said. 'You'll end up the owner of a peeling house like the one you just got rid of. This discussion is over.'

As of two days ago she had become the awkward, uncomfortable employer of a tall, strong, energetic Polish lady who smiled in delight at her suggestions and then did what she thought necessary to keep the house clean. Having a 'weekly', as Kit called Mrs Wisniewski, made her feel itchy, something uncomfortable sliding down her back she couldn't reach. It made her sound like Elsa, who'd always talked fondly of the days when her father had employed a daily and a weekly. As though it was the civilised way of looking after a house, reducing people to adjectives. Isabelle was struggling to pronounce Mrs Wisniewski's name, but she persisted. Asking Asha to help her learn it, along with some basic Polish.

Isabelle left the desk and the contracts, went across the corridor and into the new workroom, a space dominated by the large table. Kit had spared nothing in moving her, much had been lost in the reduction of space. Older machines she hadn't used for years sold, boxes relocated to the spare rooms on the top floor, even the paintings of Hester's, loaded into Kit's van and taken to Swansea. He'd shown her none of the patience Moth had. She clung to the essence, refusing to let him get rid of any of her hoarded fabrics, insisting she would need them. For the curtains for the drawing room, or Asha's wedding dress, or the different coloured sashes that she made for each chair set out in the ballroom below.

'You're the one who wanted so many colours,' she begged, holding on to her baskets.

He growled at her and stormed out the room, swearing at Ed as he passed him. Kit had set the tonal value for the wedding, wanting a multi-hued scheme on the upper edge of pastel, colours that Isabelle had been able to pull from her stocks in victory.

'Yeah boss, gotcha boss, screw you too boss.' Ed took the basket out of her hands with kindness, saying, 'another slim victory for you.'

Isabelle looked at the colour coded fabric-filled shelves on the back wall. It might have been a slim victory, but at least she'd won one, and she had the wedding to thank for it.

68 guests were due to gather on Thursday. The vicar, non-Catholic after an intense debate between Kit and Asha that had seen even Kate retreat to the fringes of the kitchen, was scheduled to marry them in the new ballroom at 4pm. Followed by a buffet dinner, and a dance in the evening. It was elegant, simple, light-hearted, warm and sincere. As Kit expressed it. It was colourful, very colourful, was how Kate put it. Isabelle felt a wobble of concern chase her gratitude out the door. It was not the first one she'd had about the impending day.

Moments when anxiety gripped her. When she saw the guest list and realised how many of her and James' old friends were on it, friends she never heard from anymore. Or when she was fitting Asha's dress and her hands glanced across the tightening belly where the baby snuggled. Or when she realised that she had not thought about her own outfit and was stabbed with a rush of panic that she didn't know what to wear. Or when she realised that she would be hosting Elsa and Nat in the newly altered house and invited Rob and Kate to dinner on the first evening. Anxiety that swept across her in a hot wave and left with a rush, leaving her reeling with the effort to adjust to the new person she was supposed to be unveiling at the event, as much as the new house.

Moments when she longed for Moth to turn up and make the day bearable. When she was suddenly, intensely lonely in her huge, hollow house and her busy, empty life. When Moth seemed such a long way away, removed to a memory that she struggled to give clear shape to. A glimpse of the person he might have been, before the will was read, before Riverdell became her every thought, before all this, when they had been about to become something other than this woman with a weekly and the half-man who'd disappeared.

ISABELLE WIPED her hands for the umpteenth time on her jeans.

'Do relax,' Kate told her. 'You'll wipe away the last threads holding those old things together.'

'You first,' Isabelle retorted. 'If you rearrange that table one more time it might look exactly how it did twenty minutes ago when you first laid it.'

'Nonsense,' Kate said. 'It looks completely different.' But she grinned all the same. 'God, I'm nervous. Why am I so nervous?'

'Perhaps because you haven't been to Swansea to see Elsa since she moved there?'

'Oh don't,' Kate groaned. 'Seven months, where has it gone!'

'Or maybe because you're finally retiring, after she leaves the county?'

'She left first.' Kate tossed her comment aside with a wave of her hand and a twitch of her hair. 'In fact, she started all the changes. Anyway, at least I haven't sold off half her assets and redesigned her childhood home.'

'I wonder which she'll be more upset about?' Isabelle asked. 'Our not going to see her, or our desecrating the memory of her life?'

A car pulled up in the driveway, its lights shining through the drawn curtains, it tyres churning the gravel.

'Oh God, they're here,' Kate groaned.

'No, it's Rob,' Isabelle said.

'You know the sound of his car?' Kate asked. 'How often does the man come?'

'It takes a lot of paperwork to cause this much change!' Isabelle could not believe how much of the stuff was generated by house sales.

'How diligent of him,' Kate said, pausing in her fiddling with the table, looking at her.

Isabelle went to open the door. She was so relieved Rob had arrived before Elsa, it was another body to diffuse the conversation.

'Something smells amazing,' Rob said as he came through the door.

'Chicken Provencal,' Isabelle told him as they walked into the kitchen. 'Kate brought it down from the bistro.'

'Rob, how are you?' Kate walked over to plant a light kiss on his cheek.

'Overworked, overpaid,' Rob joked. 'Annoyingly, can't complain.'

'Honesty from a solicitor, what a refreshing change,' Kate said with a smile. 'Wine? Beer? Tea?'

'Anything non-alcoholic.'

'Elderflower presse?'

'Anything other than that.'

'You're in a jolly frame of mind,' Kate responded.

'I've been invited to dinner. As an overworked single man, I'm grateful.'

'Yes, I can sympathise. I'm not looking forward to living somewhere where I don't have a chef on hand.'

'You'll descend to the depths of the bread bin,' Rob told her. 'Beans on toast, cheese on toast, jam on toast, even plain old nice fresh toast. I try to fit in as many working lunches as possible these days.'

'You make it sound delightful,' Kate said. 'Here, try this. A new low-alcohol beer the manager is trying out, I think it's perfectly vile.'

Rob took a long pull of the frothy glass. 'It's rather bubbly,' he said. 'Doesn't taste too bad though. They're all the rage these things, alcohol taste without the alcohol content.'

'Can't see the point myself, might as well have a cup of tea.'

Isabelle retreated to her chair during the steady flow of pointless noise they soothed the kitchen with.

'Why are you sitting there?' Kate snapped.

'What?' Isabelle jumped in her skin.

Kate was scowling at her, Rob smiling over his froth. Isabelle realised she'd retreated to her old chair, the one on the window side of the table. The chair at the head of the table that she'd grown used to taking stared reproachfully at her.

'Old habits die hard, eh?' Rob suggested.

'Oh.' Isabelle looked blankly between them, and the chair. She couldn't sit there, not in front of Elsa. She had no idea where to sit.

'Don't let me forget to get those papers from you,' Rob said. 'I'm likely to forget at the end of the night and I need them for first thing.'

'I'll get them now.' Isabelle slipped out of the offending chair and the room to the study. She picked up the papers, looking at the room, feeling a wave of panic when she realised what she'd done to Elsa's study. The study. Her study. The new desk looked wretched, all modern and rustic. An obscenity when she thought about showing Elsa.

'They're here!' Kate called from the hallway.

Isabelle heard car doors slamming on the drive. Her stomach lurched. She slipped back to the kitchen, past Kate heading for the front door, and held the papers out to Rob. They wobbled at the end until he took them.

'Relax,' he told her. 'It's Elsa, not the Queen.'

'Queenie, darling!' she heard Kate say from the front door. Rob choked on his bubbles and grimaced at her. 'And, oh my goodness, look at you, Nat! You've grown an inch for every month, surely!'

'I'll open the wine,' Rob told her, turning her towards the door. 'Go greet your guests, Isabelle.'

She walked out of the kitchen and into the hallway, her hands sweating. Confronted with the massive change of décor in the reflection of Elsa's stunned face as she took it in. Her hair as immaculate and curled as ever, not a hair out of place from the last time it had walked out the door.

'Gosh, you have been busy,' she said with a breathless laugh as she saw Isabelle.

'Kit's been busy,' Kate corrected, waving the comment aside. 'Very, very, busy. Brace yourself, this is just the start.'

'Goodness,' Elsa said, then, 'Isabelle, darling. Oh, I've missed you. You vile pair. Neither of you have come to see us.'

'Hello, Elsa,' Isabelle gave her a warm hug. 'And Nat, how lovely to see you.'

'Hello,' Nat said. Kate had barely released her from a long hug, she looked as though she dreaded the idea of another one.

'Don't worry, one crushing is enough for tonight,' Isabelle said. 'But I'm sure you'll get more before the week is over. How was your trip?'

'Perfectly lovely,' Elsa said. 'We stopped at Tintern and explored the abbey. Nat's doing a local history project, we thought we better get something done before the wedding took over.'

'How wise,' Kate said. 'Are these all your bags?'

'No, the car is packed to the brim, but these are all we need tonight. We can deal with the rest tomorrow. Whose posh car is that?'

'Rob's.' Kate looked at the gleaming new Jaguar estate on the gravel. 'He had a promotion at work, apparently.'

'Rob's here?' Elsa asked. 'How wonderful, I have missed him. Where is he?'

'In the kitchen, pouring wine and stirring the pot as though he's cooked it himself.' Kate linked her arm through Elsa's, and they disappeared into the kitchen together.

'Shall I show you to your bedroom?' Isabelle asked Nat. 'I'm afraid it's a different room to before. Kit's rather changed everything.'

'I don't mind.' Nat lifted her bag.

Isabelle lifted Elsa's and headed for the stairs. 'I put you next door to Elsa, I thought you and Asha can all get ready together on Thursday.'

They headed up the stairs and Nat paused at the top.

'All the pictures have gone,' she said. 'And there's a wall there.'

Isabelle felt her stomach lurch, she hadn't told Elsa about the pictures yet. An argument that had been lost to the storm of Kit's disbelief she was even trying to pretend she wanted to keep them. He'd removed them from the walls while yelling at her stupidity, daring her to prove she even knew the name of the old miser in the picture. She had hidden a few in the depths of the furniture stocked rooms before he found a buyer for the whole lot.

'Yes, Kit sold them,' she said, breathless and wobbling on the top step.

'It all looks very different.'

'Different good or different bad?'

'Just different,' Nat said. 'It's nice to be here though.'

'That's good. Are you looking forward to getting your dress fitted?'

'I'm a bit nervous. I haven't met the other bridesmaids yet.'

'I have, and they're younger than you, and really funny. I think they're more nervous about meeting you.'

'I can't wait for the wedding.'

'I know,' Isabelle agreed. She paused outside the door next to Elsa's, opened it. It was both under-furnished and dis-coordinated, but spotless. 'Here, this is your room, and here's the bathroom.'

'Where's yours?' Nat asked, walking through the door,

holding her bag against her knees. She had grown, Isabelle realised. Not just taller, but leaner. The stoutness of the child growing more graceful in limbs and fingers. Her fringe grown out and showing more of her face, her ponytail lengthening to keep pace with her neck, Isabelle glad to see it hadn't been crafted into a plait. She looked for any sign of Moth, but Nat had always looked different and she was growing further away from her brother, not closer to him. She wondered what Moth would see when he finally came home to his sister.

'Upstairs. In what used to be Moth's bedroom,' she cringed as his name left her lips, rushing on, 'and there's another spare one too, though it's a bit full of rubbish.'

They stood silently in the room for a moment, weighing each other up. Nat holding the bag in both hands, dangling against her knees.

'Are you ready to come down?' Isabelle asked. 'Or do you want a bit of time? Dinner will be ten minutes yet.'

'I'll come now,' Nat said, putting her bag on the bed.

They walked back down together. Isabelle showed her the new drawing room. Decked out in its fresh walls and curtains, furniture arranged to greet the guests before they headed downstairs for the actual ceremony. Nat regarded it in silence.

'The florist is turning up to start tomorrow,' Isabelle's voice echoed in the large room, she tried to soften it. 'Hopefully, it will look prettier then.'

'It looks so different.'

'You keep saying that,' Isabelle told her, cringing inside with how much she wanted to hear approval, delight, anything.

'But it does!'

'Come on, let's get some food.'

She walked into the kitchen with Nat behind her, to see that Elsa had taken a seat away from her old one. Talking to Rob, who was sat next to her, with her one hand reached across the space between them, connecting them again, while Kate was serving the food into dishes. It overwhelmed her, left her frozen in the doorway while Nat slipped past her.

'Isabelle, come and help,' Kate called. 'Nat, sit down darling, over there, that's it. You can sit next to me and tell me all about your new school. What do you want to drink?'

'Squash please,' Nat said. 'I can get it.'

'Oh, would you, lovely. Isabelle, could you strain the vegetables.'

'Of course.' She moved to Kate's side, helping, not thinking.

Through small instructions Kate gathered them, each assigned to their place, with Isabelle put in hers, at the head of the table. The table itself seemed to reproach her with its empty seats, as they huddled at the one end. It was too huge, too filled with the habits of the past. She regretted that she hadn't turned her attention to the kitchen earlier. In Elsa's presence it reclaimed her. The dresser still full of the majolica, the table and chairs leaning towards their old owner. In all the changes this had become the headquarters of operations, evading the redecoration process.

They made their way through dinner, supported by Kate and Rob's endless small talk. A chain of sentences that refused to break, to leave a moment for difficulty, or the tangle of emotions that they all held back. Between talk of the wedding and the news from Swansea, with much prompting of Nat to talk about her new life, the adults avoided dealing with any of the gaps that lurked in the shadows of the room, hovering over the table. Isabelle struck by how different Nat's voice sounded, in the absence of Moth's comments teasing her. How she sounded older, finding her own place at the table.

Afterwards, when Kate and Rob had left, with Nat in her bedroom reading, she and Elsa took a slow walk through the ground floor of the house. Looking in at all the rooms, commenting on the changes, until they ended up in the ball-room via the revealed stairwell which Elsa could recall from her childhood.

'Well, how remarkable.' She span about, taking in the massive space. 'You've left the basement and Hester has retreated to it.'

'What?'

'She's taken over the basement in Swansea. Nothing as large as this of course. But when Kit turned up with all her old paintings, she needed somewhere to put them and we hadn't done any more on the idea of a flat, so they ended up down there. Then an easel appeared. Next thing I saw her buying paints.'

'She's started painting again?'

'Yes, and she's doing a refresher course at the university. She's thinking about doing her Masters in the fall.'

'That's wonderful.'

'I know, I'm thrilled for her. And for Rob, he's more the man I remember when they married. It's been an awful disappointment for them, I do want to see them both happier again.' Elsa paused. 'Though, I am a little anxious about them both being at the wedding, I must admit.'

'Not my idea,' Isabelle said, fiddling with a sash that had slipped on a chair. 'Kit drew up the guest list with Asha and James.'

'And how about you?' she asked. 'How do you feel about being at the wedding?'

'Me? Thrilled, I'm delighted for them.'

Elsa smiled at her as she straightened from the sash. 'You've made it beautiful for them. I haven't seen this room look this glamorous for decades, it's a revelation. Is this what you want to do with the house now, host receptions?'

'It's one idea, and Kit of course has made it seem easy. I'm sure it won't be that simple if I try and do it myself.'

'I'm sure he'd help you.'

'Yes, but perhaps I ought to be doing something I can manage by myself. Kit will get fed up with looking after everything for me, eventually.'

'I shouldn't imagine so. He's been more than content organising other people's lives for decades now, I can't see him changing,' Elsa said.

Isabelle watched her walking through the room with fascination, trying to catch her thoughts from her expressions as she took in the changes. It certainly looked different to her old workroom.

The walls had been stripped back to a bare, traditional plaster and painted with a colour that she could only describe as fondant, in a paint that was dead matt and seemed to change shade as it flowed over the aged ripples. The grimy fireplace had been sand blasted back to pristine, re-pointed stone, and the wood burner removed. Replaced with a huge open basket, backed up with low level, cast iron radiators staged along the perimeter. The window frames had been painted to match the linen in a tone Kit called 'greige' and her old curtains had been taken down. In their place, she had made plain cotton voile sheers, with natural buff linen outer drapes. All festooned onto the floor and held up with bosses on the sides, their sweeping edges softened with a delicate picot trim. On the fireplace wall two ceiling-high, arched mirrors hung opposite the outer windows, reflecting their light and views through the room. Three drooping glass chandeliers hung from the ceiling, in line with the windows, and at the far end there was a small, temporary, raised platform, that was to double as a ceremony area and a band stand. Beneath their feet the wooden boards gleamed from their new coats of oil and wax. Her solid old wooden door had been removed, the space plastered up and double glass doors repositioned in the middle of the wall, abutting the stairwell as it came down from the main hall. Outside them the old garden room had been converted to provide another reception room. Furnished with comfy chairs and sofas, decked out with a bar that led to the kitchen in what had previously been the old storeroom. There was no memory of the years she had spent down here, no memory of Moth's time either. The door he'd grown familiar opening, gone. Inadequate to the new, expansive life of the room.

Elsa wandered out from the main room to the base of the stairs, she followed and pulled the glass doors to.

'It's going to make your hallway terribly draughty in the winter,' Elsa said with concern. 'I'm sure that's why it was blocked up in the first place.'

'Kit refurbished the walls in such a way to install wooden panel doors at the top.' Isabelle pointed to the ceiling as it broke into a curve to begin down the stairwell. 'See, up there, there's a track concealed behind that wooden plinth. But we ran out of time to get them made. By next winter I shall be able to shut it all up.'

'He thinks of everything.'

'He does,' Isabelle admitted. 'Though I think I'll be glad

when he can slow down a little. I find it hard to keep up with his thinking-of-everything brain.'

'He always was a bit to handle. Kate's the only one who's never been troubled by it,' Elsa paused, her hand feeling the new wood of the banister as they went back upstairs. 'Are you and Kit still, you know, together?'

'I don't know. We're all too busy with everything to think about it.'

'That's not a great solution.'

'Hmmm.'

'Mind you don't both default back to what's comfortable,' she said.

'What do you mean?'

'Evasion, in your case, and... diversion, in his.'

'Diversion?' Isabelle asked, evading the first part of her comment.

Elsa smiled at her wryly. 'Yes, I suppose now they would put a label on whatever he is, except of course he wouldn't accept it. But, back then, they didn't have all these labels, Asperger's, Autism, ADHD. They call it a spectrum now. No doubt we're all on it somewhere. Kate and I called it "boredom disorder", it was the only way we could under-stand it. Kit's never liked boredom, he needs plenty of diver-sion, distraction, challenge. It seemed to me, after you and James separated, he wanted to change that part of himself. For you.'

Isabelle didn't respond.

'But here we are, all these months and distractions down the line, and he seems to have reverted to what's comfortable for him.' Elsa paused on the stairs, took another step upwards, added in a soft voice, 'Or whom.'

'You think he's seeing someone else?'

Elsa fluttered a look at her, returned to climbing the stairs, asking in a curious but absent-minded way, 'Do you?'

'I hadn't thought about it. He spends all his time working, or here, or helping Kate. I haven't got time to think about anything else and he's running circles round me.'

'Kit's not one for solitude, darling,' Elsa said. 'If you keep evading the conversation, I think you may find he moved onward. Or backward, as the case might be.'

'I don't evade,' she protested.

'Yes, you do.' Elsa linked her arm through Isabelle's as they reached the top of the stairs. 'Let's have a final cup of tea in your new study before bed. I'm proud of you dear, even if you did ignore your promise to me.'

'I'm sorry.'

'I know and, thank you darling, but actually you've done wonders,' Elsa led them both down the corridor towards the study. 'You've been loyal to your family. You could not have done more for any of us. But it's time to start thinking about yourself, Isabelle. Trust me, this house will take over your life if you aren't careful, and I'm not sure that's what you want, is it?'

'I'll go make tea,' Isabelle said, as Elsa chose a spot on the sofa.

'Camomile please, darling, else I shall never sleep.'

'Of course.'

'And Isabelle?'

'Yes?' Isabelle stopped at the door.

'I know you're ignoring me.'

'I'm not ignoring you, I'm making tea.'

'We'll talk when you've made the tea,' Elsa said. 'I do like what you've done in here, though I'm not sure about that desk. It looks more like a butcher's block.'

'I don't think anyone does like it, apart from me.' Isabelle looked at the new desk. With Elsa in the study, she was glad she had changed it. It claimed the room as her own. There was comfort in its shape and height suited to her. In the way it discomforted everyone else.

'Well, I suppose you had to start somewhere. What did you do with the old one? No, actually, don't tell me. I don't think I want to know.'

Isabelle left the room with a grim smile and went to make tea. Elsa hadn't seen the upstairs corridors devoid of portraits. Perhaps she would let Elsa make her own way to bed.

She filled the kettle, looking out the window towards the weir, wondering if Elsa was right about Kit. Who he might be seeing? She tried to capture that thought, focus on how it made her feel. But the soothing rush of the water from the tap, and the sparkle of it over the weir took all her focus.

NAT WAS at last impressed when she walked into the new workroom the next morning, after breakfast.

'Wow, this is different.'

Isabelle laughed. 'Different good or different bad?'

'Different amazing,' Nat said, going to look at the colour-coded, stacked shelves. 'I was always a bit scared of the other room, downstairs.'

'It's a bit friendlier, isn't it?' Isabelle agreed.

'Moth preferred the other one. He always liked it down there.'

Isabelle found herself drawing a breath again, caught on the ease with which she mentioned her brother. Nat used his name at any opportunity, and Elsa was unfazed each time. Not with her tongue stuck limp in her mouth. But Elsa wasn't there now. She'd gone into town to see old friends and collect some bits for the wedding. There was only her and Nat, fitting the dress. The silence seemed to stretch while she tried to think of a response.

'Shall we try this dress on?' Isabelle asked. 'Then you have to choose what you want to decorate it with.'

'Decorate it?'

'Um, Kit wants all of you to look individual. You have to choose whatever you want out of those baskets and I'll decorate the dresses with it.'

'Why these baskets?' Nat asked, looking at the ones arranged on the table.

'Kit chose the colours.'

'Oh.' Nat trailed her fingers through the dress that Isabelle had laid out on the table. 'It's very swishy.'

It was a flowing, chiffon, full-length dress, with plenty of layers in the skirt, and a wide satin band below the bust. They were identical to Asha's dress, but less elaborate, without the lace adorned top. Nat looked at the dress and darted glances about the room, looking for somewhere to change.

'I know, right,' Isabelle took charge. Dressing flighty people was something she could handle. 'Look, you jump into it while I nip next door. Step into it, pull it up, and it zips up at the side, here. I'll pop back in, and we'll check the size. I'll draw this curtain over a little. You can change here, and no one can see you from outside either.'

'Thank you.'

'No problem. I'll be in my study, call when you're ready.'

'Ok.'

Isabelle left the room, pulling the door to and walked into the study. Her mouth was dry. Moth was closer than he had been in months. Nat spoke of him as though he was there, still part of her life. The desire to speak to him crushed her and resentment, green-hued and heart lurching, lay thick in her throat. The hard surface of her desk beneath her hands felt coarse on her skin as she tried to calm her thoughts.

'I'm ready,' Nat called, her voice timid.

Isabelle took a deep gulp of air. She had to focus on the dress, on Nat. Not on Moth. She couldn't pump Nat as a source of information. She walked back into the room, saw Nat on the far side of the table, looking down at her dress. Her fingers stroking it with delight, her face flushed with pleasure when she looked up.

'Here,' Isabelle pulled a long mirror from behind the door, walking across the room to prop it against the shelves. 'Have a look, what do you think?'

'It's so long, and even swishier now.' Nat looked in the mirror, smiling, toying with the fabric. 'I love it, it's gorgeous. Thank you.'

'You're welcome. Now stand up straight for me.' She sank to the floor in front of Nat and ran her hands along the bottom of the unfinished hem. 'What shoes are you wearing?'

'Kit sent them, weeks ago,' Nat said. 'I've had to wear them every evening since, to get used to them. Flat pumps, they don't make me any taller.'

'Are they comfortable?'

'Now, yes. They were horrible the first few times.'

'How sensible of him,' Isabelle muttered from the floor. 'May I?' she asked, sitting back on her heels, and pointing at the waist of the dress.

Nat nodded. Isabelle pulled the side hems in, focused on the fit. Young girls all had such strangely shaped bodies, wide and narrow in the wrong places. She'd designed the dresses with plenty of darts in each, and the wide band was attached at the zip seam only until she finished it by tucking it into the opposite seam. She popped a few pins in, nodded.

'Right, slip it off again, and I'll take it in.'

They worked in silence. Isabelle at the machine, pulling in the seams, letting out others. Nat at the table, rummaging through the baskets of ribbons, beads, trims, buttons and oddities. When they convened again, she'd pooled an ambitious assortment on the calico.

'Try it on again,' Isabelle said. 'I'll have a look at these for you.'

She kept her back turned, sorting the decorations into colour co-ordinating piles which laid out the possibilities for Nat to consider again. The other, younger, bridesmaids had been unfazed at running around in their underwear between fittings. Nat was somewhere closer to an awkward awareness of her own body, and perhaps she would end up with the natural shyness that some people had about sharing their skin in front of strangers. Some actresses were the same. Coy in the dressing room, where they were still some part of themselves, no matter what indecencies they had to perform for the script when the cameras were turning. If she did any more dressmaking, she would have to set up a separate dressing room for her clients.

The morning room would be perfect.

The thought struck her with singularity. Coming at her with a smug completeness. As though the idea that she might do more of this, dressmaking, here at Riverdell, in her future, was irrelevant. What counted was the sensible solution of the morning room.

'I'm ready,' Nat said again behind her, startling her from the reverie that had paused her hands.

Isabelle turned to see Nat looking pleased as punch. The

dress was a much better fit now, and seemed to belong to her, rather than hanging from her shoulders.

'Well, that's a lot better, isn't it?'

'It feels a lot more comfortable now,' Nat said. 'I wish Moth could see me.'

Isabelle paused again, she had been about to go over and check the hemline. The mention of his name held her immobile. She couldn't stand it, the lightness with which Nat spoke of him, the weight like an anchor that it induced in her.

'You must miss him,' Isabelle said, rushing forwards as the words left her, dropping to her knees to fuss with the hem. She missed the thick rug that had been in here. Elsa had taken it with her, and Isabelle had patched the floor back together with older rugs from the old guest bedrooms. It was a mishmash of colour and design, but she wouldn't spend money on her workroom. Now, kneeling, she was aware of the hard boards beneath her.

'I do,' Nat said. 'I wish he was here for the wedding. It's scary doing new stuff without him.'

'What are you scared of?'

'All the people I don't know,' Nat said. 'And being by myself.'

'You won't be alone. You'll know all the most important people, they're your family.'

'And you,' Nat said.

'Yes, of course. Though I'm not as important, certainly not a bridesmaid.'

'But you are family,' Nat said. 'I wish Moth was going to be here.'

Isabelle paused from her tinkering with the unruly chiffon hem. An air of wistfulness in Nat's voice twisting her thoughts. She reached up and squeezed her hand.

'Me too, Nat,' she said, her voice strangled, her hand anxious. 'I miss him a lot, but especially at times like this. He used to make the hard things feel easier.'

Nat squeezed her hand back and smiled down at Isabelle. 'He emails me.'

'He does?'

'Yes, and sometimes a postcard, though they're not about places, but people, or animals. And they all come from London.'

'London?'

'So we won't know where he is,' Nat explained.

'I didn't know he had an email address.' Isabelle looked back down at the hem with a lump burning in her throat, moving her hands to work the light fabric fluttering between her fingers.

'I'm not supposed to tell anyone,' Nat said. 'He sent it on one of the postcards. Elsa said it was best kept quiet. I haven't told anyone else.'

'Well, that's very thoughtful of her.' Isabelle wondered if it was true that Nat hadn't told anyone else. She couldn't imagine Nat telling her something she hadn't told Hester. 'I won't tell anyone, I promise.'

'Moth liked you best of all,' Nat rushed on, her voice rising, wobbling with doubt. 'He told me to talk to you if something was wrong. If I had a problem. But I never see you.'

'Is anything wrong?' Isabelle asked. 'You know you can always call me, anytime.'

'I don't use the phone a lot. But nothing's wrong anyway. Just that I miss him. And that's not wrong.'

'No, it's not. It's not wrong at all.' She ran the scissors one more time across the front of the hem, to give it a last tweak, and sat back on her heels with a heavy sigh. 'I wish he would send me a postcard. You are lucky.' She paused, wanting to be strong, unable to resist asking, 'Does he say when he's coming back?'

'When he's sixteen. When no one can tell him what to do anymore.'

Isabelle laughed. 'Well, that sounds like Moth. Except it seems odd, that he's not sixteen, you know. Because he's already doing what he wants anyway, isn't he?' She looked up at Nat.

'Yes. I don't want to be sixteen. I don't want to have to do everything myself. It's scary.'

'It's not scary when you get there,' Isabelle said. 'And you're a long way off. I wouldn't worry about it yet.'

'I'll be at the end of senior school then. Moth never liked school, I do though. Especially this one.'

'What's best about it?'

'I get to walk by the sea on the way there, and on the way back,' Nat began an earnest list. 'Hester or Elsa come with me. And it's got lots of sports fields and playing fields, and a wildlife garden, and the classrooms are outdoors.'

'Do you have nice teachers?' Isabelle tried to catch up. Nat moved so easily from the intangible subject of Moth to the graspable one of school life. She moved her hand up to tweak at the solid satin band.

'They're fine. Except Mrs Vaughn is a bit bossy. I like Miss Byard best, she makes us laugh, and she laughs at our jokes. Mrs Vaughn never laughs at our jokes. And Mrs Thomas is always telling us how lovely we are. And Mr Morgan shouts a lot but he's nice too.'

'You have a lot of teachers.'

'I know.'

'It's a good place, huh?'

'It's my favourite school so far.'

'You must try and stay there, all the way to senior school.'

'Elsa says we won't move again,' Nat told her, but her voice wobbled. 'She says it's important that Moth knows where to find us when he's ready to come home.'

'I don't think she will ever move again,' Isabelle said, trying to comfort her. 'Elsa's not the moving type. This is the only time in her life she ever has, and I don't think she'll do it again. You can feel pretty confident you'll be staying there.'

'I really like it there,' Nat said.

'You don't miss here?'

'Not really, but it's nice to come back.'

'Especially for a wedding?' Isabelle asked, winded by Nat's childlike oblivion to her feelings.

'Especially for a wedding, though I do miss Moth more, here.'

'How come?'

'He liked it here,' Nat said, distracted now by playing with the sash of her dress.

Isabelle stood up, not responding. Nat's sudden confidence with her was overwhelming. Especially when every other sentence seemed to stab at her with a memory of Moth, stemming from her brother's encouragement to trust her. The months of activity crumbled in their achievement, exposing it all as an excuse for not trying harder to find him. Even Kit, who had promised to try and get in touch with him but had failed. Failed even to mention it again. Failed to find time, in the time he had thrown into everything else. A distraction. Isabelle frowned. Perhaps all along he had been distracting her too. While she waited and waited to raise the concern, to bring it to the forefront. To make everyone realise that finding

Moth should be the priority, not the issue forced to the bottom of the list. Find him and reassure him they would support his choices. He could come home. Trust them. Trust her.

'I like these ones,' Nat said, from the table, where she had moved. Drawn towards the piles of colourful things Isabelle had arranged. Isabelle walked over to the table.

'Let's get this dress hemmed up, then we can put it on the dummy and start pinning these on.'

Nat slipped behind her back while Isabelle stood at the machine, looking out of the window. The sunlight was weak, the cold wind buffeting the bare trees on the bank opposite the house. The house was warm enough, but she could feel the chill in the leeched colours outside, the wind blowing through the naked trees. Winter was harsh but the house kept them safe. Where was Moth in this weather? In a tent pulled over a bike frame. Guilt stabbed through her. It had only been a summer tent. Designed with weight in mind, not insulation quality. Or had he spent the winter somewhere warm, in someone's house? Someone who wouldn't send him back to a child's life.

'Isabelle?' Nat was looking at her, holding out the dress.

Isabelle felt guilty all over again. She felt her face flush as she took the dress. Nat hadn't forgotten her brother. Nothing had pushed him out of her mind.

'I'll do this now,' Isabelle said, sitting at the machine in a daze. 'It won't take me long. Do you want to get a snack before we look at the next stage together?'

'Ok.' Nat headed for the door. 'Do you want anything?'

'I don't mind, see what you can find,' Isabelle said.

'Should I bring it back in here?'

'Yes, that'd be great.'

Nat left the door open behind her. Isabelle sat at the machine, folding the fine chiffon twice on itself in a thin line and trapping it under the foot. With her knee she lowered the mechanism and put her hands ready to run the fabric through. They were shaking. She stopped, pulling them back, clenching them into fists. Putting her head down to the cool metal of the machine head, letting it vibrate through her, waiting for her to carry on. She closed her eyes and squeezed the tears back, gulping down the lump in her throat.

Opening her eyes, the thin fabric shimmered in her sight, waiting to be sewn. The line pinned down, asking her to follow it. She unclenched her fists and began to feed it through the eager needle. Churning up and down, piercing the fabric, thread spooling out to hold it all together. In the steady pace of the machine, the quiet fold and stitch, fold and stitch, which sealed the dress hem, Isabelle resolved to finish the job.

KIT CONSUMED the room with pleasure. The swagger stick tapping against his leg. Eyes encompassing the result. He had done this.

He opened his phone, found the notes folder and typed in WEDDINGS. How had he not done this lark before? It was a whole new market he'd never touched on. He drank in the details.

The stage hovering in a cloud of white gypsophila. Each tiny bud packing a punch. Counting the cost of the multi-hued flowers that littered the tables, that draped in a garland over the fireplace, the doorway, across the head table. Flowers were big business. He had always known this, known how important they were in houses, how they worked, how to create impact. He'd never known they quadrupled in price on one day, and not just bloody red roses either. All of them.

'You are jerking me off!' he'd told his florist when he found out.

'You want a Valentines wedding, you suck it up,' Dylan had sung back at him. 'And don't even dream of trying to get them cheaper elsewhere, you owe me this.'

Kit huffed and, once again, moved on from the flower irritation. The whole room gleamed comfort back at him. A child dragged from a filthy puddle and buffed and polished to within an inch of its life. He breathed in the scent of oiled wood, polish, flowers, that subtle hint of orange essence he'd added to the starch for the tablecloths lingering beneath, bringing it all together and keeping it fresh. His hands reached out, tweaking a chair into alignment, pulling a sash tighter, running a palm over the tablecloth to straighten it.

He glanced out the windows. It was bleak and threatening, a dark sky above the river making its swirls leaden and furious. If it didn't rain it would make a great backdrop to the photos with their multiple fragile colours. And if it did, well, there was the drawing room, and Isabelle had been right about the décor, he had been able to tune it to his colour scheme.

He walked out of the main room, back into the lounge area. Consuming the details, hawking the staff. Behind the bar he could hear the kitchen staff preparing for the dinner. A light soup, followed by rare beef, finishing with miniature cheesecakes that rose in a flutter to the pinnacle of a violet topped cream swirl. A waitress smiled at him, asked if she could do anything. He shook his head and watched her return to the bar. They were waiting, relaxed but ready. Kit felt coiled. He wouldn't relax until it was all over.

He stalked back up the stairs into the main hall, eyes scanning. It had to be perfect. His first ever wedding, he wanted it to set the standard.

He could hear the photographer in the drawing room, taking pictures, moving about on quiet shoes. He'd given strict instructions to photograph everything. He wanted to look over it later, through the critical lens of the camera, to see if he could improve anything. See what to do next time. Because there would be a next time, Kit was adamant. He was too good not to do this again.

He walked into the kitchen, pushing the door open. He'd knocked aside all Isabelle's door stops that morning, closing the doors to prying eyes, marking out the public arena. The kitchen was empty. It was half-past nine. He felt the kettle. Warm. Someone had been up. He checked the coffee machine. Cold. Not Isabelle. Elsa. Retreating to her bedroom for some peace. Sneaky old bitch. He'd been there since seven, after leaving Bristol at 5am. Someone could at least have got up to welcome him.

He swapped the stick for a cloth, wiped down the surfaces. He was agitated, and he knew it. He relished it. This waiting. In his design work decisions fell into place over such a long period, there wasn't this sense of grand conclusion. It gave him the biggest buzz. Knowing the day was poised before him like a performance caught his guts up in a knot that made him want to pin someone, anyone, to a bed and release it. He wrung the cloth out, picked up the stick, tapping it against his leg again, dropped it on the table. Moved to begin making coffee, packing grounds into the filter when the door pushed open behind him.

'Morning,' Isabelle mumbled in her dressing gown, pushing her hair out of her face.

'You must have smelt the coffee,' he mocked.

'No, I heard you busting the balls off the staff and thought I better give them some back up.'

'I was not busting their balls,' he said. 'I was outlining the day's order.'

'I was asleep, on the top floor, and I heard you,' Isabelle said. 'Sounded like ball busting to me.'

'Just waking them up for the day ahead.'

'What's this?' Isabelle asked, picking up the swagger stick, squinting at it.

'It's my thinking stick.'

'As in it helps you think or calms your thinking?'

'Both, possibly, not sure.'

'It's a bit intimidating, isn't this an old army thing?' Isabelle put it down, away from her, and pooled herself into a chair.

'It's called a swagger stick, and yes, it's an old army thing. That one is from the old East India Army. Which, by the by, your father and grandfather served in the dying dregs of.'

'How exotic, it suits you,' Isabelle yawned.

'Lou hates it, but it gets rather addictive,' Kit admitted. 'Coffee, sleepy head?'

'Thank you, ummm, lovely. What's next on the itinerary?'

'You wake up, get bathed, get dressed, become the epitome of a perfect hostess.'

'That's going to take some time, we only have until this afternoon,' she mocked him. 'Anyway, surely that's your role? I just provide the house, you organised all this, right.'

'Quit with the wallflower act, you need to own this day.' Kit threw the cup at the coffee machine, warmed milk, tapping into his irritation through the process. 'I don't want you acting all backgroundish. This is your statement. Your chance to show the rest of the world what you're doing here, what your house is going to be about.'

'The rest of the world?'

'Well, Hester, for a start,' Kit said, putting the coffee down in front of her. 'No more apologies Isabelle. Be yourself, be proud.'

'Hester won't like the changes.' Isabelle made a face, reaching for her coffee.

'So?' He picked up the stick, stalking the length of the table and back, tap, tap, tapping, pulling the smooth leather through the length of his spare hand. 'She's done her thing, moved on, new life. This is your chance to tell her to stop judging yours.' Tap, tap, tap. 'Show her you know what you want.' Tap 'What you've done.' Tap. 'What you're capable of.' Tap.

'Kit,' Isabelle said, looking at him aghast. 'I think I'm with Lou, you need to put that stick down.'

'What? Oh.' He put it down, walked back to the sink, cleaned some more. 'I told you it was addictive. But that's not the point.'

'No, the point is, coffee.' Isabelle used her cup to emphasise. 'And I just got up, I need to wake up. Stop scaring me with all these things I need to do, and be, today. All I want is to get through the wedding!'

'I know but...'

'No buts, no,' she said, raising her hand. 'Nothing. Not until I've woken up and had a shower, then you can command me. Maybe go look over the flats, or see if Kate needs anything? It's too early. Asha won't be here until midday. You'll drive yourself mad if you stay this focused until then. Why don't you go find Elsa, worry her into a bad mood too? In fact,' he watched as she stood up and circled the far side of the table heading for the door, 'I'll go right now and head for the shower, then I won't be sitting here annoying you, right?'

Kit watched her retreat through the doorway. He went and picked up the swagger stick. Perhaps she was right, maybe he did need to relax for a few hours. He would go and see Kate, she was always up early. He walked through into the hall, stuck his head into the drawing room. The photographer was still there.

'Did you get the stairwell?'

'Yep,' the man said from behind his lens, pointing through the window.

'The front porch?'

'Yep.'

'Here, what about these?' Kit picked up one of the multi-coloured cushions Isabelle had made, thumping it into plumpness, rearranging it back with the others, tweaking the piping stiffened corners. 'Did you get these?'

The photographer sighed and walked over to him. Kit forgot about going to see Kate. He had told the man to take pictures of everything. What had he thought everything bloody well meant?

'YOU NEED TO RELAX,' Asha told him. 'I thought I was supposed to be the stressed one?'

'I'm not stressed, I'm focused,' Kit said, looking at her from the end of the bed. 'Does that fold need to go there? Isabelle, do you think it needs adjusting, should you re-stitch it?'

'Kit, it's perfect, stop fussing,' Kate told him. 'You look stunning my dear, doesn't she, Elsa?'

'Beautiful,' Elsa said. 'You look radiant, dear. But come on, we must let Asha have some time with her own family. I came here to drag you out, not get dragged into a debate about remaking the dress. The bridesmaids are ready too, Kit. You might want to check them.'

Elsa walked out with Kate following.

'You're sure now?' Kit asked, frowning. 'Isabelle?'

'You know I can change anything if you want to,' Isabelle said.

'Of course not!' Asha protested, looking at herself in the mirror again. 'It's gorgeous, I feel amazing. Oh, I'm nervous now.'

'I'll send your mother up,' Kit said. 'Now, no last-minute jitters? You know you can say. It's a lot easier to stop a wedding than a marriage. And I don't think James will let you go once he has you.'

'Kit,' Isabelle said. 'Behave.'

'No, I mean it. Any doubts, now's the time to say.'

'Don't worry,' Asha told him. 'No doubts at all, just performance butterflies.'

'That's why they give you a veil, darling,' Kit told her.

'Come on,' Isabelle tugged on his arm. 'Leave the woman in peace. Good luck Asha, see you afterwards.'

'Isabelle, thank you.' Asha stepped forwards to hug her. 'Thank you so much.'

'You've nothing to thank me for,' Isabelle protested.

'No, you have a whole load to thank me for though,' Kit told her. 'Seriously, James had better show some gratitude later.'

'James is always good at showing gratitude,' Isabelle told him.

'Yeah, well, he's always managed to avoid it with me,' Kit said.

Asha gave him a hug, saying, 'well, I am very, very grateful. This is going to be an amazing day, and you've done it all. It's a wonderful wedding present.'

'See, that's gratitude.' Kit told Isabelle over Asha's shoulder. He held her back at arm's length and took one more critical look at the dress. 'You could do with giving James lessons on how to show it.'

'I'll work on him, I promise,' Asha said. 'Now, go, stress someone else out.'

'He's going,' Isabelle promised, dragging Kit out into the hall. 'Honestly, what is the matter with you, you're so on edge.'

'I'm not, I'm just...'

'Yeah, focused, I know,' Isabelle said. 'Have you had a drink even? I think you need a drink before the guests arrive. At least you put that bloody stick down.'

'Elsa took it away,' Kit complained. 'Now, where are those bridesmaids?'

'Cowering in a corner if they have any sense,' Isabelle said. 'Nat's bedroom. I'm going to get changed myself. I'll see you downstairs later.'

They heard Elsa coming back upstairs with Asha's parents. Kit made a face and headed for Nat's bedroom, where he could hear Kate's voice. Asha's parents had arrived a week ago and been staying at the farm. He found them irritating, with their thick accents, and their poor English. He couldn't connect the woman they'd created with the world they came from. He didn't have the patience to try and communicate, a process that demanded slow speech and monosyllables, as Elsa executed perfectly, leading them up the stairs. He knocked on Nat's door, praying they would answer before the new guests made the landing.

'Come in,' Kate called out. 'Kit, don't they look adorable?'

'Hester?' Kit said in surprise, seeing Hester sat in a chair by the window. 'I didn't know you'd arrived.' Kate rolled her eyes at him.

'It was all so hectic.' Hester gave him a flat look, uncrossed and recrossed her legs. 'Made it easy to slip in.'

'You look... elegant,' he told her.

Which was the best thing he could say about her careful beige slip dress. That covered up her collarbones, her shoulders, and extended to below her knees. She'd teemed it with a fine cardigan that lay on the chair, in a matching shade of indifference. Even her hair had been restrained from where it normally caressed her shoulder, wrapped back in a smooth chignon, with not a whisper of decoration anywhere. She looked like she was attending the AGM of the WI, not her adored brother's wedding.

'Well, I thought something simple. Mustn't outshine the bride, right?'

Her voice was cool, displaying none of her new, relaxed ease with him. As though she'd gone back in time and assumed her normal rigidity as she'd walked back into Riverdell. She couldn't have outshone a mushroom, let alone a bride. It irritated him, this resumption of the old habits, when he'd done so much, changed so much. It made him want to return to the same hostility and, only through an intense moment of unusual consideration akin to shaving his skin with the ragged edge of a broken beer bottle, did he manage to restrain from voicing the thought.

'Perfectly considered.' He gave her a tight smile and looked at the bridesmaids, who were bunched together, playing with their full skirts. Nat had her hair down for the day and it made her look older, released from its girlish pony-tail, streaming down her back. 'Well, now, who's going to twirl for me first?'

Hester needed to watch her step. He was not about to let her ruin anything. She needed to sit in that crappy beige apology of a dress, in the corner, and stay there all day. If she put so much as an unpainted toenail out of line, heaven help her.

'I'VE a good mind to drag you into the boiler room for ten minutes,' Kate murmured, leaning across to his ear and grip-ping the inside of his thigh, tight enough to his balls to get his attention.

He'd been staring at the guests on the other table, thinking about whether the beef on their plates was the right shade of pink. Isabelle had slipped away from his other side and gone to the toilet, taking advantage of the pause between starter and main.

'What on earth for?'

'To make you bloody relax,' she told him. 'Heavens, Kit, it's all done bar the drinking. When are you going to unwind?'

'It's not over yet.'

'Yes, it is,' she told him. 'Look around you. Happy couple, thrilled family, fed guests. Everything went perfectly, of course, why wouldn't it? Yet you're still wound up. You've eaten next to nothing. Have you even touched your wine?'

'I'll be happier when the meal is over,' he said. Hoping he could then let go of the knot inside him. That the great moment of achievement would be his.

'No, you won't.' Isabelle slipped back into the chair next to him. 'You won't be happy until the last person has gone. Never mind the wine, Kate, I don't think he's even taken a full breath.'

'It's my first wedding event, that's all,' he defended himself. 'I want to make sure it goes well.'

'I hope it's your last one too,' Kate said.

'Actually, I'm thinking of doing more,' he told her. She and Isabelle groaned in tandem.

'I'd be a great wedding planner! The first is always the hardest, you make all your mistakes. Then you have something to work on.'

'Mistakes?' Isabelle asked in disbelief. 'What mistakes, it's been perfect.'

'Of course it's been perfect,' Kate said. 'Everything you do always is. That's not what's bugging you. You need a break. You haven't stopped for months. I reckon the last time you sat down was on Christmas Day.'

'And before that I think it was Easter,' Isabelle added.

'I'll get a break when I've finished everything,' Kit told them. 'I have my annual in Italy at the end of next month. Just enough time to finish you off first.'

'Are you moving me, or killing me?' Kate asked. 'Besides, you always come back frazzled from that job, I'd hardly call it a break.'

'Change is as good as a rest,' he told them, glancing at the next table being served their beef, frowning. It was barely the right shade, dangerously close to overcooked. He had wanted the perfect shade of blush. Like the inside lip of the vulva, tempting, soft, raw.

Over the table he saw the polite distance on Hester's face, as she sat at the end of the top table. Her mother next to her,

James and Asha in the middle. Him looking rigid in his suit, loosening the collar. Her looking radiant, chattering to her parents on the other side, trying to pull James in. Conversation would be excruciating, but he'd seen a wry justice in getting James used to it. His new wife would be interpreting the rest of his life, why not his wedding dinner too?

On the table next to the happy couple, James' best man and many of the couples he and Isabelle had been friends with for years were talking and laughing with the bridesmaids. At the table furthest away sat Rob, making the best of a difficult table of older couples and singletons. Hester had refused to look at him, turning her head away when he reached her in the family line-up to greet the guests. Kit had felt a moment of sympathy for him, an urge to twist Hester's nipple until she showed some emotion. He tapped his fingers on the table.

'Kit.' Kate leant forwards and said in a bright sweet voice. 'If you don't drink a glass of wine, right now, I shall seriously embarrass you.'

'You couldn't,' he told her, but he did manage a smile. 'You're too socially elegant.'

'I shall stage a dramatic fall down the grand stairwell,' she declared. 'Screaming blue murder as I go and taking the flowers with me. I'm old enough now to get away with such a thing.'

'Nonsense,' he told her. 'You're not old, you simply grew laughter lines.'

'That's the definition of age,' she told him, gripping his thigh beneath the tablecloth, her hand inching higher.

'No, it's not,' he said, but he did pick up his wine glass. 'Elsa got old, you got better.'

'You make me sound like a vintage whiskey,' Kate

complained, her voice rising enough that the people on the other side of their table stopped talking and looked at them. 'Isabelle, did he just make me sound like an oak-aged barrel?'

'I'd drink up if I were you,' Isabelle said. 'You know she'll do it.'

'Alright, I'm drinking.' He admitted defeat, taking a large mouthful. 'I was only trying to stay sober until the pudding.'

'I can't believe you're worrying about the pudding,' Kate said.

'I'm not.'

'What are you worrying about then?'

He paused, about to say her, Hester, sat there with her cowpat of a face, emanating misery and disdain, when he wondered, why was he worrying about her? What on earth would she do? Apart from scowl, and condemn, and smile that polite, disinterested smile at everyone who spoke to her. And when had he ever let Hester bother him?

'I don't know.' He let out a deep breath.

'And... he breathes,' Isabelle said.

'You should be proud.' Kate let go of his thigh, leaving a chill in her absence. 'Your happy couple look ecstatic, what more could you want? You've given them a wonderful day they'll never forget. That all the guests will remember. You should be delighted.'

'I suppose I thought it would feel happier than this.' Kit let disappointment slide across him. Admitting how he was holding out for the climax of the day, only to realise it had gone. 'It's supposed to be the best day of your life, right?'

'And it probably is, for them,' Kate said.

'I thought it would be for everyone.' Kit could hear the dejection in his own voice, took another sip of wine to drown it. 'I mean look at her, what's the matter with her?'

'Who?' Kate asked.

'Hester. Anyone would think she was attending a wake, not a wedding.'

'She's in the process of a divorce,' Kate said. 'You can't blame her for not jumping with joy.'

'And she hasn't mentioned a word about the house!'

'For which I am so grateful,' Isabelle said.

'You sound so bitter. Because she hasn't read the script for your happy-ever-after,' Kate agreed.

'It's a fairly universal bloody script!'

Kate laughed. 'You sound like a frustrated romantic who's found himself embedded in a horror movie.'

'What's wrong with romance?' Kit asked.

Both Kate and Isabelle grinned at him.

'Neither of you are being very kind,' he told them. 'Everyone's a romantic at heart.'

'Everyone's a cynic at heart,' Kate countered. 'They just can't admit it.'

Isabelle was distracted by an old couple friend of her and James' walking up. Saying hello, congratulating her on the venue, inviting her to join them for a drink. She agreed, and stood up, following them to the bar area. He watched her go. She shouldn't be following. She should be leading, like the hostess she was.

Kit took a larger gulp of wine. A great gulp of air, pulling him up to the surface of a huge lake he was drowning in. 'Sod it, even Asha and James don't look that happy.'

'Stop whinging,' Kate said with an impatient tut. 'They look like any other couple on their wedding day. Busy looking after everyone else when they want to be alone together and dazed as hell. Let's face it, they didn't even know each other a year ago, now they're married, with a mortgage and a baby due. Come on, Kit, what did you expect?'

'I don't know, more than this.' He plucked a discarded cocktail umbrella from the table. They were pastel-hued rainbows. He'd hunted high and low to find them. 'I wanted it to be, amazing, you know? The most romantic day ever.'

'You softy,' she teased him, reaching a hand to touch the back of his, removing it before anyone noticed. 'Perhaps you have some unexplored ideas about love you need to think through.'

'What's that mean?'

'Next thing you'll be saying you want to get married yourself.'

He looked at her, grimaced. But she was right, in a way. He was disappointed with something. He took another sip of wine. Something that was always lacking at weddings. The sense of incomparable, all-consuming, overwhelming love, that made you want to give up your freedom for the chains of forever. Something he'd always assumed missing from other weddings because of the poor planning, or the lacklustre venue, or the cheap flowers. Not his weddings. Because they would be the intimate backdrop, the perfect, crafted setting for the purest love. Kit felt his chest cave in. The room was full of people, and they all seemed happy, but no different to the guests he'd sneered at through other weddings. He twirled the rainbow umbrella in his fingers, watching as the colours merged into sludge the same shade as Hester's dress. Full of the tiredness of love, not its grandeur.

'Look,' Kate nodded to the couple. He turned to look at James and Asha again. Their faces were bright, but tired. Listening to everyone around them, ignoring Hester's silence, their fingers laced together on the table between them. 'This is their brightest moment. They're both themselves, in love with the other. They don't know the distance they have to move towards each other. Or that, in doing so, they'll lose themselves. That's what marriage is; the loss of two people into something lesser than the sum of their parts.'

'That's a bit depressing.'

'But true,' Kate said. 'Look at Hester, she never made the journey, marriage failed. Look at Elsa, she's never been herself since she lost Richard. Since she married him. Is that what you want? To be part of something lesser.'

'You're so cynical today.'

'Being honest is not the same as cynical.' She gave him a strange, crooked little smile. 'And, honestly, aren't you already a little bored?'

'Bored?'

'With us?'

'I've never been bored by you,' he told her.

'I said us, not me,' she corrected him, turning away to look across the table, smiling falsely at another guest. 'Admit it, you don't cope with us this, well... this normal. This predictable. And what about you and Isabelle? You still think you want this permanent thing with her? Or that she wants it with you?'

'You're spoiling my wedding debut,' Kit complained.

'You're deluding yourself,' Kate said. 'There's nothing ahead of you but these decisions, and you can't face it, which is why you feel deflated.'

'Is there no part of this that appeals to you?'

Kate looked over at the newlyweds. 'I don't want that, for sure. I tried it once, used to gag on the word "Mrs", it never did suit me.' She shuddered, turned back, toying with her dessert fork on the table.

'What do you want?'

'I suppose I want what we've always had.' She paused, the prongs of her fork resting on the table, her fingers holding the shaft, pushing it into the cloth where four dimples appeared. 'Ourselves, unapologetic, getting on with who we are. Except...'

'Except what?' He leaned towards her, the wine kicking in, pulling them away from the others at the table.

'Except... not this secret nonsense of it anymore.' She lay the fork down, covering it with her hand. Kit felt an urge to put his over hers, knew she'd remove it. 'Maybe I'm getting too old to keep secrets. I worry it will come out, in an embarrassing senior moment of some sort.'

'And Isabelle?' he asked. 'What will she say if you tell her?'

'I don't know,' Kate retorted. 'What will she say if *you* tell her?'

'Touché.'

Kate's jaw tautened down the side of her face, her finger tracing the ridge of the rising fork. He moved his hand under the table, placed it on her thigh. She dropped the fork, moved her hand to her lap, laced his fingers between hers.

'What do you want?' she asked without looking at him.

Kit looked across the guests' heads, taking in the room hovering above them, all the wedding details he'd laboured over. He had wanted this to feel epic. To make him feel alive. Full of love and joy. But it was a wedding, same as any other wedding. Most couples not talking to their spouses, the bridesmaids were the happiest, the single women the sourest, the married men the drunkest. The weight in his chest slid beneath the table and sulked away.

'I want Hester to cheer up.' He felt her fingers unlacing

from his and pulling away. 'I want the beef to be a tad rarer. I want the waitresses to be quicker. I want Isabelle to stop acting the wallflower.' He gripped her hand tighter and, leaning closer, whispered in her ear, 'I want you, naked, spread on the table while I eat pudding from between your legs. A whip of violet cream on each nipple. With everyone watching. Except I don't think James would thank me for it.'

Kate laughed out loud, the whole table looked up as one, wondering what she was blushing at. 'That's my Kit.'

'But perhaps in the meantime we could find somewhere a little less public?'

'Now?'

'Oh God, please. Save me from this insanity.'

'Happens there's an empty flat upstairs,' Kate told him, eyes sparkling. 'Though I'm afraid it's rather cold and unfurnished.'

'I'll get pudding and meet you there,' he told her, standing up, pulling her chair back. He let her walk out of the room, turned and walked over to Nat, who was sat with the other bridesmaids. Crouched down beside her and took her hand. She turned to look at him.

'You couldn't do me a small favour, lovely girl?'

'Of course, Kit.'

'Your Aunt Hester is looking a bit lonely,' he said. 'You wouldn't go and join them at their table. I know you're having fun here, but I think she'd enjoy your company.'

'Of course. But I haven't had pudding yet. Will I miss it?'

'I'll tell the waitress to bring it over to you. Come on, let's find a chair.'

He took her hand, apologised to the others for dragging her away, and walked over to the main table, grabbing a spare chair in his hand from the edges of the room.

'Shift up, darlings,' he announced from behind Elsa. 'Someone wants to join you.'

'Oh, lovely,' Elsa said, with a hint of relief. 'Darling, how are you? Have you been having a fantastic time?' She made a space between herself and Hester and Kit squeezed the chair in between them.

'Pudding is on its way,' Kit told Asha. 'There will be a break while the band set up, and then the party can begin. I hope you're ready for your first dance?'

'It will be quite simple,' James protested.

'What a surprise,' Kit told him.

'I like simple,' Asha said.

'That's good then,' Kit said. 'I've got to sort the band out, I'll be back in time for the dance, but don't worry if you can't see me. You carry on.'

'Don't forget to enjoy yourself too,' Asha told him.

'I won't,' he promised.

Kit put his hands on Hester's shoulders. They were rigid, solid with discomfort. She was the old Hester, her armour tight about her. There was nothing of the woman he'd seen in Swansea. He leaned forward and spoke close to her ear, away from Nat. 'It's nearly over, don't worry, you can leave again soon. But it is your only brother's wedding. You might try and enjoy it, perhaps a little bit.'

He wove between the tables, into the garden room, towards the bar. Isabelle was sat on one of the sofas talking to her old friends, oblivious to him. Cushioned between two other women he knew only by sight, their partners stood beside them talking. She looked relaxed, indifferent to her own gooseberry act, glad to be out of the main room. Kit wondered, if he called to her, would she look up and smile? Leave them, come to him. Slip away to find comfort together.

Her head turning from one woman to the other, managing the conversation like a metronome. Doing what should be done.

From the kitchen he gathered cheesecakes, a bottle of wine and two glasses, and made sure a waitress knew to give Nat her pudding. He told another member of staff to go and greet the band and get them set up, not to ring him. He needed an hour's break. Then he left the party behind, shedding his sense of disappointment as he took the back stairs to Kate's flat, two steps at a time.

9

D earest Elsa,
What a year you are having. I can sense the frown between your eyes from here.

I am sorry to hear of your father's ill health. A suspected stroke is not the most useful of diagnoses, is it? Your father has always been the sort to prefer a proper problem he can get his teeth into, not some wishy-washy medical maybe. You say he is unaffected but appears diminished. I cannot imagine him ever diminished. He and Ted are so alike in that way. They both have that same unstoppable belief that they can set their course and steer to it. During those years at university, when Rose and Kate encouraged us to embrace feminism, I almost believed it myself. But now, well, the truth of the female body has forced itself repeatedly upon me. I feel keenly for your father. It is a vile thing to have your body betray you and be unable to do anything about it. Remain positive though, Elsa. If anyone can overcome health issues it will be your father, and he is yet only sixty-eight. At least there is the bonus that, as his health is affected, he is drawing you more into the running of Riverdell. You have a steadiness of mind and heart which well suit you to the task and I know you are going to be a wonderful successor to all that he has done. It must give him such pride and joy to have you close, and your help will relieve him from some of the work and aid his recovery. I hope Richard is coping with your absence during the day and is still full of his love for the farm. You sound utterly contented, even with your concerns and worries. I can imagine you now. I bet you still carry a novel wherever you go, just in case.

Thank you for the news of Kit. Rose is a tardy writer and sends me occasional flurries of photos and very little news of her dear boy. How he has changed already, and I love that you say he is a fierce poppet and full of laughter. I am glad that they have been often to Riverdell and your father grows fond of him too. Trading toffees for stories of guts and glory. What on earth can a toddler want to hear of an old man's stories? And surely most toddlers would refuse to hand over a toffee to anyone? He is already a chatter box. I can imagine Rose talking politics to him while she breastfed! Dear Lord, this boy is going to be unstoppable.

I am devastated by your news of Kate. How awful for her. She wrote nothing of the matter, and to be that painfully close to the line of legality. It must have been infuriating for Rose, to be so close to helping her and a step too far away. To have to go with her to such a place and watch Kate going through that... I must stop, I will be weeping over the page. I am so glad she came home to you to recuperate. That she has you there to support her, and Rose to stand beside her, gives me the greatest comfort. ~~You cannot imagine how much I long for you all here, beside me.~~ And as for Patrick, I take all my good opinion back. How despicable, to have told her

whole family behind her back. No wonder she threw him
out. She never had the easiest relationship with her grandmother, but now? To be making such a difficult decision like
that and have to deal with her family abusing her. Rose
always had her concerns about him. Must she be right ALL
the time? I guess no one knows the depths of their faith until
it is tested. Once a Catholic, always a Catholic, as you
suggest.

Kate wrote nothing of his work issues. I did not know that
she was the only wage earner, and then he expected her to
quit to raise his child? What on earth sort of life would she
have ended up with? But I suppose we all write a shine on
our lives. It's hard to see the truth down in black and white,
isn't it? As for trying to talk her into going home to live with
you permanently, I am not sure. Perhaps if she returns to
London, she might yet resolve her marriage. Though I know
divorce is becoming socially fashionable, there is the inner
voice of failure to overcome. Is it our place to try and
persuade her of anything other than her own wishes?
Perhaps give it a little more time? These last few months must
have been raw for her.

I have returned to Kashmir, which I confess to feel more
my home in India than Bombay. Our own news will, I fear,
only add to your frown, but please do not dwell on it. We
were delighted to discover I was pregnant again, in December. The long rest in Kashmir last year seemed to help my
health, and the pregnancy, though difficult, blossomed
through the winter months. You will forgive me for not telling
you, Ted and I both felt ragged with hope, and did not want
to jinx the process. It was a precious time together. He was so
devoted. Home from work more often, taking me out to see
more of Bombay than I have yet explored. I had even decided

to stay there for the duration, for better access to doctors, and to avoid the long trek up to Kashmir.

Sadly, my body had other ideas. I miscarried in late March, just as the weather was getting warmer. A nineteenth week miscarriage is no fun. Did you know, if it had happened but a week later, I would have officially had a stillbirth infant? The doctor seemed to think that information would be some comfort. I cannot begin to tell you how awful I felt. What a failure this body of mine is, that it cannot even fulfil its most basic function. I knew something was wrong for a few days, my stomach felt too quiet. I was holding my breath waiting for movement. It was as though I could hear the baby saying goodbye. I did not tell Ted, I am so anxious that he will end up treating me like a china doll and I was right for, when I did, it was straight to the hospital. And hospital in India, even the private ones, are no joy. The doctor said 'no heartbeat' – how lightly they dismiss your months-long hopes and prayers with a few brutal words – and insisted on a D&C. I will not go into the details of that. I had to stay for over a week, the bleeding was so bad. And it was many weeks before I left my bedrest.

Ted was devastated. He was horrified by the gore of the medical side. Even though I told him to stay out of the room, he insisted on being with me. ~~But I fear his seeing me, my pathetic dignity exposed, our tiny child scraped from my womb broken piece by piece, has left a distance between us. How does a couple recover from such a thing?~~ Afterwards, as work called him back to his normal hours and the heat of April became purgatory, I think we both felt the need for a sojourn from each other and the sadness of our loss. Now, it is July, and the Valley has restored my spirits. Kish is the most wonderful woman, she seems to know exactly how to care for me, to restore my spirits and health. In Bombay, Sai treats me like a broken vase, in need of coddling, while not quite looking me in the eye. Kish always looks delighted to see me, shows me what needs doing, and immediately we set ourselves to the new task.

Ted has yet to join us. His work has kept him long hours, even during the rains. When he does come, I know we will be better again. So, although my news is tinged with sadness, do not worry for us. Restored to health I am determined to keep trying for a child. It is natural, is it not, to feel troubled after the late loss of a pregnancy? It is far more common than people think, and I will not sink into despair. I wonder if it would be better for me to stay in Kashmir, rather than returning to Bombay. I know this would hamper our time together as a couple, but if it helps me bear a child I would do it for a short while. I will speak with Ted and see how he feels. ~~Perhaps you could speak with him, but no.~~ Please, do not tell Kate about the miscarriage. With all that she has gone through herself and her own courage, I do not want to trouble her with the news. The doctor called my loss a spontaneous abortion. It comforts me to know that, even this far away, I am connected to all that is happening in your lives, but I doubt this would bring any cheer to Kate, and her own experience would be a far worse one.

All winter I had hoped we might return to England this year, with a grandchild for your father and a play mate for Kit. How I dreamed of that return to see you all. For now, the issue of coaxing this reluctant body of mine to do its duty is my highest priority. I will not risk travel until I have seen a pregnancy through to the end. It will be a while yet before we see each other, and all so busy in our lives that the distance is prohibitive. Rose with Kit, you with your father, and Kate with her career. ~~I begin to understand the great loneliness that has been part of Ted's life, and the sense of insuperable distance between himself and his home and family. It leaves a hollow place in the heart that yearns to be filled. Perhaps it was only this which attracted him to me? A sense that I was part of Riverdell and could comfort him.~~

I remain your dearest friend and miss you all so much. Forgive the messy letter, I have scribbled over the worst of my grammatical errors to save your syntactical distress.

LOVE,

BETH x

10

He blinked. Ached. Stirred. Light and the noise of traffic flickering through branches.

It was late afternoon. The homegoing rush on the roads across the fields had woken him. He made himself move. Twisted by the pains in stomach, chest and at the base of his spine where they all seemed to be having a party. Spent an hour drinking water, eating crumbs. Listening, breath held, hands stilled, to the few cars that pulled up by the copse, turned into the lodges. Car doors banging. People calling. Letting out his breath when the sounds dispersed.

He traced his next move out on the crinkling surface of the map. There was a wide old bridge below him that had been made redundant by the new road. He waddled a painful crouch to the far edge of the trees, looking out. It would have once been a major road bridge, now it was sealed to anything bar foot traffic. Weeds growing inwards from the edges. It would save him a long retrace and miss the main junction across the river with its busy traffic. Back in his makeshift nest, he added the information to the plan. Over the bridge, across the main road, straight onto the route through the southern mountains. They weren't as big as the ones he'd come through, and the passes were a lot lower. He had to get over one big uphill and the road would take him down, curving its way along the quieter valley floor.

Moth tapped the map in comfort. He was tired, painful, numb with the desire to not move and starving. But he had a plan. And hunger was good. It meant his stomach had settled.

You're getting better.

When the quality of light dipped low enough to make people concentrate on the road, he left the copse and wheeled down to the bridge. Across the road. Hit the new route. Within 100 metres the incline hit his leg muscles and he realised how weak he was.

His plan for a restful day with three big meals had ended in a day of puking and stomach cramps. With nothing but staling bread in his bag and some oat flakes to keep him going. He passed a supermarket, stopped, went back. It was a quick five minutes. Coke poured into his water bottle, and a bag full of boiled sweets tucked into the front bag. Pastries, fresh full-fat milk for the oats that night, a seed mix, dried fruit. No more than that, feeling the added weight in his aching spine as he pulled back onto the road and started focusing on the climb.

Houses thinned and disappeared as he hit the first switch-back. He set his eyes on the road and watched the tarmac crawl beneath the tyres. His legs screaming at him, his stomach clenching, hunger fading into pain.

You can do this. You can do this.

He put a sweet in his mouth. Sucking until the outer coating cracked and released the nugget of juice inside. The burst of flavour and sugar battling the pain. When the sweet ran out he took a tiny sip of coke, counted to a hundred, popped another sweet in. The road passed, the sweet bag diminished, and Moth kept cycling on dead legs and a wrecked system.

What would Luca do if the fifteen applications were turned down? Would he keep going? Or give in and remain a barista?

It's not much of a plan.

Moth pushed himself on. It was all well and good having an impeccable plan, but you had to have a system in place for when the plan got crumpled. Beyond even a Plan B. An underground system to keep on going when the plan got hijacked. Like counting names when he had to overcome a reluctance to mount up. Or now, cycle, eat sweets, drink coke, count and repeat. With a destination ahead. Over one hundred and seventy kilometres to do.

But you'll get there.

He had two days left of hard cycling to get to Kit. It wouldn't be the gentle cruise down the valley he'd expected.

But you can do it.

He was later than late, but hopefully Kit would be there.

There or not, you're going anyway.

Moth popped another sweet in. Lovere would be as good a place as any to stop and recoup. Before he moved on with the plan. Maybe not to conquer the UN, but to conquer Asia.

Cycle, eat, drink, count. Repeat.

Somewhere in the rhythm, images crept in. Mila. Luca. Nat. Isabelle. Kit. Moments and words popping through the pumping of his legs and the sweet drizzle of sugar down his throat. He tried to push them all back, but they were stronger than him. He downgraded his expectations, peeling them away one at a time. Putting them in their place.

Kit he would see soon.

Or not, what's the difference?

Nat he would see again, though she wouldn't look the same. She would be older.

Nat's fine. Nat's with Elsa. You sorted Nat.

Luca. Mila.

Hopefully, you'll never see them again.

Maybe on the front of the news a long time in the future. In a flash office, with a smug quote attached.

Isabelle. Isabelle he couldn't picture in the future. Only in the past.

It's in the past. You don't need to go back there.

Perhaps he might see her again. When he returned home, or back to England anyway. When he went to see Nat.

It's in the future. It's not today.

The incline bit in as he rose through the chilling night air. The space between thoughts condensed.

By midnight he'd crawled up the ascent and was riding fast through high, fine air thickened with the sluggish scent of moist fir trees. The road undulating along the side of the mountain as it took him south. The relief from pain and mind-breaking, soul-carving physical effort giving him a high. Fuelled on the empty bag of sweets and the coke.

He passed hotels, villages, road junctions. Cars came past him both ways with pitiless intensity. The road was not as fast as the one he'd moved away from, but it was narrow. The cars indifferent. The odd one gave him the full width of the lane but most swerved past him with barely an inch to spare, even on an empty road. As night deepened, they got nastier. Tooting their horns in a long screech as they went past.

Ignore them. They've got nothing better to do. This place is their life. You're just passing through.

Moth sensed local frustration with the presence of cyclists. Though he hadn't seen many, perhaps he was an early reminder of the tourist influx that would come in the following months. The tension of it, of waiting for the next one to wobble him in the blast of air, bit into the place of feeling high.

Mila crept back into his head. Her breasts disturbing him. How they squashed against her arms when she wrapped herself up. How they pushed at the buttons on her shirt. The loose breasts of the girl in the tent that morning, swinging against her shirt. The flattened breasts and nipple eyes of the girl on the beach. A car roared past, taking another drop of his confidence with it.

Bastard bloody drivers.

Moth squeezed the handlebars tighter. Luca overrode the breasts. His apron strings sitting above the line of his jeans. The way he glided across the floor. Effortless. Making the world pause around him. The way the bike made life still, while he floated through it. The curve of his forearms, the tattoos on them. He wondered what the tattoos meant.

Why does it matter?

He focused on Isabelle. Because when the other girls disturbed him, she could calm him. Her hair falling over her face as she sat on the stool. Her legs twisting like a puppet's as she pulled her feet up beside her. Always struggling to look comfortable on a chair. The oddity of the shapes she made with her long limbs. Knees making mountains as they reduced a place or time to a position all her own. The same shape Luca made, propping his foot against the wall, sticking his knee out to the side, watching Moth puke. Their thin bones drawing shapes in the air. Fascinating him. Making him look, making him...

... a car blasted its way by in a rage of noise. Close and fast enough that the bike wobbled in the rush of air...

Goddamn wankers!

... making him, making him wonder...

Never mind, just bloody focus. Get off this road now.

The strain of the bike, the fading sugar rush, the nerves sent soaring by the cars. Moth buffeted between memory and sensation. Funnelling into an intense painful pressure on the saddle. It was gone 2am, he'd made at least forty km that night. He pulled into the trees, hauled the bike up above the road, sweating with the effort, and found himself a green padded space. Huddling into the curved roots of trees. Staring, exhausted, into the black space above and inside his head. Trying to shut his thoughts down with his hand.

It was not good. He needed a piss and the conflict of interests had him up, leaning against a tree with his eyes clamped shut. Managing a trickle of urine through a sore dick and a pained hard on he couldn't ease. Pain intensified throughout his body. The desire for relief etching into a deeper discomfort. He gave up trying and wrapped up in the sleeping bag instead. Leaning back against the tree, too tired to manage the tent.

You should get the book out, write the day in.

He wasn't sure where he was, which would mean pulling the map out too. The bag was tucked behind him, cushioning his back from the tree. It would all mean moving. To write those few pathetic words, dates, numbers.

You can do it tomorrow, pick the next place name.

The trees were huge above him. Swaying in the wind. Their branches whispering to each other. Shy touches. It was comforting, pushing aside the sensation that his body was trying to come apart. Reminding him of people talking at a distance. Good people. Old men in the squares arguing. Children running and squealing.

How do you know good people from how they sound?

How could he know Luca was good? Or Isabelle? How could he know Hester was damaged, or Elsa sound, or Kit trustworthy? How could you know anything about anyone? Except with experience.

He focused on the moving screen of branches and the glimpse of stars teasing behind them. Not constant enough to catch his gaze. The wind pulling the trees in eddies that his mind wanted to make a pattern out of and couldn't.

There were too many thoughts he couldn't put to bed.

Too much flak in the plan.

It's all too much. You've got to let something go.

Awareness of the density lifting it in an instant, into the night sky.

He made a decision.

He would email Mila when he got to Lovere. He would find out if she had taken the tickets or not. Then he would forget about her. He had given her a chance.

One chance is all it takes.

Luca's words floated across him.

Oh, stuff Luca. He's nothing.

Some smug dreamer stuck in a dead-end job.

He would contact Mila and find out what she'd done. Then he could move on.

One less thing to fret over. You should put the tent up.

His eyes drooped at the thought of the effort needed.

He fell asleep thinking about Luca's apron strings. The intricacy of the knot tightening as he pulled at it, tired hands finding comfort at last. Moving beyond the exhaustion of his body. The wind irritating him even as it lulled him to sleep.

· · ·

HE WOKE on the edge of a grey dawn, as the first raindrops began a threatening crash through the trees. The stars had gone. The wind was whipping the treetops across a dark dawn. He rolled out of his bag in a start, got it away as the drops turned to a cruel, quickening persistence. He yanked his cycling cape out and over himself and the rucksack. The panic ending with shaking hands and his heart booming in a chest that was struggling to catch breath.

Relax. Breathe. You'll wake up in a minute.

He tugged the bike back down to the road, slipping on the damp ground, and over the barrier. Rode away as the rain grew vindictive. His legs were soaked, the damp splashing back up under his cape. He was drenched in sweat again and his stomach was numb with hunger. Two km of soaked riding and he found a bus shelter. Ate breakfast beneath its false cover. Cold porridge oats in creamy milk. Freezing in his damp clothes. Cold from lack of movement. He waited twenty minutes to see if it would come back up. When his stomach held it together, he smiled. It was a small precious victory. He was good again, back on the road.

Able to eat.

From the narrow shelter he watched the rain nibbling into the small dry patch it created. Consumed by the shining damp of the road, the coursing water gurgling off the mountain. A car went past, the water surging upwards in its passing, collapsing back onto the road.

It's going to be a wet shitty day.

There was no point in changing, he'd stay warm with the pedalling. He wheeled the bike out and started off.

The damp road threw rain up at him as fast as it was

falling down the back of his neck. The helmet channelling rain in a wind tunnel down his cape where it chilled his back. His legs were cold from the thigh down, the constant slight abrasion of his moving legs rubbing the hair sore where the wet cotton extended over the Lycra. Clothes that helped him look local didn't work well when the weather got wet. Now he needed base layers and clip shoes.

His control on the bike was thinner than normal. The odd slip of the tyre on the deepening puddles. The pull of the bike as its wheels slid out of harmony with one another. The strain in his feet to keep his shoes on the pedals. The damp weight of the day a constant additional drag on his muscles. He left a wake behind him of wind and water.

It was nothing compared to the deluge that went over him when cars swerved past. Going fast on the steady decline. Hugging close to him on obscured bends rather than waiting to pass on the straights. If there had been no straights he would have understood, but there was a constancy of them. A long steady gentle downhill, the straights long and dependable, the bends sharp but infrequent.

With arseholes in cars determined to be annoying.

All of them drenching him. It was intentional. Their way of telling him he shouldn't be out here.

Moth retreated into a world of sound. The rain pelting against his back and on the bike, sluicing past the frame, morphing him and the bike in to a tunnel. The suction of sound away from him as a car approached, passed, roared away. The silent second before the impact of water. Watching with dripping eyes the retreating cars with their indifferent dry occupants. Cursing them to hell and back.

Not back. May they never come back.

It was bike-hating turf. He'd gone through similar in

Wales, in Ireland, in France. The local economy must have decided to cash in on their cycling heaven landscape without consulting the residents.

The residents are an inbred bunch of ignorant arseholes.

The long hours of the morning stretched out along the road. His pain began to tease. An ache that if he concentrated on would move, disappear, settle elsewhere.

There were moments of emptiness. When the sounds and the focus pushed out the rest. Long straight stretches of no cars. Him moving through the world, numb to the damp or the cold. Floating free from the pain in his body. Brief seconds when he knew his feet might slip, or his wheels spin. That the edge of the road might throw up a bump and send him careening. That a car might come past too fast, too close, and send him surging in the aftermath. But they were distant thoughts. Flying backwards with the water. No one in front of him.

Alone in the world. Free. Unfettered.

As free as the motion that took him along. When the confusion of Isabelle's connection or the irritation of Kit's selfishness disappeared. When Mila's vulnerability didn't worry him, or Luca's brilliance overwhelm him. When he hadn't a worry in his head about Nat. When his mother didn't look at him from the front door as she slipped out of it for the last time. Moments when his father had never existed.

This is why you do this. For these moments.

Moments when the past was all behind him. Sound slipping into stillness. Him hurtling through the frozen space into beyond. Beyond the person they'd all made him, into his own bright space. Pure, clear, fresh as mountain air.

Moth tried to focus on those moments, clutching at them. But another car would come. His stomach would clench. The pain would move inside him and grab his focus. Faces would impinge themselves again. In those moments he was overcome with fear.

That the stillness would never come back. That there was nothing beyond. That he would always be dragged back to those memories. To the murk of those days. That old, tight place where he couldn't breathe, couldn't think, couldn't dare.

It's just a shitty wet day. It will end.

He pushed himself past hunger, waiting for a village or town to appear and give him a chance of lunch. By the time it came he was soaked through and frigid. His hands protesting as they uncurled from the handlebars. He sat, the bike beneath him, leaning over onto one foot. Breathing short, sharp, hard breaths and trying to persuade his body to straighten up and dismount.

Shops, cafes and lodges herded along the main road like cattle at a trough. He could see them trickle out at the far end of a straight run of tarmac. Cars parked in neat angles like arrow fletching. Bigger trucks abandoned where it suited them. All shining bright from the deluge that had turned him to a dripping lump, smug and sparkling in their complicity.

He scanned the nearest windows, steamy with occupants getting out of the rain. Eyes looking out at him in bemusement at his choices. The doors looked indifferent, unwelcoming. None of them with that crisp sheen of paint that had tempted him into the café in Male. Luca might have made him feel pathetic yesterday, but Luca was impressive. Luca had been a vision of self-mastery even before Moth had started hurling.

As bad as Kit. Never a hair out of place.

Today he would be a drowned broken rat in front of much lesser people. His reluctance to move increased.

You need food. Go get food, get back on the bike.

The rain streamed across his vision and blew a gust of water into his face. He wiped his eyes. Without taking a room there was nowhere he could rest and dry up. He eyed the nearest café.

A hot drink. Some warm food. A quick exit.

He looked down the road, considering how far it might be to the next town. A longing to get away pulling at him. It was too wet to get the map out. This crushing place was the best he could hope for.

He propped the bike up outside, his fingers too cold to try and chain it up. Pulled the helmet off, clipped it over the saddle. He smoothed his drenched hair over his head, felt it dripping down his neck. With a grimace he peeled his dripping cape off, threw it over the bike and went in.

He walked into a room full of men who all looked up as he entered. Watching him drip on the floor, his clothes sticking to him, his face red from the cold. The door swung shut behind him. Moth felt the collective sneer of disdain as they turned away from him. The only woman in the room was stood behind the counter. A young woman full of contempt for his presence and his dripping.

Great. A bit more contempt. You could do with some of that.

He ordered a hot chocolate and a toasted panini, speaking in quiet Italian. Picking a bag of sweets from a basket and some milk from the small fridge that fronted the till. There was nothing to do but stand and wait. No spare seats even if he had the courage to drip on one of them. He could feel eyes boring into his back. Murmuring and laughter escaping his understanding. The sense of their dislike was framed in the frown on the face of the waitress. In the way she dropped his change into his outstretched hand, keeping her distance. Her silence as she took his order and served it to him.

At least you won't be wasting any time rescuing this one.

At the door he fumbled with the hot drink, his cold hands and the tight space. Struggling to turn the handle and open the door. He spilled a bit of the chocolate onto his wrist and wiped it on his drenched shorts to prevent it dripping on the floor.

The chair nearest him scraped backwards with a tut from the occupant. He heard speech directed his way. Laughter rippled out across the room in response.

Moth never looked at them. He wasn't sure what it meant, something about a shower, and didn't want to engage in finding out. He opened the door and walked out.

Inbred idiots. Ignore them.

Sucking his spilling fear back inside with great gasps of needy air. Sweat rushing over him, making him gag. His shaking hands trying to pour the hot drink into his bottle on the rack, struggling not to spill it, to be swift and get away from the watching eyes. Rain pouring back over him. Running off his hand into the bottle. He squashed the plastic cup and the food into his rucksack and pulled the icy, limp cape back over him.

He pushed the bike out onto the road and left. Full of a vile taste in the back of this throat and a throbbing hatred in his head. His chest wrapped up in a grip of pain, lancing down his spine and into his legs. His fingers numb, gripping the handlebars and his feet heavy with water, struggling to stay on the pedals.

You need to get out of town. There'll be another bus stop to shelter in.

He needed a rest. Rest and a chance to eat and drink the

hot chocolate. Its scent wafting up from the rack between his legs. Sickening in its sweetness, making his mouth water. He cycled down the long straight stretch without another sideways glance. The trees closing in as soon as he left the shops and the grey sky overhead disappearing to a narrow strip between their high wind-tossed branches.

There's going to be a place to stop just up the road.

But no respite appeared. The sides of the road trapped by high banks that had been cut out of the rock. The road inclining uphill, the water running down it in fast shimmying ripples beneath his tyres. It was a battle to keep the bike on the road and no option to get off it.

Just get to the top of this hill, there will be a lay-by, a bus stop, something.

The hill increased its demand on his legs. He was wracked with pain, trying to focus, fumbling on the pedals. He stood up on the pedals, pushing his anger into the work. Hunger turning his stomach to mush in the rising scent of the hot steam. Pushing away from the café full of men, the town full of men, the roads full of men.

You're not one of them.

Hatred for them. Hatred for how weak he felt. Hatred for the bike. For the painful turn of the wheels rubbing on his raw skin. Hatred for the tears that were blurring his vision and wouldn't... just ...

... stop. You're not the same.

All of them, all thinking they knew better, they were better. Tears mixing with the rain, and if it would all... just...

... stop... you just need... to stop.

Moth never heard the car roar up from behind. He felt the deluge that surged towards him as it passed and the splintering sound of laughter. Lost in the impact of water. The bike rocking beneath him. He saw the crude gestures they were throwing at him.

Saw the sparkles, lost and tumbling in water.

Falling from the hand hanging out of the driver's window. Heavier than water.

Saw it pulling away from him, the windows closing against the rain.

Get off the bike! Get off, now!

Watched the glistening points as they tumbled down the road toward him and felt the wheels crumple beneath him as they punctured.

Watched the bike tip him over the handlebars and pitch him into the air as it flipped out from the road.

Watched the slender metal frame of his free life crumple against the bank and ricochet backwards as the dark, wet bank of hewn rock came towards him.

Watched the drinks cup crush and the hot liquid erupt into the air, steam spiralling through the damp cold rain, as his head impacted.

He felt it ripple through him. Shuddering along one agonising vertebrae at a time. Himself following the crumpling bike. The crushed bottle. Collapsing on to the road. Landing on the sharp sparkling tacks that littered the roadside. The multiple points stabbing his skin even as the tarmac shredded both away.

The sound of the rain falling retreated from his ringing head. Sound morphing into an explosion of light. The cold of the rain, its wetness on his skin, the tarmac under his helmet, he could see them, but not feel them, hear them. Only sight worked now.

The bright blood covering his hands and legs didn't hurt. The tacks in his skin were shiny, not piercing. The rain was falling in front of him, not touching him. He lay on the tarmac. Black, endless, gleaming in the wet. Watching the spinning back wheel of the bike, lying on the far side of the road. Its flaccid tyre warping the movement in a fascinating imperfect arc.

Oh. No. No. No. Hell. No.

Warmth washed over him. A blissful relief to the day. No sense of cold or damp or pain. Sweet, encompassing warmth.

At least if you're going to die, it'll be warm, not wet.

It was a shame about the hot chocolate though.

He lay back, waiting for the warmth to take over. Knowing no pain was a good sign. It meant he was done. Wanting the images outside to stop and let him go. He closed his eyes to stop looking at the busted bike. Watching the sky dancing over the valleys. The white Mont rising against the blue sky. The grey road disappearing into motion. Lying with his fingers touching Isabelle's under the wide bay window. Hoping death would be a longer version of those brief peaceful moments he'd known. That they'd been preparing him for this longer endless peace.

It's been such a shitty few days. Death seems fine.

Behind his eyes sweeter images danced.

Cool, this is definitely how death is meant to be.

Luca was first. Looking down at him in the road. Seeing all his filth. His bloody hands and legs. His drenched arse sticking up. His stupid hair sticking out from his hat. His dumb face pressed to the road.

Luca, looking too cool and perfect.

Moth wanted to smack him. The crispness of his shirt against the ripples of his hair catching his breath.

Then Mila. Standing watching him as he rode circles

around her. Looking out the window of her poky little flat over the dark alleyway. It had been raining on him then.

Nat. Trying to skim stones across the river at Riverdell.

Isabelle. Close beside him in the river, hands and bodies touching in the cold water. Stood soaked against the tree in the garden, their bodies hot and wet and icy.

Luca. In the shower this time. His clothes wet through.

Why's he wearing his clothes in the shower?

Nat again. In her bedroom at home. Their old home. Before Riverdell.

His mother. Stood at the door, about to go out. Her eyes frowning at him. Her mouth a disappointed line.

Not that.

The closing door. The smell of dinner cooking on a Sunday.

His father. Stood by the study door.

Don't do it.

Moth opened his eyes and dragged a deep breath in.

Get the hell up.

He didn't want any more memories. If dying meant going back through those memories, he would leave it for now.

Get up, dammit.

Ringing sound returned, hammering into his head. Sound too big for the space it needed to be in. Pain pretending to be sound.

This is going to hurt.

Luca came back. Shimmering between the rain and the glittering tarmac, backed by increasing ringing noise. Luca again. Somewhere between the memories he had to go through on the way to death and the pain that was trying to break through the sound barrier in his head, Luca was the freshest memory to try and focus on. That crisp white shirt. Which had to come off to get Luca in the shower.

Why can't you bloody well focus.

He raised a hand to his head, rain washing his blood out of the long gashes across his palms and knuckles. When he managed to get his monumental, gargantuan, ten-tonne hand as far as his head, the simple touch connected all the fragmented parts of the moment back together.

Moth groaned. Pain ripping outwards from the touch of hand to face. Blood washing down his dripping face with the rain. His shoulders were agony. His knees shredded on the tarmac. His hands lacerated.

You should see the bike.

He looked across the road. His stuff was collapsed on the opposite side. This lane was covered with shiny tacks and his bloody body. Sound came back with the exhalation. Followed by a wave of panic. Warmth chased out in shaking cold.

He looked up and down the road. He had seconds maybe before a car came. He looked sideways. High banks both sides of the road, higher than he could climb.

Damn. Damn. Damn.

He pulled himself up to his knees, gasping as his head rocked him in the opposite direction. If someone came now and saw this, they would try to help and call the police. Or they would blame him and call the police. Or they would see the tacks and call the police.

He scrabbled about on the road, trying to gather the tacks up. If he ignored it and someone else got injured, it would be his fault. The rain falling fast, the tacks slipping out of his hand. He managed to stand up, throwing a bloody handful of tacks against the far bank. They scattered again. Rebounding from the hard rock barely hidden under moss.

What a waste of time. Give it up.

Moth watched the sparkles rise in the watery air between him and the bank. Fall back onto the road. Not enough to cause a problem to anyone except a cyclist.

Yeah, great, they were clever. Just great.

He looked up the road where they'd gone.

You hope they've gone.

Hoped they weren't going to come back to see how successful they'd been. Or waiting further along to add to his bloody humiliation. He hobbled over to the bike, picked it up from the road. The back wheel was bent from where it had hit the bank. Both tyres were limp. The lights were smashed up. He tried to straighten it out. The handlebars were bent. There was something else. A kink that wobbled the wheel as he spun it.

At least the chain's intact.

The bags were clinging to the panniers, though scratched and dented. He picked the bike up, its weight making his injured shoulders scream. Causing pain to lance across his chest, underneath the pain that had been there for days, making breath hurt.

Great, more pain. On top of the pain you already have.

He staggered under its weight, back over to the right side of the road and past the remaining tacks he could see. Put the bike down and began to push it uphill. His shoulders were splitting apart, his hips wrenching, his head bursting. The limping kink of the bike causing a rhythm to how the pain lanced through him. The hands on the handlebars getting sticky with his blood. His clothes were soaked through and his helmet was loose. Jarring on his forehead, and against his ears. Feeling even more broken than him.

Better it than you.

A car came up the long tree-tunnel road and passed him. Moth cringed inside, praying it wouldn't stop. It went past in another backlash of rain.

You needn't worry. You're nothing more than an obstacle.

Three more passed him, a truck went downhill on the opposite side. Eyes firmly averted.

Within 30 yards the pain had intensified to agony. Fear of passing motorists reducing to grim hatred of them.

Of the whole inhumane human race.

Panic reducing to a shaking awareness that he was lucky to be alive. Coupled with a rage that he couldn't just be dead. That even being dead was as much wrapped up with his father as being alive and in this mess.

His legs turned to jelly, and the dead weight of the bike on flat tyres was pulling his body back down the hill as he pushed himself up it. As he crept to the top the banks lowered, and the road came out into the forest again and opened out into a long straight. Each step a sworn expression of hatred.

Urging himself on. Taking the next step.

As soon as he could he hauled himself and the bike into the soft earth under the trees and worked his way back from the road. Further and further from the tarmac and the passing cars, up and above them, where he had the vantage. Where he could look down on them.

He found a large rock thrusting up out of the ground, covered in moss with fallen trees leaning against it. He tucked himself behind it. Under the lee of the trees. Snapping away dead brittle branches to make space for himself. The bike leaning against them, covering over the gap. His hands raw with the tarmac scrapes, reacting to each piercing fir needle. Huddling into himself, wrapping his arms about his knees.

Tucking his head onto his chest. Letting the rage vent and spend itself. Curses turning into hated tears ending in shaking humiliation.

You could've done with that chocolate now.

When the shaking lessened, reduced to no more than pain consuming his body, he crawled out of the woody pit and took a long hard look at the bike.

It's not going to fix itself, get on with it.

It took him over two hours to repair the inners. To get the tacks out and, with brittle fingers, patch the inner tubes and get the tyres back together and back on the bike. The rain worked its way through the shelter of the tress, forming bigger drops that he couldn't avoid. Fat juicy drops of freezing pressure that hit him from all angles. His whole body was shaking.

Junked out, scared out. Post-adrenalin.

He tried to eat, but his body rejected it. Left him puking his guts out on the soft forest floor. When it stopped, he stood up, felt a worse pressure, hurried to squat. Waves of cramps leaving his legs screaming from the position. Hobbling to get away from the stinking piles before the next ejection.

Oh, this gets better and better.

Returning to the bike, his fingers slipped with the tyre levers, opening fresh wounds with a pain that reduced him to sobbing and clutching his hands in agony. Wiping away the tears, hating them, hating them, hating them.

You said you wouldn't cry. Stop bloody crying.

The same grey tinge that had started the day began to edge back into the sky. The pressure of trying to get the bike back together and back on the road before dark fell pushing him on.

He needed to find a town, get the bike fixed. Somehow.

You have to get out of this valley of bike-hating arseholes.

He had to get to Lovere. If he could get there, he could rest, recover. He focused on the bike. It didn't matter if he was broken.

You can fix yourself later.

If the bike was functional, he could keep going. Finally, it was enough. The bike was back together.

Barely enough.

He was maybe five hours ride from a decent enough town to get some help. He would ride through the night until he got there. Riding would warm him up.

If you stay here, you'll freeze in the night.

Moth worked his way back down the slope. Each step hurt a new part of his body. Trying to keep the tyres up was torture. Throwing his leg over the frame sent shooting agony up the length of his back. He pushed on, feeling each turn of the pedals wrenching the pain in his hips. Images tumbling through his head. Grating through his mind at the same pace as the pedals. Glimpses of people. All smiling at him.

What's so funny?

The pain in his body moved to surround them. The intermittent rain lashing him, picking up on a wind that he had to ride straight into, chasing them all away. The weather slackening and letting the images tumble back. The slow descent of the road kept him moving forward. The valley floor coming closer one excruciating rotation of the wheel at a time.

All you have to do is stay on. Just stay on.

He stopped three times before he made it to the outskirts of the town, Tione di Trento. The bike fighting back. The tyres going flat on him. The chain staying on but grinding through a gut-wrenching stammer that pitched the bike sideways at random moments. The handlebars no longer aligned to the wheels. The whole effort of keeping it going forward making him gladder than he'd ever been to get off it. Pushing it through the streets.

It was well past midnight. The streets were deserted. He was starving. Soaked from sweat and rain. Cold the moment he stopped. There was nowhere to get dry, to get food, to get sleep.

Urban stealth mode. Great.

He turned down a quiet back road. From that into a quieter alleyway, filled with security fencing and large roller doors. Rammed the bike against a crumbling stone wall between two industrial waste bins. Crouching down in front of it, his back against the pannier, shoulder against the metal bin. Pain shooting through his legs as he tried to force them into the new position.

At least it's cold enough the bins don't smell.

The wounds on his hands were chapped from the wind and his raw face dried into a position that wanted to break. He prised the helmet from his head. It was held together by the inner lining of its hull. A long clean break down the solid case. Fibres teasing apart at the back join. He put it under his butt and sat on it to save the muscles in his screaming legs. It crunched as his weight landed on it. Useless now, he'd need to replace it in the morning. He curled himself round the backpack on his knees. Rested his chin on the front bag. Let his body sag into their support.

Opposite him a cat sat on the wall of an outbuilding and stared back. He knew what the cat must think. He'd seen himself in the dark reflection of windows as he rode into the outskirts.

Mangled.

He couldn't think of a better word.

A mangled tramp.

Out in the dark with the grim night-walkers. Except the cat looked slicker and fatter by far.

More loved. More belonging.

Moth smiled at the cat. It was even better-looking than Luca. At least he didn't want to punch the cat.

'Puss, puss,' he called, trying to tempt it. The cat looked at him, turned its head down, hiked a leg up and began licking its arse.

Puffed up fur ball.

Agile puffed-up fur ball.

Moth stayed there, letting the rain run off his cape. Making a mini tent, warming up in the foetal curl of his body. Listening to the rasp of the cat's tongue in the silences between distant traffic. Too tired to get the notebook out and write in it.

The blinks lengthened and became slower, longer. Focusing on the repetitive movements of the furry neck until the last minute, defeat and exhaustion sliding over him. The numbness extending. The sound of rain falling on his head, soaking down beneath the cape. The sensation of water puddling under his trainers. Consuming him with a creeping, weighted chill.

ISABELLE SIGNED the final paper and pushed it across the table to Rob. It was done.

She had signed the farmhouse over to James and Asha. Mr and Mrs J Threlfall.

On this, the first day of March, in the year twenty thirteen.

If any of her doubts over what she was doing had woken

her in the early hours of the months gone by, they were stamped out by the newlyweds' signatures. A careful blueprint claiming their future. It took away the painful knowledge that had crept over her yesterday. The day that hadn't been there, that missing leap day anniversary of David's funeral. When her mind had been full of Moth and Nat, and all the grimness they must have gone through.

She leaned back in the study sofa and felt the thrill of relief seep into her. It was done. The wedding debris was swept away, the farms were sold, the flat conversion was being painted, and Kate was moving in in two weeks' time.

'Well, that's it. All done, for a bit at least,' Rob told her, putting the top back on his pen and folding the papers back into their neat manila case. 'How does it feel?'

'Unbelievable,' she told him. 'Surreal, actually.'

'It's good to stop for a bit,' he said. 'You've done a lot in a short space. Kit's wise to make you draw breath.'

'I'm looking forward to doing something else,' she admitted. 'Just got to get Kate moved now, and that's it. My future is empty.'

'You haven't been to India for ages, will you go back?'

It had been April last year when she'd come home to Riverdell, almost a year since. It was hard to reconcile, the time passing, the things achieved. Back to India? She hadn't thought about that. Work had become something else.

'I'm not sure. Perhaps. It's been nothing but Riverdell for so long. I want to work out what I do next.'

'Isn't this enough?' Rob asked, gesturing at the pile of documents, the room behind them, the ceiling above.

'No,' she said. 'That was Elsa's life. I can't be her. It would be like trying to live her life, but I don't have the same reasons. She had a family, and it guided all her decisions. I need to work out how I look after this, but also, why I'm doing it.'

'Well, at least you'll have the time to do it now.' He began to pack away the papers into his briefcase. 'I won't be troubling you for any more signatures for a while.'

'I'm sure you'll find something for me to do,' she mocked him. Rob had a precise way of going about life, careful, measured, calm. She'd always thought him a bit bumbling before. Now she'd seen how proficient he was, yet humble. If Kit could summon a royal banquet with the snap of his fingers, Rob would pack you a working lunch. No waste, no unnecessary packaging, every nutritional need considered. She would miss his regular visits. They were part of what made up her life now. 'You'll come over for dinner anyway. Won't you?'

'I don't think I can keep imposing working dinners on you, Isabelle,' Rob joked. 'I'll have to find another client to keep me fed and watered.'

'I never thought of them like that. You're part of the family.'

'That's kind, and it's been appreciated not to be cast out, but...' Rob paused, pulled his glasses off and closed the arms into themselves, tucking them into his shirt pocket.

'But?'

'... but I must face reality, Isabelle, and it resembles Hester's face at the wedding.' He dropped his eyes to his hands, rolling his thumbs along his nails until they wrapped into fists. Releasing them. 'Our nisi is due through any time. After that it's a matter of weeks to the absolute. We won't be family anymore.'

Isabelle watched him back. Strange. Hester hadn't felt part of the family at all at the wedding. She'd arrived without fanfare and left without farewell, while the band was playing the wedding dance song. Unnoticed until several hours later. Asha had been tight-lipped about it, Elsa had been apologetic, James had been sympathetic. Isabelle had taken it as normal. In all his calm assistance over the last few months, Rob had been more a brother to her than anyone. And here he was telling her he wasn't family.

'Well, you're a friend, by choice,' she told him. 'And don't try and weasel out of it, because I don't have that many friends now James and Asha have nicked them all, I can't afford to lose any more.'

'Yes, friends disperse quickly when you separate, don't they?' Rob said. 'Most of ours seem to feel the need to invite me but are embarrassed when I turn up. I've started making work excuses and declining the invites.'

'Well then you can't avoid to decline mine,' she argued. 'Contracts, nisi, absolute or not, you're to keep in touch. In fact, you're invited to Kate's housewarming.'

'I didn't know she was having one.'

'I mooted it with her.' It was a shallow rendering of a conversation Kate had pushed away, but Isabelle was sure she would relent, and Rob's inclusion was a good enough reason to argue for it. Weren't both she and Kit always telling her to be more commanding? 'Saturday the 23rd March, she should be done by then. Kit's flying out to Italy on the 24th, he's booked the movers for the week prior.'

'Ehm...'

'Thanks for the invite, Isabelle, I'd love to,' Isabelle mocked him in a man's voice.

He smiled, said, 'thank you, Isabelle, I'd love to.'

'That's better.' She stood up, stretching. 'I can't believe it, all the work done.'

Rob stood up, collected his case, and followed her out of the room, saying as they walked down the corridor and past the old silk map of India hanging in its new space, 'It's been a lot to sort, you've done well. Stayed calm with it all.'

'I don't know about that. I could have stabbed the builders in January, not to mention Kit, at least a few times.'

'But it's all good now, you and Kit, right?' Rob asked behind her as they emerged into the hall.

'I have no idea,' she admitted. 'Kit's focused on work, and, if I think about it, I'm not sure I want him to change focus.'

'Why's that?'

'I don't know that I want to be back in his focus.' Isabelle stopped in the hall, turning to Rob. Enjoying the sunshine that flooded the decluttered centre of the house, the pale walls echoing the lightness of her relief to be shod of assets, to have secured the farm for James. Surprised at how readily her words came out. 'It's so intense with Kit, like wearing blinkers. Everything else seems to slide out of sight.'

'It was the same with IVF,' Rob said with heavy, slow sympathy. 'I began to feel that life had slipped away, and the only thing left was this intense need to make a child. Until I realised it wasn't the thing I wanted. I missed going out for a meal, or going on holiday, or even, just reading a good book.' He blushed, shrugging away the weight of the admittance.

'I understand.' Isabelle laid a light hand on Rob's arm. 'Kit has an absolute sense of what he sees as a priority. I get a bit lost in that.'

They paused together on the hall rug, its colours brightened from dry cleaning. Their honesty rising into the clear light, floating up to the ceiling's witness. No response came, and they both smiled, unsuspecting of how good it felt to voice those thoughts.

'Well, time to go,' Rob said.

'Great, we'll see you on the 23rd?' Isabelle dropped her hand.

'I'll look forward to it,' he told her.

'Take care.'

'You too.' He leaned forward and kissed her on the cheek, as he had always done. She walked him to the doorway and watched as he drove away.

In the passing of his car Isabelle could catch the bass beat of decorator's music in Kate's flat. Carpets were due to be fitted in three days' time, the electrician was turning up intermittently to finish small jobs, and the plumber was back daily with gleaming fittings that fixed niggling issues. They were no longer her concerns. Kate was in charge, coming and going as she pleased. Supervising, observing, considering. Isabelle noticed a change the morning after the wedding, a space widening between them, as each tried to work out where they fitted. Kate asked her less about the flat, told her more. Three days ago, they had signed the tenancy contract. Rob instructing her not to give the contract to Kate until the date the tenancy was due to start, the 15th March. As she couldn't give Kate the keys and did not want to restrain her access to the final stages of the flat conversion, Isabelle left a set beneath a pot of mint on the porch, for the builders, and retreated from going there herself as much as possible.

She was using the front door more and more. In the porch she'd placed a boot rack, and a bench, to throw wet coats over if needed. She found neglected pots from the garden and created a circle of exclusion within the open sided porch with them, buying a tragic looking herb when she went shopping and transplanting it into fresh compost. They waved back at her, glad for the rescue, not knowing any more than her if they would thrive or wilt in the space. Happy to try marking out a territorial difference between the porch that accessed Riverdell House and the adjacent doorway that marked the entrance to Flats 1 and 2, as yet untouched.

Isabelle turned from the altered view and walked back inside, letting the door swing shut behind her. Fifteen more days. Upstairs she could hear movement and singing.

Mrs Wisniewski had extended her weekly visit into an arrangement that suited her own convenience. Calling in for a few hours several times a week, her incomprehensible songs becoming the marker of those days, post-wedding, pre-Kate. Settling into domestic acceptance of each other's peculiarities that might stem from a cultural difference or a bacterial one. Like the horror expressed in rapid Polish when the oven door was opened; Isabelle had never thought of cleaning it. Or the day she walked into the kitchen to find the table covered with bags of icy food from the depths of the freezer, lambasted in the same swift Polish for the dates on them; Isabelle hadn't looked in the freezer beyond the level where she added fishfingers or frozen vegetables and removed them. Their learning a way around one another unfolding into a new rhythm, while the coffee machine whispered at her and the pages of the diary turned their way to the fifteenth and Kate's arrival in the flat.

Kit rang and asked her about possible events she could host, but she pushed back any decisions until after Kate was moved. He swallowed his irritation and told her about his work schedule. Elsa rang, urging her to think about the summer months and booking events, to think beyond Kate moving in. Isabelle asked how Nat was, and if they'd heard from Moth.

Isabelle looked at the fifteenth in the diary whenever she

went into her office. At the writing, her writing, increasingly
circled, outlining the event, 'Kate moves into Flat 1'. Staring at
it, thinking about the house jobs she should do, the thoughts
about the future she should organise, the gardener she
needed to think about hiring. Sipping coffee after coffee and
when decisions didn't come, wondering instead about where
to make curtains for next. It was as though she couldn't think
beyond that date, beyond the final hurdle. Something about
it teased at her concentration.

When the coffee cup emptied, she walked into her workroom. Fingers caressing the folded shades of fabric, pulling
out a fond memory, laying it on the table, wondering how it
might combine with another. Packing them away. Wishing
Asha would call in and motivate her again. But Asha was
juggling work and moving into the farmhouse with James.
Moving aside generations of stored affection to make way for
the swelling new life. Dropping in for fleeting herbal teas,
scrunching her face in distaste, stroking her belly and leaving
the cup unfinished.

Ten days passed in this way. Time in which the weather,
wet and windy and spiteful, hemmed her indoors. Where the
house was calm. Not quite empty, nor quite in silence, but
stiller, lesser, than the furore that had been the past few
months. Waiting for her head and body to adjust to the new
strangeness. Waiting to see who would descend and make
their demands first. Waiting for the fifteenth. An emptiness in
the rooms which echoed the emptiness in the house, which
began to speak of the emptiness inside her.

On the Sunday morning she rose and dressed, pulled to
her window by the swishing sound of the trees across the
river, whipped by a strong wind she couldn't feel. Watching as
the weak sun glinted back from their young, lime green

leaves. The morning was light, fresh in the way of early spring. Too fresh, hopeful after days of overcast weather. Ignoring the likelihood of worse to come before it really did improve. The valley curved away, and in its stretch towards the hills made her recall Moth, as it always did. She left the bedroom and was about to go downstairs when a thought, a nudge, a memory pulled her up at the top of the stairs.

She stopped, looked across the hallway and went towards the spare bedroom. Opening it she found the baskets of collected scraps that Kit had made Fred and Ed haul up here when they could get no more in the old sitting room. She knelt on reverential knees, rummaging. Hands finding memories. People and places that felt such a long time away. Finding, buried beneath the surface of her latest basket, where she had tucked it to keep it safe and not had time to recover, the scrap that Moth had given her. Her body leaning back onto her feet, her mouth expressing a long, slow silent out breath.

She took it in. The swallowtail pattern of the cross weave. The rough shadow of the grey weft. The welts of scarlet stripes softened by the hovering surface threads. Recalling the train station. His words as he left. The scrap given knowing he would be leaving. She could place it now, as she hadn't been able to before, the woollen coat of his school uniform. Cut knowing he wouldn't be there to face the backlash. Memory unfolding in her mind as she folded and unfolded the scrap like a childish wish maker. All the way back through those days, to the time when he had been here. To the days before she came home. To the last 15th of March. His birthday. That she had missed. The scrap lying open in her palms.

She had forgotten his birthday.

It had become Kate's moving day instead.

She couldn't believe it. Pushed away the shame of failure. No, it couldn't be. Felt memory sink back on her again. Hot in her stomach. She was certain. She had to check.

Isabelle ran downstairs with the scrap in her hand. On the shelves behind her desk in the study were the rows of diaries that Elsa had kept. Sharp spines all the same size, holding a page a day, with meticulous notes recording the life of Riverdell. On her desk, the current year lay open. Elsa had sent her a new one for Christmas, to continue the habit.

She reached for the spine that said 2012. Flicked backwards, pausing to register the gap in silent pages when the confident handwriting had changed from Elsa's to hers, hesitant and self-conscious. Moving beyond it, to the careful neat lines that sometimes filled the page, sometimes scratched the surface. Isabelle home from India. Moth and Nat arrive at Riverdell. Moth's birthday, 14 yrs. David and Sandrine's funeral. David and Sandrine's accident. But there it was. The fifteenth of March. His fourteenth birthday. No comment on what they'd done, or how they'd celebrated. Bracketed by the immensity of the other events.

The emptiness of it appalled her. She recalled telling him, the first time they'd met, that he got to hope for better the next year. Isabelle felt sick to her stomach.

She snapped the diary shut and put it back on the shelf. In the open one on her desk, she flicked again to the fifteenth, finding its well-worn corner only five days away. Beneath the circled note that had overtaken it, Isabelle wrote in large letters, Moth's birthday, 15 yrs. Her pen hovered over it, wanting to write more, desperate to write more, drooping in despair.

She stood back, closing her eyes, pushing away the

horrible truth. She had forgotten. He would think she didn't care. She didn't know where he was, how could she even hope to show him she cared.

It was the most awful thought. Emptier than the house, emptier than the rooms, emptier than herself. It made all she'd done feel foolish, petty, selfish. Her, Kit, Elsa. All of them burying themselves in work, giving up on Moth.

Isabelle's eyes opened wide. Not all of them. Nat. Nat had said she emailed Moth.

Isabelle grabbed her phone. It was mid-morning, they would all be up.

'Hello,' Hester's voice replied.

Isabelle rushed on, 'Hi, Hester, it's me, Isabelle.' Cringing, feeling an idiot.

'Hello, Isabelle,' Hester said. 'I'll fetch Mother for you.'

'I wanted to... speak to Nat, actually, if she's there,' Isabelle interrupted her.

'She's here.' Hester drew in a breath as though to carry on, pausing. Isabelle could hear her battling the desire to ask why she wanted Nat, being protective but resisting the engagement that asking would achieve. 'One moment.' She let out the breath and went away from the phone.

Isabelle waited, heart pounding. She had never asked to speak to Nat before, didn't know what to say.

'Hello?' Nat said into the phone, voice shy.

'Hi Nat, it's Isabelle. How's your week gone?'

'Good, thank you. We went to the museum with school, and I got Child of the Week at assembly.'

'That's great.' Isabelle searched for words. 'I remembered what you said, when we were fitting your dress, about keeping in touch. I thought I'd ring and say hello.' Isabelle paused, searching for words. Looking round the study for inspiration. 'Things have become less hectic. It's been quiet here all week, the workmen have pretty much finished and Kate moves into the flat next week.'

'Is she excited?'

'I think so,' Isabelle said. 'She's certainly busy.'

'Are you?'

'Excited, or busy?' Isabelle teased.

'Excited?'

'Yes, I'm looking forward to it, but I'm enjoying the quiet too.' Isabelle went quiet and realised how hard it was to talk to a child on the phone. Nat waiting for her to continue. 'What are you planning to do today?'

'We're going for a walk in a minute,' Nat said. 'It's not raining for a change.'

'Oh, I better let you go. Say hi to Elsa for me, will you?'

'Ok.'

'And Nat?' Isabelle fingered the rough scrap between her fingers.

'Yes?'

'When you email Moth, will you wish him Happy Birthday from me, please.' She faltered, not wanting to say more. Knowing she shouldn't even know they were in touch. 'Tell him that, from me, please?'

Nat paused, said 'Ok', but with a happier tone than the rest of the awkward conversation.

'Can I call you again?' Isabelle said. 'To see how you're doing?'

'Yes, I'd like that.'

'Thank you,' Isabelle told her. 'Have a nice walk.'

'Ok.'

'Bye for now,' Isabelle said.

'Bye.'

Isabelle ended the call. Stood by her desk, holding her phone in her hand. Longing to say more. Tell him to call me, tell him to come home, tell him I miss him, tell him I haven't forgotten, tell him I hope it was better. Happy birthday was the least of it.

She looked about her, head cocked, eyes squinting. The days dissolved in this way, Isabelle realised, looking at things and wondering what to do next. While the doing of things got pushed back. Unlike Kate. Or Kit. Or Moth. Who seemed to push back time itself with the doing of things.

She held the small scrap, felt its weave. In five days, he would be fifteen. A year on, if Nat was right, he might even come home.

She pulled a pin from the pincushion, harpooned the scrap to the centre of her desk, and stared at it. Moth wasn't the only one who needed to find his way back. She had been something, before all this chaos was unleashed. Perhaps by the time he made it back she might work out what she was doing. Decide if she was going back to work in India. Or building her own life and work here, at Riverdell. Five more days, and it would stop, this waiting for other people.

She remembered her suggestion of the house-warming party to Rob and grimaced. Why had she done that? She counted on her fingers, five to the fifteenth, eight more to the 23rd.

Thirteen more days.

And she would begin again.

KIT LAY IN BED, propped up on pillows, holding onto Kate's hips as she straddled him. He was worn out and feeling lazy with it. She was anxious and bad-tempered. It wasn't the best combination of his life.

They'd bickered during sex the night before, falling asleep more out of irritation than satisfaction, until she woke him with her hand round his nuts, moving astride him when he grew hard but refusing to otherwise respond.

There was something homely about it. This last shag in the old flat before the removal trucks arrived. Behind her swaying body he could see the boxes piled up on the floors, the empty shelves and open doors of the wardrobe. This was something she needed more than him, to say goodbye. He'd already christened the new flat and simply wanted to get the mattress there.

'Concentrate a minute, would you,' she murmured down at him. 'I can't keep this up all morning while you budget a client's swimming pool refurbishment.'

He grinned up at her. Raised a hand to support her breast, lowered one to tease her clitoris, feeling himself sliding in and out of her as she rose and fell. She responded with a finger exploring the rim of his anus. That caught his attention. He raised her up, turned her over and pulled her waist into him with one arm, keeping a hand on her breast, leaning back and probing more deeply.

'Thank you,' she said. 'My hips were on fire.'

'Happy to serve, ma'am.'

'You do it so well,' she replied and, closing her eyes with a contented sigh, leaned into the pillows, raising her hips higher towards his delving dick. He stroked them both to a happier mood and, when they were done, pulled her down into a close cuddle. Kate smoothing his chest while he cupped and stroked her breasts. Aware of his sperm leaking out of her. A warm trickle against his thigh, her leg tossed over it.

Kate's breasts had always fascinated him. Through the years he'd had many arguments with numerous gay friends over his bisexuality. Bi made no more sense to them than it did to his straight friends. How could you be one or the other, or even both? Many gay blokes he knew had an intense dislike of breasts, of their movement, of their weight. They couldn't understand how he could hold one, take one in his mouth, taste it, get a hard on. Kit was hard from the first moment he'd noticed Kate's breasts, back when his mother had brought him to Riverdell one summer in his early teens. They'd consoled him at night when he'd moved to live with Elsa and life in general, plus the specific departure of his mother, enraged him, pushing sleep away and turning him to masturbation. Wondering to himself if it was normal to be fantasising about her breasts and the new PE master's packed crotch in the same wank. Not much caring considering how hard he was with the thoughts. Teased by the way they moved with her, with her deep breathing and her expressive shoulders. How they had a weight that had seemed disproportionate to her fine neck and sharp collarbones. How you could see the lines of her bras under the fine blouses she wore, the clip holding it all together at the back when she leaned to get something. Kit had dreamt of her breasts with a painful obsession until the day she first let him hold them. Even now, slackening with age, her breasts retained a bounce he adored.

'Looking back,' he murmured over her hair. 'I think there was something unsavoury about our early relationship.'

'Having regrets?' she asked, a finger trailing a lazy pattern on his chest.

'Regrets?' he scoffed. He turned her head up to look at him. 'The entire dorm handed themselves to sleep at night while I was learning how to please you. What regrets am I supposed to have?'

'Well, you mentioned unsavoury.'

'In the sense that I was working for you and making out with you, from breakfast until closing down.'

'I had to do something to stop you bloody running away. Besides, it was obvious you were going to be in someone's bed, at least I knew you were safe.'

'How maternal of you,' he teased. Remembering the day that he'd threatened to run away, because he wasn't wanted. Sulking his way into her bed because he didn't know how else to achieve it. Would he have done it, as Moth had? Up and left, entirely alone.

'Well, I did promise your mother,' she responded. She sat up, swung her legs to the floor, paused on the edge of the mattress, looking out of the window. Bare without its curtains, the spring sky dark. Lights on in some of the windows across the square. 'But you aren't, are you? Having regrets?'

'I don't have regrets,' he told her. 'Waste of time.'

'Glad to hear it.'

He reached a hand to touch her side. Tracing the curve of her body down from her breasts to her hip, to the bulge of her thighs spread on the mattress edge, holding her attention one more moment.

'You're not having any, are you?'

'Me, about us?' Kate asked, incredulous, turning to look at him. 'Are you kidding?'

'About leaving here,' he corrected. 'You were rather tetchy last night.'

'I was not,' she denied, grimacing at the righteous tone of her own voice, 'Ok, maybe a little, but no regrets. Anxieties maybe, but no regrets.'

'What anxieties?'

'About what comes next,' she said, looking back out of the window.

'Worried about going public?' he teased.

She stayed silent.

'Or don't believe I will?' he asked.

He saw her smile, but she didn't turn to face him.

'Or not sure you really want to?'

Her head flicked that one away, as though outrageous.

'Ah,' he murmured. 'There's the rub.'

'Alright, Shakespeare,' she complained, standing up, reaching for her dressing gown. 'Perhaps a little bit of all those.'

'Don't,' he said, hand motioning the covering gown away.

'I have to get dressed,' she evaded, reaching her arms into the sleeves.

'Kate, please don't.' He leant on his elbow. 'Let me see you. In all your anxieties.'

She paused, her hands stretching to seek the belt. He knew he'd hit a button.

'It's alright for you,' she muttered. 'Your skin hasn't started land sliding down your bones yet.'

'Kate, please, show me.'

She left the dressing gown open, lifted her chin and turned to face him. Kit followed the lines of her body. How it fascinated him, how it made his tired dick twitch even now, how it had changed, softened, wrinkled, moved, as she said, lowering itself into comfort on her ribs, her hips, her knees.

'Does nothing make you anxious?' she asked.

He stood up beside her. Pulling her into his body, wrapping her body within his arms until she softened and blended into him.

'Being alone,' he told her. 'The people I love dying.' He kissed her face until her eyes closed beneath his lips. 'Things I can't control.' He cupped her head in his hand, pulled it into the crook of his neck until she rested it on his shoulder. 'Some low-life scratching my Bentley.'

She snorted on his skin, nestling in even closer.

'Come on.' He soothed her hair, his hand following the curve of her neck down across her back. 'Let's make out in the shower one more time and go show the world what we are, warts and all.'

'I do not have warts,' she complained.

'Not yet,' he teased. Kate stood back and glared at him. 'I tell you I won't miss this shower. At least there's a big enough one at the flat that we can get a safety handle for you when you need it.'

He ducked from her hand and flicked her on the bum as she turned away. She sucked her breath in and marched from the room into the bathroom. Kit reached down, stroking himself. He was tired, nothing there but spent spunk and poor effort. He followed her into the bathroom. One day, maybe, he wouldn't be able to get it up again, but it was not this day. He checked his watch, 6.35am. 25 minutes before the vans pulled up. It was going to be an intense day.

'BOSS, THIS CUPBOARD WON'T FIT.'

'What do you mean it won't fit? The rooms here are all larger than the ones this stuff has left,' Kit challenged the call echoing from the top of the stairs.

'I know,' Lou said. 'But it won't fit. Come see for yourself.'

Kit walked up the stairs. He rounded the bend and came up against the problem. Fred was in front of him, sweating and supporting a heavy wardrobe that was wedged against the wall.

'Well, cat in a cradle,' Kit said.

'How is that relevant?' Lou asked from the other side of the wardrobe, leaning over the banister.

'You ever tried to get a cat out of one?' Kit asked. 'Have you marked the new paintwork?'

'Yes, we did,' Lou said. 'But concentrate on the issue. This bugger won't go round the corner. The rooms might be bigger, but the access is not.'

'And it's not getting any lighter,' Fred grumbled.

'Where's Kate?'

'In the kitchen with Isabelle, unpacking.'

'Ask her how precious this wardrobe is.'

'I did, she said her grandmother adored it.'

'How much did she adore her grandmother?'

'Oh, I didn't ask her that,' Lou admitted. 'Hang on, I'll be back.'

Kit looked up at the bulk that was Fred. Frowning at what he saw. 'Have you put weight on?' he asked. He put his hand out and squeezed Fred's middle line, gathering up the loose dry flesh hanging out of his swinging T-shirt like dried icing folded over a too small cake.

'Not an inch,' Fred grunted. 'And keep your fingers off my tickle zone or you'll have me and the wardrobe on top of you.'

'You have put on weight,' Kit told him. 'You need to get back to the gym, you're losing shape.'

'Go stick it,' Fred told him. 'I've not put on a pound.'

'Well, it's changed shape, you've lost muscle.'

'Is Lou back yet?' Fred whined at Ed, who was relaxing over the bannisters.

'Nope. I think he's right, bro,' Ed replied. 'You're sweating more, that's normally a sign of muscle loss.'

'I don't see either of you holding this cupboard up,' Fred told them.

'I thought it was stuck?' Kit asked. He put both hands up on Fred's torso. 'Yeah, definitely lost shape. Shame on you.'

'It's stuck going up, not coming down. Needs me to stop it from taking the wall out, and the stairs, if it goes. And will you get OFF my arse.'

'I didn't touch your arse, I was checking your back muscles. Unless your arse has expanded?' Kit mused. 'What have you been doing?'

'Fat feeding woman,' Ed chirped in. 'Ego-busting nasty this one.'

'Oh Lord, not another one.'

'Will you shut the heck up,' Fred complained to his brother. 'He doesn't need to know every detail of my love life.'

'What, like the fact she's always on top?' Ed asked.

'No wonder you've lost shape,' Kit said in disgust.

'He's not lost shape,' Lou called over the bannister.

'See?' Fred said. 'What did I tell you? Thank you, Lou.'

'He's just lost focus on which shape he's meant to be,' Lou added.

'Screw you,' Fred told her, sweat beginning to drip down his chest, making his trouser line slip. 'Will someone, please, sort this effing cupboard out.'

'She hated her grandmother's guts,' Lou announced. 'Something about catholic hypocrisy and unchristian charity. Or some such. Saw or mallet?'

'Well,' Kit said. 'If Fred were at the top of the stairs, we could throw him on it.'

'How about I let go and it flattens your pretty face on the way down?' Fred retorted.

'It will make a terrible mess of the banisters too,' Kit said. 'Ed, if we get it past the bend will it go through the hall and turn the next corner?'

'Yeah, easy.' Ed leant over the banisters, looking down at the wardrobe. 'I say cut the legs off, if they won't unscrew, and take the ornate bitty thing off the top, scrape the walls a bit more, but they can be fixed. Better up than down. We're all up here, it's just you two down there.'

'It's a plan,' Kit said and turned down the stairs, pausing to say, 'Fred, hold it there a bit longer. Count it as your workout for today.'

Fred grunted hard at him and shifted his frame.

'Seriously, bro,' Ed told him. 'You need to get shot of this one, she's ruining your physique.'

Kit ran out to the van, found the toolbox, and went back upstairs with a saw and a mallet. 'Hold on chunky, I'm going in.' He ducked beneath Fred's heaving frame and set to, knocking away the Queen Ann feet without even needing the saw. 'Jesus, this is ugly.'

'Shut up,' Fred told him. 'It's not my best angle, alright?'

Kit tickled his belly where it hung out from under his shirt. 'I meant the wardrobe, gorgeous.' He emerged from under the cupboard, threw the tools up to Ed who knocked away at the cornice that decorated the top of the wardrobe. It splintered into three unhappy pieces.

'Oops,' Ed said. 'That won't be going back on in a hurry.'

'Here, pass it out, she'll never notice,' Kit told him.

'Notice what?' Kate's voice came from the top of the stairs, behind the others.

'Nothing, my sweet, how's that kitchen going?' Kit called up. He backed down behind Fred and took a position next to him, taking some of the weight. 'Wow, this is heavy.'

'I know!' Fred told him, his shoulders slacking as Kit took some of the weight.

'You should have said,' Kit teased. 'Right, on three. Ed, get ready. Girls, step back, it's not going to be pretty. One, two...'

His phone rang. They all groaned, not least Fred.

'Oh, come on,' Lou complained.

'Hang on,' Kit said.

He reached into his pocket, levered his phone out, checked the screen. It was a Skype call. Unidentified. He went to ignore it, knowing Fred was at his limit. His hand paused on its way towards his pocket, the indecisive sun reaching through the window lighting up the stairwell, dust swirling from their movements. People didn't Skype him often. And not without caller id. He let go of the wardrobe, heard Fred grunt and took a few steps down the stairwell to take the call.

'Kit de Lavelle,' he said, exuding confidence for any situation. There was a moment's silence. A long-held breath. He couldn't decide if it was his, the others on the stairs or the person on the other end. He took another step down.

'Hi,' said Moth's voice. His face appearing on the screen as Kit was trying to identify the known voice.

Kit tried to take it in. Watching the dust spin through the seconds it took for his brain to register, to recognise the voice. To take in the face. Now? Nine months he took to call, and he chose now?

'Boss,' Lou hissed. 'Hurry up.'

'Hey.' Kit clattered down the stairs, hand gripping the banister. 'Hey, I wasn't expecting this.'

'Yeah, right,' Moth said. Moth. Said.

'Christ, you're a stubborn bastard,' Kit told him as he reached the outside driveway, stepping away from the house. The stair window was over his head and he felt the pressure of people waiting for him. Isabelle, inside. Isabelle, who he'd sort of promised to tell if Moth called. 'I've been busting your mate's balls to get you to call me. Nothing, not a whisper.'

'Yeah, he told me to call.'

'But you didn't?' He could see Moth's face, his hair longer, his hand covering the side of his face. Leaning in towards the computer, trying to block out the background.

'Ben likes people to dance to his tune,' Moth was keeping his voice low, making Kit strain to hear it. 'I thought it would do him good to dance to yours for a change.'

'Ha,' Kit said. 'Excellent. Maybe I won't tell him you rang, after all.'

'I didn't ring because of him anyway.'

'Why did you ring?' Kit could make out a café. Noise in the background blurring Moth's soft voice.

'Wanted someone to wish me Happy Birthday,' Moth joked.

Kit let that sink in. Let the memory of it wash over him. He wanted to close his eyes, push away the rush of guilt that warmed him. But Moth was watching.

'You want birthday cake and wishes you get back here,' he said. 'Or tell me where to send the card to.'

'Fair comment.' Kit thought he was going to say something else, but he didn't. Same old guarded Moth. Don't ask a question that might lead to one he didn't want to answer.

Kit tried to see more in the background behind him. He couldn't tell where it was. Moth was being careful.

'How's the coffee?' Kit asked.

'Not great. You make better.'

'Glad to hear it.'

'What are you doing?'

'Moving a client into a new house.' Kit felt aware of how much he'd have to explain if he even offered the smallest piece of information. Aware of noises from the stairwell.

'Sounds fun,' Moth said, not meaning it.

'You could have tidied up for your birthday,' Kit told him. 'You look rough as hell.'

'It's been a while since I showered,' Moth said. 'Besides, I'm celebrating alone, and I don't mind how I look.'

He looked like a kid who'd buggered off with no explanation. Unsure why he'd rung home, wondering if he'd regret it. He also looked older, tougher, less nervous. More feral. It looked good on him. A deeper shade of don't-give-a-shit-itus. Apricot hair framing a wind-kissed face. He looked not unlike a young Greek god. Shimmering in a golden halo, rising against a stained backdrop. Making him feel sweaty and tired from the long day of humping stuff around.

'Well, whatever you're doing, it suits you.' Kit held shy of a compliment, no need to actively encourage his behaviour. Not in a way that might get back to Elsa, anyway. 'Is there anything you need?'

'No. Unless you fancy treating me to a hotel for a night?'

'Birthday treat?'

'Something like that,' Moth quipped.

'Of course, tell me where, and I'll book it.'

'And you'll tell the rest of them where too?'

'You think I'd do that?' Kit asked. He paused. It was

bizarre, seeing his face. It stung at him, the reality of something that had become hypothetical. 'It's amazing to see your face,' he added. 'I've missed you. We've all missed you.'

'Shouldn't think you've had time to miss me, I hear you've been pretty busy. Swansea, weddings, Riverdell.'

'Someone keeps in touch,' Kit said, mentally strangling Elsa.

'Nat. It's an eight-year-old version of the world. The details get lost in girly issues.'

'You've missed a lot,' Kit said. 'How about we catch up sometime? I'll fill you in.'

'I'm not coming home yet.'

'How about I come meet you?' Europe. If he had to stab a guess, he'd say Moth was somewhere in Europe.

'You don't know how far away I am,' Moth told him.

Kit could swear he was being smug.

'Well, no, but there's a plane to most places these days. I'm not even in England next week.'

'Where are you?'

'Italy.' Kit could hear grunting and squealing from the stairwell, they were either calling for him, or trying without him. 'I'm flying out to northern Italy on the 24th, Lake Iseo, in Lombardy. I can come meet you on the way back, have a coffee. Hang on a sec, don't go anywhere.'

He flitted back to the stairs. Fred was going a strange shade of purple at the top, intriguing under the black skin. Lou swearing beguiling tones of abuse at him and his phone. He held up two fingers and ducked back outside.

'I'm going to have go in a minute, Fred's about to have a heart attack under a wardrobe. Look, I don't know where you are, or how you are, and I don't want to, because I can't tell anyone anything if you tell me nothing. I really hope you're

Ok though. I'll be staying at the Hotel Castello, Lovere. You can get in touch with me there or call me again. I can come meet you. Then I'll leave. No pressure. No nagging. And I'll bring cake, alright? With candles.'

'I'll think about it,' Moth said.

'And email me anytime. I'll send money or book you a hotel.'

'You better go rescue Fred,' Moth said. 'Do me a favour, don't tell anyone, that I rang.'

'Yeah, he's more reliable than you,' Kit agreed, deflecting the request. 'Look after yourself, call me again. It's amazing to see you. Alive is a bonus too.'

Moth cut the connection. Kit winced. Damn it. He'd said nothing right. He turned and ran up the stairs. Fred was wheezing in a puddle of sweat.

'... three,' he yelled and put his shoulder to the wardrobe.

They pushed with a joint grunt. There was the sound of squealing wood, scraping plaster and with a rush it fell forward and twisted into the space at the top of the stairs where Ed braced it with a grunt. Fred sat down on the top step, panting.

'If I had the strength, I'd take that phone and shove it that far up your arse,' he told Kit.

Kit patted him on the knee, 'There's my pissy little Hercules. All done. Right, let's see what's next.'

He squeezed past the wardrobe, along the hallway and past the bottom of the stairs that rose to the top floor flat and through the wide-open front doorway of Kate's new home. The stairwell was undeniably a bit narrow. They'd had to sacrifice space there to create a private internal hallway for the first floor flat. Whoever took the top floor would want flat pack. And preferably move themselves.

He turned right, away from the master bedroom and walked down the hall. Past the spare bedroom and bathroom, into the kitchen. It wasn't the lightest room first thing in the morning. The window faced west, and the sun was young enough in the year not to be reaching with much strength. Light from the hallway windows helped though and the room was generous, newly fitted and shiny. More than an improvement on the old cupboard Kate had cooked from before.

Kate was reaching up into a wall cupboard, arranging china. Isabelle was cross-legged on the floor, hidden by a door, emptying three large boxes stacked beside her.

'What have you done to my grandmother's wardrobe?' Kate demanded.

'Harmonised it with your new home,' Kit told her.

'Is that the sort of nonsense you tell your clients?'

'Pretty much.' He paused, trying to pull his mind together, resisting the urge to spill the momentousness of the recent call. 'I didn't know you hated your grandmother. Why did you end up with her furniture?'

'My beloved brother's new wife sent it all over when she died, in a rush to redecorate the old farmhouse, no doubt. I wasn't flush enough to turn away furniture in those days.'

Isabelle stood up from behind her cupboard door. She'd welcomed them with the first load at 10am, made coffee, opened the flat, propped back doors, latched the windows. Making it fresh and breezy for the sweaty work, bringing cups of tea out from her kitchen with every load they brought down. Moving smaller boxes and unpacking where she could. She'd been quiet all day, waving away his concerns with a 'girly stuff' comment when he'd asked.

'I don't suppose you could find a glass?' he asked her. 'Fred could do with a long drink of cold water.'

'No problem. I can make tea if you all want a break.'

'No, just water for Fred. We'll have a break after we get the last of this heavy furniture unloaded. We'll all be ready for it.'

'Of course,' she said, filling a large glass with water and taking it out into the hall. He waited until she'd left. Kate looking at him with a raised eyebrow, unwrapping a china saucer. He grimaced, walked over to her.

'What's up?'

He bent over and spoke in her ear. 'Swear you won't tell anyone?'

'Hmm, depends, I might have to. Have you murdered someone?'

'Moth rang.'

She looked at him in surprise, the saucer held out on its way to the cupboard, a filigree leaf pattern curling its way across the rim. She frowned, put the saucer in the cupboard, asked, 'Is he alright?'

'Didn't say much, but I think so.'

'Is he coming home?'

'He didn't say.'

'Does he need help?'

'He didn't say.'

'Then I didn't hear that.' She unwrapped a matching cup. 'And you'd best keep it to yourself.'

'I sort of promised Isabelle I'd tell her if I heard from him,' Kit murmured. 'He asked me not to say anything. To anyone.'

'Have you got anything to tell her?'

'Not exactly.'

'So, you've got exactly nothing to say.' They could hear

Isabelle laughing with Ed in the stairwell. 'It won't help anyone, Kit, least of all her. Best left unsaid.' Isabelle began walking back down the hall. Kate put the cup in the cupboard.

Kit stepped away from her, leant against the work surface, twisting his watch. Stuck between a promise and a favour.

'He says it better have been the bloody Queen of bloody England on the phone,' Isabelle told them as she walked back in. 'With a request to redecorate the palace.'

'No one so important,' Kate said, unwrapping a sugar dish.

'An old friend, wanting a favour,' Kit added.

'Always annoying,' Kate said, forcing the conversation onwards. 'At least you can delay it until you're back from Italy, right?'

'Hopefully.' Kit watched as Isabelle returned to her space on the floor. Kate glanced at the door.

'Right, let's get the rest of this van empty. Fred, are you talking to me again?' He moved out of the door, back into the hall. Glancing at Isabelle, back behind the kitchen door, amongst the boxes. At Kate, stood upright in front of the window, fitting the lid onto the sugar bowl. The day seemed full of awkward choices.

'Depends what we're moving next?' Fred asked from the stairwell.

'The beds,' Ed answered for him. 'Not much left but the beds, and they're heavy old bastards too.'

'There's nothing wrong with being heavy and old!' Kate called from the kitchen. 'Show some respect you two.'

'Nothing wrong with being a bastard either,' Kit added as he walked down the corridor. 'Some of us are just born that way, right?'

'Not going to argue with you on that one, boss,' Ed said.

'Lou, are you there?' Kit called down the stairs.

'One step ahead of you, boss,' Lou called up.

ISABELLE SPRUNG the idea of the housewarming on Sunday evening, over a quiet dinner in the kitchen at Riverdell.

On Friday evening, after they'd moved the last van load, Ed, Fred and Lou spent the night in Riverdell's spare bedrooms. He and Kate spent the first evening in the flat. Exhausted, falling onto the un-made bed together and wrapping each other up in the bare quilt, feeling their naked skin exposed in the new surroundings. Listening to the strange sounds. Trying to register the change in the shape of life. Its outermost dimensions in the dark, its new windows, its door frames, the wardrobe in the wrong place to the bed.

Saturday, they worked all day again. Mending the damage from the moving in, rearranging furniture as Kate needed it and spending most of the time up at the bistro, cleaning the empty flat out.

'This isn't cleaning, this is decontaminating,' Lou protested. There was a lot of dead wildlife in the abandoned corners. Kate tartly responded that she'd been too busy working to do domestic chores.

Sensing fraction between Lou and Kate, Kit sent Kate down to direct Ed and Fred in relocating all the flowerpots from the extended roof terraces of the bistro to the small section of garden she'd commandeered at Riverdell. She'd chosen a spot visible from her kitchen window. It sat at the bottom of the stairwell, outside the garden door in the lower ground floor basement, chosen for commanding a view of the weir.

When Kit popped his head down there, he'd looked at the mass of overgrown bushes and asked, 'Weir? What weir?'

Ed and Fred turned furious glances on him, seething looks behind Kate's back. He guessed the pots had already been moved several times.

'Shut up,' Kate told him. 'You know nothing about gardens. Houses, maybe. Gardens, no.'

When he opened his mouth to differ Ed had coughed and Fred had asked Kate a distracting question.

On Saturday night they ate at the bistro, courtesy of the new managers. A late night, in which Ed and Fred ended up arm wrestling, and taking it in turns to dance with Lou and Isabelle to the aged rock band whose sound level was rocking the too small space but suited the clientele. While Kit and Kate were saying goodbye, Isabelle walked down to Riverdell, supporting Ed, while Lou gave a steadying arm to Fred. When they arrived, Kate's arm tucked through his as they crossed the courtyard, they could see the party had moved to Isabelle's kitchen.

Kate squeezed his arm and pulled him up to the flat, locking her front door behind them. Turning all the lights off and kissing each other with agonising slowness all the way to the bedroom, removing the clothes that lay between them, abandoning the layers. Making up for their exhaustion the night before with lovemaking that surprised them both with its tenderness. Its pauses for touch, sweet soft kissed and long looks in the darkness swallowed up by more kisses. Kit could feel her hand on his chest, unmoving, as she fell asleep, long past midnight. Returning there to wake him well past 9am in the morning. They lay in bed, silent, holding each other and listening to the world again. He wanted to say something. Tell her not to be anxious. Tell her

it was all going to be fine. Wishing she would do the same
to him.

The others woke late. Kit was working upstairs when he
smelled bacon cooking, wafting up through an open
window. He went downstairs to Riverdell, found all four of
them quiet and nursing hangovers in the kitchen, laughing
at their misery. He'd finished cooking their breakfast for
them and sent them home with the vans, telling them to
drive slowly. Isabelle retreated to her study, to sleep on the
sofa.

He spent a quiet morning with Kate. They walked up to
the bistro, swept down the empty roof terrace and handed
over the flat keys to the excited new managers. It was a
subdued moment. Watching Kate hand across the old key
that had been guardian to her home and life, seeing her final
look of anxiety. They walked back down to the house,
through the frail spring pleasure of Sunday lunchtime,
mingling with people strolling through the town. White and
blush cherry blossom peeking out between the bare branches
of trees. His arm tucked through hers, their feet pacing out
the length of the distance from one ending to a new beginning in perfect harmony. People content in their world, in
their company, in their day. He felt the same vibe. Unpacking
Kate's new home, helping her settle, feeling replete. Sitting
down to a late afternoon meal knowing he'd achieved
wonders that weekend.

Content, right up until Isabelle said, 'I want to throw a
housewarming party for you.'

Contentment turning to confusion, because Kit wasn't
sure if "you" meant them, him and Kate, or just Kate, and he
didn't know what to say. Didn't know where they all stood yet.
His contentment a thin-skinned thing. Peeled away by the

suggestion, fork on the way to his mouth, looking to Kate, who looked back at him in mirrored bemusement.

'Oh, how sweet,' Kate said. 'But there's no need, darling, and anyway, who on earth will we invite?'

'Everyone who wants to wish you happiness in your new home,' Isabelle said. 'James and Asha for a start, and Elsa and Nat. Your friends from town, and Mrs Staines and Marge, and Rob, lots of people. Kit, you'll come, won't you? And the boys, and Lou. It would be fun.'

'Sounds a blast to me.' Kit lied, voicing the other end of Kate's instant discomfort. 'But I'm not sure when. I'm away from next week and not sure when Elsa will be up next. Why don't you ring around, see who's free? Maybe when it's warmer too, we can enjoy the garden as well.'

'That's why I thought next weekend. Before you go away. Besides, if I give you a chance, you'll procrastinate your way out of it.' She said that part to Kate, who smiled, trying to deny the truth of it.

'You don't have to do anything,' Isabelle added. 'Nor you Kit, I know you're flat out all week. I'll ring everyone, and I'll do the food. We can keep it simple, just a little get together if you prefer, but something to mark the occasion. Please say yes.'

'A small one,' Kate protested. 'Close friends and family only. Leave the rest. I shall invite them in my own time, once I've settled in. But Asha and James, and Elsa, if she can make it. Perhaps not Rob, if Hester can come.'

'You want Hester?' Isabelle asked.

'You don't want to invite her?'

'I already mentioned it to Rob,' Isabelle confessed.

'Perhaps not Hester,' Kit said, though why Rob was already invited was beyond him. She hadn't thought that through. 'Why not. I'm back up this weekend after all. Not sure the boys will be free, but I'll ask Lou. It's not a bad idea, and you're right, if you leave it too long, nothing will get done. So long as I don't have to do anything, I'm too busy.'

'Looks like that's sorted then.' Kate tried to hide her irritation.

'If it's warm enough we can use the garden,' Isabelle enthused to Kate. 'I'll make up the spare rooms, people can crash here if they want.'

She stood up from the table, gathering the dishes, taking them to the sink. Talking about bunting. Kit watched Kate put her cutlery down, her dinner unfinished. She wasn't happy about the idea. No doubt he would hear all about it later. He looked at Isabelle. Wondering how long before she wondered? Before she asked. Before she knew. That Kit didn't just hear all of Kate, he saw everything too. Isabelle was oblivious, chattering about her ideas. He speared the final piece of beef, popped it in. She'd moved onto asking about music. Since when had Isabelle been a chatterer?

She had never asked about them. Not since the argument. Not since he came back. Not since the wedding. He thought she might never ask, even when she did begin to realise, to understand. For a moment he felt better that he had kept Moth's phone call to himself. Kept it between him and Kate. Where confidences now belonged. He pushed the plate away from him. He never could stand an empty plate that lingered.

'Come on,' he said. 'Let's have coffee in the study and then I'm done. I want a good night's sleep before I head back first thing.'

No one asked him where he was sleeping.

.   .   .

HE LEFT before daylight on the Monday morning. Kate was stirring in bed when he walked in, fresh from the shower, dressed for work. Putting a coffee on her bedside table, sitting down on the edge while she dragged herself up in bed.

'Have a lazy day,' he told her. 'There's nothing much left for you to do but get used to the change.'

Kate put a hand to cover his. 'You've been a star, as usual. Made it all look a complete doddle.'

'People do make a fuss about nothing.'

'Thank you, and don't forget to bill me for the work,' she said. 'I don't expect you to foot the bill for all this and it's not up to Isabelle to pay for my moving.'

'Don't worry, I'll bill you. Intimately.' He leaned forward and kissed her sleepy lips, laughing at her frown. 'You bore, it would be much more fun paid that way.'

'I'm not shagging Ed and Fred, or Lou, for that matter, to pay for moving my ornaments. Send me the bill.'

'Oh, if you insist,' he said.

'I'll see you this weekend?' she asked. 'For this bloody party I don't want?'

'I'll be back,' he kissed her fingers. 'You can announce our engagement.'

She looked hard at him.

'Joking. But we ought to make a start, don't you think?'

'Well, I suppose we could.' She looked down at her hands sitting cupped in his, on the bedclothes.

'You don't have to, take your time,' he said. 'I was thinking...'

'Thinking what?'

'About you coming to Italy, afterwards. I'm busy out there, you'd have a lot of time to relax, get used to the idea of retirement. And we'd see each other in the evenings.'

'You want me to come scrub your back in the bath at night?' Kate asked, amused. 'A faithful little woman?'

'No, I want to show you the Italian Lakes,' he told her. 'And take you into the mountains and make love to you all night under the stars. Some time away, the two of us. Get used to the idea, maybe, before we do announce it to the world.'

Kate sat, lips pursed, thinking.

'You aren't the most decisive in the mornings,' he told her. 'Have a coffee, think about it, call me later. You don't have to decide yet. I'll book an open ticket to Milan, you can come for some of the time, or all of it.'

'It's a gorgeous idea.' She lay back against the pillows, softening. 'I'm not at my best first thing.'

'You look divine to me,' he leant over in the bed and kissed her again. 'Were it not for a tonne load of appointments I'd get back in there and wake you up.' He tweaked open the neck of her nightdress, kissed the curve of her breast. 'Hmm, I have to go. You're going to make me late.'

'Work hard,' she told him.

'Retire gently,' he said back, giving her nipple one last gentle flick with his tongue and standing up, his trousers taut.

'You better go, before I wake up and decide to do something with that.'

'Think about Italy,' he said as he left, peering back round the door. 'I want to fantasise about your naked body in the swimming pool at the villa.'

'Ooh, a swimming pool. That is tempting.'

Kit left her. The sun was scraping its way upwards through thick clouds, the courtyard lit from the porch lights. He swung into the Bentley, looked up at the bedroom window, saw Kate looking down at him. She dropped the neck of her nightdress, showed him her cleavage with a smile, disappearing with a swish of the curtains. Isabelle's side of the house was in darkness. Well, things never did go as expected. You had to know how to run with a curve ball. He drove off the gravel in his usual spurt. It was a busy week. Time to focus. He flipped on his phone.

'Morning, boss.' Henri's voice was weary. As sleepy as Kate's. Moderately less arousing.

'How's that mission board looking?'

'I don't know, boss, I'm in bed.'

'Well, get the heck up,' Kit said. 'It's been a busy weekend. I want to know what's going on. Who's this woman Fred's losing shape over?'

11

D ear Kate,

How cool and elegant London sounds. You moan about the indifferent weather, but I would trade cities with you in a blink. Bombay in August is unendurable. The streets are turned to rivers of sewage and the humidity sits on your lungs like a suffocating iron weight.

As for your news, I have never had so much admiration for you. You've always been strong, same as Rose, but... to find the courage to end an unhappy marriage, set sail into the world all on your own once again, and be able to know you are your best self, outside of such an age-old tradition, well... what can I say? ~~You fill me with hope and courage.~~ I am unbelievably proud of you and wish I could be there to give you a great big hug and cheer you on. I know Rose is often with you, there when I cannot be. The thought of you two sharing a bedsit does make me laugh, it will be a complete domestic wreck. I hope she is spending lots of time at home with Kit, and not losing herself in her latest project. But perhaps it is bliss for you both. To have that space to share where you need think of no one else, no man or child, and focus entirely on your work. You truly are the epitome of all that women should be, and Elsa and I have slid backwards into the soup of tradition.

Patrick sounds the worst sort of man. One that starts out shining and ends up croaking. I am glad I shall never meet him now. Although he might have gambled all your savings away at least you had the sense to hold on to your job ~~and not give up your independence~~. To find out in such a way that he was cheating on you too, with your boss. What an utter pig. I despise what he did with your family, dragging them into your personal affairs, when you had already made your mind up to divorce. Though, please do not cast them all into the abyss... you don't know what time might heal and they remain your family. That age-old adage seems to fit us all so well; you can't choose your family, but you can choose your friends. How lucky we have been with one another.

My trip to Kashmir this year didn't happen, and I could weep over it. How much cooler and sweeter it seems compared to this sweating monster of a city. But Ted and I are determined to try what hope medicine can offer, and that means my being present near the hospitals for our weekly visits. I tried to persuade Kish to come and stay here for the summer, but Sai sulked for a week when I told her, and Kish replied to say she could not endure the travel.

From day to day, I am not sure what my problem is. The doctors toss descriptions back and forth in such rapid speech, I only occasionally catch a word. Hyper-thyroid, Grave's disease, Lupus, diabetes. Oh Lord, you name it, they think I might have it. The cocktail of medicines changes monthly and all of them make me feel sick. My periods go from drought dribble to tsunami flood. I have fainted numerous times and woken up in hospital with enough instruments attached that I might as well be with Armstrong on the moon. I have come to the private conclusion that my greatest problem is not having a problem, but don't wish to suggest this to the doctors, or to Ted. Between his determined positivity and the doctors', with their constant burying of faces and probes in my nether regions, I feel not unlike a precious, prize cow. But what if there isn't *a* problem? What if *I* am the problem? Perhaps my body won't sustain a pregnancy for a reason, and this is nature's way of telling me my child would not survive in the world?

You would not think it such a hard thing to make a child. Here in India, I am swamped with daily evidence of how readily most women can reproduce. How much they worry about the next child arriving, how much I worry about no child ever arriving. There is this great wasteland of infertility between me and the world and I feel undone in its stare. It is hard to see daily so many impoverished children in need of loving without wondering if Ted and I would not be better to adopt. I did raise it with him. He looked bemused. I guess it is different for a man. I know I could love any child put into my arms, that the love itself would build that bond of motherhood. Ted sees only the genetic legacy of his loins as worthy of the love that makes him a father. So, adrift in Bombay, in the hinterland of medicine, without the joy of our home in Kashmir to cheer me, I am most fed up. Your letters keep me smiling and positive.

I am glad you are enjoying your new job. And that you managed to get a new job after smacking your last boss with a skillet. I know you had provocation, but it must have made references awkward! Do you hope to stay working in London? Or do you have dreams of your own sweet place one day? A restaurant of your own and no boss but yourself? London would be a tough place to compete in, I guess. Send me more news, I love to hear how you are getting on. And don't forget to go visit Elsa. She misses you too and Riverdell is even more your home now, since falling out with your family. I know you are unstoppable, but the odd rest and recuperate at Riverdell will only recharge you and give you time to focus on where you go next. You can't share a one room bedsit with Rose forever. And though I know Patrick might have put you off marriage for life, I hope you are enjoying your freedom and dating lots of interesting people. I'm sure Rose is dragging you out on double dates all the time. She does not write much about her love life, but I can't imagine her ever being lonely. Leaving Kit in Bristol with Grandma and nannies to work in London must be such liberty. What fun you must both be having.

Perhaps next time I write, I might have good news of my own to share. Meanwhile, it's back to the prodding and poking for me. Honestly, this search for a medical cure to my infertility might put me off intimacy ever again. It's the least erotic thing in the world to have your legs hitched up and apart in a room full of curious men pulling on their plastic gloves. Sometimes I wonder if they don't fancy having a poke themselves, to see if they're any better at the task than Ted. Why are there no women in infertility work? My body is a thing I wrap in many layers when I can.

Much love to you and Rose,

Beth x

12

A car started. It was strange. Mechanical. He was too used to birdsong. His eyes opened. The jaundiced glow of streetlights mingling with the hidden dawn. Creeping across the rim of the bin.

He was in a town. The early birds were commuters setting off for the nearest cities and better paid jobs. He lifted his head and regretted it. Pain lancing down his spine, curling through his butt, shooting into his legs. His face flattened from its perch on his arms. Arms numb from the weight of his head. Fingers tingling with the rush of released blood. He sat up against the wall and let sickness and a thudding ache wash over him. His throat thick and dry, hands stiff with pain. He screwed them into fists, loosened them into claws.

At least it's not raining.

He peeled himself up from his helmet perch and pulled himself up on the edge of the bin, leaning against the wall and letting his body grasp the level of pain he was going to have to negotiate. The cat was gone. The bike was there.

Of course it is, who'd want to steal that?

He had a brief, flashing desire that someone had taken it. That he didn't have to face the day ahead. By the end of which he might have to get used to life without it.

It might be beyond repair.

Or, at least, financially beyond his repair. He was going to have to sweet talk someone into letting him use their kit.

But first, breakfast.

He peed against the back of the bin. It took ages to come and when it did it was weak and painful. He threw the helmet away. He didn't want to have to explain to anyone what might have caused the damage. It was Italy; he didn't have to wear one by law. No one would question its absence, only its condition. He would get another as soon as he could.

At least you can tell Kit you were right about that.

It was a slim victory to cling to.

It's about all you've got.

He shoved his hair under the beanie hat, found some cleaner clothes in his bag and changed. The sky was getting brighter, the cars more frequent. His hiding place was getting less safe by the minute. He wheeled the bike out of the alleyway and went into town. Fingers crossed for a bike repair shop. Hoping he had enough money. Hoping the town didn't hate cyclists too. Hoping the bike wasn't as busted as it looked.

Well, it can't get any worse than yesterday.

Moth found a small park with a fountain before the town woke up. The Italians put fountains everywhere. Took a surreptitious wash, trying to clean the dirt out of his grazes. Wondering what bacteria he was rubbing into the wounds. Taking his top off and scrubbing at his pits. He sat down on the rim of the fountain, pulled the small stashes of money from the corners of the panniers, the front bag, the rucksack.

Loosened the seat off the bike, pulled his emergency roll of cash out. Started counting. All his dosh for the next month's riding.

You can sting Kit for some cash.

He'd have to steal food and have no campsites until he'd covered the loss. He wouldn't ring Ben for extra again. He wouldn't ask Kit for help.

What if it costs more?

He looked at the pile of notes. It looked meagre. His whole life for a month balanced into a pile that might not be enough for a bike patch up. He'd deal with that crisis if it happened. He kept out enough for breakfast, painkillers and deodorant. Put the rest into his front bag, slinging it across his chest for added security.

It took him an hour, but he found two bike shops. One that looked downright pompous. Spanning two faces of a corner of one of the main roads into the town centre. Announcing itself with great signage, a rack of posh bikes out the front, and matching overalls for the mechanics, visible opening up the cavernous workshop on the other corner. Moth could smell his scent rising with the sun. A dose of strong deodorant failing to mask it.

They're going to take one look at you and tell you to sod off.

The other looked humbler. On an older industrial estate towards the fringes of town. With a simple sign over the roller door, and louder music. Younger guys tossing banter across the dusty concrete floor of the shed.

They're going to take one look at you and laugh.

He looked down at his hands. Cleaned of dried blood his wounds looked raw. He covered them with his gloves, forced himself into a cheerful posture, and led the bike up to the door. A large bag of fresh pastries in his hand and a smile on his battered face. Two guys looked up from their work as he pushed the bike in.

'Ciao,' he said. 'Hey there.'

'Ciao,' one returned. 'Can I help? You are booked?' His glance at the closed office door suggested that he needed to be.

Moth played dumb, with gusto. He couldn't afford to try for subtle.

'I am sorry to trouble you,' he started talking in fast English, telling them all about his night cycling through the rain, about slipping off the road, puncturing the tyres in the forest, the state of his bike, his lack of Italian, his girlfriend back home, not to mention his mother and sister.

They tried to interrupt him. Moth ignored them. They looked into the workroom with discomfort, Moth kept talking. With a long sigh, one of them went into the office and came back out with an older guy. The older guy looked him over, looked the bike over.

'I'm sorry, Signor,' his perfect English was accented, indifferent. 'We cannot help you today, we are too busy. You can book it in for another day?'

Moth told the new guy the same story all over again. How he needed a few tools, he could do the work himself, he had to keep going that day, he was so sorry to trouble them. All the while hating the upper-class accent and mannerisms that he knew from school. The assumption that the world was good and would help you. The embarrassed condescension with which it was delivered. Suggesting that you were being polite, waiting for the other person to catch up with the inevitable. The most important thing, Moth knew, was never to flash money. You must never suggest that money would be the answer, you had to prove you knew they'd help you from the goodness of their hearts.

The whole time feeling his body start to hurt from the sheer ache of being so polite. Of talking so much. Of standing so straight.

With an exaggerated sigh the older guy held a hand up to stop him talking, waved the hand at one of the workers to help him, said 'Va bene, a bene, abbastanza,' and retreated with gusty irritation to the office.

The guys in the workroom warmed up when they could see he knew what he was doing and wouldn't take their time up. When he offered out the pastries, they made coffee. Gathered round with strong tuts of commiseration. For an hour Moth forgot the pain in his body and the general doubt about his life. An hour of trading stories about a mutual passion for cycling. About places they'd ridden, swapping achievements.

It's all bullshit. Keep smiling anyway.

The bike looked less damaged in a workshop full of tools and clamps than it had in the dripping forest. The savaged inner tubes replaced with new ones. The chain removed, its crushed links appraised, replaced, reattached. The kink in the wheel they couldn't straighten, and he couldn't afford a new one. Between two of them they got it wobbling a bit less. The bike wasn't perfect, but they helped him get it more roadworthy. It should get him to Lovere at least.

You'll have time to get it sorted there.

By midday he was gone. Into the valley floor. A long sweeping road that wound through small villages. Passing over narrow bridges that were centuries old, and between the close-hemmed buildings of main streets. He blended into the background of a tourist realm again. The rain from the day before gone. Taking the grey threat with it, leaving smiles of contentment and genial humanity.

They were trying to kill you yesterday.

He smiled back at the locals, threw greetings in response over his shoulder as he passed by.

He ignored the tension that was back in his chest. The pains shooting down his legs. The bike had developed a sporadic lurch, a result of the slight kink in the wheel. He had to concentrate hard on the road, trying to work out what exacerbated it. An abrasion in the tarmac, a small rock, a weird camber in the pitted roughness of the edges of tarmac where it flowed into the stone supporting it. After several hours he realised there was nothing specific. It was a flaw. It would be a real pain to fix. The anxious focus faded, leaving a tiredness behind his eyes.

The tension grew, building on the pain in his shoulders, the cramps in his stomach, the knot in his chest. Finding weak points, building them into an unrelenting wall. Pressure bubbling behind it. The miles getting harder.

He was a hundred and twenty km away from Lovere. From Kit. It was the 29th already. He didn't know how long it would take him to get there, with the bike in this state.

With you in this state.

Twenty-five km from Tione his legs were shaking. The pain shooting through them had advanced up and into the curve of his back, embedded in his hips like hot knives. He pulled the bike into a lay-by and negotiated his stiffened body off the bike. Lay down in rough grass to try and ease the pain.

It's muscle ache. It gets worse the next day, you know that.

It was mid-afternoon but already the mountains towering into the skyline on both sides of his painful eyes were brighter at their tips. The sun beginning to slink into the

valleys west. Iseo was in those valleys. Behind those mountains. Moth closed his eyes in frustration. If he could breathe
properly, it would help. His in-breath straining, out-breath
rushing to release the pressure.

You probably bruised ribs in the fall.

He was disjointed, unfocused. Knowing where he needed
to be, without the determination to get there. He wanted it to
be over. The endless cycling, forever trying to move forward.

It's better than going backwards.

It was comforting to lie down, to let his body relax. The
hum of engines and stirred wind lulling him.

Another twenty kilometres today at least

He fought against it. He couldn't afford to be more than a
few days late. He had to hope Kit had given him that much
grace, but he couldn't count on more.

Better hope he's there.

If he wasn't, if Moth had heard him wrong, if Kit had gone
when he made it to Lovere, then...

... then the whole trip's been a bloody waste...

... and he had a busted bike to fix...

... and how are you going to get out of Europe...

... with no money and no transport.

Moth groaned as he pushed himself up. His back muscles
flinched and contracted. Reducing his determination to a
crouch, waiting for the pain to lessen so he could make it all
the way up. He looked at the bike for long minutes before he
got back on.

One more mile.

Get on the bike.

The hardest bit is getting on.

After that it's easy.

Get on the bike.

It's not even a mile, it's a kilometre.

You can do this the easy way or...

The system had to work every time, or it wasn't a system. He mounted with gritted teeth, his body reacting with another wave of sweat and nausea.

Fifteen km later, with the afternoon closing in on him, he was cycling at a speed inadequate to keep the bike from swaying. On ground that was level. Even the campervans were overtaking him. He'd been shouted at several times by motorists annoyed with his pace and his stability. He was too tired to hate them back. Wanting to stop. To sleep.

He passed the far end of a crescent lake. The road curving round its outer edge. Three lay-bys along it were crammed with campervans. He prayed each time for an empty spot. Peering through the wooded sites, seeing white box after box. Knowing he couldn't face people. Imagining the comfort within those worlds.

The road left the lake, heading into open fields. Ahead two hillocks shaped the disappearing apex of a rise. The road piercing the cleft between them. He stopped, slid a foot to the floor. Stared at the distance, knowing he needed to keep going.

It's not enough.

He slipped another foot down. He was done for the day. He chucked the bike over a gate, fell over the top rail, found the tallest bit of hedge he could find and threw the tent over the bike.

Crawling in, clutching the front bag to his wheezing chest, his body seeking the floor. Breath hanging in his mouth. Full of pain and spit. Tasting rank and metallic. Forty km in seven hours. Less than six km an hour, on flat ground. If he did the same as today, it would be three days to Lovere.

There're some big climbs ahead.

He would be three or four days late at least.

If you can keep this up.

Silence leeched in from the edges of the tent. Light ebbing as he blinked. Wishing the pain away. All his limbs remote from feeling, closing to a final thought.

You might not make it.

He might be too late. A slow spreading despair, seeping into him as the painful breath left him. Closing itself round the pain in his chest and squeezing hard. He clutched hard against the bag on his chest.

You should write in the book.

He needed to write in the book. He would forget. What day it was. What day was it?

29th March.

Where he was. Where was he?

Some sad backwater between Tione and Lovere.

He tugged and pulled at the zip. Fingers sore with the effort. Pulled out the notebook. It fell open to the right page, pushed apart by the whiteness of Luca's paper. Moth stared at the number, eyes struggling in the fading light. The dark lines against the crisp pale slip. Behind it the lines of his notebook. Dim, tarnished, recording the last entry. Made the night before Male. Before meeting Luca.

Before all the bad stuff started, you mean.

He read the name, the number.

You should write in the book.

His eyes couldn't move beyond that slip. He closed the book upon it. Luca could mark the place for now. He closed his eyes, holding the book on his chest, feeling it rise and fall. A hard, solid shape he could pin himself too, while the pain swirled outward and filled the tent.

. . .

WHEN HE WOKE the pain had settled onto him. Light and air rushing at him. The brightness of the light in his eyes, the agony of the air in his lungs. Pain oozing out of him with the breath. Banging against his head, shooting across the bridge of his nose.

It's always worse the second day.

The full impact of the crash was coming through. He couldn't move. He couldn't think. He couldn't breathe. The final thought of the night sat above his head in the groggy thick air of the tent and laughed at him.

Forty km a day? Fat chance.

He would never make it out of the tent, let alone onto the bike.

He rolled onto his side, his ribs screaming at the effort, to try and get away from the pain. Two minutes later he rolled back. On the third toss he realised that no position was going to give him relief from the pain.

You can't sleep. You're not dying. Might as well get up.

He fumbled and fought his way out of the tent on his knees, his hands wet in the dew. It was bright already. He'd slept late. Cars whizzing by on the road behind the hedge. He blinked in the sunshine, looked over the hedge.

The sun was rising over the mountains, cutting the tops off in its bright haze. Fog cradling the sides with the valley road clear beneath it. He was hemmed in by it. White haze looming down on him. The sun trying to burst out over it. Birds screaming back at it. It was a day trying to be gorgeous and he hadn't the heart to want it. He wanted darkness, soothing darkness and silence.

His chest erupted in a hacking agony that doubled him

over. When it finished, he was desperate to pee, dropping his pants and trying. Overtaken by stomach clenching. Squatting on agonised legs as stinking liquid squirted out of him. Pissing between times, liquid rising in the dew, puddling under his trainers. The stench rising to taunt his weak stomach.

Jesus, you pissed all over your trainers.

It took him ages to fumble his way through packing up and getting the bike laden. The lingering scent of his stained trainers making him retch. His hands unable to warm up, to function. He stood and tucked them under his arms, holding his body together with crossed arms. Waiting for some warmth to spread. Thinking about how Isabelle used to wrap her arms round her waist.

Time to get on the bike, let's go.

The white mist hovered over his head, a cool weight above him. Thoughts stuck beneath it. What was she doing? What was the weather doing? Back there, at Riverdell. Was it warmer in England? Had the magnolia bloomed yet? A high white campervan side trundled past the hedge, catching his thoughts.

Road's waking up, let's go.

He pushed the bike back to the gate. It was quiet. A back road through lesser mountains that didn't go anywhere. He looked at the fog crawling up the sides of the mountains, waiting for the fog inside him to lift with it. His hand held the bike upright, its crumpled scratched mess standing beside him, balanced beneath aching fingers. He had to swing the bike over the gate, put his leg over the frame, push off and the day would start.

As all the other days have started.

Him, the road, the bike, all poised to go.

Moving forward.

The intense light was thickening through the fog. The solidity of the mountains fading in the glow. It was an uncanny emptiness. Beautiful, poised, stilled. Moth could feel it beside him, inside him. Stillness nestled with the pain. No desire to take the first push on the road ahead. Light and pain ebbing and flowing, drifting in the morning air.

If only those birds would bloody shut up.

If the noise would stop, Moth believed he could conquer the pain and find a vein of peace so deep he would never hurt again.

It's time to go.

He gritted his teeth, hefted the bike and hauled it over the gate, holding onto it as it landed. He put his leg on the second rung, lifted himself to the top. Another campervan surged out of the light. White sound and size rushing by. He saw the smiling faces of the couple inside. Enjoying the day. Looking at him with bemusement as they passed.

One day. One day, you're going to do it their way.

He watched it ease away. Crawling up towards the buttock hills. Swaying in that soft way they had.

Must be nice, that sway. No pedalling. Swaying along.

He let go of the gate, flung his leg over the frame and wobbled away on the road west. The warmth of the sun weak on his back as it battled its way through the mist. He would make it to Lovere, not on time perhaps.

But you will get there.

Just keep pedalling for a few more days and he would get there. He adjusted his expectations. Perhaps thirty km a day.

One mile at a time. That's all you need to think about.

The two buttock shaped hills he followed the road between set a new tone. Turning north. Furrowing between two wooded ridgelines. Rising in crevices, rolling backwards and upwards. Revealing the higher reaches of the mountains as the mist swirled and lifted. Their high tips touched with an unworldly white glow rising above him. Leering down on him.

And a great big climb at the end.

The one between him and Lovere. He pushed the dread of it away. Focused instead on each fold of the road. Taking him into the rising fog, dipping back down to the floor. Twisting past a farmstead or a fierce outcrop of rock. Swinging him back, leaving the compass needle rocking on the handlebars.

At least it's better than yesterday.

The vicious cars had gone. The road seemed a secret must-visit destination for campervans. Crawling along it and admiring the view. Sitting in the nooks and passing places as he passed them. Catching him up when the incline slowed him down. Pain nuzzling into his buttocks. Breath tearing at his ribs. Waving and cheering at him in oblivion.

Moth shut down, swamped with pain and the intense urge to stop. He focused on the compass, on the dark tarmac in front of him, sweat dripping. His head vulnerable without the helmet. Feeling the surge of air when a vehicle went past him.

One more big climb.

One agonising push at a time he began the ascent up away from the valley and into the beginning of the mountain pass. Focusing as hard as he could on the small space he was in. Keeping the bike steady within it, not swaying towards the rough edge of the road, or into the middle where traffic over-took him.

At the outer regions of his blinkered world, he could see

them passing him. The slow battered trucks, dirty old farm trailers, swaying polite campervans, all giving him a wide berth. A tractor went by him in a wave of stinking air. The back draft making him choke. He swallowed water to take the taste away, but even the water seemed tainted with the odour.

You got overtaken by a tractor.

He tried not to think about how slow he was going. Pickups went by him in a range of colour, age and condition. Red, silver, black. Brand new and shiny, beaten and rusting in little sprays of damage that nibbled at the edge of door panels. Red seemed the most popular. And the busiest. He was sure he saw the same battered door panel go past him twice. The moments of loud and fume-laden ugliness made worse by the intense beauty of the road he was on.

Shame you feel like death warmed up.

If his breath hadn't already been short, it would have been stolen by the view. The thick trees speared through with the sunshine. Light refracting in the space he rushed through on the bike. Dazzling him. A fast-flowing river raced towards him going into the valley. A lake appearing in a moment of calm, sky-reflecting surprise. He paused, taking a breather beside it, watching how the mountains peered into the edges behind his own face. His battered, pale face and dark eyes. Picked up a pebble and threw it in. Watching the mountains laugh in the ripples, subsiding into stillness. Watching his own shape heave and shake, return to stillness. When he got back on the bike and turned to go, he saw a camper van on the opposite side of the road. Two people with steaming mugs looking back at him, a hand raised in greeting. He tugged the beanie cap tighter, ignored them and rode away.

Houses and farms perched in pockets of green meadows. The tarmac grew ragged, cracked from winter, resisting the sideways slide down the mountain. The roughened sides bouncing through his sore muscles and along his nerves to rattle his head with a vengeance.

You had to pick a road to nowhere to try and get somewhere.

It was a stunning road. Closer and more real than the high road through the Dolomites. That had been a challenge to overcome. This was an experience he wanted to bask in. Once he got to Lovere, saw Kit, got himself back in shape, he might come back this way. Pause. Enjoy it. Park up next to the numerous campers. Doors open, folding chairs set out.

You're getting soft. Next thing you'll want someone to share it with.

It took all his determination to keep going, and there was nothing left to control his thoughts. Vivid memories sluicing between the pounding waves of pain. Nat was there today. Nat at Riverdell, with Hester. Nat playing at home, before his parents died. Nat drawing, always drawing. Paper and pens strewn behind her wherever she went. Nat asleep in her bed the night their parents died. Asleep and safe while he sat on the bottom of the stairs. Fighting sleep and praying they never came back. When they didn't and the hours crept on, he crawled up the stairs, curled up outside her door. Dozing until the doorbell woke him.

Don't open that door.

His mother. Standing between what was bearable and what was not.

You need to stop right there.

If she stayed in place, he was held together. If that barrier broke, all he'd built was washed away.

Moth couldn't seem to get away from his mother as the road swept him upwards and cut into his body. The bike dragging him backward, the effort pushing him forward, pain breaking him apart in the middle. He tried to barter her off, with thoughts of Kit, or Isabelle or Nat.

Maybe you should think about Luca.

She stood too strong to avoid. At the front door, looking back at him. Trying to be comforting and strong, ravaged by the anger that raged between him and his father. Her dark hair scraped back from her face. Her eyes creased with disappointment. Following David into the car and away into the dark. Moth looked at the back of the front door that closed behind her for long hours. Both that night, and on the way up the mountain. Hoping it might open.

Hope it bloody doesn't.

He passed out of the trees in a breathless agony. The road disappearing into little more than a single-width lane across high meadow grass. His pace slowed even more. Vehicles reduced. The spaces between them lengthened.

Na, it's you slowing down. Not them.

He sipped again and again at his water bottle. The road kept going uphill. The bike did not.

Are you giving up? Don't stop. You can't stop yet.

He didn't stop. Not consciously. The pedals slowed to the point where he couldn't keep the bike moving forward. Gravity pulling him to a hushed stop in a sun-streaked section of road. Beneath towering pines on precipitous slopes. His breath ripping in and out of his body in great gasps of insufficiency.

You're going to topple over, idiot.

Moth would have rather toppled over than admit defeat, but habit slipped his foot off the pedal. The bike leaned to the road beneath him, his hands gripping the handlebars, his back slung low across the frame.

He looked up. Out from the images that were playing in his mind. Ahead the road took a sharp bend, along the edge of another mountain meadow.

You might as well get off and push.

Coordinating thought into action. Peeling himself from the bike. His legs as weak as mucus. Humiliated by his failure. He walked along the road to the curve of the switchback and took four steps downhill onto soft short grass. Full of slender plants fluttering in a gentle wind. The mountain tops at eye level. Staring him down. Counting his failure. Reflecting his stillness.

Positively gloating at you.

He couldn't hate them. They were glittering in the spring sun. As perky, fresh and unconquerable as Luca. He propped the bike against a boulder, sank down onto the grass. His body stiff and resisting, stretching out. The warmth from the sun hadn't penetrated the ground. Chill seeping into the comfort of being horizontal.

This is not going to help.

He was too tired to get up and do anything about it. The crush of his body releasing oils from the plants. Acrid and cloying before they dissipated. Exhaustion pulling his eyelids down.

You need to get up. Move away from the road.

He laced his fingers through the spokes of the wheel. His eyes weighed down beyond his efforts to keep them open.

You need to get warm, get some food.

Drifting into a doze fractured by birdcalls. The rolling waves of traffic. The rustle of grasses beside his ears.

The squeal of old brakes on the tight switchback jarring him out of another lull.

He twisted his head to peer at the road and saw another

red pickup pass him by. Going down into the valley. The driver's head turned to look at him. Moth's eyes couldn't focus. Couldn't see more than a moving head within a moving shape. There were too many red pickups on this road.

Must have been a good deal on a bad paint job.

He grasped at the thought, using it to focus. Making himself get up. He pushed the bike away from the boulder. Into the meadow. Further away from the road. He couldn't get right out of sight. His throat aching, needing water.

He tried to eat. Picking at plain bread. His stomach roiling.

Maybe you should stick with the water.

His bowels fought back. He crabbed away from the bike on shaking legs. Holding himself up on his hands while his guts erupted.

Yep, you should have stuck with water.

Afterwards he sat cross-legged, freezing, shaking, eyes shut against the view. Stuck inside himself, arguing the toss.

You've got to get back on the bike.

Not yet. Not a chance. No way.

If you don't make that pass, you'll be sleeping on top of this freezing mountain.

He'd rather die here in a meadow than get back on the bike. He was freezing anyway. What difference would it make? Ten more minutes.

Ten minutes is up.

Just ten more minutes. The sun crawled over the southern mountains while he tossed it back and forth. The chill in the ground seeping into the wind.

Get up, you loser!

No. Not yet.

Is this it? Giving up? You bloody wimp!

He pulled himself to his knees, bending over the pain in his chest.

That is not up. That is arse up.

Moth dragged himself into a crouch. Rose onto his feet. Pulled the bike up. Packed it, pushed it back to the road. Tears mixing with his loathing. He was cold through. He would walk.

Walk a few metres, until your muscles loosen up.

Then he'd get back on the bike.

Walk past that first bend.

Then he'd make a start.

He was so shocked when the pickup pulled up alongside him that he nearly lost the bike. It rolled backwards down the road in his hands, the weight pulling at him. He turned to catch it, wobbled, tried to right himself. The battered panel next to him familiar. That growth of rust sucking at the edges in a flame pattern.

'Ciao,' called the driver, the window rolling down beside him.

Moth looked up from the panel and the car to see the face. An older bloke, about Kit's age. A week's worth of growth on his chin and a dirty shirt rolled up his arms. Moth was too tired to speak or think.

'Di dove sei?' the driver asked.

Moth tried to focus. Where was he from?

Don't answer.

Fear seeping into the exhaustion.

'Non locale, solo in viaggio,' he mumbled, trying to find some confidence.

'Ah, you English!'

'Canadian.' He tried to thicken out his accent.

'Ohh,' the driver said. 'I see you today many times, you come long way!'

Moth stared at him.

'I work this road, back, forwards, back, forwards,' the guy said, his hands emphasising his journey. 'I see you many times, going up, up, up!'

Moth tried to relax. The man was kind enough. He was the one acting weird.

He must be bored stiff, travelling this same road all day long.

A local, looking for a chat, a chance to try out his English. Moth tried to smile. It hurt too much, cracking his lips.

'You work near here?' Moth asked.

'Yes, yes, I work here, moving stuff for the ski slopes,' the guy pointed to the piles in the back of the pick-up. 'I am Bino,' he added.

'Bino.' Moth tried to think of something to say. 'Nice day for driving.'

'Yes, yes, beautiful today, most sunshining.'

His English was not great, a mash up overcome with enthusiasm.

It's better than your Italian.

'You are going over the tops?' Bino asked, leaning against the steering wheel, nodding his head forward.

Moth nodded.

'You have long climb yet.' Bino looked forward out of the window, shaking his head as he weighed up the road ahead. 'You keep going or camp tonight?'

Moth swallowed, looking at the road, back to the meadow.

This guy asks a lot of questions.

'I don't know yet, see how far I go.' Moth shrugged his shoulders.

'I give you lift?' Bino said. 'Is no problem, take you over the top, you go whoosh down the other side, yes? I would like to do that, but not this bit. The up is hard work, yes, you want to lift?'

Moth wanted to be sick. His stomach was churning. His head was pounding. He wanted the man to drive away. He wanted to curl up and go to sleep. He wanted the pain to end.

No one ever offered you a lift before.

Not many pickups that could take a guy and his bike were going slow enough to offer. Not many saw him several times in one day to care enough. Moth's head pounded.

It will get you over the pass.

'I not going too far, to Bazena, on the other side of the mountain, and I have to come back, yes, I cannot take you all way.' Bino frowned, emphasising his limits. 'I go Bazena last time today. I have to go home, my wife waiting, Ok?'

Moth could see Bazena on the map clear as day in his head. It was the start of the downhill journey to Iseo. He'd never wanted to be somewhere this much without having to get there himself. He looked at Bino, looked at the road ahead curving upwards and his body won the debate.

'That would be amazing,' he said. 'You sure it's no problem?'

'No, no, no problem.' Bino opened his door and got out, came and helped Moth put the bike in the back. Stopping to ask a few questions about the gear. Moth was about to lift the front bag off the handlebars out of habit but stopped himself, not wanting to make a fuss about any part of the gear.

Don't draw attention to what might matter.

The inside of Bino's truck was full of discarded food

wrappers and receipts, an assortment of tools and tape measures. A thick layer of dried mud across the dashboard, the door ledges, the floor. The windscreen had a grimy rim, with an indistinct wavy line where it had been wiped by the edge of a sleeve many times. It smelt stale. Moth's stomach heaved as he opened the door.

This is filthy.

Moth didn't think his wife would get in this truck much.

Bino pushed and pulled the rubbish out of the way to create space. Despite its mess the bench seat was luxury compared to the hard bullet of the bike seat. His body sank back into the ripped cover and disintegrating foam with relief. Watching out of the windscreen as the mountain rolled backwards with no effort. Bemused by the motion.

It's been a long time since you sat in a car.

Bino drove with gusto. The winding narrow road up the pass became more potholed and Bino threw the truck through the ruts with equal indifference to the effect on the truck or his passenger. With the doors closed and two bodies inside, the cab began to heat up and a faint odour crept across him. Stale and moist at the same time.

That smells familiar.

Moth couldn't focus. The twists and speed of the road rushing towards him a shock to his battered system. He couldn't hear anything. Not the wind, or the steady approach of other traffic. Bino chattering away in the driver's seat with enthusiasm, switching between Italian and English in the effort to communicate. Moisture tickled at Moth's scalp, sweat dripping onto his temples. His hand gripped the door handle.

'Hey, you Ok?' Bino asked. 'You need to sick?'

Moth shook his head but didn't answer.

Don't throw up now.

Bino stopped talking to him, peering across at him, his erratic driving turning haphazard. The truck swinging over the entire width of the road. Moth's stomach began to clench in panic.

'Hey, no sick in my truck, yes? Ok?' Bino told him. 'I know is messy, but no sick, yes?'

You'd be doing him a favour, make him clean this dump out.

If he could hold onto his guts, they were covering road and height fast. Moth waved his hand at him in reassurance. Didn't trust himself to open his mouth and respond. He longed to be back on the bike. They came out of the final clumps of trees and onto the mountain proper. Coarse clumps of grass and flowers broke up the glaring bare rock.

'We stop soon,' Bino told him. 'You get some air, some rest, you feel better, yes?' Moth nodded at him.

That's great. That will help.

A couple of minutes fresh air. If he didn't feel any better, he could always not get back in. The road was going by fast. The kilometres ripping through him.

Bino swerved into a narrow opening between boulders that opened into a large lay-by looking out across the mountains. A spectacular viewpoint, but there were no other cars there. It was hard to spot from the road, full of potholes and mounds of salted grit. It looked like a storage depot rather than a viewpoint. Bino rocked the truck through them.

No wonder nobody parks here. Is he even trying to miss them?

Circling round the large space until he was on the far side of it. Pulling up with Moth's door to the barrier looking over the edge. Moth was weak and shaking. Moments away from throwing up. His hand scrabbling to find the door handle.

Sweat dripping off his brow, stinging his eyes. Bino jumped out and ran to open his door, pulling him out of the seat.

Moth fell to his knees and vomited over the wooden barrier. Clinging onto it. The hard, angled edges sticking into his ribs. The sound and taste of his own filth spewing out of him. The smell rising to fill his nostrils.

He could hear Bino swearing behind him.

He might take the bike. The bike's in the truck. With all your money. Your card.

He couldn't do anything. Pinned against the barrier while he threw up again and again. He heard Bino pulling the bike out of the back of the truck. Swearing, slamming the tailgate shut. Altogether less helpful.

Yes, leave the bike. Just leave it. Go.

He felt the retching begin, the dry heaving of nothing left to come up. The convulsions moving down his body. He clenched as hard as he could, but it was coming anyway. It wasn't controllable. Moth crawled over the barrier. Into rough ground and boulders. Behind the nearest big rock, away from Bino and the truck. He fumbled to pull his pants down, desperate not to soil his clothes.

Just drive away. Just leave.

Moth hated the fact that he was there. Heard a door opening, closing. No engine starting. He crawled into a squat against a face of rough rock, his guts opening so fast it was all over his feet. Catching the edges of the shorts and pants caught upon his knees. He had to put a hand down to the ground to steady himself, feeling the gut cramps turning him inside out, hurling again. Sweating, crapping and puking all at the same time. The fresh mountain air hitting his raw skin, his stinging throat. When it quelled, his body going from aggressive ejection to shaking exhaustion. Tears coursing down his face from the pain. The acrid taste in his mouth overwhelming.

Moth collapsed and crawled away from the stinking pile. Cold dry earth beneath his hands.

You need to get up. Check the bike.

If he could only lie down.

You can lie down if he's gone, if he's left the bike behind.

If he made it through the next ten minutes he would camp here for the night, start again tomorrow. He tried to get to his knees, the clumps of grass beneath his hand ragged and breaking.

Stuff Kit. If you miss him, you miss him.

He would get down off this mountain on his own. No more free rides for him.

Same as you made it here. On your own.

He didn't need help. He'd proven it to himself.

Same as you got out of that mess. You'll get out of this one.

Hands grabbed him from behind. Strong hands that pulled him up. Moth tried to resist but he had no energy, no strength.

Bino.

'It's Ok,' Moth tried to mumble. His mouth was swollen and dry, his lips covered in sick.

He's not listening.

Moth smelled the same odour he'd noticed in the cab, but stronger.

You know that smell.

He knew it, his brain clocked it, but couldn't tell him what it was. He was pulled up, pushed forward towards some boulders.

No, no, no, this is not good.

He needed to lie down, not get up. His shorts fell down the rest of his legs, caught on top of his trainers. He was naked from the waist down, stumbling over his own clothes, trying to push away the helping hands.

'No, no, I'm Ok,' Moth mumbled.

Bino slammed him against the rock with such force that Moth heard his ribs crack. An odd crinkling sound that bemused him, a split second before the pain ripped through him, taking all sense with it. His face was smashed against the rock with crippling pressure, hips crushed into the rough surface. One hand in his hair held him immobile, pinioned over the freezing stone, tasting his own blood flowing from his nose. He tried to get his legs up under him but Bino kicked them straight back out, tangled in his clothes and trainers. The smell of booze washed over him.

Dutch courage.

Moth knew that smell.

You know what comes next.

The pressure against him. The scrabbling of his panicking body. Moth tried to breathe, tried to shout. Wounded breathless by the burning sensation as Bino forced himself inside him. His body tightening in resistance, even as he remembered to ease the pain by making himself relax.

This isn't happening. It's not happening to you. It's not you.

Moth was slammed against the rock again and again. Pain matching pain breeding pain. He tried one last time to push himself up from the rock, his hands scrabbling to lever his body away. Bino knew what he was doing. He had him pinned, spread-eagled, speared through. The hand wrapped in his hair slamming him back down on the rock. The breath bashed out of his body. His lungs gasping and useless. The moment intensifying in his head.

The grunting of a man.

The smell of sweat and sex.

The birds disturbed from the trees.

The bright light of day blooming, raging, fading.

Moth saw his mother looking at him from the door again. Seeing him. The disappointment on her face changing to horror. Seeing her husband. The door changing. Not the front door closing. The study door opening. To see what her husband did during Sunday lessons. She never opened it.

She couldn't open it. He made you lock it.

Their special time together. A secret game. Keeping the girls out. Doing man stuff. Moth could hear the click of the key turning in the lock. Keeping them safe on the outside. Keeping the world away, where it couldn't see. To keep Nat safe. To keep his mother from seeing what he did...

... what he made you do...

... if she'd ever opened the door, if she'd...

... what? What if she'd seen?

... she might not have looked at him, that last time, with that disappointment. Seared into his memory. If she'd known why they fought that night, that he did it to protect Nat, she might have...

... might have...

... might have... forgiven him.

Moth clung to that thought as the pain of his body seeped away. Numbness edged in, leaving the inky blackness and the comforting warmth of blood against his skin.

'I CAN'T BELIEVE Elsa never did this before,' Isabelle said.

'She never was a gardener,' Kate said. 'Loved her house too much to think about her garden.'

'She always said the river was too much of a risk to justify the cost.'

'That's because it reminded her of her mother.'

'What?'

'The gardening. Her mother loved gardening, spent hours out here. I think she always felt sad when she came out here, that's why she stuck to the house.'

Isabelle stepped back, looking at Kate, who was sitting on her knees patting down soil in the dozen pots they'd replanted. In less than a week Kate's garden had already changed, not least in the sense that it seemed to be her garden now.

Since Monday morning Kate had advanced on the neglect with grim determination. Reclaiming the patio, the long-lost stone wall, the second set of steps and hacking her way into the rhododendron den, discovering the hidden lower level of the terrace. At which point, somewhere near the middle of the week, with face and arms scratched and sweaty, she swept into the kitchen and demanded they negotiate a gardener between them. Isabelle was making her third coffee of the morning and thinking about whether to order pink rose or white prosecco for the party.

'What?'

'You drink too much coffee, and we need a gardener.'

'I thought we had a gardener.'

'We have a lawn maintenance guy,' Kate told her. 'Because that is all Elsa had, a great big bloody lawn. With trees and shrubs trimmed once a year in the late autumn, which you probably didn't even know happened.'

'Kit did mention something about it,' Isabelle admitted. 'I was a bit busy with Rob, and Asha, and the sales.'

'True,' Kate said, breathing out a bit. 'I'll have one of those coffees while you're making it. But anyway, we need a gardener. I can't cope with looking out over the state of this garden every day.'

'You've only been looking at it for three days!' Isabelle tried to think which day it was. She'd had a hideous period from the morning of Kate's move. The time had warped. Thursday. 'Three and a half days.'

'Yes, and it's irritating me already. The sooner we discuss this and come to an arrangement, the better.'

'I get the feeling we're not really discussing this.' Isabelle sat down.

'Nonsense, of course we are. Now, I know the perfect person for the job but, before I call him, I want to know how we're going to share the cost. How much scope I have to... improve the gardens? I don't expect you to pay for it all, obviously.'

'Obviously,' Isabelle said. 'Don't you have anything in the flat you need to think about?'

'Heavens no, Kit arranged it all. Not a hair out of place. I've nothing to do, bar look out the window and bother you.'

'We better get a gardener then.'

'It's not funny, Isabelle,' Kate said. 'I've not had a quiet moment in my life, now here I am supposed to do nothing. The garden is driving me insane.'

'Perhaps you could take up a hobby, join the WI or something?'

'Oh, please,' Kate's voice pushed the idea away, loaded with swirling tones of contempt, as strong as the spoon stirring her froth.

'No, you're right, the WI don't deserve it.'

'You're evading the discussion,' Kate told her.

'Yes, a gardener, ask Kit. I don't know who the lawn men are. If we're contracted to keep them on, or if you can change them too.'

'Kit's too busy. We can decide this between ourselves. We should keep the lawn men on over the growing season and get a gardener two days a week. At least to start with. Split the cost. When we've got it in shape, perhaps we can cut back.'

'Your shape, or my shape?' Isabelle asked.

Kate grinned at her.

'Let's try it,' Isabelle had capitulated. 'For the first year anyway, and then we'll renegotiate.'

Watching Kate dust soil from her knees and stand up, Isabelle reflected that she might have made a mistake. She had a feeling the garden was no longer hers. She had a feeling that Kate's spread outwards from the rear garden door was going to keep going, and going, until it hit the river. Then God help the river.

Gardening was addictive. She could see that too. The patio looked amazing, and it was not even a week old.

The new gardener, Martin, a stunning man with huge, soft, languid eyes framed by drooping, indifferent hair who arrived in a battered VW van with the slogan Keep Calm and V(eg)an On hand painted on the side of it, had set to with calloused hands, a guttural chain saw, and merciless aggression. Hacking back the rhododendrons to reveal two spindly, strangled cherry trees framing the entrance to the lawn proper, leaving the hidden cherry blossom falling in his wake while Kate and Isabelle watched in fascination.

Isabelle had made bunting and hung it from the house walls to the patio and, on the lower terrace, from the stone wall to the cherry trees. Isabelle wasn't convinced they'd survive. The bunting was the only thing holding them up. She'd raided the Christmas decoration boxes in the top-floor spare bedrooms and filled their thin branches with fairy lights, hoping they could last twenty-four hours until the party tomorrow evening.

'It's the perfect time to start a garden.' Kate stood up, stretching her back. She squinted out into the garden. 'Well, perhaps not perfect. That peony should have been trimmed back in the autumn, and the beds needed cutting out of the turf weeks ago.'

'Beds?' Isabelle asked.

'Yes, the flower beds,' Kate said.

'Are we having flower beds now?'

Kate glared at her. Isabelle remembered its power from her days at the bistro.

'Sorry, I meant where,' Isabelle countered, 'where are we having flower beds, now?'

'To break up the lawn, create smaller areas, pathways,' Kate said, turning and gesturing her hands over the lawns. 'I mean, look at it. It's nothing but grass.'

Isabelle looked. It was nothing but grass, but it was beautifully kept grass, and it did roll down to the river most greenly. 'I see your point.'

'No, you don't,' Kate said. 'But never mind, I can forgive your indifference as long as you indulge my interest.'

Isabelle smiled and went to give her a quick hug. It came unbidden, swift and simple, and Kate looked surprised when she stepped back.

'What was that for?'

'I'm glad you're here. I don't feel abandoned with it all myself now.'

'Good, I'm glad it's not feeling too awkward,' Kate said. 'Though, for the record, I'm only dealing with the garden. The house is all yours to contend with.'

'That's a shame, I'm sure you'd do a much better job than me.' Isabelle looked round the patio.

'Nonsense, you're doing a fine job.'

Isabelle felt less sure. 'Don't you ever...' she began to ask.

'Ever what?' Kate prompted, picking at a few plants, snapping away browning or wilted stems.

'... ever doubt yourself?' Isabelle finished.

'Oh, all the time,' Kate said, glancing at her. 'But I don't let it stop me from making decisions. There's something enervating about overthinking a thing, you lose the inspiration of the moment that way.'

'How much do you know about gardening?' Isabelle asked.

'About the same as I did about running a business when I took the bistro on,' Kate flicked soil off the wall. 'Bar the pots on my roof I've never dug a hole in the ground, let alone planted a bush or tree in one. But I've read a lot, and looked a lot, and I have a willing pair of hands to help me.'

'And that's enough to convince you to have a go?'

Kate turned away from tinkering with plants. 'What other option is there?' she asked. 'I can't keep looking out the window and wondering what to do with myself.'

Isabelle knew it was true, but all around her people seemed to be busy grasping the details of life, and she couldn't decide what it was she should be focusing on.

'It's not enough to say you don't know what to do. You have to recognise what fascinates you in life, seek it out, absorb it. You've been so busy dealing with this beast,' Kate nodded at the house, 'from the moment it was foisted on you, but look at what you've done. You made choices, you did things, without anyone else telling you to. And now it's time to get back to where you were. Decide which thread to pick back up and weave with.'

'I'm not sure what to do with the sewing anymore.' Isabelle pulled a string of fairy lights into neater order.

'I didn't mean the sewing,' Kate said. 'I was trying to be clever. I should stick with being plain. You're adrift darling, and things adrift get snagged on flotsam. You need to know which direction you're going in. Other than hosting parties for people. Do you think it will be alright?'

Kate had returned her attention to the patio, eyes screwed in consideration.

'Alright?' Isabelle scoffed. 'It's better than alright, it's wonderful, it's you.'

'You made the bunting, and you've done all the planning.'

'It's a small party, hardly a wedding to plan.' Only James, Asha, Kit, Rob and a few of Kate's friends from town were attending. Elsa had been unable to get away from Swansea, and Kate had refused any of her other suggestions.

'It's a retirement party, it should be discreet.'

'Well,' Isabelle looked at the patio, 'if this is a retirement party it says as clear as day that your idea of retirement is no different to your idea of work. But with a new focus.'

'Wonderful,' Kate said. 'How perfect. Come on, let's go think about lunch. You can tell me what you're up to in that new workroom of yours.'

THE EARLY SETTING sun put on a sublime display over the stone patio before plunging the guests into a shivering appreciation of the fairy lights and candles. Reminding them all it was after all only the 23rd March and they were being more optimistic than the evening was long.

Isabelle came out of the back door with her arms full of blankets nabbed from the sofas in the ballroom. She distributed them to appreciative murmurs, keeping the final four to take down to the lower terrace where she'd settled with Asha, James and Rob.

There was a sharp difference between those settled in the chairs on the lower level and those talking and admiring up above them. Kit and Kate forming a formidable hosting double act. Commanding a loud chatter of excitement and enthusiasm, accompanied by the constant tinkling of glasses being moved, emptied, refilled, swirled, jabbed into the air for emphasis.

Kate's friends were an odd, loud mix of characters, gleaned from her many years as a landlady. She'd shown them her new flat before herding them outside. All of them avid gardeners, bright with ideas and optimism for her plans. Martin was amongst them, with a limpid slip of a young girl barnacled to his side. They weren't the only younger people. One couple seemed to have walked straight out of a boutique, filled with immense enthusiasm for all things Salopian. An intensity achieved only by those newly arrived from London to the shire where, as one older friend declared in loud derision, 'all dreams come to die.'

Kit had arrived with Lou, Jamie and her husband, Rick, and two other friends that Isabelle had never met. A man whose physique seemed made to perform. All muscle and sinew poised to pounce, his movements hypnotic. His skin emphasising the extraordinary whiteness of his eyes and their brown pupils, dark and intense. When Kit had introduced her in the hallway, his handshake filled with the knowledge of his own strength. Commanding and gentle, clasping her single pale hand within his cool brown grip, enveloping his spare hand over it.

'Isabelle, right?' He looked her over, comparing her presence to the image in his mind. 'Kit's told me lots about you, it's good to meet you at last.'

'And you,' she paused for his name, wondering if she'd know of him.

'Jay.'

'Jay, oh good to meet you too at last,' she gushed, covering over the fact Kit had never mentioned him.

'Kit likes to keep his friends apart, right?' Jay muttered, holding onto her hands, smiling to show he saw through her polite nonsense before letting go. A smile that seemed to pull all the planes of his face into its depths. 'He quotes you to prove he's not the racist scum I accuse him of.'

'Me?'

'You're his India girl.'

'I was only born there,' she protested. 'Afraid I'm as white as the next scumbag.'

'As I suspected,' he murmured, but his eyes were still smiling when he let go of her hand. 'But I can't even claim that much so perhaps he has a point.'

His girlfriend was a different matter altogether, bouncing from the balls of her feet through to the wild curls of her blonde hair. Offering the tips of her fingers in greeting and a smile as shallow as a cat's saucer. Chattering with false vigour, flitting from one subject to another. Lydia, that was her name, she said it often enough you couldn't miss it. Jay a tempered shadow to her bright light. Isabelle had watched as Jay circled the hall, looking up at the high, coloured window of the landing, peering through the door of the drawing room. He had a curiosity greater than his sociability and, while Isabelle tried to engage with Jamie and her husband in welcome, she saw him look down the eastern corridor, tilt his head with curiosity and leave their group to take a few steps that way. She'd stepped towards the stairs to get a better glimpse and seen him looking at the India map. Watching him watching it, she had felt an uncomfortable shiver down her back. Was he looking for somewhere familiar, and personal, or questioning her right to have a map of India in her huge home? The chance to ask wasn't given her, for his bouncy girlfriend had spied him hiding and dragged him back to her side.

About to go back down to the others, Isabelle was tempted to invite him down to join them. There was something about his stillness, the way he observed rather than engaged, which reminded her of Moth. But engaging with Jay would mean talking with Lydia. She was about to slip back down to the others when Lou came up and said, 'mind if I join you guys?'

'Of course not,' Isabelle said, grinning. 'But we're being terribly boring.'

'I could do with some of that, these guys are exhausting. Here pass me a blanket.' Lou went down the steps in front of her. 'Any more room at the knackered inn?'

Isabelle realised someone would have to share and wondered whether she should go back and get more blankets.

'Plenty of room.' Rob pulled a chair from another table, making her welcome. 'We were admiring what retirement looks like.'

'Pretty amazing, right?' Lou said. 'Though I'm not sure it's retirement as much as ample money. Did you know that guy with the checked scarf is a Lord? I mean who actually knows a Lord?'

'Lord Clive.' Rob told her. 'Yes, he has money. Never spends it though, except in a pub, which is how Kate knows him. Mansion falling down around his ears. Blames a brutal divorce for it all. The Threlfalls are distantly related to the Clives, a long way back, if I remember correctly.'

'Good an excuse as any I suppose.' Lou sat down with a happy sigh. 'Jamie is loving this, despite Kit having to drag her here screaming. Made Fred look after her kids for the night and told her she needed a night away. Now look at her.'

They all looked up at the balcony. Jamie and her husband were waving glasses and discussing something with the young couple from London. As though they too had lived here all their lives.

'She's going to have a savage hangover tomorrow,' Lou said, shaking her head.

'It's a shame you have to go back tonight,' Asha told her.

Isabelle offered a blanket to Asha, one to Rob, the last one to James. He waved it away. She retreated with it in gratitude to her chair by Rob.

'I don't mind,' Lou said. 'Kit's got to stay sober for his flight first thing, we all get a good time and a free ride home. There's enough space in the van we'll be asleep before we get back.'

'There are some advantages to having a partner who can't drink,' James agreed.

Asha snorted.

'Not for much longer, eh love?' Lou commiserated.

'Long enough.' Asha touched her belly. 'First week of July.'

'You've done most of the hard work now, well, except the

last bit, of course. May I?' Lou reached out an enquiring hand.

'Of course.'

Isabelle watched Lou place her hand on Asha's protruding stomach. It was only a month since the wedding and her belly had arrived. It was a strange thing, this laying on of hands. It left Isabelle hiding a shudder of... of what? She wasn't sure. Discomfort, intrigue? Perhaps her own emptiness?

'Still as a frog,' Lou said. 'I like it when they're kicking, impatient little feet itching to get out. Boy or girl?'

'We don't know,' Asha said. 'I wanted to savour the mystery.'

'I think a boy. The way it's sitting, surely a boy.'

'That seems to be the consensus,' Asha said. 'But who knows?'

'What do you want?' Lou asked.

'A girl first, then a boy,' Asha said. 'To start with.'

Isabelle listened to them, withdrawing into her blanket. They created a bubble of baby-ness that made her feel lost and out of place. Isabelle could sense Rob's silence, polite and frozen. She reached out a discreet foot and touched the side of his, caught his attention. She wasn't the only one who felt excluded from this world.

'Kate's done an amazing job on this.' He turned towards her, lowering his voice to be respectful.

'I know, right?' Isabelle replied, leaning closer. 'And she's been here a week! Hired a gardener. I think she's going to spread rapidly.'

'I suppose it was foolish to think she might take up baking or knitting?'

'Go figure.'

'Do you mind?'

'What, the gardening?' Isabelle asked.

'Hmm.'

'No, not at all, though I don't suppose it will stop there. In fact, I'm glad. I feel less lonely now she's here. The house seems happier for it.'

'And you?' he asked. 'Are you happier?'

'I think so,' she said, her head cloudy with wine. 'It's lovely to have her here, I'm glad she came.'

'But what about you?' he persisted. 'You said you wanted to work out what you wanted, now all the rush was over. Have you had time to do that?' His hand reached out and touched the arm of her chair.

'Well, I've had more time, but I'm not certain I'm any closer.'

'And Kit? Is he any clearer now?' Rob asked, nodding his head in the direction of Kit. He was stood with his arm draped across Kate's shoulders, and she had leaned into him in laughter. He was being the most supportive demi-host, despite his protestations, determined Kate enjoy the event.

'Oh, not really. Maybe it is what it's always been. Half of something, a bit of nothing.'

Rob looked at her with a raised eyebrow. 'Six of one, half a dozen of the other, you mean?'

'What?' Isabelle asked, confused, trying to focus.

'What about a holiday?' he changed subject. 'Have you thought any more about travelling? Taking a break?'

'Not yet. I want to help Kate settle in first.'

'I'd say she's pretty settled.' Rob looked back up at the crowd above them.

'How about you?' Isabelle asked. 'How are the new client dinners going?'

'Ahh' he said, looking out towards the garden. 'I'm becoming the cunning singleton. I can eat without ever cooking these days. Which is good,' he turned from the distant darkness of the garden, 'our nisi came through yesterday. Six weeks to the absolute.'

She reached out, touched his hand where it gripped the curve of his chair arm.

'That must hurt, I'm sorry.'

'Oh, no need.' He patted her hand. 'It's what I wanted, right? A chance to move on, for both of us. To find happiness with someone else.'

'It can't be nice.'

'It is what it is. The damage was done. We have to focus on the future. I can't change the past.' He let his hand rest over hers. 'We all have to move on, right?'

'I suppose,' Isabelle said, her hand warm beneath his. The night was cooling rapidly. Even with the blankets any warmth was noticeable. 'That's what Kate says.'

Rob's words were brave and real, tingling with truth. She looked up at Kit. Perhaps he was right, perhaps she was waiting for Moth to come back rather than facing he wasn't going to. Elsa had saddled her with a responsibility for him, and she hadn't been able to let go. She was waiting for Moth to tell her it was okay to let go. Except he had. By leaving. Moth had shown he didn't want any of them being responsible for him. Whether she liked it or not, even if it stung inside when she thought about him. He had gone.

'What are you two whispering about?' Asha asked them.

She looked across to see all three had finished talking babies and were watching them. Isabelle felt Rob remove his hand, take a drink.

'The future,' Isabelle said. 'There seems an awful lot of change in the future, we were talking about it.'

'Seems to me it mostly stays the same,' Lou said.

'Not true,' Rob protested. 'Seems to me you never know what's coming round the corner.'

'I'll say,' Asha added, rubbing her belly.

Isabelle followed the curving, possessive fingers flowing over the swollen future.

'I reckon we don't know what's coming at the end of the hour, let alone the next corner,' James said.

Up above them laughter broke out again, they all looked up. Kate and Kit were leaning on one another, spluttering at something the old Lord had said. Isabelle watched them. Kit had been distant all night, rapid-fire exchanges, queries, compliments. Back in work mode, monitoring the evening though she had promised to manage it all.

She looked back, caught Asha glancing at Lou, raising her eyebrows. Lou rolled her eyes in reaction. Asha caught her watching them and smiled, a slight blush rising in her cheeks. Isabelle smiled back, wondering what she was thinking about. Too relaxed to really care. She'd ask her another day. It was such a peaceful evening, the party was going well. She was relieved. Relaxed. Rob was right, after tonight, it was time to move on, think about what came next. She'd promised herself she'd do that. If she wanted to, she could even focus on finding Moth. Going to meet him rather than expecting him to come home. Make sure he was alright rather than hoping it. Put her sense of responsibility to bed and move on.

'I'm going for a top up,' Rob said. 'Anyone care for another?'

'I'll have one.' Isabelle held out her empty glass.

'Me too,' Lou said. 'Make the most of the boss driving.'

'I'm fine, thanks,' Asha declined. 'I can only take so much water in one evening. I'll be up peeing all night.'

'I'm good, and anyway, we ought to think about getting home,' James said to Asha.

'I know but I'm so comfortable.' Asha snuggled deeper into her blanket.

'Come on,' James said, getting up. 'Or you'll be asleep, and I'll have to carry you both up those steps.'

Asha groaned but heaved her way out of the chair.

Rob and James said goodnight as Asha came over to kiss her goodbye. Isabelle was left with Lou, who slumped back in her chair and watched the trees above them.

'I swear he's more erratic than ever,' she muttered to the sky, as Kit's voice crackled out from above them.

'He seems pretty much the same to me,' Isabelle replied.

'Hmm.' Lou squinted at her with one eye, closing it again. 'Seems to me you miss a lot of stuff, must be that creative streak of yours.'

'He's not that different,' Isabelle protested.

'It won't last, nothing ever stays the same with him,' Lou said. 'Boredom threshold of a two-year old. Not that most men aren't the same, but he's definitely the worst.'

'The worst what?'

'Self-serving,' she said, nodding upwards.

'Not all men are the same.'

'No, perhaps not,' Lou admitted. 'I hate that generalisation stuff too but I've yet to see the exception to the rule. Like that fella just left, he knows he's scored gold there. That girl he's got ticks every box he needs but can he tick hers?'

Isabelle sipped from her emptying glass.

'And the other one, he's no different. Sniffing the wind, catching the scent.'

'Rob's coming out of a divorce, I suppose it's natural to think about his choices,' Isabelle defended Rob. She had never heard Lou this cynical before.

'Rob?' Lou looked up. 'Wasn't he Hester's husband?'

'Yes.'

Lou snorted. Upstairs she could see Rob heading their way. Lou shook her head, dropping her gaze.

'Don't mind me,' Lou said to Isabelle. 'I'm weary of the lot of them, but only tonight. Tomorrow I'll no doubt be looking too. It's what we do, isn't it? When one fire dies, you go light at another hearth. Nothing wrong with that.'

Isabelle was relieved when Rob arrived, setting three bottles down on the table. She felt uncomfortable sat there with Lou by herself.

'I'm being economical with my energy,' Rob said. 'Thought I'd bring a bottle back for us.'

'That looks like one each, to me,' Lou said.

'I wasn't sure which colour you wanted,' Rob said. 'I brought all three, red, white, rose.'

'How practical,' Lou said with a snarky tone and a wink at Isabelle. 'I'll start with white, by the time I finish that, I won't mind what I drink. I've never been fussy on colour.'

Isabelle felt an uncomfortable shudder as her comment span loudly up through the sharp air to the upper level and Jay's presence. It must be a successful party, people were starting to get drunk and embarrassing. She decided it was time to stop worrying about food and catch up. Up above she could hear music, pouring out from Kate's window in her kitchen.

'Excellent, dancing by moonlight,' someone called out.

'Hardly moonlight,' Lou scoffed.

'Get up here and dance,' someone called over the stone wall.

'You want to get Jay dancing,' Kit called out. 'Come on Jay, show them how it's done.'

'Later,' Jay retorted. 'I'm not drunk enough yet.'

'I'll dance,' Lydia called out.

The calls and laughter increased, and the music was notched up.

'Well, at least the neighbours won't complain,' Lou said, standing up with a sigh. 'Oh well, might as well go for it, you two coming up?'

'In a minute, maybe,' Isabelle said.

'Not me, thanks.' Rob sat down.

'Your loss,' she said. 'I promise I won't tell them you're cowering down here.'

They watched her go back up the stone steps, grinning at the shared dodging of the dancing. They sat sipping and talking, about the house, or legal details, or Nat. Bubbles of conversation that hung between them, growing, floating, popping. On the patio wall, the candles were fizzling out in a haphazard fashion, drawing their eyes, wondering which one would go next.

Isabelle became aware that Kit's loud voice had disappeared. She listened for a moment, waiting for him to come back from the toilet, but couldn't hear him, or Kate either. Saw Lou dancing nearer to the wall with Jay, moving away. Kit was right, the guy could seriously move. Hands spinning Lou with ease, a touch to her shoulder, to her hip, controlling where she moved, a kind wide smile and easy laugh encouraging her. Lou, for a woman who'd seemed prickly and negative towards men before she stood up, looked high as a kite in his arms. Isabelle envied her. She would have loved to dance like that and never had the confidence to try. In Mumbai, she had always watched from the side of the shot, adoring the big Bollywood dance scenes on set. Wishing she could ever do such a thing. The closest to a comfortable dance she had ever come was her and Moth shimmying on the rug in the garden under starlight. She watched Lydia ease Lou out of the way and throw herself into a flamboyant display with Jay. Jay's smile diminishing, his movements reducing until he eased his way out of it, disappearing past the corner of the house towards the drive.

Rob asked her about the possibility of another hosting and pulled her thoughts away. When their conversation ebbed again, she heard Kit and Kate were back. Jay had returned with an enormous dog on a lead. A darker shadow beside his quietly leaning frame on the stone wall, a long bushy tail swishing against his legs when people drifted closer to them. Lydia made a huge fuss of the dog and danced away with her high laugh. Isabelle grew aware of dislike growing in her. There was something demanding about Lydia, a constant need for attention and high spirits. She couldn't imagine how they had got together. What a strange combination they made. Watching Jay from the safety of her lower bower, Isabelle wondered again what he had thought of the map. Of the house. Of her. What people thought, meeting her for the first time this way. Owner of such a place. Up until now she had only had to deal with the change of circumstances in front of people who had always known her. Watching Jay reach a hand down to pat his dog's head, she felt pushed outside the circle of what was familiar. Rob, a comfort at her side she was glad she had invited. They talked their way through more of the evening, until the noise diminished, along with the emptying of their wine bottles. She became aware of people looking for her, to say goodbye. Heard Lou say something about looking downstairs.

'I think you're wanted,' Rob told her, glancing at the stone steps. 'Looks like they've had enough.'

Isabelle rose from her chair, felt her thick head waving in the sudden height.

'I'll go start on the washing up,' Rob said. 'You do your hostess of the mostess bit.'

'God, I feel drunk,' she said. 'No more parties for a bit.'

She negotiated the unfamiliar blurred steps, found people beginning to leave. Swamped by the sudden intensity of their heat, and presence, after the cool quiet of Rob and the lower terrace.

She could see Kit saying goodbye, 'Darlings, another time,' Lou trying to round up Jamie, 'Jesus, you are wasted,' Lydia leaning on Lord Clive and laughing at his every word, Jay waiting for Lydia, silent.

She reached a hand to the dog at his side, let it sniff her fingers and, when he put his muzzle into her hand, tickled his chin, asked, 'What's his name,' and folded a palm across the top of his shaggy head.

Jay, an even deeper smile on his face as he looked at the dog beneath her hand, said, 'Uggs, short for Ugly.'

'Oh no, he's beautiful, I've never seen a dog like him. Poor angel, what an awful name.' Jay, folding her hands up in his again in farewell.

His skin on hers a crisp moment in the mayhem. Taking her back to some part of her old self, away from here, in India, at work. A lucid drop of recollection swept away in the swirl of alcohol as he let go.

Kate was saying goodbye to everyone at once, a vibrant

blue scarf draped across her shoulders. It glinted in the way only silk could, catching the light and holding it, clutched close in Kate's hands to keep her warm. Isabelle caught it in passing, felt the way it dissolved between her fingers, springing back as she released it, 'Wow, where did that come from?' watching as Kate caressed it, 'A house warming present, gorgeous isn't it,' replying, 'I'll say, it's stunning, the exact shade you love,' and turning to the next person, 'Lovely of you to come, so glad, yes, I know,' and the next, 'Oh, thank you so much, but it's really Kate's work,' and, 'Lovely to see you too, yes, goodbye,' while all the time she tried to catch up with the rush of people leaving.

The confusion on the gravel driveway, trying to make sense of who had to go first, which close-packed car could get out, who was waiting for whom, watching Kit give Kate a fierce embrace, feeling his fleeting kiss on her own cheek, helping others negotiate the drive and out onto the tight bend of the road, feeling Kate plant a happy kiss on her cheek and tell her she had to lie down, seeing Kit back out the van with his friends singing inside, while she held back the impatient Lord who was too drunk to drive and being dragged out of his car by a friend and given a lift, and all the noise and the happy farewells, until she realised they had all gone.

She was alone in the night on her empty driveway.

Feeling the chill of the March night.

Realising that Kit had gone.

With the merest goodbye.

Same as Moth.

And inside her something snapped. Some little thing she hadn't known was there. A miniscule piece of elastic that was doing its job and holding her together, where the world couldn't see its simplicity, or its essential integrity to her.

The night sky stretched empty above her, reeling and absent of cloud. The twinkling distant stars diffused by the glow of streetlights from the town above. Herself as untouchable, untouched, as the glinting sky.

She turned and walked back into the huge echoing house with tears in her eyes. Drunken, hot tears that hated the emptiness of the vaulted hall. Tears she couldn't wipe away, couldn't stop.

And there was Rob, at the sink, washing dishes. Turning with a warm smile when she came in, seeing her useless, unstoppable tears. Putting his warm fingers to her betraying cheeks to wipe them away, with gentle clucking sounds of sympathy and understanding.

THEY TAUNTED him all the way home.

'Boss, she's retired.'

'So what?' he said.

'I have a friend who retired at 32,' Lydia said.

'She's not 32,' Jamie mocked.

'What's age got to do with anything anyway?' Kit complained.

'Maybe not now,' Jay said, gentler than the rest. Sat beside him, sober, with his ugly panting dog between them, while the rest threw drunken abuse from the back. 'But it will show.'

'Like what's the difference, 40 years?' Jamie asked, she and Lou howling in the background.

Jay cast him a kind look with a raised eyebrow. Kit kept his eyes on the road, ignoring the calls. Drunk, the lot of them. Uggs seemed to sense his distress, nuzzling his elbow. Kit stroked the dog's head, catching his ears, which he loved.

He might be the ugliest dog in existence, a mismatched, ill-considered hodgepodge of breeds, but he was loyal. Having decided he liked someone, Uggs never changed his opinion. And Kit had worked on earning his loyalty with sirloin steak the first time he'd had to dog-sit for Jay.

'22,' he muttered under his breath.

'As in, you should be shagging a twenty-two-year-old?' Jamie's husband asked.

More laughter.

'It won't last,' Lou said. 'But, what the hell, enjoy I say. Whatever floats your boat, right?'

'It might last,' Kit said, thinking about the long years behind them.

What did they know anyway? He hadn't seen anyone else slipping away from the party, making the most of time. No one had even noticed they'd gone.

They'd both been high and brave. Kate drunk enough to hold his hand in public, him brave enough to pull her close, kissing her. Seeing the surprised looks of Jamie, Lord-what's-his-face, the rest who'd seen. He'd never felt as invincible. Kissing her in public, knowing Isabelle was below and visible if he'd got the spot right, if she'd been looking in the right direction. He'd had to drag Kate away, the rush of it giving him a vicious hard on. Hard to hide, even in the dim lights.

'Meet me in the ballroom, two minutes, not a second longer,' he whispered in her ear.

He went to the van, pulled out the present he'd bought her, walking back through Isabelle's front door. Down the new stairs into the darkened room, grabbing a blanket from the sofas, on into the ballroom. Waiting for Kate, hearing her quick steps down the corridor.

She unwrapped the gift with happy hands as he

unwrapped her clothes, dropping his own to the floor, kissing her skin as she pulled the fabric out. It had cost him a fortune, from a boutique in Bristol that specialised in hand-made items. He took it out of her hands, slipping it round her shoulders. Pulling her close in it as they shagged, breath-less, ragged, brave, listening to the noise of the guests filtering in from the garden. The blue of the scarf catching the blue of her eyes, the moonlight catching the sheen of her hair, blue and silver running through him as her hands ran over his body. Reminding him of the long-ago night on Swansea beach. Thinking he would burst with the intensity of it. The knowing that this was it. This was what they were. What they'd always been. Matched, in a stunning harmony of need. Her teeth sharp on his ear, her breath hot on his neck as they grew warmer together in the chill air of the vaulted room. He'd always wanted to make out down here. To feel this close to someone. Wrapped up in someone. Skin moving on moist skin. Warmth encasing his dick. It felt glorious. Amazing. Endless. Kit gripped the steering wheel and let that feeling wash through him again. Lost for a moment in the thick intensity of what Kate made him feel. How she had always made him feel. Alive. Riding the moment with an edge of fear and glee, and never an ounce of remorse.

'Last?' Lou choked on her laughter.

'Who can tell where love will start or end,' Jay said in his thoughtful way.

Kit looked across at him, grateful for an ally. Jay was cool. Jay was an awesome mate. It had felt good, bringing him, introducing him to Kate. Jay was also blind as a bat. Lydia was going to destroy him one day. How Uggs had decided to like her, Kit would never understand.

'Love?' Lou asked and cracked up again. 'Kit? Lasting love?'

'Love's not his calling card,' Jamie added, trying to soften her laughter. 'Right, boss?'

'Love, anyway, yuck,' Lydia added, sat beside Jamie's husband, bored that she didn't have Jay's attention.

'Love's cool,' Rick said. He'd been ignoring her flirting all evening. Rick was solid. Solid in the way some men could only ever love the woman they'd bred with. Rick would be dull if it wasn't for his passion for the outdoors. A man who'd go away, climb a mountain, come home and build Lego with his kids. Even Lydia's low-cut blouse and roaming hands couldn't catch Rick's attention.

'Oh, please,' Lou jibed. 'You're telling me this is the one for you? She's old enough to be your mother. You'll be burying her before you have the chance to know if it's eternal love.'

Silence echoed through from the back. Lou could be vicious when she was drunk if she was single. At least she wasn't shagging Henri. Of that he was now sure, having got Ed to check on it. One less thing to worry about. Something was up with Lou, though, she hadn't been the same since Swansea. Kit let her bitter comment melt into the knowledge it had little to do with him.

'Maybe I already know.' Kit let the truck bite into the curving A roads, watching Lou and Jamie take the brunt in the swinging back, grinning at their banging heads in the mirror. 'Maybe we've already had a chance to prove it to ourselves. Maybe that's how I know.'

'Oooh, tetchy,' Lou tossed back. 'Nah, what the hell boss, I'm only teasing. Long as you're happy, I'm happy. Like I said to Isabelle, we're all the same right?'

Kit's heart leapt. Lou had been sat with Isabelle, when he kissed Kate, just before he dragged her away.

'What did you tell Isabelle?' he asked, keeping his voice neutral. Gripping the gear stick tighter. He saw Jay glance down at his hand. Observant twat, why couldn't he get drunk same as everyone else? Kit could count on one hand the number of times he'd successfully steered Jay past his child-hood hang-ups on alcohol and into a solid hangover.

'We're all looking right?' Lou said. 'All looking for the next ride. Keeping our options open.'

'Not all of us,' Rick countered. 'Some of us are content where we are.'

'Nah,' Lydia teased, stroking his thigh. Kit could see the flash of distaste in his face in the mirror. He wondered if Jay had seen that. 'We're all looking, even when we're happy. It's human nature.'

'That's what I said,' Lou agreed.

'What did Isabelle say?' Kit asked.

'I can't even remember, boss,' Lou complained. 'I've drunk too much. Do you have to sway the van this much?'

'Get the sick bags,' Jamie called forwards with laughter.

'Aw, don't be sick,' Lydia complained. 'I can't bear watching people throw up, it makes me...'

'... nauseous?' Kit offered with a grin in the rear view.

Lou mock hurled in the back and everyone groaned. They piped down though, getting quieter and sleepier as the road sped by.

Had Isabelle seen? What had she said to Lou? He hoped she'd seen. Hoped they'd answered the queries without any outright questions. Was it cowardice to end his maybe with Isabelle this way? Or gentle kindness? After all, she'd retreated first. Disappearing into Riverdell. Ignoring all his attentions. Wasn't this what she had made perfectly clear she wanted? He hoped they'd done enough. That it was clear, out there in the open, like Kate's skin in the ballroom. Wrapped against his, kisses that fused them together, breathless with the ending, the new beginning. Her happiness when he gave her the ticket to Italy, whispering in her ear about making love to her in the pool.

'I like her,' Jay told him in a voice quiet enough not to travel. 'She suits you. About the only person I've ever seen who stands a chance of keeping up with you.'

Kit glanced over with a grateful smile, took his hand from the gear stick. They fist bumped in the middle of the seat, hidden by Uggs' chest fur.

'Cheers, bud.'

'Ignore them,' Jay added. 'They're all drunk anyway.'

Kit hoped Isabelle was drunk too. Drunk enough not to notice how swift his goodbye had been. When it came, holding onto Kate had been natural, but saying goodbye to Isabelle, stilted. Reminding him of James in the kitchen the morning Asha told them she was pregnant. He'd mocked James, rigid as Isabelle congratulated him. He'd been no better. Brusque and uncomfortable.

Kit drove into the darkness. Perhaps it hadn't been his best farewell. But, thinking of Ms Suzanne Harper, it hadn't been his worst either. It was what came next that mattered.

And what came next would be Kate, in Italy, beside the pool.

Right beside the pool if he could persuade her. In the pool. Her breasts floating on the top of the warm water while he kissed her. And, with Kate, he knew his own desire had a chance of being matched.

13

Dearest Elsa,

Oh, my wonderful friend, congratulations! So many congratulations from us both!

We are thrilled to hear your news. Ted was delighted for you. A boy, no less. Your father must be over the moon, and Richard. What bliss it must be to have your first child in your arms. I am relieved to hear the birth went well and that you are finding motherhood such a joy. Take plenty of time to let your body recover, won't you?

It is such a shame to be so far away. Ted is swamped with work, and it feels like forever since either of us were in England. Six years. Where has that gone? David's birth seems to have emphasised how long I've been away. I have missed seeing your sweet little bungalow, and now you are already gone from there. I have missed seeing Kit too. Can he possibly be five already? Missed seeing Rose as a new mother. Missed seeing Kate go through this exciting time. Oh, how much I have missed and now your own new baby too. I wish I could say we will be there for the christening, and thank you for the invite, but Ted says it is not possible. Our medical bills are extortionate and keep him long hours at work. I shall send gifts with this letter and you must make sure to take lots of photos to send me.

Your father must be over the moon to have you back at Riverdell and with his first grandchild too. I hope Richard is settling into the house and managing to find his own place between there and the farm. It can't be easy to have to suddenly share his wife and new-born child. But it must be bliss for you too. I could never see you anywhere but at Riverdell. You are the anchor that holds us all down and keeps us steady. How exciting that you and Richard have moved into your mother and father's old bedroom. I always adored that room. Do you remember how we would all lie on the bed as girls and dream all such fanciful nonsense up? Those days seem a world away now.

I am thrilled to hear about Kate. Your father is such a wonderful man, and he has always had a particular soft spot for Kate. Only he could have seen through her resistance and independence to give her a greater challenge to rise to. A restaurant of her own, and she is only twenty-seven. I suspected from her letters that, despite her protestations of loving London, there was something lonely about her life. A big city can make you feel so insignificant. ~~Yes, they are wonderful to live in and visit but, after a while, there seems to be a siphoning away of your character into some shapeless mass of humanity.~~ Kate was never going to fit into a crowd and now, in Ludlow, with her own place, I think she will truly have a chance to shine. Do you know when it will be definite? Have all the details been sorted? How exciting it must be at Riverdell. You with your new baby, back at home. Kate living there with you and waiting for the mortgage to go through.

What a busy, hectic, delicious time of it all. I am glad for your father, to take his mind off his health, and it must be a relief for you to be there with him daily again.

I am waiting for March. Breathlessly. I cannot wait to go back to Kashmir. It is December '68 since I left there and these two years in Bombay have been... difficult. There, I have said it. The doctors say that the medical treatment itself brought on my depression. That the combination of drugs can do that sometimes. I suspect it was more the continual act of trying to achieve the impossible. I conceived twice last year. First in January, with a bloody miscarriage in March, my worst yet. Secondly, somehow, my body recovered, and we found out I was pregnant again in July. You will forgive me not sharing the news, as you did of your own pregnancy a few months earlier. I hope you understand the terrible fear that sits over us with each new hope. In the end I think it was all too much on my body. Which is, sad to say, that while you were getting ready to welcome David into the world, the doctors scraped the stillborn remnants of our fourth pregnancy from my useless womb. A third trimester dead foetus takes a lot to get rid of. I prefer to think it was that which brought on the depression. I have not strayed from the house since returning here and refuse any more treatment for now.

Either way, I am glad to be looking forward to Spring with positive news on the baby front, even though it is not mine. I never really thought of us as being in a race, but when Ted received your news about David, I felt as though a great weight, or hope lifted from him. The pressure to provide your father with an heir, to somehow put right the mistakes he made in his youth, seemed to expend itself in the few bare weeks between losing our child and hearing of the safe delivery of your own. Nature makes its own choices, doesn't it? Tests on our baby revealed chromosomal problems that develop in the third trimester. I am convinced now I am not meant to carry a healthy child. There is relief for me in accepting this. But the depression, that arises I think from feeling the great weight of failure. That I cannot give your brother a child. Cannot do this one simple thing my body is meant to do. I need some time away from Bombay and think it will do Ted good as well. To put this great disappointment behind him. Let us move forward considering what other hopes we might fill our lives and marriage with. I long for the trip to Kashmir which, normally, is an evil necessity of getting there. Travelling, I can slough the physical skin I have developed through these years in Bombay and remind myself of who I am when I arrive.

Now, enough maudlin, I wanted to write only of your own joy, forgive the bleakness. This depression is a vile thing, my body feels drenched in treacle it cannot escape. I know time in Kashmir with Kish will completely restore me, and my next letter to you will be more positive.

Send news and photos, especially of the christening. Give your father and Richard our warmest love for this exciting time in their lives too. I miss you all and look forward to coming home to England to visit you in the next few years, I promise. Let us get our finances more stable and we have both agreed it is to be our next priority.

ALL MY LOVE and hugs to your adorable little boy,

BETH x

14

H e heard them coming through darkness. Sounds. Echoing and massive sounds that he couldn't grasp hold of.

Sounds and cold.

A throbbing icy darkness.

Moth listened to the rhythm. It was steady and comforting. A drum far away. Rumbling across a vast distance. The sounds intruded again. The distant drum got louder and faster. Sounds turned to voices and the drum exploded right on top of him.

It's your heart booming.

He opened his eyes. Nothing but darkness.

The sound wasn't comforting anymore, hammering away at him. The voices coming closer. He tried to open his eyes again and breath left him in a groan that hit the earth beneath him and died. The voices increased, how many, ten, twenty. How many? Who?

Bino.

His heart exploded beneath him. Moth tried to move.

Nothing worked. There was nothing but pain, no response from any part of his body.

Bino again. He's come back.

To finish him off. To bury the evidence. Moth tried hard to move.

Are you already buried?

Were the voices leaving, not coming. Sweat and fear broke out of him. He could smell it. Sweat. Dirt. Fear. He could smell his own body. Smell Bino's on it. He retched. If he could get away from his own body, he could get away from that smell.

Hands found him again. Rage overtook the fear. Rage hurling out of him. Rage that would kill them all. A gurgling whimper emerged.

Pathetic. You are so pathetic.

Convulsions racked his body. Hands upon his back, his body. Voices talking to him.

Two voices. Two lots of hands.

Turning him over. Wiping away the dirt and congealed blood that covered his face. Light burning through his sticking eyelids. He tried to open them again. Nothing but a glare of light and shadow. One voice that called to another. He was shaking all over. Frozen. Something was thrown over him. He couldn't feel anything except the cold and the pain. He was lifted by the shoulders, someone knelt behind him. Warmth oozing through from them against his back.

This isn't Bino.

He tried to twist away, tried to move. Nothing, no response. He was immobilised between the warmth behind him and the shaking of his body.

Voices talking. Two voices. Italian. He thought it was Italian. Rolling tones of language in kind voices.

The voices drowning out the throbbing in his head, the sound of his heart racing, the agony beating itself out of his skull. Gentle hands gripping his shoulders. Resting on his bruises with the same hardness as the ground under his arse.

Your naked arse.

Awareness seeping into his growing senses. He was covered on the top, but the brutal cold of the mountain was seeping straight into his buttocks through a thin scraping of grass. That's how they would have found him. Naked from the waist down. His exposed privates to the air.

Covered in blood and spunk and dirt.

Moth squeezed his eyes shut. He didn't want to open them. He didn't want to ever open them again. He didn't want to let the tears out. The ones building behind his eyes and in his throat.

If you let even one out, you're done.

His humiliation complete. If he let one out, he might not keep the rest back. He focused on the battle. The great lump forming in his chest and throat. The tickling behind his eyes. He swore them down in silent fury.

Not. Even. One. You understand.

The voices carried on talking but he pushed them back. He didn't need their kindness. Kindness wouldn't win this battle.

You need rage.

Rage, hatred, fury huge enough it could turn back an ocean.

Don't you dare cry.

He heard the word 'polizia' and froze.

Police. No, no police.

He tried to open his eyes. Light again, and shadows in front of him. He tried to sit up.

Get up. You must get up.

He had to get away from them. No police. No police. Something must have made it out of his mouth. Something spitted and garbled. The voices stopped talking. He struggled again.

'Hssshhh,' a voice spoke to him.

Moth heaved again, tried to get up, away, 'no police, no police,' he heard himself speak.

The hands on his shoulder held him back, he cried out against the bruising they gripped. The two people tried to calm him. He tried again to open his eyes and hold them open. One side of his face felt swollen. The eye slower to focus. Numb.

The glare receded to a bearable level. It was evening. The sky not yet dark. He managed to focus on the figure in front of him.

Great, another bloke rescuing you.

Moth could see him now. A middle-aged man. Fit and sharp. Well-trimmed hair and clean shaven. Wearing walking gear, worn but clean and tidy. Moth looked, saw a kind face looking back at him with anxiety.

Anxiety for you.

Moth could read it on him. He must look like hell.

Great, you had to get screwed up a mountain and rescued by decent people like this.

He could sense the person behind him, propping him up. A woman. Her finer hands, her softer voice.

Ok, it's no better being rescued by a woman.

The man looking at her over Moth's shoulder, a thin line of anger on his lips beneath his anxiety.

Is he angry with you? Or with his wife, for making them help.

'I'm sorry,' Moth tried to say, 'mi dispiace.'

'Non devi dispiacere!' the woman said from behind him.

'La polizia,' the man said in firm tones. 'You need help, paramedici.'

'No, please, per favore, no polizia, no medici,' Moth mumbled.

Silence and a frown greeted him. Moth closed his eyes.

Please, please, please let there be a God somewhere.

If God had sent someone to help him, please let him have the sense to have sent someone who would not call the police.

Come on. Surely, he can do that much!

'Per favore, no police,' he muttered again from behind his eyelids.

Neither of them responded. He felt the body shape of the woman behind him. She was slim, her firm legs bony beneath his body. He must be heavy on her. He must get up. He had to get up.

Prove you can get up.

Get away from these people. Prove he didn't need the police, or medics. Moth put his hands down on the earth and began to move his body upwards. His ribs screamed at him in complaint and he groaned at the fact that pain could increase in his body. They both started fussing and complaining. Trying to settle him. Moth persisted. The blanket, it was a blanket, load across his lower body slipping as he made himself move.

'Clothes?' he asked. 'Abiti?'

'Bicicletta?' the man asked.

'The bike?' Had Bino left his bike? 'The bike is there?'

'Yes, bike, in... parcheggio, yours, yes?'

'Yes, si, si, bicicletta, e mio. Clothes, yes.'

'Ti abbiamo visto, prima, sulla strada. Ho visto la bici...'

The man lost him in swift Italian, nodded at the woman, easing the weight of Moth's body onto his own arms. She slipped out behind him and scrabbled back to the car park. The man fussing to hold the blanket around him. Moth could feel the warmth of it on his skin. He could smell himself. The blanket would smell too now.

You've ruined their blanket.

He was so grateful for it. The blanket between them a fragile shred of decency in the horrible moment. Moth clung to its soft edges.

Sunset tinging the sky into a welter of glowing colours. Orange, pink, purple, all slipping across the horizon, pushed down by the great descending darkness above. It would already be dark in the valleys. They had stopped at the viewpoint to see this last amazing sight of the day. Braved the potholes for a view. Found him instead.

Another twenty minutes and it'll be dark.

He would have frozen overnight if they hadn't found him. Not even conscious he was dying, or maybe conscious and unable to move, to stop it.

'Grazie,' Moth murmured to the man.

The man tightened his grip on his shoulders. Moth was on the knife edge of this guy's sense of duty.

'Mi chiamo, Tim,' Moth told him. The name weird in the air. 'Grazie per l'aiuto.'

'No grazie, ovviamente, e terribile, no grazie,' the guy returned, trying to make him understand. 'No thank you, eh, Tim?' and he squeezed his shoulders again.

They sat looking at the obscene beauty of the clouds, waiting for the woman to come back. It was surreal. Awful and stunning in the same breath.

This is one viewpoint they'll never forget.

The woman came back, slipping down the rough ground. She'd found trousers and pants. A woman used to caring for men. Retreating while her husband helped Moth to fumble his way into some clothes. Unable to stand. His trainers making the job awkward. Moth couldn't see his shorts, Bino must have kicked them off him when...

... when he dragged you across the ground like a trussed chicken and...

... and threw him onto the rock. The rock that Moth could see to the side. A blood stain where his nose had exploded. To be washed away in the next rainfall. Clothed, he hugged the fabric to himself, waves of gratitude rising in him. The gross reality of his nakedness hidden. Fabric encasing his body had never felt so close to making him human.

Really? This, all this, and you're going to cry about the clothes?

Moth rubbed the tears away. The guy offered him a hand. Moth looked at him, dreading the moment.

The guy smiled back, 'Ok, pronto?'

Moth gave him a hand, the skin raw and broken.

This is going to hurt.

He put the other hand on the ground beneath him and pushed.

Nope, it really bloody hurts.

Moth groaned between gritted teeth and felt his body collapse in wobbles. His ribs were agony, his legs, his butt, his head. He tried again, lurching up through a thin screech of pain. The woman stepped forward to try and help but her husband waved her back. Protective of her. Caring for him.

Another scrap of dignity but Moth clung to it. They made it two steps across the rough ground before he staggered back to his knees, groaning, crippled over with waves of pain. She stepped forward again.

'No, va via, va via,' the guy muttered at her, shooing her away. She sighed and walked back up to the barrier, shaking her head.

'Dai, Tim, dai, alzarsi.' The man offered his hand. 'Tu e me, o la polizia?'

Moth took his hand and gritted his teeth. He swallowed the groan as he was pulled upright, the guy holding him steady before moving away. Moth hanging on his slim build. When they reached the barrier, Moth started to cough. Heat lancing through him, collapsing his chest. Making him cry out, struggling to breathe. Falling onto the barrier, curling over himself.

The woman came forward with the blanket and pushed it against his ribs. Holding it there. Keeping the pressure strong until the coughing stopped. Moth was breathless by the end, gasping for air that wouldn't come. All three of them wretched by the time he stopped groaning.

This is a mess. This is not good. You are trashed.

It took two of them to turn him about on the barrier, his sight blurring with the discomfort. The guy supporting him while the woman reached down and lifted first one leg over the barrier, turning him, lifting the second. He could see a looming white camper van filling his vision. His bike in front of it, thrown on the ground in a wretched heap. The bags had been opened and thrown about.

Did she do it, looking for clothes?

Or had Bino gone through his stuff too, hoping to find money? It was a mess.

But at least it's there.

Even the front bag and the rucksack. Moth looked beyond the bike. Saw flattened birds fluttering across the ground.

Oh no. Oh not that. No. How could he. No.

Moth looked again. Not birds. Postcards. Floating through the potholes. All his precious postcards. Dirtied and crumpled.

Where's the notebook. Where's the bloody notebook.

He tried to see the notebook, his tears blurring the search. Luca's number. Moth stared at the pieces of paper, trying to find the small card. Tears splurged over the edge.

Where is it? Where is it?

'Alzarsi, alzarsi,' the guy said beside him.

Moth couldn't move.

The man looked at his wife, nodding, she stepped forward and took his other side. Between them, with Moth groaning in pain and a dead weight, they dragged and staggered with him across to the camper van, inside the doorway and collapsed him onto the floor of the van.

Waves of nausea and pain were rolling over him and he fell onto the carpet, letting them pull and push him inside, stretching him out.

Sound retreating in waves again. Ebbing and flowing. The wavering mountains outside the door, and the heads bobbing in front of them. Pain crashing from one side of his body to the other. Tossing the points of his injuries about until he could no longer tell where it was coming from. The pain, the sound, the light. Back and away. Out through the narrow door of the camper van and into the stunning sunset.

It's better out there. Away from you.

Inside, the worn carpet of the van beneath him and the distant ceiling with its pretty ridged wallpaper. False flowers on ocean waves. He drifted away on them.

It's a lot nicer than the inside of Bino's truck.

HE HEARD the engine start from somewhere inside the dark numbness. Doors opening and closing. He even felt air sweeping over him. It all sat at a distance. A gentle swaying began. Not the sickening swing of the pick-up. A soothing calmness. Floating along on it. He could cope with this.

One day, you can give up the bike, get a camper van.

When he had enough money to pay for fuel. A job. A life. Something he could look Luca in the eyes and be proud of. Soft swaying. Soft talking.

Luca.

Moth absorbed it all from a distance, barricaded behind the wallpaper. Hands on him again. Soft, remote hands he knew but couldn't tell. Touching here, there, rearranging him.

Luca setting out his coffee cup.

Turning the handle to perfection. Moth let the hands wash over his body. The far-away outside body. Inside it was numbed out. No one troubled him there. Kind hands on the outside, and a known voice whispering to him, calling him, demanding him.

Moth tried to open his eyes. Eyes swollen and blurred. Eyes that lied to him. Seeing Luca's face peering down at him.

That pretty face is laughing at you. Again.

Dark eyes, improbable cheekbones, full lips drawn into a tight line. Moth closed his eyes again. Lying, lying eyes.

'I told you to let me help, Sick Boy, now look at you!'

Luca's voice washing over him. Talking in Italian to the other soft voices. Talking to him.

He'll seduce the United Nations with that voice.

Moth felt sorry for them. They wouldn't even know he'd whispered his way to the top. Moth kept his eyes closed.

Wait. Luca. Talking. Here.

He opened his eyes again. Luca looked back at him.

'You need a doctor, Sick Boy, no arguing,' Luca told him. 'Not to mention the police.'

Doctor. Police.

Moth's comforting numbness slipped away from him. He scrabbled with his hands, trying to grip Luca, grasping pain instead.

Luca. Here. What. Focus.

'Luca?' he tried to say. Slurred gasping coming to his ears.

'Oh, now you use my name!' Luca took the flailing hand that Moth tried to grip him with. 'You are ill, proper sick now. Broken ribs, broken nose, temperature, maybe bleeding inside, who knows what.'

'Luca?'

'Yes, it's me, they found my number.' Luca told him. 'You kept it?'

Luca, here, how.

He tried to grasp it, tried to make sense. Nothing worked, his eyes couldn't focus, his voice wasn't his, his body wouldn't respond.

'No, no doctor, no police,' Moth mumbled, struggling to rise.

'What have you done?' Luca asked him. 'Why no police?'

'Lovere,' Moth said, 'friends in Lovere.'

'Is that where you were going?'

'Yes, yes,' Moth said. 'Please, no police, no doctor. I did nothing wrong, I, I...'

He watched with useless eyes as three people looked back at him with worry. Light blinding and jagged behind them.

His throat was thick and tasted awful, his breath was ragged. They were trying to help. But they would mess it all up, and he was nearly there.

Kit would help. Kit would know what to do.

'Kit, my friend, in Lovere. He is waiting for me.'

Luca held up his notebook and read, 'Hotel Castello, 24th?'

Moth nodded, heart pulsing, sick inside at seeing the notebook in Luca's hands. It was there, it wasn't lost.

What did they read? What else would make sense?

'You know you are late?' Luca asked. 'It's already the 30th. Will he be there?'

'Yes, yes. I think.'

Three worried heads looked away from him to one another. Luca spoke in quick Italian to them. Low and fast. Too fast for him to catch.

'If I take you, and he is not there, I will take you straight to the doctor in Lovere.' Luca told him.

Moth gripped at the hand that held him.

'What's his name, this friend?'

'Kit de Lavelle.'

Luca turned back and spoke some more. Moth watched in exhaustion, trying to listen, struggling to catch a single word. The man was worried, arguing back. The woman quiet and watchful. Luca was calm and confident. Talking to them with conviction.

He's going to win. Smooth talking bastard.

Moth clung to him. Watching as best he could. The man shaking his head. His wife putting her hand on his arm, pulling her husband to the door. Luca soothing them with his lush voice. He watched as they stepped outside the caravan, heard them whispering outside. Luca looked back at him.

'Two things,' he said in a low voice. 'First, your name, your real name, is it Tim?'

Moth shook his head.

'Well?'

Moth stayed silent, resisting.

'I can change my mind, Sick Boy. I don't have to help someone who won't trust me,' Luca told him. 'I left my shift and drove two hours to meet these people when they rang me. You owe me that much.'

It was so difficult to give that one thing away. To be that person. Luca staring at him, demand written in his pout. Moth wished he could be anyone else, someone he could be proud of. But he wasn't, he was himself, trying not to be himself.

Jesus, what choice do you have?

'Moth,' he said. 'Moth Threlfall.'

'Not Tim?'

'Tim-Moth-y,' Moth explained. 'Timothy Threlfall. Moth.'

'Ah,' said Luca, happier.

'What's the second thing?' Moth asked.

'After I take you to Lovere, find your friend...'

'... and don't call the police,' Moth added.

'*If* I find your friend, and *if* I don't call the police,' Luca stressed, 'you must tell me what happened to you.'

Moth looked at Luca with near hatred in his eyes. Nothing, but nothing, would make him do that.

Tell this man-god what a fucked up useless life you've got?

No, never. He would not do it. Would not. Could not. Moth looked away from him, shook his head, tried to voice his refusal. Nothing but unspeakable lumps in his throat.

Luca looked long at him, sighed and grinned in defeat. 'Well, at least I have your name, right?'

Moth breathed out a grim breath, and started coughing, the pain ripping through him. Luca grabbed a cushion and held it to his ribs.

'Broken ribs, you need to support them if you cough,' Luca told him. 'Now come on, let's get going, before this couple change their mind about letting me take you.'

'My bike?' Moth asked.

'Don't worry, we'll take the bike too, somehow.'

'My stuff?'

'They brought what they could find, it's all packed up. Stop worrying about your stuff, start worrying about yourself.'

Luca stood up. Moth tried to focus on his form as it moved away. The wallpapered ceiling came back into focus above his head. Daylight. It had been night when he got in the camper van.

'What time is it?' he asked Luca.

'Late-morning,' he answered. 'They rang me first thing, drove you down the mountain to meet me. We are not far from Lovere, a few hours, we will be there. Now, stop talking, I'll be back.'

The door closed behind him. Wind gusting through the cabin as he went. He had to try and sit up at least. Moth took a deep breath and started to roll, making it onto his side with his teeth gritted, the breath hissing out between them. It was agony. He gritted his teeth and kept moving. He would not be helped up again.

You need to at least stand up alone. Prove you can do this.

He made it to his knees before the coughing reduced him to a crumpled heap again. He heard the door open beside him. He was gasping in agony. Hands reached out. Voices told him off in Italian.

'Come on, Tim,' Luca said, 'let's do this together.'

'Alzarsi, Tim,' the man added.

They pulled him up between them in the tight space. Encouraging one another, manhandling him. His body explored in bruises where it pressed up against them, squeezing out of the narrow door.

A woodland lay-by. His bike hanging out the back of a battered old Fiat, the hatchback door tied down over the protruding tyre. The woman held the front door open while Luca and the guy dumped him inside. He gritted his teeth and gurgled at the pain that sitting down caused, trying not to groan in the face of all they were doing. Luca closed the door on him and hugged them both goodbye. He could see the worry in their eyes as they watched the car move away, the woman turning and putting her head on her husband's shoulder.

'I ruined their holiday,' Moth said.

'Yes, you did,' Luca agreed. 'Good people, you were lucky they found you.'

Moth was silent in response.

'It might not have been anyone,' Luca added.

'Not too fast,' Moth begged him as the road began to blur in front of him. His stomach churned. Empty, nauseous, scared.

'What?'

'Not too fast, please,' Moth nodded out of the window. 'I feel sick.'

Luca slowed down, looking at him for reassurance, until he nodded. Luca grinned at his discomfort.

'You have been on that bike too long. I'm driving like an old woman now.'

'It's better, no faster.'

Moth watched the road, battling the sickness and pain. Waves of sweat washing over him, his hands fisting on his knees. He felt Luca wind the car in a bit further. Beside him the trees flashed by, hurting his eyes. He focused out the front. Saw a pick-up go past in the direction of the mountains, silver, tidy. Cold washed over him at the sight of it. Anger rising to hold back the flood again. Luca beside him, glancing at him, watching the road.

What must he think?

How bad did he look? Moth looked down at his hands. Clutching his knees. They were bleeding. Raw and damaged, painful and swollen. He looked in the side mirror. His face scraped and swollen, the eyes puffy and red. His lips were scabbed and bleeding.

Your nose is wrong. It shouldn't be over there.

Moth put a hand up to touch it and felt pain explode in his head, making him gasp.

'I wouldn't do that,' Luca told him.

Moth tried to push his hair back from his face, it was crisp and tangled. His scalp hurt, raw where Bino had used it to pin him down.

'I look a mess.' Moth explored the less painful parts of his face.

'Your friend might be a bit shocked,' Luca told him, watching his attempt to tidy his hair up.

He might indeed. What would Kit say? Would he even be there?

Be there. Please, please be there.

What happened beyond that moment was too hard to

focus on. Better a shocked Kit than no Kit, Luca dragging him to a hospital.

The road passed. Its hypnotic soothing effect striated by the conflict of Luca beside him. Moth watched his legs working the pedals, his elegant hand on the gear stick. Soothing movements that caught his tired eyelids. His own legs too long for the small vehicle. His hands on his knees ugly, nails ripped and ragged. Luca had the tidiest nails, trimmed close. Quicksilver hands. Tapping and flicking at the wheel. The scent he remembered rising to meet his own.

You stink. Not like you smelled bad yesterday. You actually stink.

Moth could smell his rank scent rising in the small space, with Luca's scented screen of decency holding it back. Moth wanted the journey to end, to get out and away from himself. To put Luca back where he should be. Somewhere clean and decent and normal.

Away from you. Your filth.

He wanted to be clean, to be decent, to be normal. Somewhere pleasant where Luca belonged. He let his eyes close. Succumbing to the sway of the road.

Anywhere but here.

'MOTH, LOOK,' Luca called to him, flitting a hand across his knee to wake him.

He opened his eyes against the fall of light and dark flashing against his eyelids and looked out over a wide lake.

Luca pointing out the window, 'Lago d'Iseo.'

Behind Luca the lake stretched by the side of the road. The high sun falling on its surface and bouncing back into the car. Moth blinked against the brightness, trying to focus on the water.

Two weeks of trying to get here.

Here you are.

The water reaching away to the high hills on the far side, disappearing into the horizon further along the road. He pushed the button to open the window and let the air flood in. Sun-warmed, spring-fresh, stirring the stiffened vileness of his hair. Luca opened his own window too, the breeze rushing across them. Moved his hand from the gear stick to tap comfort on Moth's ragged knees.

That fine hand, light and fluttering. Moth wasn't sure if it was meant to be reassuring or concerned. Inside he could feel the walls against the ocean quivering. That dancing hand would break them down with one more flutter. He clenched his fists against the wall, digging filthy nails into the raw wounds.

You will not break. Not here. Not with him.

Closed his eyes again and let the breeze fill his mind. He longed to be on the bike. Alone. Beside this lake. Letting it wash over him. Clean him. Wash away what had happened.

Luca moved his hand to change gear. Moth felt the ocean inside him surge again.

'You will be alright Moth, we are nearly there.'

Moth couldn't speak, the great lump in his chest a barricade. Speak, and he might break. Silent, he could resist. Wind and silence holding him together.

Luca drove down the main road into Lovere. Fluid in the traffic, muttering under his breath, 'Castello, Castello, dove sei?'

Moth ignored him. Letting the lake ebb in and out of

view. It would have been amazing, riding this road after the heights of the mountain passes.

You can do it soon. By yourself. When you leave.

He heard Luca exclaim, pointing out past his torso, muttering at the traffic. He pulled into a carpark, exclaiming in satisfaction.

Moth tried to focus. Was it the right place?

Will Kit be here.

If Kit was here, Luca would go.

If Kit's not here, you'll be left with the police.

Fear stirred, a need to get out. To get away. Not to be stuck with the result of what might happen. Without any control over where it ended. He pushed at the door handle, trying to open it. Luca complained at him, but he persisted. Twisting his body through the open door until he had his legs on the pavement and the door had banged shut on them. Moth hung limply on the threshold of the seat, trying to find the momentum to get up. Luca appearing beside him, trying to encourage him back in the car.

You need to get out of here.

'No,' Moth said. 'No, I have to get out.' His head was spinning, he tried to push forward. 'Please, Luca, help me up.'

Luca hesitated, looking about them. Moth could tell what he was thinking.

This posh public place and you looking a beaten wreck.

Not an ideal combination, but he wanted out of the car. He was sick of it. He didn't want to be left in the car while Luca went looking for Kit. To be sat there, broken and useless, if he came back with Kit.

Buggered if he comes back with the police.

He wanted to stand up and face whatever was coming.

'There is a bench over there,' Luca gave in. 'I will put you there, but you must not move.'

Moth nodded, his eyes downcast, chewing on his lip. Luca was not convinced.

'You are not well, you must listen,' Luca told him. 'Please, Moth, let me help you. I will find your friend if I can, I promise.'

'I know,' Moth told him.

'Don't run away again,' Luca said.

Moth didn't respond.

'I shall lock the car, with your bike in it,' Luca told him.

Moth looked at him, furious.

'You must not try to run away, Moth.'

He wanted to tell him to leave. To give him his bike and go.

Sod off with this rescuing hero, caped crusader stuff.

He wanted to be able to stand up. He would have given anything for the energy, the health, the willpower, to stand up, to walk away. Even arguing with Luca was robbing him of breath.

'Help me out, I don't want to be left in this car.'

'You won't run away?' Luca demanded.

'I won't hobble away,' Moth confirmed.

Luca got his arm beneath him and pulled him up. Moth gasping at the effort of trying to move his body. They took slow painful steps across the car park to the benches by the lakeside. It was even more beautiful outside the car. Walking through the air, not driving through an unfeeling tunnel of speed.

The ground solid beneath your feet.

Luca strong beside him. Slim frame or not, Moth was

supported. Surrounded by the subtle waft. Perhaps it wasn't aftershave, maybe it was Luca.

All that goodness washing out of his pores.

As if there was too much beauty inside as well as outside, and the excess had to evaporate. Out of the car Moth didn't smell as bad.

Or perhaps you do but can't smell it.

Or perhaps all he could smell was Luca, tight up against him. One hand holding his arm across his shoulder, the other cupped against his waist.

'You smell good,' Moth said.

'Hmph,' Luca grunted by his side. 'You think?'

'Yes.'

'I'm surprised you noticed.'

'I noticed. In the coffee bar. When you came over to the table.'

'Yeah, you looked better then.' Luca flashed a vivid white smile at Moth, their faces close in the crush of support.

Seriously, this guy brushes his teeth in Persil.

They edged closer to the benches.

'I did?'

'Much better.'

'Didn't I throw up in front of you?'

'Well, yes,' Luca admitted, 'but before that, in the coffee bar.'

They passed a couple walking back to the cars, expressions of concern on their faces. Luca smiled at them and wished them a confident greeting in Italian. Pretending it was the most natural thing to escort a beaten wreck to sit beside the lake. They smiled a little back, not much.

'Better how?' Moth pressed him when they'd passed.

Focusing on the excruciating progress of his steps and not the faltering conversation.

'Nice. Enjoying your day.' Luca explained. 'No phone, no rush, no bother. Content, you know?'

He said nothing about looks.

Moth tried to ignore the sting of noticing that. A little jolt in some part of him that hadn't hurt before.

Nowhere doesn't hurt.

'You looked strong,' Luca added. 'Fit from all that riding. All muscles and chill. Like you belonged anywhere, wherever you decided to go.'

Moth chewed that one over.

'Not so strong now,' he mocked himself, clinging to Luca.

'You looked better in the coffee shop,' he agreed. 'Your friend will not be impressed.'

'Tell him I had a fight.'

'What?'

'Tell him I got in a fight, over the bike, please?'

'Is that what happened?' Luca was staring at him, close and determined. His brown eyes tightening, trying to look intimidating.

'You need to work on looking scary.' Moth grinned and tried to move forwards. 'You won't conquer the United Nations with that look.'

Luca squeezed him round the ribs. Not letting their walk continue. Moth felt breath rush out of him and refuse to come back. He groaned, trying not to draw any more attention to himself.

'Any better?' Luca asked.

Moth nodded in a head rush of pain and dizziness. 'You nasty...' he muttered.

Luca grinned at him and squeezed the curse short. 'Well?'

'Well, what?' Moth said, trying to breathe again.

'I asked, "is that what happened?"'

'No.'

'You want me to lie to your friend?'

Moth didn't respond.

'That's not what friends do,' Luca told him.

'That bench seems a long way away,' Moth said.

They walked on in silence. A fountain crept into sight, overlooking the lake. Behind it the road swept past between the plaza and a grand building with tall windows lined up between columns. The words 'galleria' emblazoned on fluttering banners across its front. Light rippling on the fabric reflecting the light on the lake.

'Trust the Italians to put a fountain right next to a lake.' He was tired now, bone tired. Head rushing with light and pain. His feet a long way away and heavy on the ground. Luca grunted beside him.

'We need to get you sat down,' he told Moth. 'You should have stayed in the car.'

'There,' Moth suggested, nodding his head at the low wall of the fountain. It was no more than four steps away.

It will do. Not the lakeside, but sweeter than the car.

They staggered the last few steps and collapsed onto the wide ledge together. Beneath the scent Moth could smell warmth coming from Luca. A warmth that taunted him, leaving his own mess colder and uglier than ever. Luca took his arm away, checking to see he could support himself upright on the stone ledge.

'This is not ideal,' he said. 'Come, we will find a bench in a minute.'

'No, it's fine, it's good.' Moth couldn't move another step. He was awash in pain and trying to keep it to himself. He could feel blood trickling inside his nose. He tried to ignore it. 'Leave me here, I like the water.'

Moth trailed his hand in the fresh water of the fountain, the coolness biting into his fingers and taking his mind off the pain. Luca anxious, looking down at him.

'It's Ok, go. I'll be right here,' Moth told him.

'But what if someone...'

'Look at me?' Moth gestured to himself. 'No one is going to come near me. Go, find the hotel, come back.' Luca took a step back, wavering, his hand reaching back to Moth. 'Go,' Moth insisted.

'Be careful... don't do anything stupid... or attract attention to yourself?'

Moth gave him a grim smile and two false thumbs up. Pain swamping him as Luca ran away across the park.

Nope, not going anywhere. Not yet.

He needed to catch his breath first. He squirmed his way across the stone surface of the fountain ledge. Water bouncing off the surface and splashing his back, droplets falling on his hands. Icy pinpricks of sensation that helped keep him focused. Putting himself closer to the lakeside. Further away from the road and the big gallery.

Get behind the fountain. Get some privacy.

The view of the lake was worth the effort the walk from the car had cost him.

You can get up in a minute.

Moth couldn't move. He was done in. At least here he felt less pathetic if Luca did find Kit. It wasn't even a year since he'd left home.

Home. Whatever that is.

It felt longer. A whole life he'd crafted for himself between leaving there and arriving here.

Not the reunion you planned.

Not how he'd wanted to see anyone. Maybe Kit was the least of all evils. Anyone else would use his state as the swiftest reason to drag him back.

He promised not to do that.

Moth looked over the glistening lake. It was ruffled on the surface, playing with the light. The mountains and hills behind rippling in reflection, tossed about by the wind.

You need to get up, get moving. Look stronger.

He put his hands against his head and pressed into them to silence the pain. When he took them away, he'd blinded himself. The pressure of his hands and the brightness of the sun warping his sight.

He watched a woman walk across the railings in front of him. Following the curve of the path as it chased the outside edge of the little garden. She had a blue headscarf pulled up over her head, cradling her throat and trailing across her shoulder. A long loose dress floated about her ankles in the breeze from the lake. Her shoes were clicking a slow, slip slop pattern.

Mules.

What.

Mules. Kate wears those.

Moth squinted. She paused at the outermost point of the circular barrier, where the pathway turned up through the middle and came to the fountain. Watching the lake. Her shape hazy in the brightness.

Something about her.

She turned and looked past him, up to the pinnacle of the grand building behind him. Moth looked at her face. Let his eyes catch her features. While inside, pain rose to a grim pitch. Sensation blotted out. The wind ceasing to touch him.

The glistening lake disappearing behind her. Her eyes dropped.

To the high spouting water.

To the rearing fountain.

To the basin.

To him.

Her eyes locking onto his. His staring back at her. He watched understanding register. Shock. Doubt. Certainty. Horror. Her mouth fell open in a cry and she started towards him, the scarf falling backwards as she darted forward.

Time slipping with her. Light sliding behind her. Moth saw her move, but she was stuck. In the act of reaching out for him, going nowhere, while he fell backwards. The vivid, blue sky cartwheeling over his head as water exploded around him. He heard the distant sound of his head striking stone. Heard Luca calling. Saw hands reaching. Watched bubbles rising through the water as it coursed over him. Some of them red and lazy, filled with blood.

Bubbles of life floating upwards through the churning sky-filled waters.

'ARE YOU OUT OF YOUR MIND?'

Isabelle winced. Her head was pounding. The kitchen table was swaying, and the floor seemed intent on tripping her up. The sunlight pouring through the tall kitchen windows with as much aggression as Kate's voice.

'Sorry?'

'I said, Are You Out Of Your Mind?'

Isabelle flinched in the onslaught. She hadn't meant it to happen.

'I know it's not ideal,' she defended herself. 'We were both rather drunk, it was a mistake. It'll be Ok.'

'Ok?' Kate scoffed. 'OK!'

She had come pounding into the house on fast feet the moment after Isabelle had shut the door on Rob. Not giving her a chance to think through the night before.

'You think he's going to see this as a one-night stand? A drunken mistake?'

'I'm hoping he's going to be as mortified as me,' Isabelle said, her throat swollen with discomfort, pulling a chair out at the end of the table. 'And try to forget it just as quickly.'

Kate stared at her in amazement. 'You think Rob is going to admit he used you for a commiseration shag, Isabelle?' Kate pointed out the window at the empty driveway. 'Or accept that you used him? Our Rob? Mr Decent himself. You've made a mess, and you need to sort it.' The hand slapped down onto the table.

Isabelle felt it reverberate through the wood, put a hand to her head. Rob. Of all people. What had she done? Too much wine, and that awful goodbye. The utter loneliness crashing down on her.

'I'm sure he'll see how stupid it was,' Isabelle protested.

Kate harrumphed in response. 'We'll see about that.' She stormed from the kitchen.

Isabelle watched her go, heard the back door slam. Perhaps having neighbours was not such a hot idea. Not when they could look right onto her drive and see a man kissing her goodbye in the morning. A gentle respectful kiss on the lips. So, well, so positive, so optimistic.

Isabelle put her head on her arms on the table and begged it to stop moving.

. . .

'Now, do you believe me?' Kate asked.

Isabelle crossed her arms over her chest and leaned her hip against the kitchen work surface. It was Tuesday morning. Rob had been two evenings on the trot to see her. She had tried to let him down, tried to suggest it was a huge mistake. Rob was firmer. He said it was emotion, and it was real, and he had no worries about telling anyone. But they – they, when had they become they? – should let his decree absolute come through before starting a new relationship. Out of respect to Hester.

'It's James all over again,' Isabelle said. 'Like I can't say no, I can't bear to hurt him.'

Kate put a finger to the centre of her forehead. Suppressing the irritation that was sitting there. Isabelle could tell she was trying to be patient.

'I can't believe I let this happen. I'm useless. I'm worse than useless, I'm pathetic. I mean, it's not Rob, he's nice enough, but God, what is Hester going to say?'

'I shouldn't worry about that. I don't think her opinion of you could sink any lower.'

'Are you trying to reassure me?'

'No, I'm trying to help you. Look, you're not the first woman to make a gargantuan mistake in a drunken moment. Certainly not the first woman to put herself in the wrong man's bed.' She flicked her hair back with a swift hand. 'But it's what you do next. I mean, is this what you want? Him? You and him?'

'No,' Isabelle groaned. 'No, no. I mean he's lovely, but I don't even really fancy him, I just feel, I suppose, relaxed with him. Rob is so easy to be with. God no, I don't want to get tangled up in another relationship.'

'And let's face it, your skill in extricating yourself is already proven.'

Isabelle tugged her arms tighter and raised her eyes to the ceiling. Self-loathing seemed to have got there first, she looked back at Kate. Leaning on the far side of the table with both hands splayed to pin the surface down. Worry and determination etched on her skin as clear as the lines engrained on the wooden surface.

'What do I do?' Isabelle asked.

'You have to go away, leave.'

'Run away? That's even more pathetic.'

'Not run away. Give him a clear message. It was a mistake, you're not interested.'

Kate took something out of her pocket, held it in both hands, looking at it for a long minute.

'What's that?'

'A ticket,' Kate said. 'To join Kit, in Italy. He wanted me to take a holiday, while he was working there.'

'Well, he didn't ask me.' Isabelle felt the same emptiness reaching into her from the night of the party. 'He wanted you to go. He won't be happy to see me.'

Kate walked round the table and looked at her, held the ticket out. 'Nonsense, Kit will always be happy to see you.'

Isabelle looked at the ticket in doubt.

'Isabelle, come on, you know Kit, he's only every wanted to help you. He adores you. You have the chance to crush Rob's illusions kindly and maybe even save your friendship with him.'

Isabelle reached out for the ticket, took an edge of it.

'It's open, you can go any time,' Kate said, her hand firm on the other side of the ticket. 'Go. Pack a bag. I'll speak to

Rob when he comes. Because he will come, you know that don't you? Until you give in.'

'And you don't want to go?'

'Oh, I can take a holiday anytime,' Kate's fingers released the ticket. 'Besides, think what I'll get done in the garden while you're away. Now, go, pack. I want to get something for you. You leave in ten minutes, no longer, or you'll think it through and get stuck again.'

'What about...'

'What about nothing! Go, pack, ten minutes, the rest can wait. I'll look after it until you get back.' Kate walked out of the room without giving her a chance to respond, leaving Isabelle looking at the slim chance in her hand.

ISABELLE STOOD ON THE DRIVEWAY, the old, patched handles of her travelling bag stiff in her hand. She'd rejected the case in favour of what she could grab and walk with. She felt the pressure of not having a car of her own. Envied the ease with which other people seemed to open a door, sweep across the gravel and onward in their own life. She had to walk to the station, wait for a train, connect to others, make her slow painful way to Liverpool airport. When she came home, she promised herself she'd get a car.

Kate had left her waiting under the porch, staring at the budding magnolia about to burst into flower, listening to the traffic outside the gate. Anxious to be gone. Hating the creeping sense that her home had become not her own again. That she had let someone else into it, into herself, hurt more than any of the shame she felt when she thought about that night with Rob. Most of which she couldn't remember in detail, only anxiety. She wanted to come home and not feel this horrible cringing dread when she heard a car slow down outside the gates. So much had happened since she last came home and yet here she was, wondering what right she had to be there again.

Kate opened the back door. In her hands the folded blue scarf Isabelle remembered from the party.

'Here, take this,' Kate said. 'You'll enjoy wearing it in Italy.'

'But it's yours,' Isabelle protested as Kate put the soft fabric into her hands.

'And I'm lending it to you, bring it back for me. I hate things sat unused on shelves, bring me back something nice in return.' She gave her a small envelope. 'Here, pass this on to Kit for me, and tell him "perhaps another time". He'll understand.'

Kate paused, looking down at the sharp edges of the paper between them as she handed it across, saw the light sandals on Isabelle's feet.

'Are those all you're taking?'

'What?'

'Those shoes?' Kate tutted. 'It's Italy, darling, in spring, not India. Did you pack anything else... no, of course not. Here,' she held onto Isabelle's arm, slipped her shoes off, popped them on top of the scarf, 'take these, until you can buy something more suitable. And have fun, put this behind you. Come back ready to get on with what you want. Will you do that? For me.'

'I'll try.' Isabelle looked down at the soft blue silk, and the small envelope pinned down by the mules.

'Go on, and call me when you get to the airport, let me know you're on your way. Leave a message if I don't answer, I'll be in the garden. It's going to be a gorgeous day.'

Isabelle gave her a hug, crushing the scarf between them, tears of gratitude surging upwards. Kate held her for a moment before pushing her away with two firm hands on her arms, and Isabelle could see wetness gleaming in her eyes. She lifted a finger to push Isabelle's hair back.

'I do love you, hopeless darling. Now, off you go. I'll deal with everything here.'

Isabelle stepped away, holding the gifts to her chest, hefted her bag and walked out the gates of Riverdell.

KIT LOOKED AT THE ENVELOPE, speechless. He took it from Isabelle's outstretched hand and tucked it into his pocket.

He looked again at the blue scarf wrapped round her head and shoulders, her face hidden within.

'That's a beautiful scarf.'

'Kate lent it to me,' she said. 'It was a housewarming present. I hope you don't mind it being me? She said to tell you, "perhaps another time". I think she thought I needed it more.'

'Did she indeed.' Kit was light-headed with the moment, a sense of something slipping away from him. Perhaps this is how Kate felt, he thought, that last morning in the bistro. Trying to catch hold of something that had already gone.

'I'm sorry if you're disappointed,' Isabelle's voice wobbled in a way that made his breath catch in his chest. 'I hated how you left, after the party, it left me... well, I didn't know what I was doing.'

Kit could feel the busy airport surging past him. People rushing through life, and he'd been sitting, watching, waiting for Kate for over an hour. Excited from the moment she'd texted him telling him the plane and arrival time. Focusing through all the crowds, feeling the flow of their happiness and the tension of airport stress, trying to find her face. The sight of the blue scarf had been electric, warming him down to his neatly clipped toenails.

He was trying to process that Kate had given it to Isabelle, that Isabelle was wearing it here, and that Kate hadn't come.

His head couldn't work out how those all points fixed together and, with the constriction of confusion throttling his earlier excitement, all he could focus on was the scarf.

She hadn't even told Isabelle it was from him. Before she gave it away.

Whatever was in the letter in his pocket, she had made her message clear. Kit drew a breath. It hurt. Breath had never hurt like that before. Like he was alone, and that last breath had held him to something. Evaporating into the air of Milan airport. He reached out a hand, took Isabelle's.

'Of course I'm not disappointed. Surprised, that's all.'

She squeezed his hand, eyes downcast.

'Why so sad?' Kit asked.

Isabelle remained silent. He reached out and pulled her head up with his other hand. Her eyes were damp, and she looked exhausted. White with tension.

'Perhaps Kate was right,' he said. 'You look shattered.'

'I'm such a fool, Kit.' She was struggling to keep tears back. 'I can't believe how many mistakes I make.'

'Oh, you don't get the prize for screwing up,' he said. 'We all share that one. Come on, let's get out of here. I know a great place for lunch, then we'll leave Milan behind and head up to the Lakes. You'll feel better before you know it.'

He took her bag in his hand, tucked an arm through hers, and guided them towards the exit. The letter in his trousers felt heavier than its pathetic size permitted. Trust Kate, the apocalypse reduced to a pocket-sized perfunctory.

KIT LOOKED in the mirror in the gents. Surprised to see himself staring back. It wasn't even warm, but he could see the sweat beading on his temple. He wiped it away, threw the paper towel in the bin. Looked again at the note. It's white paper dazzling.

Trust me, it's better this way. You'd grow bored and I'd grow old. Let's not kid ourselves. Don't be a stranger. K x

But it hurt. Jesus it hurt.

It hurt like the morning on the beach when he'd seen her fierce, naked and impetuous and not had the courage to speak up. Hurt because he knew it was fear inside that stopped him then. Hurt because the same fear lurked now. Go back out to Isabelle, tell her the truth, that he and Kate were, were what? Something? That he had to go back and make her believe he wouldn't grow bored, or she old. And could he tell her that? Or accept the note, the returned scarf, the crystal-clear message. Kate didn't want him. Not now. Not how he'd thought. Maybe not at all. And the thought of facing that made him more fearful than the rest.

Kit put his hands on the rim of the sink, squeezed his eyes shut and tried to push the fear away. Do it, you gutless, spine-less waster. Go out there and tell her the truth.

But for what?

Her pain. Kate's rejection if he did turn up at Riverdell, demanding an answer. Kit felt the sweat beading on his temples, he gripped his hands into fierce fists. Heard the door to the restaurant opening. He straightened up. Turned on the tap. Tried to ignore the sound of urine hitting the pan behind him.

He slipped the note in his pocket, looked in the mirror. Wiped the sweat from his brow again, cooled his face with water. Turned and walked out past the bloke zipping up his fly.

'WHERE ARE WE GOING?' Isabelle looked away from the countryside and towards him.

'Lake Iseo,' he said. 'One of the less famous lakes of the famous lake region. I've booked... you... into a private villa, in the hills outside Lovere. I have a lot of work to do, I'm a bit here and there.' Kit flexed his hands round the steering wheel, warm, slippery. 'I've got a room in town, and sometimes I stay on the job, but I'll be around.'

'Why don't I stay at the same hotel as you?' she asked. 'Wouldn't that be easier?'

Kit paused, a tiny flicker, too much to explain and none of it would be good. He'd chosen it for Kate. To start as they meant to go on. To make her feel special. To convince them both. He'd only kept the other hotel in case Moth left a message.

'It's gorgeous, you'll love it, and it will make me get away from work too,' he reassured her. 'Within a few days you'll feel completely refreshed.'

Kit pressed the throttle of the old Alfa. The engine well-cared for, the boss indifferent to fuel consumption. He'd borrowed it for the day to impress... Kate. Its bloody bonnet stretching out in front of him. The depths of the paint flickering the passing landscape back to him. Isabelle looked in the side mirror. Kit could see her raise a finger to her eyes, puffy with tiredness and whatever else she'd been crying over.

'I could do with a bit of that,' she said. 'I look shocking.'

He looked across, grinned, 'You do look rather British.'

The villa was as stunning as he'd promised, cheering him up as he sped up the curving driveway. The old stone house set on a hill, rising to a low-roofed cube of precise assurance, softened by vines and presenting itself at the end of the long cypress-lined driveway. Bougainvillea and clipped yew surrounded the terraced lawns.

He pulled the car up outside the entrance.

'Wow,' said Isabelle. 'Kate would have loved this, it's amazing.'

'Hmm, right? Come on, let's find... your... room.' He grabbed her bag from the back seat, trying to cope with the stumbles in conversation. 'Is this all you brought?'

'It was rather short notice.' She swung her legs out of the car, put the backless mules on the gravel with an air of embarrassment. 'I didn't have a lot of time to think about packing. Kate even leant me her shoes.'

Kit looked at the shoes sticking out from under her creased trousers. They looked preposterous.

'How thoughtful of her.' He took her hand and pulled her out of the car.

He walked up to the entrance, through the open doorway, calling out in Italian. No one answered, but he knew the room anyway. He grabbed the key from behind the desk, turned to see Isabelle taking in the details. Oblivious to him, her eyes drinking in the décor, mouth agape. He led the way up the wide stairwell.

He hadn't thought about it from her perspective. Had seen the view from the bedroom window that looked out over the gardens crowning the high hill, down to the lake at the bottom. The lake which glimmered as seductive as a jewel in sunlight. A view Kate would have adored. He'd not registered the rich tapestries hanging between the windows, the ornate thick curtains, the sprawling damask bed dressings that Isabelle now took in, feeling them between her fingers in joy. The blue scarf falling upon her shoulders as she looked upwards at the painted ceiling.

'Didn't I tell you you'd love it,' he said.

'It's stunning. This must cost a fortune.'

Which was what he'd wanted Kate to think, along with the scarf. That he would spare no expense on her. That he'd give her everything. He put Isabelle's old threadbare bag down on the bed.

'Well, have a bath, settle in, look around. I'll find the owner and tell her you're here. I have to go into town now, but I'll be back this evening. We'll have dinner together.' He started towards the door. He had to be clear what he was doing. He would call Kate. It might be a moment of panic. It might be nothing. He had to be sure.

'Kit, don't go.' Isabelle reached out to catch his hand. 'I mean, do you have to, go, right away? Can't you stay a while?'

Her hand was shaking where it held his. He squeezed it, tried to reassure her. He had to leave her for a little while, get it clear, come back when he knew. Turned his shoulder to leave.

'Please, don't go,' she said. 'I don't want you to leave again. I'm... I'm scared.'

'Scared?' Kit asked, his hand trapped by hers. He turned away from the door. 'Scared of what?'

She reached for his other hand, taking a step out of the distance between them.

'I don't know. The future, you, me, life. I can't make sense of it. I don't know what to do.

Kit stayed rooted to the spot. Fascinated by the open window, the sun shining on the lake below, the cool of the deep rooms and the quiet, the intense quiet of the bedroom, where all he could hear was breathing. His own tightening him up inside and Isabelle's, shallow breathing droplets between them. He moved a tiny mouthful of air closer to her. Not even a step, involuntary, like breathing.

'You don't need to be scared, not of me.'

She took one more step out of the space between them, those ridiculous mules on the wrong feet inching towards him.

'I'm scared of me,' she said, not looking at him.

'How can you be scared of yourself,' he asked. 'Especially you. What's to be scared of?'

Her hand reached out, stretching through those final globules of space between them, landing on his chest. First one, then the other, pulled from his hands, touching his chest.

Kit felt his hands on her waist, pulling her towards him.

Knowing he was going to leave, walk out the door, come back later, when he knew what to do. Even as her head found the crook of his neck, and his body felt the intense pull of her warmth. Even as he knew he was too scared to ring Kate or walk out the door.

He was going to do it, even as she lifted her head and he kissed her.

KIT WORKED RELENTLESSLY all morning and through lunch, which he didn't let anyone else at the island take either. Mid-afternoon, he threw himself into the boat and pushed the throttle hard up, roaring out across the quiet waters, where a casual wind ruffled the perfect surface of the lake.

He had felt the pressure all day of leaving her by herself. Even with plenty of ideas, amusements and things to do. Enthusiasm hadn't been much evident in the last three days. More a fearful hanging onto him, gladness to see him that evaporated into a hesitant lovemaking.

A patient, calm, brittle lovemaking where he had to hold back, rein in, subdue himself, to find her level. Trying to value it as a respite after the intensity of his working hours, with a villa full of decorators, cleaners, and sundry staff issues, all waiting for him at the end of a short boat ride each morning. He had less than another two weeks to go, and he couldn't help but wonder if he would manage such restrained lovemaking for that long.

At the edge of his thoughts, somewhere during the boat ride back from the island, Kit felt a discomfort twisting through him that he'd made a mistake. A mistake which Isabelle clung to. A mistake he might not be able to unmake. But the boat ride was exhilarating, pushing back the discomfort.

He had to stop in at the hotel, check there was no message from Moth.

He'd said nothing to Isabelle, assuming as the days rolled on that the little shit wasn't going to ring anyway. Besides, it was easy enough to arrange separate trips back home, she didn't even need to know he was going on somewhere else if Moth did call.

Check the hotel, pay for the room for another week, go meet Isabelle.

A fine sheen of sweat was blown away by the breeze from

thrashing the small speedboat across the waves. The petrol engine leaving a multi-hued frothy skin in its wake. Kate would have loved this. She would have made him take her out to the deepest part and swum naked in the freezing waters. Made him warm her up on the floor of the cockpit. It amused him, that it was called that. Cockpit. How appropriate. He moored up, jumped onto the jetty and walked down the road to the hotel. Checked his watch. Ten minutes, he was doing fine. Perhaps time to buy some flowers.

'Signor de Lavelle,' the concierge greeted him. 'No messages I am afraid.'

'I didn't expect any, never mind. I'll pay for another week. Oh, and a flower shop, where's the nearest flower shop?' I've got five minutes, is it close by?'

He would surprise her with some flowers.

'Round the corner, Signor de Lavelle.'

'Mr Lavelle?'

Kit saw the concierge frown over his shoulder. He turned around. A young local guy looking at him. Stunning. Dark hair, dark eyes, cheekbones you could hang a hat off. Skinny runt mind, all limbs, loose hair and clinging trousers. Reminding him oddly of Isabelle. He certainly caught the eye. Relaxed and confident in the hotel entrance, indifferent to the concierge sniffing at his presence.

'De Lavelle,' Kit corrected him. 'Can I help you?'

'My name is Luca Moretti, Mr de Lavelle, I was looking for you. For a friend.'

'What friend?' Kit asked.

'Sir, can I help?' the concierge enquired.

'No, it's fine,' Kit said. 'How do you know me?'

'Your friend asked me to find you,' Luca said. 'Moth? Moth Threlfall? He says you know him.'

Kit paused. Not a flicker this time. A long pause. Breath-less. Something was going on. Again. Something he wasn't in control of. That rising sense of something awful, curdling his toes.

'You have a message for me, from Moth?' Kit asked.

'No Signor, I have Moth for you, here.'

'Moth?'

'Yes, he needs to see you. Can you come?'

'Here?'

'Signor, are you sure this man is not bothering you?' the concierge asked.

'Here. Right here?'

'Yes, here, right now.' Luca turned and took a step towards the door. 'Please, you need to come.'

Oh God, Isabelle was around the corner. Visiting the museum. It had taken three days to tempt her away from the villa. The anxiety of plans unravelling hit Kit in the guts. A vile, unusual feeling, distasteful. Souring his mouth. An oil slick across the waters.

'What's he doing here?' Kit snapped, following Luca out of the building. 'He was supposed to call me, not come here.'

'He said he was supposed to meet you here,' Luca said in concern. 'But he is not well, he needs a doctor.'

Luca strode up the street, refusing to wait, Kit chasing a pace behind him. Away from the hotel and over the road towards the gleaming railings that fronted the lake. Kit saw the banners of the museum fluttering ahead. The taste in his mouth grew stronger.

'What's wrong with him?' Kit asked, trying to stay focused, to keep up with the swift anxious stride of the long-legged, younger man. 'What's happened to him?'

A cry came towards them from the lake. A sharp, female

call of distress. Kit looked past the young man as he broke into a run towards the fountain, his own feet faltering on the pavement at the sound of that well known voice. Heard a splash and a sickening thud. Saw the blue scarf unwinding from Isabelle's shoulders as she ran from the lake towards the fountain. Stumbling in the wrong shoes. She'd promised to replace them today. He walked forward, curving round the side of the marble basin, his feet refusing to go faster.

Saw the blue scarf floating downwards. Lingering exquisitely on the slight breeze. Expirating on the ground.

Saw Luca, soaking wet, trying to pull someone from the water.

Saw Isabelle reach out to help.

Saw Moth rising limp between them.

A bloody Lazarus.

15

KASHMIR, INDIA. 3RD JULY 1972

My darling Rose,
How wild and erotic your letters are! Though I am rocked by jealousy, how much I adore these long, intimate letters you send. They remind me of a diary entry, and I think perhaps some days you reach for a loose sheaf of paper and write to me instead of in your scrappy notebooks. I feel close inside your life and heart, not pushed away at a bitter distance.

I remain in Kashmir. It has been a joy not to return to Bombay. Ted visited late last year, in November, after the weather had become particularly intolerable in Bombay. It was not a successful visit. His attempts to rekindle our love life came up against my own physical distress at the memory of all that my body has been through. I know he is my husband, and that I should be warmer to him. But, well... I cannot. It is that simple. ~~The thought of his hands on me, even now, makes me cringe.~~ This is not Ted's fault. I have recovered from the depression and exhaustion I came home to Kashmir with, but only if I remove myself from the

drudgery of our marital relations. But that was not an easy
thing to try to explain to him. I guess the age difference
between us didn't help. He is one foot closer to the world of
his father than to me. I bemuse him with my talk of platonic
love, or other purpose and passion in life. Suffice to say, he
left after only three brief weeks and has not returned since. I
get a missive from him once a month to keep me updated
about the house and his business matters.

Kish tells me he probably has a lover now. At first, the
idea shocked me, but I suppose it is quite natural. Do I mind?
Only in theory. We are still married but, beyond the shock, I
am relieved. How can I explain this? This sense that a barrier
has risen through my skin, pulling me firmly away from all
contact of an intimate nature. The depression left the day I
allowed myself to admit this. That I do not enjoy a man upon
or within me. From that day I shed the belief I am a failure
for not bearing a child and decided to see what else I might
yet become in life. My hair, once my pride and joy, ravaged by
the drugs of the last few years had grown sallow and limp. I
made Kish cut it all off. Rose, you would be shocked. It now
nips at the base of my neck, a whisper reminding me of what
I once was. Weighed down by expectations and failure. When
I catch my reflection, I am reminded of my own agency and it
keeps the depression at bay. How can I resent Ted the choices
he makes? Your letters fill me with a warmth that has long
been missing in the bedroom of my marriage. Is it not fair for
Ted to feel the same, and pursue his own pleasure as he
needs to?

How you inspire me! How open and fierce you are.
Switching your passions between lovers, between men and
women, between controlling and being controlled. You write
as though your body were an experiment, to see how far you

can take the pleasure you crave. The world you describe seems another life altogether. How different we have become. I love nothing more than the solitude of my bed, the sense of my skin being mine alone to caress. Your desire was always a thirst and now seems an insatiable well you cannot fill. Lying in bed at night and re-reading your exploits makes me warm with happy memory. How glad I am that we had those wonderful years. I do not mind the great disappointment of my married life, with such thoughts to recall. In fact, I count myself as lucky. How many women have only ever known the grunt and thrust of a man's love, with no idea how their own pleasure is roused or fulfilled? Does Elsa even know how much you taught Richard? Do you remember that time they caught us in the bird tower? Elsa's face a picture of self-righteous shock, as though she hadn't been coming to do the exact same thing. And Richard's narrowed eyes calculating what he might be able to learn. Does she have any idea that you have had as much an influence on her love life as mine? Keep your gorgeous exploits coming. They are my companion in the long hours of the night, and my gentle longings are satiated in dreams of the adventures you have.

Kish worries that Ted will divorce me, and I will be thrown out of this villa. A divorced woman in India is a pitiful thing. Homeless, unprotected, without finance, she is subject to a great deal of scorn, abuse and physical violence. She is nothing. Perhaps it is naïve of me to think that I will be in any different position. But, while I know Kish is rightly worried, I cannot live with that fear over my head. I have tried everything to be the wife and mother that Ted wanted. If he chooses to divorce me because I failed, I cannot blame him. He remains, as he always was, honourable and caring, and I cannot believe that he would abandon me without the means to support myself. If all else fails, I will return to England and be at last with all my friends again.

Though, there is my dilemma. I confess, I adore Kashmir. With as much passion as I have come to hate Bombay, through no fair distinction. I guess Bombay is the seat of all my failures in life. I returned here to walk at last among the flowering almonds of the Srinagar parks and felt myself released, as gloriously free as the mountains reflected in the lakes. An almond tree is a beautiful thing, it bears blossom and yet produces not fruit, but the most adorable, furred pod of a nut. Here, I am making something of myself and would not be ashamed, as I once was, to stand beside you all again. I thought once, such a silly and long time ago, that coming to India would be the beginning of my journeys. I hoped so much to see the world. All of it, I imagined. Now, I hope only to stay here in Kashmir. If I must leave, I would be overjoyed to see you. If I came home, I would be heartbroken to leave this behind.

You should see all that we are doing, Rose! You would be proud of me. Kish and I have cleared the entire villa. The damp and rot have all gone, replaced with calm, soothing walls of whitewash. We have begun working on the court-yard, fixed the old fountain and are now moving out into the extensive grounds that surround the house. Much of it is overgrown and inaccessible. A wall of neglected greenery that forbids entry. In our own way we are explorers too. Hacking paths into the shrubs and diverting them round trees, fanning out from those paths. There are over 100 acres of neglected land here. Even Ted is not sure of the full extent. Land reform in India would make it impossible for a non-national to purchase this sort of land now, but as Ted acquired it just after partition it is apparently acceptable. He has done nothing with the land since he bought it in 1948. Nearly 25 years of neglect is a lot to nature's ingress. Though he used to profess a desire to retire here, I worry he is more interested in selling it to fund his retirement in Bombay. Perhaps my determination to prove the place worthy is a foolish hope to change his mind. I have planted a young almond sapling in the courtyard. It reminds me of Riverdell's magnolia, and I feel closer to you all. I tend it daily, wondering if I shall still be here when it finally bears a pod, hoping it will remind Ted of his original hopes for this place.

The best part of all this is that we are not doing it alone. Kish has organised a classroom for me in the west wing of the villa. We do not charge for these lessons but the children (and adults) who come for lessons, work for us instead. I do not want you to worry! This is not a cheap labour trick. It is a genuine exchange. All the children who come are either homeless or working to support their families and have no chance of school. They arrive barefoot after a long early walk, are dropped on mopeds, or even delivered by passing trades-men. Sometimes they stay an hour, sometimes a week. Some-times I see them once and never again, and that is hard to bear. The vast majority are girls. Some of them are Dalit, reduced to the lowest caste level, often by virtue of the jobs their parents do for other Indians. To be Dalit and female in India, is to be worthless. You belong to your father or husband or brother. It is unedurable. Two girls have now joined our home permanently. They help Kish cook and clean, and work to organise the lessons. Leaving me to concentrate on teaching. They have been rejected by their families and live in terror of honour killings.

The mother of one, Madhuri, brought her here herself and begged Kish to take her. She refused to marry when her father insisted. She is fourteen. Her groom-to-be was fifty-two and twice widowed, with nine children he needed a wife for. Madhuri, a much-unwanted third daughter, was covered in bruises when she arrived. When the mother left, she told her daughter that she was dead to her and must live in the world alone, and never to contact her or they would both be killed. Kish tells me this is an unusual act of maternal love, that in many cases the mother too would have conspired in the killing.

And then there is Laksha... she is seventeen and made the mistake of falling in love with a Dalit. Her face is ruined. Her nose and ears cut, her hair burnt from her scalp, her breasts slashed. She is crooked from the beating she was given, walks with a twisted limp and cannot sit in comfort. She was found unconscious in the street. Kish says death would have been a kindness. Death is what was dealt to her Dalit lover. He was beaten, castrated and hacked to death in front of her. The police brought her to us, and that is all they will do. They do nothing about these honour killings. They say it is a family matter.

Beneath the layers of her clothes, I think Laksha feels like me. That our failure is the beginning of our freedom. Laksha has the chance of a life her own with us, and what price beauty to escape the life so many women in India suffer? Though Kish encourages her to veil herself during the day (despite my protests), in the evenings we will sit and prepare food together on the wide verandah and she lets her layers fall. There is a strange and luminous peace behind the scarring and her smile is the deepest of many crooked things in this odd life.

Who knows what Ted will think of this ragtag band of misfits who renovate his house for free? The boys who chop the trees down and clear the damaged land. The girls who sweep the aggressive garden back out beyond the courtyard, cultivate the vegetable plot and string flowers from the windows? Weekly, we take offerings from our garden down into the city, sell them at market and give some of the money to the local police force to foster good relationships. This is bribery, I know, and you would scorn it. But not all of them are bad people, though there are enough, and we hope to build a network that might help us aid other victims such as Madhuri and Laksha. Though it is wrong, there is weight behind Ted's name as a white man, and I use that name with what weight I have left to claim it my own. What will Ted think of the woman his wife has become? The golden hair she has chopped off. The sanctuary his house has become? He is at heart a good man, and I hope he will see the good that we are doing, as he once did by Kish.

My love, time drifts on, and I am needed. When Ted returns, I shall speak to him of our return to England for a good visit. It is long overdue, and I am desperate to see Kit and David and be with you all. To walk the green lawns of Riverdell, idle beside the gleaming river and talk nonsense long into the evenings as we once used to.

Give a huge cuddle to your wild boy for me. If you can pin him down long enough. Take care too of your beautiful body, for it is precious to me, even if you see it as a commodity to utilise.

MY ENDURING LOVE ALWAYS,

YOUR BETH x

16

I t wasn't difficult to arrange.

Three phone calls took Moth from the public lake side, to the private villa on the hillside, to the very private doctor's attention. Kit's thoughts focusing as the fountain water collided with the pavement, picking up the prostrate blue scarf, watching Moth's bloodied head on Isabelle's sodden white linen lap, pulling out his phone.

Get it away from public view. Put it somewhere safe. Fix it. In that order.

ISABELLE SAT IN A SHADED, discreet corner of the verandah. Oblivious to the blood on her linen top. Distressed that she'd left Kate's scarf behind.

The lost shade of blue silk haunting her in the glistening waters of the lake below. Its shimmer dance hypnotising her eyes, the reflection glimmering behind her lids when she closed them.

Kate would not be happy she'd lost the scarf, even under

such circumstances. She felt unveiled and exposed before the naked lake, seeking refuge from the fulsome sun in the shade of the tall potted trees and hanging climbers. She wanted to go back, find the scarf, rescue it. Wrap it round her head and cover up the roiling emotions careening inside from the moment she saw Moth's face falling backwards. She closed her eyes, saw the glinting waters seared upon her vision.

Moth. What was Moth doing here?

KIT WAITED at the back of the dark room, watching the doctor work, watching Luca stood near the bed. His fingers twitching a dance along the length of Moth's arm, the bed covers, his own pulsing wrist. Listening to the doctor's diagnosis. In Italian too fast and mumbled for Kit to understand.

He would have rather sent him away, this unknown young man who knew too much, but his own Italian was limited, and Kit wanted to know what the hell was going on. Besides, Luca didn't look like he was going to be told to go anywhere. Only the arrival of the doctor had stopped him from calling an ambulance and the police.

How had Moth ended up here?

Some sludgy shade of filth that shimmied in the light from the window.

What was it with him and Isabelle? Every damn time.

Nothing but murmurs from Moth, or yelps of pain, or low groans of agony or silent limp stretches. The doctor had been pumping drugs into him for the last hour, Luca their unhappy translator. The names of the drugs didn't mean much to him. He'd made Luca write them down, to get them checked later. Not that he distrusted the doctor. Just the doctor's irritation with being called to attend on not much more than a tramp.

A knock on the door. He went to open it a crack. The owner of the villa herself, alerted by her staff.

He slipped outside. Into the wide decent corridor they'd had to drag Moth along that seemed as unperturbed as the owner, a crinkle of distress between her eyes hidden by a smooth practiced smile. He reassured her in gentle tones, 'a family friend, yes, attacked, no, we are not sure, you are so kind,' offering her his hands, unsure of who was giving out the sympathy, mentioning the name of his employer again. That flat-lined smile, the short nod, the withdrawn hands.

His boss out here was well known, if not well liked. However the family had accrued their wealth it had left them more respected than loved. The private doctor arriving not ten minutes after they, Moth, Luca and Luca's car had arrived at the villa. Kit demanding an empty room. Stalling Luca's swift-rising panic with his clacking leather shoes on the stone hallway.

Moth. How had Moth ended up here?

LIGHTS. Moving. Brightening. Overwhelming him. Sharpness that hurt where he couldn't reach. Lights and sound.

Sound. Lapping against the shore. No, not water. Sound. Moving against him, touching his skin.

Luca's voice.

He could recognise that.

Memory stirred. Isabelle. He couldn't hear Isabelle. Had he seen her?

Waves of warmth in his limbs. Softness beneath him.

Himself merging into the softness. Losing focus on the contact.

Explosions inside. Heat, searing heat.

White coldness washing over it.

Lights. Moving away, growing darker.

He was losing the sound. Voices whispering. Luca. He couldn't hear Luca.

Where was Luca?

Where was Isabelle?

WHERE WAS ISABELLE?

Kit stood outside the door, watching the owner retreat. He had to face her sooner or later. Moth was out of it. No point waiting there. He walked to the top of the stairs. Looked down at his shirt, stained and filthy from manhandling Moth.

He turned back to their own room, ripped the shirt off and threw it in the laundry bin. Slipped the belt on his trousers and pulled open the armoire, took fresh clothes out, shut the door, halted by the mirrors. Stung into stillness by the reflection from the bed.

Kit turned, walked across. Dropping the clothes, picking up the scarf.

There was a speck of blood on it, he hadn't been able to keep it away from the mess that Moth had made. He wiped at it, frowning.

Pulled it up to his eyes and drowned the moment out in its oceanic vastness. Felt Kate far away on the other side, lost beneath waves of confusion.

Fear stabbed him in the chest. Fear. What was this fear? It had no place being there. He clenched fists in anger at the vile taste of it. Hating that the scarf smelt of everything other than Kate.

He folded the scarf up, found his bag and put it at the bottom. Piling clothes on top. Pulled fresh clothes on, straightened his belt. Checked the mirror again.

First, Isabelle.

Then, Moth.

Then, then?

ISABELLE HEARD HIM, the hard shoes coming across the stone, stopping beside her chair. His hand resting on her shoulder like stabbing flint. She shrugged it off.

'You knew he was here?'

'No.' Kit sat down opposite her. 'I told him I would be here.'

'But you spoke with him?'

Kit paused. Took a breath to say something and let it out.

'And you didn't tell me,' she finished.

'I did what I thought was best for Moth.'

She looked at his fresh pressed shirt blocking out the lake below, sunlight dazzling on the brightness of the cotton, its clarity offending her. Looked down at her own bloodied clothes. Moth was lying injured in bed, the world had exploded with the fountain, and Kit still came up looking immaculate.

'You did what you thought was best for yourself.'

Kit didn't say anything in response. She looked past him into the dark interior.

'Has the doctor finished yet?'

'No, he's still with him.'

'We should arrange to take him home,' she said.

'Home to where?' Kit asked. 'Where do you think home is, to Moth?'

'He's sick,' Isabelle protested. 'He needs to go home, get better.'

'He's been beaten up,' Kit countered. 'He's a mess, but he's not dying. Moth won't thank you for dragging him home when he's too drugged up to fight it. Let's patch him up first and find out what he wants.'

'You think that's what's best?' Isabelle demanded, staring at him, waiting for him to respond. He didn't.

'Where did you get the doctor from?' she asked.

'He's my client's doctor,' Kit said.

'Who is this client of yours?' Isabelle asked.

'I told you, I can't say. I'm bound by confidentiality.'

She heard the precise way he deflected her. Saw the exact edge of the collar, the neat fingernails. Kit's perfection. Shining out of him with self-confidence, arrogance even, that lashed at her. Moth unkempt, bleeding, unconscious, drenched. She stood up.

'I'm going to see him.'

'You should wait,' Kit said as she stepped up from her chair and towards the doorway. 'Give the doctor a chance.'

She paused, stood with her back to him, feeling the sun on her shoulders, looking into the darkness of the interior. Wait. Wait for what? All this time she'd waited. For Moth to get in touch. For Kit to find him. For something, anything, to show her the way.

'I'm done with waiting.' She walked into the dimness of the room ahead.

. . .

SOUND BOOMING OUT OF HIM. Rousing him. That inner drum exploding in fear. Hands, strong hands on him. Turning him over, feeling down his back.

He surged. Muscles battling, pain exploding, hatred flashing.

Resistance. He felt resistance.

Hands again, touching, pinning, probing.

Heat. Searing hot pain firing through him, chased by numbing cold. Ice crawling through his blood. Taking his legs, his arms, his hips, his back.

Soft hands. Cool soft hands on his. Fingers wrapping through his.

Focusing the pain, right there. On those fingers. Sat in the chair at Riverdell, the grip keeping their arms taut between the chairs. Free to break away whenever they chose.

Isabelle.

He breathed out. Felt the numbing cold reaching into his chest. Up his neck, sweeping past his eyes. Great heaviness shutting him down. Soft, sucking, deep weight, pulling him in.

ISABELLE SAT beside the bed and held his hand in hers.

When he settled, stopped writhing, the shouts turning to gulping soundless breaths and ending, pinning it between her other hand. Stroking it, stroking it, stroking away the fading shouts. Keeping her own distress in control.

Moth's face blank on the pillow facing her, his wide shoulders stooping towards her. Luca stood next to her, holding Moth's limp weight on his side. Face pinched from the thrashing they'd restrained. Lip bleeding where Moth had smacked him.

On the far side the doctor put the syringe down on the bedside cabinet, tutted, continuing his examination down Moth's back. Pushing the cover back as he probed ever lower. Muttering in angry, rushed Italian to Luca.

She could see more of Moth than she ever had. His shoulders were knotted with muscle, thicker and broader than they'd been beneath the shirt on the day he left. His pulse twitched the muscle that lay down the side of his neck. His chest was wider, more filled out. His fingernails coarse and broken, blood caked on his skin, seeping from grazes. Not even a year had passed, he was barely fifteen, and she didn't know his new shape. She'd lost touch with time, but time had swept Moth forward. Moulded him into a man. The door opened and she sensed Kit slip inside, watching them.

'What's he saying?' Isabelle asked Luca, nodding at the doctor.

He looked at her, shook his head. She looked at the doctor. He ignored her, spoke again to Luca, anger on his breath.

'Tell her,' Kit told Luca.

'He is ill,' Luca said. 'Broken ribs, on both sides, broken nose. Something wrong with his shoulder blade, possible internal bleeding, high temperature, infection maybe, and... and lacerations.' He practically spat the last word out.

'Lacerations?' Isabelle asked.

The doctor spoke again, hushed, intense, inspecting. Luca shook his head when Isabelle looked at him.

'I told you to tell her what he said,' Kit spoke from behind them in a voice that hurt Isabelle to remember. A voice that brooked no argument. Except perhaps from Kate. How she wished Kate was there.

'Please, Luca,' Isabelle pleaded.

'He has been... attacked,' Luca said, angry, distressed. He shook his head again, refusing to speak.

'What do you mean?' Isabelle insisted.

The doctor stood straight from his inspection. Leaned a hand across the bed, too wide for a patient, meant for a loving couple, and laid it on Luca's forearm where it supported Moth and gave him a gentle pat. Encouraged him to help get Moth back on his back. Isabelle tucked his arm onto the bed beside him, kept her fingers wrapped round his unresponsive ones.

'I suspect your friend has been assaulted,' the doctor explained in slow but impeccable English. 'Raped. It is a matter for the police.'

Isabelle looked down at Moth's hand in hers. Her eyes tracing all the wounds in need of treating, wrapping up. She wrapped her hands over the skin. Shock taking the warmth from her limbs, until she thought the only warmth left was the point where she and Moth were connected.

'We'll take care of that,' Kit told him.

'I must go and get medicine,' the doctor said. 'And a nurse is needed. He must be bathed, but not before the police see him. His wounds cleaned, his nose reset, his shoulder bound, his chest strapped. He will need an x-ray.'

Isabelle felt lost between the four men. The doctor angry, firm. Luca shaking, upset. Kit quiet, precise. Moth. Silent. Accusing. She heard the doctor leave, Kit speaking with him by the door.

'He insisted no police,' Luca muttered as the door closed behind the doctor. Moving to the other side of the bed. 'We tried to persuade him. They found him... undressed, but we did not know... about this.'

'He wouldn't have thanked you for calling them.' Kit crossed to the bed.

'We have to call them now,' Isabelle said. Moth's hand weighing down hers.

'We call the police now and you take Moth's choice away.' She could sense Kit looking down at her, sat beside the bed, holding Moth's hand. She did not look up at him. 'He asked Luca not to call them. That was his choice.'

'But the doctor insisted.'

'The doctor is paid to do as he is told,' Kit said. 'Whether he likes it or not.'

'You wash him, you wash away the evidence,' Luca said.

'We can sort that,' Kit said. 'Unless you call them yourself, I'm not involving the police without Moth's permission. We need to let him choose what to do.'

'He's a child,' Isabelle protested, looking up at him. 'It's our responsibility, Kit.'

'He's not a child,' Kit snapped at her in the same voice he'd used in her bedroom, that long-ago day of their argument. Their argument over Moth. She looked back at Moth, away from Kit's harshness. 'Look at him! He doesn't look anything like a minor, how would anyone know?'

'How old is he?'

Isabelle looked up at Luca, hearing the squeak in his voice, smothered by firmness at the end. Wondered how he even knew Moth, what their relationship had been? How much they could trust him or what he said?

'He just turned fifteen.' She watched Luca blush in discomfort. 'Two weeks ago.'

'He looks much older,' Luca protested. 'I thought, at least twenty-two. At least. He looks older than me.'

Kit stared at her with a grim look on his face. Silent

vindication.

'I'm going to speak with the doctor,' Kit said. 'I'll be back.'

Isabelle and Luca looked at each other across Moth. Luca reaching his hand out to touch his shoulder, adjust the sheet that covered him. His hands reluctant to leave Moth's form.

'I only met him a few days ago,' Luca said. 'He came into the café where I work, for breakfast. He left his bag behind. I took it out to him, and he was sick. I tried to help him. He wouldn't let me.'

Isabelle watched the small touches with which he tried to make Moth's mess better, the matted hair moved, the speck of blood on his cheek wiped away.

'If I'd tried harder, this might not have happened.'

He looked even more vulnerable than Moth. Isabelle took in his sweeping hair, thin frame, elegant fingers. They all held guilt for how they'd failed Moth. It wasn't only her. Even Kit, she thought, and pushed the thought far away. Kit she couldn't work out yet, but this strange boy looking out for Moth, someone he'd only met a few days before, he pierced her heart with guilt.

Isabelle leaned across Moth to touch his shoulder in comfort. 'You did more than us.'

MOTH FELT THE COLD LIFTING. Peeling away from his eyelids, hovering hard inside his mouth.

He could smell it. Smell it on him.

The filth.

The filth of what he was doing. Sweet and sharp at the same time. The sweat on his skin. He couldn't move, pinned between the sharp table and the hand digging into his shoulder, pincer firm. Trying to raise his head, trying to see the door, pushed back down. He flickered his eyes open, someone leaning over him, reaching for him. Familiar eyes.

It can't be. He's dead. Dead in the car crash.

'No, no, no,' he tried to say, his tongue stuck to the roof of his mouth. Heavy, difficult.

'You're dead, stop it, you're dead.' Hands on him, those bloody hands, shouldn't be doing this.

'Get off me, get off.' His tongue moving. His voice working. Nothing else. Eyelids too heavy to stay open. No hands, no strength, no way to push him off.

'Stop it, stop it, please.' Tears coursing down his face. Crying, swore he'd never cry in front of him.

'Stop it, stop it, please stop it. You're dead, you're dead. It's wrong, it's wrong, stop it,' he sobbed.

Words he'd never been able to say. Too scared for Nat. Take it like a man. That's what his father had told him. You or her. Your choice, Little Timmy.

The cold seeping back upwards, his mouth full of salt, full of that vile taste. The sweetness, the sharpness. His tongue cleaved to his cheek, pushed aside by the hardness. Choking, choking on it. Take it like a man.

'Please Dad, please, please, I don't want to, it hurts.' Sobbing.

Stop crying. Stop crying.

You swore you wouldn't cry.

KIT OPENED the door as the shouting stopped. He'd heard the weak edge of it from the corridor. Christ, he thought the Doc had knocked him out cold. He saw Isabelle sit down hard on the chair next to Moth. Saw Luca's shocked face. His shaking hand on Moth's shoulder, soothing the inert form.

'What happened?' he asked them, closing the door, moving closer.

Isabelle raised a hand to her mouth. A shaking hand. Why was everyone shaking?

'What?' he insisted.

Isabelle wouldn't speak. She was crying. Silent wretched shoulders bent over him, her head hanging behind that wall of hair.

'What the hell happened?' Kit demanded in a voice that split the air between them, making them wince.

'He was crying out, trying to make him stop, begging him to stop it,' Luca explained.

'He said a name?' Kit asked.

Luca looked up at him, swallowed in discomfort.

'Who?' Kit demanded.

Luca looked at Isabelle in distress.

'Luca, who?'

'Dad,' Luca said, the word poison in his mouth. 'He called out 'Dad', begging him to stop.'

Kit looked at Moth on the bed. Watching all the pieces shift. Pulling out of their hidden places. Bruised words dropping from conversations. Yellow. Purple. Blue. Dropping into sight. Into an ugly shade with a single name.

David.

SHE WAS WAITING by the bed.

Again.

Waiting, when she said she wouldn't wait anymore.

Waiting.

The weight of the past seeping into her like poison.

The weight of Moth's past.

Waiting while it settled onto her, pinning her down.

Every regret she had pitiful in the waiting.

MOTH WOKE UP IN DARKNESS. Warm soft darkness. Light teasing against the edges.

Nothing else.

No pain, no cold, no hard.

Warmth and soft light.

He felt the light drawing him on. Soft, soft light, soothing. He opened his eyes.

'NO MESSAGES, SIGNOR DE LAVELLE,' the concierge said when he walked in.

'I know.' Kit put his bag down on the floor. 'I'll have my key please.'

'You are staying with us, sir?'

'I am.'

He took the key and turned away. Taking the stairs one shallow tread at a time, each turn coming seven steps ahead. Three turns, four, the second floor. Shut the door behind him. Bag on the bed. Looked out across the lake. Over the distant fountain.

It had been the longest bloody day.

He opened his bag, pulled out the few clothes, tossed them aside on the bed. Found the blue scarf, unravelling from its crush at the bottom, billowing up towards him. Sat down in the chair by the window with it draped across his knees. The blue scarf bleeding into the blue lake hovering outside the window. Something sweet tantalising him, out of reach.

He pulled the phone out of his pocket, found her number, leant back looking at it, his finger hovering.

Call her. Make it right.

But he couldn't. It was too late.

He'd made his choice. He hadn't known Moth was going to take it back from him.

Kit put his phone down on the table, pulled the scarf up over his face and slumped back, letting it cover his sight and blot out how hollow the glistening lake made him feel.

'ISABELLE?' Moth said, voice dry and reluctant.

She looked up at him, took in his open eyes, his moving hand. Saw his dazed face taking in the room. The close drawn curtains, the light seeping in through the edges where the fabric sat against the wall.

She reached forward from her chair, took his hand where it fumbled on the bedclothes.

'Hey,' she said. 'You kept me waiting long enough.'

'Waiting for what?'

'To see you.'

To see you.

Stating the obvious that made no sense to him.

He felt her hand in his. Remembered it. Light and free, floating in the sky above the garden at Riverdell, feeling the warmth and softness. He watched tears form in her eyes. Saw them swell, wash over the edge. Drip onto her hand.

'What?'

'Oh, Moth.'

Too much in it he couldn't understand. Strange memories of where he'd been.

Oh, Moth, what?

What did she mean? Her fingers pressing into his and holding on. The warmth began to slip away. Something heavy and old and ugly coming towards him from a distance. Pushing aside a distant door. Careening down a long corridor in his mind.

Oh, Moth. Breaking the ocean wall.

Why is she crying?

Stop crying. Stop bloody crying. You swore you wouldn't.

But the waves were stronger.

Pushing him apart at the seams.

KIT SAT DOWN BESIDE HIM. Moth looked better, despite the strips holding his broken nose back in place, the padding on his chest, the grazes on his cheeks. Cleaner at least.

Four days of near constant medical attention had worked wonders. Not to mention Isabelle's endless devotion. Not to mention the stunning view from the bedroom window. Kit grinned at him.

'Well, you look moderately less grim. How are the ribs?'

'Weird,' Moth said. 'Like they should be hurting, but I can't feel them.'

'Nothing but the finest drugs money can buy.'

'I can't thank you enough.'

'You could try,' Kit replied.

'You're not here much.'

'Someone has to pay for your recuperation,' Kit quipped.

It wasn't true, that he hadn't been here much. But Isabelle had made it clear she didn't need him. Or was it want him? Talking to him outside the door as they managed the details of Moth's care. Making it clear she was in charge. From the day he'd moved back into the hotel in town. The day she paid for Moth's bedroom herself. Marshalled Luca to see to x-rays, medicinal supplies, a nurse, fresh clothes. Instructed the doctor to take swabs. She only let him in today because of her request. Calling him in for the dirty jobs. Well, he was used to that.

'Why is she here?'

'I don't know how that came about.' Kit smoothed the back of his hands, adjusting the watch, flicking invisible lint from his trousers. 'Any more than you being here. Laps of the Gods, I'd say.'

Moth stared at him. 'Why are you here?'

'I told you, work. I come every year.'

'You didn't come last year.'

'Yes, I did. Had to keep flitting back home, courtesy of your arrival at Riverdell, and all that.'

'Why is she angry with you?'

Kit sat back in the armchair, laced his fingers together, and held them in front of his mouth. 'I broke a promise to her, about you.'

'Me?'

'I said I'd tell her if you got in touch.'

'And you didn't?'

He nodded.

'Why didn't you?' Moth asked.

Kit looked at his hands, lowered them to a less defensive position, smoothed the knees of his trousers. 'You asked me not too,' Kit offered. 'Seemed the right thing at the time.'

'Not working so good for you now?'

'Not everything turns out as you hope,' Kit said.

'Tell me about it.'

'How about you tell me?'

Moth stared at him, looked away to the window. Kit had

pushed the curtains back the moment he walked in. Someone might as well be enjoying the expensive view.

'She's treating me like a broken thing she's got to fix.'

'She thinks she let you down,' Kit said, ignoring his evasion. 'We all do.'

'Why?' Moth demanded. 'None of what happened to me was your fault. Or hers.'

'She thinks otherwise.' He watched Moth retreat into the angry shell of a teenager. 'She's telling herself you're a kid, and she's supposed to be the adult. It's up to you to make her see.'

'See what?' Moth asked, his voice loaded with irritation.

'See you're no kid. Haven't been for a long time either, right?'

Moth stared back at him, if you could call that blinking flat wall of defiance an expression. Kit held the gaze. Evasion was never something he struggled with. Though Isabelle could push anyone's boundaries on that point. Most people had the capacity to evade, but not the determination to lie.

'We're going to talk about this. One way or another,' Kit told him.

Moth turned his gaze back to the window, his head on the pillows, focusing on a point somewhere between the view and the window frame. As far away from Kit's gaze as he could get.

'I wish that hadn't come out. I never wanted anyone to know about that. All those drugs screwed it up.'

'I can sympathise. There's some stuff we all want to deal with in our own time.' He watched Moth's hand clutching at the bed sheet. 'But out it is, so make sure you put it behind you, not back inside?'

'Meaning what?'

'Meaning perhaps stuff comes out when it has to, not when we want it to. Don't regret it. Put it down and walk away.'

'More life rules?' Moth asked with a short bark of a laugh.

'No. You don't need me giving you advice. I don't know jack about what you've been through.' Kit stood up, moved from the bed to the window. It hurt that Kate hadn't seen it. The way the sky and the lake spoke to one another. The hills rising away from the water, reaching for the clouds. Kit turned away from the light drenched land, back to Moth, positioning himself where Moth couldn't avoid seeing him. If he looked away now it would be weakness.

'But Moth, don't regret it. Don't pretend it didn't happen. Put it down and walk away. Not because it ends that easily, but because each piece you drop makes the burden lighter. That's all I can say. You choose what you do with it.' Which was what he had to do. Kit knew that all the regrets in the world wouldn't change what was done.

'You sound like you're saying goodbye.' Moth tried to turn the conversation.

'I'll be back, but not much.' He crossed his arms over his chest. 'I'll finish my work and come see you before I head home. You've got about ten days left. That should be enough to get you back on your feet. You have to choose what to do next.'

'Put it down and walk away, right?' Moth said with sarcasm.

'A couple of things, before I go.' Kit ignored him with a stretch, yawning. 'I have to ask if you want to change your mind about calling the police, finding the man that raped you?'

He put it out there, broad as the daylight behind him.

Where it belonged. The ugly truth shrivelled by exposure. Not left in the dark where disease bloomed.

'No.' Moth wouldn't turn his head away, but his mouth twisted around the words. 'Not now. Not next week. Not ever.'

'Someone else could get hurt.'

'That's someone else's problem.' Moth's face was tight with fury. 'Don't ask me again.'

Kit resisted the urge to persist. He knew Moth was too wrapped up in refusing to be a victim, and that had everything to do with David rather than the bastard who'd raped him. One day, he would regret the decision. Want to be the avenging angel. Get himself in a fresh mess trying to hide from the regret. But Kit knew you couldn't force someone's recovery. Isabelle had made him promise to try one more time. Well, he'd tried.

'And as for David,' Kit carried on, watching Moth's jaw work to the point he wondered if it was possible for a jaw to snap. 'It's a good job he's already dead.'

He watched Moth blink in surprise.

'But don't expect others to hide what you feel you have to.'

'It's nothing to do with anyone else.'

'I can understand where you're coming from,' Kit told him. Moth looked at him in outright disbelief. 'Oh, I know, I've never been raped.' He used the word like a hammer, watching it hit Moth, refusing to pretend it was otherwise. 'But we all have things we'd rather keep to ourselves, and the older you get the heavier the history. I've had lovers who were raped, abused as kids, and it's a heavy weight to carry alone through life.'

'That doesn't give you the right to tell me...'

'... jack. I know. Like I said, not ten minutes ago.' Kit

smiled at him, reminding him of the precise words he'd chosen to use.

Moth looked down at the bedcovers. Kit waited, grinning when Moth raised his eyes back to him.

'And I get that with him being dead, there's a sense of relief. The truth gets buried too, right?'

'Maybe.'

'But it doesn't,' Kit said. 'You're going to spend the rest of your life trying to bury it in yourself. And,' he held a hand up to stop Moth's protest, 'you don't know who else you might be burying by keeping that silence.'

'What?'

'I get it, your choice, about this one,' Kit chucked his thumb over his shoulder outside the window, indicating the recent incident. 'I don't agree, let's be clear, but I get it. But David, you must understand, it might not have been only you and that's an awful lot closer to home.'

'What are you saying?' Moth asked. 'That my silence might have let him hurt others?'

'No, your silence was a child's silence. The only one abusing anyone, or perpetuating silence about it, was David. But if he did rape anyone else, your speaking about it might unlock their silence.'

'That's not my problem.'

'Even if it was Nat?' Kit stopped smiling. It was the last tool in his bag.

'He never touched Nat,' Moth spat at him. 'He gave me the choice. Me, or her. Why do you think I stayed so long? To make sure she was safe. Why do you think I'm glad he's dead? Not for me, for her.'

Kit looked at that statement, sat in the air between them. It looked solid, that statement. Formed of hatred, with fear shining at the edges. It looked like the only belief holding Moth together.

'There might have been others,' he finished. 'Other people close to him.'

'Anything else?' Moth demanded. 'Anything you need to talk about while I can't get up and get away from you?'

'Don't ignore Luca. When you're done here.'

'Done here?'

Kit had thought about it for days. What to say? How to say it? Not wanting to admit it. Angry it had to be him who voiced it. But guilt over Moth had spread across all of them, and even though he knew he was compensating for a past he had little to do with, the oil slick had reached out and tainted him.

'In Italian law, you're a consenting adult. Back home, you're a minor. When you're done here, when you and Isabelle have sorted out whatever you need to... and I won't pretend to understand what the hell is going on between you two... don't ignore Luca.'

'Why not?' Moth demanded.

'Really? You want me to spell it out? Because I will, if you need me to?'

Moth's eyes flickered. His mouth reaching for the edges of a denial that he wanted to fling back at Kit. Kit stared him down, raised one eyebrow, quirked the side of his lip. Daring Moth to contradict what he'd seen each time Luca turned up. Darting into Moth's room while he stood outside arguing with Isabelle, hearing the happiness in Moth's voice notch up.

'You're either talking in riddles, or these drugs are amazing, because you're not making much sense.' Moth said at last, plucking at the bed covers again.

'Look at it like this,' Kit said. 'You've been through some

bad stuff, truly frigging awful bad stuff. The sort that can turn your mind inside out and backwards, and leave you convinced up is down. Now, you need to go through some good stuff.'

'Those scales again?'

'Yes, scales.' Kit leaned against the wall by the thick curtains. Moth staring back at him as only a mutinous teenager could. Might as well be speaking to a brick wall. 'You need to work out why he keeps coming all this way to see you. Every bloody day.'

'I don't ask him to come,' Moth's voice rose in a querulous whine that made Kit grin and raise his eyebrows with a smirk. Moth blushed. A soft heat that spread across his cheeks, suffusing the nose under its plaster strips in an angry scale of denial. Looking hideous as always under that apricot hair. How satisfying.

It was time to go. He'd made his point. Moth would have to figure it out for himself. There was nothing else he could do here. Oh, except, one thing. He held his hand out to Moth.

'Come on, time to get out of that bed.'

'Isabelle won't let me,' Moth groaned. 'Or the bloody nurse.'

'You're listening to them?' Kit taunted him.

Moth glared at him with something near hatred, struggling to throw the bedclothes back. He was dressed in pyjama bottoms, his ribs bound with thick padding. He tried to sit up by himself and gritted his teeth, swinging his legs to the side and rolling upwards with a groan. Kit walked over, gave him a hand and pulled him to his feet.

'That's more like it,' Kit said. 'Come on, we're paying enough for this view, you should at least admire it.'

He helped Moth over to the window, left him leaning on the frame and stood back.

'Great view,' Moth muttered from between gritted teeth, his hands clinging to the curtains.

'Told you.' Kit backed away to the door, Moth watching him go.

'Oh, and Moth,' he said, hand on the door.

'Yeah?'

'You're welcome.' Kit pulled open the door and stepped out into the hall.

ISABELLE WAS WAITING FOR HIM.

Kept there when she wanted to go in and join them. Kept there because Kit had been quiet when he arrived, looking more worn out with work than she had ever seen him. Not even in the height of the development at Riverdell when he had thrown teddy out of the pram at the announcement of Asha's pregnancy. He had listened, actually listened to her, and gone into Moth's room with no more than a focused nod, asking her to wait outside.

She watched him go with an unwelcome rush of guilt. Aware she'd ignored him since Moth arrived. As she'd ignored Rob. Running away and not even calling home. Aware she was asking him to help, having pushed him away. Not even for Moth, but for herself. Because she felt dirty inside with the hideous truth. Emptied of significance in the drip feed of details as she peeled back Moth's reluctance and came to understand all the reasons he'd run away.

She held herself together as if she might be able to hold back the discomfort trying to get out. Hold in some sense of her own worth. Watching Kit's upright back, hearing his silence, she could feel the future coming towards her and it was terrifying. As it had been on the drive the night of the party. Blank, empty, vast. With no compass in it. No James, no Kit, no Elsa, no India, no known points between which she could ricochet. The emptiness filling with the distress of Moth's... experiences. She, sinking under the oppression of his voice, his past. Scared her own voice might never work again. That if she spoke, there would be nothing. No direction, no choice, no hope that might push back against the overwhelming reality of his past.

She looked up with a jump when the door opened. Saw Kit walk towards her. Felt that surge of warmth at seeing him come into the immediate clear vicinity of her space. Not the comfort James had given her; a soft blanket to wrap herself in. With Kit it was a physical thrill, a shiver down the spine from looking at his extraordinary body. As he swam into sight she wanted to reach out, pull him close and hold on. Push back that great tide of emptiness she had seen in the contours of his back. She didn't. She kept her arms held tight.

Kit stopped in front of her. Stopped, not reaching out or pulling her in to command what happened next. The emptiness grew bigger than the foot of space between them.

'He's adamant,' Kit said. 'No report.'

She frowned.

'You can't force him Isabelle. He's an adult in the eyes of the police here, they will do nothing if he doesn't report it. More to the point, he doesn't want to. He wants to forget it.'

'And you think that's acceptable?' She fought the urge to use the word 'best'.

'I think, no, I adamantly support that it's his choice,' he said. 'You asked me to ask him, I did. I won't do it again. We've done everything we can to make sure he is physically well. It's his decision, about this, about David. About if, and when, and how he wants to talk about it. Stop treating him like a child. You never did before and it's the last bloody thing he needs. Why are you starting now?'

'I'm not,' she protested.

Kit looked at her, stepped closer, eating up the inches. She ached for his comforting presence. The solidity of his chest closing out the world.

'Yes, you are. You're doing it because you're afraid.'

'Afraid?'

'Terrified.' Kit leaned forward. His face close enough she could see the pores on his nose, the individual eyelashes, the searing blue of his eyes seeing through her. 'You want Moth to be a child. It would be so much easier.'

'Easier than what?' she asked, pulling her head up, resisting the urge to step away.

'Easier to keep that barrier between you, be the good adult. Do what's right.'

'I don't understand.' She stared at him. Battling the temptation to reach out and pull him closer, out of sight, into intimacy.

'You'd come back to me now like that.' He clicked his fingers by his side. Subtle, not aggressive, but she flinched all the same. The sound echoing in the empty corridor. 'You're so scared of what happens next.'

'I don't know what I'm doing.' The words were compressed, her breath tight in her chest, stretched out along the line he'd made in her future. 'From one minute to the next I don't know what I'm doing, but I seem to get everything wrong.'

'Not everything.' He shrugged her worries away, like they were nothing. This fear of what was coming for her, of whether she made the best or worst of decisions. The crippling desire to both run away and hold him as close as she could. 'There was never anything wrong between you and me. I guess we both needed to learn it was never quite right, either. Same as with James.'

She looked down at her feet. Solid on the long runner of the hall carpet, apologetic in their unsuitable India sandals, but settled. Attached to the solidity of the building while her head floated away in a mist of uncertainty. Kit had always been there for her. Every time life, and James, crashed, Kit had picked her up and held her close, sent her back out into the world. Each of them pivoting back to the other. She couldn't imagine that not happening again. Kit moving on as James had, into a full life while she was left behind making sense of the pieces again.

'I'm sorry,' she whispered. 'I thought it might be different. Hoped it might be.'

He took one of her arms, peeled it away from her body, laced her fingers through his. She couldn't help but keep the other arm firm against her torso. Her own warmth needed to shore up the panic inside.

'You know, a long while back, way, way back when I was about Moth's age, there was this woman. She was amazing, stunning. I was besotted with her, thought I'd die if I didn't have her. From a burst heart, or penis, or whatever unrequited crap teenage boys die from. She thought I was nothing more than a child.'

'What happened?' Isabelle kept her eyes on the carpet. How the pattern seemed to flow exactly around neatly about her feet as though they had been designed for her. A curl of fern behind her heels, its opposite cresting her toes. While she stood in the blank space between.

'I convinced her otherwise,' Kit said, peeling her other hand away and taking it in his, holding her hands together until she followed the tug of kindness in his voice and looked up from the ferns to his face. 'And it made me believe in myself from that day on. I've often wondered since, if I hadn't convinced her, who I might have become.'

'You'd always have been you.'

'Perhaps,' he shrugged. 'Maybe not. I wish you'd found that someone in me, someone who made you believe in yourself. It's a powerful thing, to know what you're capable of and to believe in it. But, perhaps, it might be you who is that person to someone else?'

'If you're suggesting that...' she began to say, pushing away the uncomfortable combination of connections in his words.

'... what I'm saying,' he put a finger to her lips, 'is that Moth needs time and opportunity, to understand himself, to let go of the past. As do you. This is where you need to be, right now. There's something here, between you two, and I'm damned if I understand what it is, but I'm done standing in the middle of it, taking the punches.'

'Are you leaving?,' she asked, her fingers squeezing his.

'You two don't need me.' Kit stepped back, drawing his hands away, her fingers held on. 'And I have an awful lot of work to do.'

'Don't go.'

He reached up and touched her cheek, two light fingers. She could feel them as she'd felt James' beside the river, stinging a farewell into her skin.

'I won't be far away.'

'I'm scared,' she choked.

'Good,' he said. 'You should be, that's real. Fear is life.'

'When will I see you?'

'Soon enough. When this is over and you go home, I'll come see you and Kate. If you need anything, just call me.' He let go of her hand. 'Remember, Isabelle, he doesn't need someone treating him like a child. His childhood is long gone. He needs people with the courage to help him be an adult.'

He kissed her on the cheek and walked past. His scent, that clean fresh scent that could reorder the universe, lingering with her. She closed her eyes against the urge to run after him, heard his steps clattering down the stone stairs, away, out of the villa. The car roaring to life and leaving, gravel falling back into the silence behind. Rearranged in a new constellation.

Opened her eyes and saw the long corridor stretching to a hazy finish in a bright window. The door to Moth's room cracked open at her side, darkness filling the room between the door and the light glaring from the window that looked out over the lake. Blinding her poor eyes.

She longed for Riverdell. To be stood in its hallway, listening to the house breathing above her. Fixing her in place in a world that seemed monstrous and confusing. She longed to return home, to see Kate waiting for her, to call Rob and put right what she'd left in a mess. To walk into the study, tidy her desk and pick up her next job. All she'd wanted all year was to have Moth come home and make Riverdell feel complete again. To make her feel liberated as he had done when he had been there. Keeping company with her strange hours and odd ways. Not demanding adult things of her as James and Kit had.

She peered into the dark room behind the doorway. What was it between her and Moth?

It wasn't what Kit thought it was. The only way that Kit understood things, intimately. Though the fear that it was for Moth confused her. The memory of their sodden trip down the river, shivering behind the chestnut tree, pricking her with guilt. Making her wonder if Kit knew her better than she did herself.

But she did know herself. She knew as she did with a scrap of fabric, where it fitted, where it didn't. She knew intuitively, without being able to explain it, that some wefts ran together, and some fibres knew each other. The person she was with Moth made sense to her, as it did not always make sense when she was with others. She turned to look down the empty hall where Kit had gone. Looked back at the doorway.

The shape of her future was on the other side of that darkened room.

She walked in, saw the bed empty as she went closer. Her eyes roving to the window, finding Moth. His outline blurred by the sharp light. He held his hand out, seeking her and she took it. Found it trembling with the effort of being out of bed, upright. She resisted the urge to scold him, remembering what Kit had said.

Isabelle raised his arm gently across her shoulders and let him lean on her. Placed her hand on his bound chest and felt the rise and fall of his lungs, the swift padded thud of his heart. The sound of it echoing through her fingers. The doorway swinging open against the wall, the stretching hall of light beyond it. Them leaning upon each other against the folds of the encompassing, rustling curtains, looking together over the sky expanding into vastness outside the window. The details of the room within drowned out by sound and light. She was here for him, that was all she knew, and Isabelle felt relief settle across her with his weight, keeping her tethered.

17

D ear Kate,
By the time you receive this, you will already know of my absence.

I am devastated not to be there with you.

I am sure Elsa is wiped out with grief. That I cannot be there to support her is beyond painful. I pray you will not all be terribly disappointed in me for not coming home. ~~I am furious with Ted. That he gave me no choice in the matter. His letter claimed time did not allow any other option. I try to think he genuinely believed this and was not punishing me for staying in Kashmir this last winter and not returning to Bombay.~~

By the time I knew of William's passing you had probably already buried him. What terrible luck that such an urgent need to return to England, overlaying all our financial considerations, should happen when I am not in Bombay. Ted will have explained to you, I hope, how remote Kashmir is from the main transport links. It would have meant many days delay to our arrival for Ted to wait for me, and I am sure he was anxious to be with Elsa and help arrangements for their father's funeral. Still, it hurts to receive news of both his father's death and his immediate departure for England, a week after the event. ~~Ted could have contacted the local offices of the businesses he has dealings with in Srinagar, and arranged for me to be informed much earlier than by letter. There was at least a small chance we could have come together. But I suppose I must bear my disappointments as he has tried to do in me.~~

I am sure the funeral was a grand affair. I hope it was held at St Laurence's, for William always adored that church. I remember him saying on Elsa's wedding day, that he had been blessed with three weddings at the church and that he hoped to know many more happy events there before he passed beneath the high tower for the last time. At least he had the opportunity of David's christening before that day came.

It is impossible to think of him being gone. Elsa's father always seemed such a solid and reliable presence in our lives. There for almost as long as I can remember, binding us together, keeping an eye on us. I wonder what our lives would have been without Elsa, Riverdell and her father? ~~If all those consequences were positive.~~ Please do me the great kindness of sending me a copy of the funeral service. It would mean much to me to have it and I doubt Ted would think to bring one back for me. Post it here to the Kashmir address for I do not know when I will be in Bombay and Sai is indifferent at best about forwarding my post.

I hope that Elsa is coping. How sad, to have David only a toddler and lose her father. He will surely be too young to remember William. To lose him from a massive heart attack, both awful for her to have found him and surely some relief

to know he did not suffer? Please, give her a long hug from
me. I will send a note with this letter to convey my condo-
lences, but please, please, make sure she is aware of my frustration at not being with her.

Please could I ask a special favour, if possible? Would you
give your time to Ted, in my absence? Ted will always try to
be the strong brother but, though he and Elsa have always
had grief in common, he has rarely been able to talk about it.
I fear I have let him down as a wife, not being there for him.
Our difficulties on the children front have left us in a troubled place these last few years and I wonder if... He was
always fond of you and I know will find your strength a
boon now.

You must feel the loss of William at least as much as
Elsa. He was always supportive of you and to have aided you
in setting up your venture so generously was entirely in
keeping with his devotion. When you wrote to say that he
had waived the repayment of the deposit he lent you, I was
not surprised. It is not a reduction of what you will achieve
in any way, but a statement of the love and admiration he
felt for you. William adored you, Kate, you must know this. I
think he would rather have had you for his daughter-in-law
than any of us. You must go forward with that thought in
your heart. Life has been unkind enough, you should
welcome the love which is unexpectedly given to you and
richly deserved. He will rest easier in the ground knowing
that you are firmly a part of his daughter's life, there in
Ludlow to help her with Riverdell in ways that Rose and I
cannot. If you did not have the chance to come to terms
with his generosity and thank him before he died, do NOT
carry that regret forward with you. Give all that you can to
Elsa and Ted now, and you will find peace with the strange-

ness of life, that both gives and takes when we least expect it.

Same as my life in India, not what I expected in any way; disappointing in some and rewarding in others. If I had managed to conceive and become the mother I longed to be, would I be here in Kashmir now? Finding such purpose in my life? You, with your grand venture, your inspiration and growing business, you would probably understand this. We cannot have everything, as the feminists of our youth would have had us believe. Rose, of course, has done both. Tossed a child out and gained a career while barely breaking stride. But we are not all as indomitable as her. Perhaps there is yet a chance for us? I have spoken to Ted about adoption, but he is not keen. ~~It left a wall between us that has kept us apart for the last twelve months.~~ I hope he will come around to it. I have learnt of myself that I do not need something to be mine, to be able to love it absolutely. A child, any child, would be a miracle of joy to me, but for Ted? To raise someone else's child? Well... time will show.

Give my love to Rose. She wrote a vile letter to me last year telling me I was being a white saviour, whatever that is. Told me I should wake up and come home where I belong. I guess it is hard to understand if you are distant from what is happening. Would she rather I did nothing? Who knows, with her? She has not written since, and I have missed her letters but continue to write. She will forgive me whatever I am doing wrong one day, I hope, and send me news of Kit. If you have any photos of him, please do spare me a few. Tell her I miss her, and know she is mad at me for not coming back to England since I left. It is not because I do not care. In fact, out here, away from you all, I feel like the keeper of all our old memories. For I do not have the daily life of our friendship going on to share with you. I know how hard it is for all of us to make the time to travel and meet up. But this is no excuse, and Rose begrudges me not giving up my time, which seems frivolous and spoilt to her.

I meant to send this small gift on when I next wrote to you, now it seems the perfect thing for such times and I am glad to have it ready for you. These are the seeds from a grove of Kashmir Rowans we found while clearing the ground here. They had naturally grown in a stunning crescent shape and have the most unusual white berries, so different to our native Rowans. I hope you will plant them and get a sapling for your new roof garden, which does not sound ridiculous at all. Do let me know if you succeed. I would like to think you are reminded of me when you see it as I am of you when I see the almond sapling in the villa courtyard.

I hope this letter arrives in time. Ted did not write how long he planned to stop in England. I assume it was only to be until after the funeral. If it had been any longer, I think he would have arranged for me to follow on.

Write me a good long letter in reply and tell me the news of the funeral. Please put flowers on William's grave from me and let me know how Elsa is adjusting to the momentousness of now being owner of Riverdell. It must have given her father great comfort to know that he had a grandchild growing up to one day carry his name forward as heir. ~~There was a while, I suspect, when Ted thought that our having a child might change his father's heart about his will. Now that pressure is gone, perhaps Ted and I can consider our family choices more openly~~. No one deserves Riverdell more than she does.

You will excuse the mess and scrawl of this letter. My mind is shocked by the news. If I had time, I would rewrite it, but I must catch the evening trip to the village to get the letter to the post as soon as possible and compose my thoughts to send a note to Elsa without weeping over it or making such a mess.

All my best wishes for your own precious endeavours, make sure and send me all your news.

WITH LOVE,

BETH x

ell?' Luca asked. 'Where to?'
'Venice.'
'Really?'
'Uh-huh.'

'It's vastly over-rated,' Luca sounded disappointed, but put the car into gear and let the clutch out.

'I hear it's who you go with that counts,' Moth said.

Luca laughed at him. 'Last time I went, I was a horny teenager stuck with my parents and younger sisters.'

'Yeah, that would be enough to leave a bad memory,' Moth said. 'But maybe, before Venice, a few other places. Anywhere you fancy?'

'Florence,' Luca said with conviction. 'You need to see Florence. Not Pisa, now that is over-rated. Perhaps Tuscany, no, I know, Umbria. We will do Orvieto, Assisi, oh, but Amalfi. We should do the coastline. It's breath-taking.'

'How long have you got off work?' Moth asked.

'A week. How long do you have?'

'Me?' Moth asked. He watched as the villa fell behind

them, the long driveway twisting and turning as it took the car away. 'As long as I want.'

'Sure you're ready to go?' Luca asked, and Moth looked back at him.

'No,' he said.

'She must go home?'

She would have stayed if he wanted.

If you'd asked.

'No. It's just time to go.'

Moth didn't know how else to put it. Something in the way the sun lit the lake. In the dimming pain in his body. The need to get back on the bike. He'd spent a few hours in Lovere getting the damage assessed, come back with pain punching holes in his ribs. Not ready to be back on it, but sick of the walls and doors of the villa. Pulled between the urge to move on and the need to mend. Stuck between the comfort he found in her company and the sensation that he was trying to stop time. Time that swept in with dark brown eyes and waves of gelled hair that barely stopped in place. Twitching fingers that made him truly restless.

'Will it always be like this for you?' Luca asked. 'This moving on from one place to the next, on a bike?'

'I've been thinking I might get a motorbike, or a campervan,' Moth said. 'One day.'

'That's not what I meant.'

'I don't like getting stuck in one place.' Moth watched the drive descending in front of them. 'Bad things happen to people who get stuck. Like this bloke I know, got stuck in a coffee shop waiting to hear back from the United Nations. Never went anywhere.'

Luca flicked his leg in response. 'It's my car you're moving in now, Sick Boy.'

'And I'm so grateful for not having to ride all the way to Venice.'

Which he was. Kit had been right. It was beyond irritating how right Kit was. Moth wanted him to mess something up, prove himself human. Luca's visits had pulled him out of the murky depths he and Isabelle swam through.

It was Luca who'd taken him out for the day on the lake. Luca who made him talk about Beau, and Mila, and all the places he'd been. Luca who'd sat with him to read the emails, from Nat, from Mila. Luca who smiled and laughed at the picture of Mila's happy face beside Beau's wrinkled smiles, while he held his breath and tried not to crumple as he read the email about her journey. Luca who'd yelled at him, well tried to yell, as yellish as Luca could possibly be, when he'd told Kit to shove the money from Mrs Staines' furnishings where the sun didn't shine. All £10,000 of it. Until he'd hurt his ribs laughing at Luca's attempt at anger and agreed to take the money. Not that he had any intention of using it. Luca who'd found the bike shop. Not been fazed by the extent of the damage, arranged to send it to Venice for rebuilding. Said he had a week's holiday due, he'd drive Moth over to Venice to pick up the bike. How about they went exploring Italy before he left? Luca, making life normal and wholesome. Luca, in those skinny jeans barely caught on his hips, who made him want to move on.

They swept down the driveway to the gates. They reminded him of Riverdell, the same fierce curves of iron-work. He could imagine Isabelle up there, hearing the car fade away as she packed her bags to go home. Tidying away all his ugly truths, the ones he couldn't share with Luca. Packing the past away, closing the gates and locking it behind them. His gatekeeper.

Moth took a deep breath. He missed her. Missed the way her hair fell across her face when she lowered her head. Her touch, tracing lines across his skin, not letting go. Her silence listening to him when his voice ruptured and broke with recollection. Her legs tucked beneath her on the bed, exposing her thin ankles and bare soles. Holding her legs crossed like a crucible he poured himself into. Each memory, unspoken secret, hatred and regret. Everything he'd done, not done, should have done. Released. The bubbles escaping into the air as she demanded to know. Rising out of the ripped apart memories. Until he felt as clear inside as the lake outside the window. The tight breath lighter in his body. The ache of his healing bones lesser.

But it is time to go too.

Leaving her was leaving the past behind.

He was excited.

More than that, he was eager.

To find out what came next.

Going because he wanted to, not because he was running.

'All good?' Luca asked, a concerned hand leaning across the divide between them and landing on his knee.

These light touches of his, the way his hands fluttered out for contact. Asked for permission. Expressed concern, happiness, opinion through skin. These moments he might have once shrunk from, had become something else to Moth. Something he wanted to explore.

They are pleasant.

'All good.' Moth sucked in his courage and reached for Luca's hand. He had the most fascinating fingers. Curious, reaching-out fingers. Wanting to touch the world, make it better.

Luca looked at him in surprise. A smile puckering the

wide edges of his mouth. His eyes fluttering as they dashed from watching the approaching gates to look at Moth.

And you do feel better.

Inside, around the tender muscles and rebuilding bones, he felt so much better. He put his head back against the seat, let his fingers curl around Luca's. Feeling how they fitted into his. How the slim fingers were strong and flexible. How they built a space between their palms. Trapping clean, fresh air.

'You choose where we go,' Moth said. 'But don't go...'

'... I know, I know, don't go too fast. I got it.'

ISABELLE SAT at the head of the table. It felt awkward, sitting here with Elsa on one side and Kate on the other. Their places in life rearranged.

Reminding her that she hadn't done anything about the kitchen. That, of all the house, it remained most familiar to the old owner and ways. Doubting her place in what had always been Elsa's chair. How had she done so little in this one pivotal room when so much had been achieved elsewhere? Even the dresser loaded with the awful majolica service was silent, guilty judgement of her and Moth's misuse. It was time that stuff was sold.

She glanced out of the window at the driveway. Autumn had come early. It was late September and a first, eager frost had nibbled at the edges of the borders. The rich green leaves of the magnolia were losing their freshness, rubbing together and making clicking sounds in the wind as they dried. She couldn't wait to see the small buds hidden beneath, to watch them swell over winter, waiting for the spring. She'd begun to notice these things in a way she'd never thought of before. Life, waiting to become life.

'Well, it's not what I thought you'd do next.' Elsa pulled her attention back to their conversation, leaning over to put a warm hand on her forearm.

Isabelle turned away from the window and smiled at her. 'I hope you aren't upset with me.'

'You worry far too much about my approval.'

'See, I told you,' Kate added.

'I have never been disappointed in you,' Elsa continued. 'Not once. But this is the first time I've been completely surprised and, as I get more used to the idea, I'm rather excited about it too. I think it will be good for you.'

'See, I told you that too.' Kate reached over and picked up the wine bottle. 'Besides, more wine for us, right, Elsa?'

Isabelle looked back at the window, biting her bottom lip. Wondered how it was going. The conversation she wasn't having. She'd done it again, let someone else take the task she was too scared to do. Wishing she'd been stronger with Asha earlier that afternoon, when she and James came to collect Nat.

Asha had taken her sleeping baby out of Nat's arms, where she was swaying her to and fro, saying, 'You're a natural. You can come and baby-sit any time.'

'She's adorable,' Nat said, looking at the scrunched-up eyes, the fists nestling defensive beside the head.

'Particularly when asleep,' Asha agreed.

'She has James' eyes,' Elsa said, watching from the sofa as Asha swayed her daughter against her chest. 'And your chin, and nose, I think.'

'She looks like herself to me,' Nat said. 'Deryn Rose, I love the name.'

'The name was the hardest bit,' James said with feeling.

Elsa, Kate and Asha looked at him in contemptuous unison. 'I mean, after she arrived, obviously.'

Asha rolled her eyes at him from her perch on the arm of the sofa in the drawing room. The velvet nap bristling the wrong way under her firmly perched bottom. Though it had been over two months her back still hurt from the delivery and couldn't bear sitting on soft furnishings. For a small baby, Deryn Rose had made a big entry. Sixteen hours in labour, blue light transport to the county hospital and forceps before it was done. Her stitches were excruciating and going to the toilet had become a trial of necessity over agony, details which she shared in acute detail with Isabelle. She had stayed in hibernation with Deryn for weeks. Resisting coming back out into the world, pushing the family visits away until she was ready for them. If Asha had been confident before motherhood, she had re-emerged invincible. With a healthy dose of contempt for near everyone.

'It's a lovely name,' Elsa said. 'It's worth the arguments you might have had. And it's wonderful to have another grandchild.'

'And a cousin for me.' Nat perched on the edge of the sofa by Elsa, watching Asha and Deryn. 'Moth will be excited too.'

His name fell into the awkward space where no one felt comfortable touching it. Asha smiled at her. Elsa and Kate cooed over the baby. James blinked. Isabelle smiled to herself. Talking to Nat about her brother when she rang weekly to share what news they both had made it even easier for Nat to talk about him. It was a small victory.

'You must send him a picture,' she encouraged Nat.

'Well, we'll have to make the most of you while Deryn has you to herself,' Asha said to Elsa, her tone brisk. Isabelle cringed. Asha had acquired a new habit of making things public, whenever she felt it was appropriate. Throwing out her opinions with the same ease she nursed in public. James fidgeted. For a farmer he was unbelievably uncomfortable with breast feeding. Asha raised her eyebrows at him, but James looked away. Isabelle dropped her eyes before she too got a scathing look, she knew Asha was beginning to think her new family were hopeless.

Kate said, 'Well, hadn't you all better be heading home? Little Deryn wants her bed. And I'm sure Nat will be too excited to let her sleep if she wakes up again.' Knowing how to distract a new mother.

'You're right,' Asha said, cradling the child as James and Nat stood up. 'Nat, will you help me put Deryn Rose to bed?'

'Oh, can I? I'd love to.'

'Here you go,' Asha slid the blanket-wrapped bundle into Nat's folded arms. 'Keep rocking her and hum until we get her in the car, she'll sleep all the way home.'

Nat walked out of the room rocking the baby and humming, as James followed, fumbling with the car seat. Elsa tagged along behind them with Kate to say goodbye. Asha waited with Isabelle.

'Well?'

'Tonight, at dinner. I promise.'

'I'll be here at breakfast with Nat,' Asha told her.

'That sounds like a threat.'

'Good, I'm glad that's clear,' Asha said. 'And I'll make James tell Hester.'

'Must you?' Isabelle begged. 'Can't she find out from Elsa when they're home?'

'You mean when they're safely back in Swansea?' Asha asked, putting her coat on over her sagging belly and enormous, full breasts. Looking at Asha's post-baby body unnerved Isabelle more than watching her bump being stroked ever had. 'Not a chance. James can tell her tonight, and deal with the drama too.'

Isabelle knew there was more than friendship in her determination. Asha hadn't forgiven Hester for leaving their wedding without saying goodbye. Expressing the opinion that it was a good job Hester had moved to Swansea, she was a sister-in-law who improved with distance. Asha wasn't about to miss this happy chance for revenge.

'Remind me never to upset you,' Isabelle had whispered in her ear as they hugged goodbye. Asha had grinned at her.

Isabelle turned back to the women at the table, trying to listen to them. The thought of Hester staying with James and Asha for the night was overwhelming. She toyed with the remains of her dinner. It had been impossible to eat with Kate prodding her to get on and spill the beans. In front of Elsa's shocked expression, the recovering conversation. Her effort to be engaging but not to pry. Under the thought of Asha gloating at breakfast.

They were talking about the garden, Elsa expressing her amazement at Kate's progress, when they all heard tyres erupting into the driveway.

'That sounds like Kit,' Elsa said in surprise.

Isabelle and Kate both flinched.

'I do hope not,' Kate said.

'I wish it were,' Isabelle said in misery as the front door banged open and steps came hard across the hallway. She had a feeling there was going to be little pleasure in telling Asha she'd been right. They should have waited until Hester was out of the county. Possibly the country.

Hester burst into the kitchen in a fury of decades, making all three women jump in their skins. Isabelle felt her heart sink to her feet and her evening tumble into dread.

'You're PREGNANT?' Hester screamed. Her face twisted into an obscenity that Isabelle felt she'd been holding back since they were nineteen.

'Hester!' Elsa protested, sinking back in her chair with a hand to her throat.

'Yes, she is,' Kate spat back, starting up out of her chair. 'Not that it's any of your business, and how dare you come storming in here like this.'

'Kate!' Elsa reached across the table to try and grab Kate's hand.

'You're pregnant?' Hester repeated. Face contorting, struggling to express herself, stuck on the fact she could not grasp.

Isabelle sat leaden in her chair, shocked with the flood of shame flushing through her. Heat suffusing her through the layers that she wore to cover her changing body. Leaving her weak with uncertainty and self-doubt, her mouth awash with acrid saliva. So much had changed and yet so much remained the same. She might be sat at the head of the table and Hester an uninvited guest in her house, but she was the one feeling guilty. Elsa, speechless with distress and the inability to help, while Kate was on her feet and moving to defend her. She felt the intense absence of her mother. Crushing down on her with longing pressure, while inside the baby who pushed her towards motherhood made her feel short of all the skills she needed. Skills like Kate's, who knew when to stand up for herself. Skills like Asha's, who knew what needing saying.

She pushed her chair away from the table and stood to face Hester, her hand moving to her belly and the quiet swell hidden beneath the loose layers. She was tired of this dread that had sat on her for so many months. She missed her mother more, in this moment, with a grief that was hard and long boiled in her bones, than she ever had as a child in this house.

Hester's face twisted as she saw that protective hand sweep. Isabelle watched the emotions warping her, the disbelief, the shock, the hatred.

'Yes, I'm pregnant,' she told Hester. 'And I'm keeping the baby.'

'You're keeping it?' Hester threw at her from between clenched teeth.

'Yes.'

'What happened?' Hester asked. 'Did you get sloppy and miss your usual deadline to murder it?'

'Hester!' Elsa gasped.

'Hester what?' Hester demanded. 'What exactly, Mother?'

'You can't talk to Isabelle like this,' Elsa told her.

'Why not?' Hester asked, her voice bursting open with pain. 'Why is it, Mother, that I can't tell her what I think?'

Elsa looked away from them both to Kate, tears springing into her eyes, shaking her head. Outside Isabelle heard more tyres on the driveway.

'You can't come storming in here, throwing your disappointments in life at others,' Kate told her, slamming her hand on the table. 'It isn't fair on anyone, least of all your mother. And it's not Isabelle's fault you can't bloody conceive. That doesn't give you any right to tell her what she can and can't do with her body, or life!'

'Kate, don't,' Isabelle told her. 'You don't need to sort this.'

'Really,' asked Hester, 'you're going to sort this out yourself, are you?'

'There is no sorting this out,' Isabelle told her.

'Really,' Hester spat out, 'really? You think not? You don't think you can sort out how the hell you dare to stand here and explain to me that you're having a baby with that freak of nature when you murdered two babies? Two babies. You killed two babies. My brother's perfect babies. You screwed-up, self-centred, murdering bitch. And now, now, you want to have a baby!'

Isabelle stood and watched the tirade build against her. Watched Hester's mouth open out into a spitting white vessel of overflowing abuse. The heavy table rocking against her thighs as Hester leant into it. Watched the kitchen door behind her open in a rush and James come hurling in and grab his sister, turning her into a crushing embrace on his shoulder, stifling the words.

She pressed the hand she held upon her stomach, hoping in some way that it would block out the hatred from pouring into the aching emptiness that her baby was nibbling away at.

She watched James, his face wrinkled with distress, looking at her over Hester's hysterical, sobbing form. Felt Kate moving towards her, pushing her back down into the chair. Hands staying on her shoulders, a weight holding her down when she would have rather run from the room. Saw Asha walk into the kitchen, hand supporting her back, rolling her eyes at Kate in impatience.

Would she ever do anything that didn't hurt this family? The only family she had. Isabelle's own hopeless sense of ineptitude brimmed up inside her, pushing tears ahead. She felt useless, sat at the head of the table and unable to fathom how to fix it. Which was the first time she'd ever understood how Elsa must have felt. Trying to hold a family together that was fraying apart at the edges. Unable to get up and walk away.

'Oh, enough already!' Asha broke the shocked silence. She walked across to the large dresser. 'This family has some really ugly habits,' picked up the large platter that sat pride of place on the middle shelf with its curving horn arms, 'and even though you know you should get rid of them, you can't bear the thought of breaking anything, so you cling onto what you know.' Her hands let go, allowing it to fall and explode on the stone floor, noise and debris spreading out in a shockwave.

Everyone flinched. Except Asha, who looked grim and satisfied.

'Now, there's a whole new generation on the way, and it's time to face it.' She picked up a two handled soup tureen that hadn't been used in decades, held it over the floor, loosed go, took great delight in the distance the pieces spread, the dust rising from the damage. The way her noise and anger commanded the room, held them all in her focus.

'You,' she told Hester, 'sit, there. James, sit with her.' She pointed at the two chairs at the end of the table. 'Whatever you said can't be unsaid and probably needed to be said, but now you have to finish it. There's a baby on the way, and there's no going back. Whatever else you need to say, now's your final chance.' She held a third piece of china up but didn't let go. 'Now, Hester, ask a question. But ask nicely.'

Hester sat in the chair that James pulled out for her, her face streaked with tears, white blotches turning red with anger. 'Why?' she spat out. 'Why now?'

Isabelle raised her head and looked down the table. At the edge of her sight Asha held the china higher. Isabelle would have let her smash it all, but she couldn't bear the noise as it hit the floor. The way they all flinched. She felt Kate squeeze her shoulders in encouragement.

'I don't know,' she said, the words torturous. 'It just feels right now.'

Asha dropped the tureen. 'Terrible answer, try again.'

Isabelle drew a shuddering breath, thought about Moth and how hard it had been for him to tell her his truths. How he'd wept and shouted, shoving her away and wept again, but told her. Because she'd insisted. She'd needed to know. And it had helped. She knew it had helped him. She'd watched him walk out of the hotel, get in the car with Luca. Joking in a way that had been young, light, free. She tried again, for Hester.

'It's different. Before, having a baby meant a different life.' She looked at James, knowing there were things she'd never explained to him, for fear of causing pain. 'It was about marriage, and moving to the farm, and those choices forever and it was overwhelming. All that time it was us I didn't want,' she said to James, who sat close to Hester, not responding, 'and I'm sorry that I didn't know that before. It's something I don't know how to do. All my life wrapped up in someone else's. And I could never say that. To myself, let alone to you, James.'

She took another deep breath, shaking with the difficulty of trying to say enough. To make sense of it for them. Something she could barely see the shadow of, in the swirl of emotions that being pregnant had brought upon her. The surge of overwhelming joy she'd felt when she realised. In the strange new shape of herself – alone, holding her flat stomach, looking at the blue line – that had made utter, absolute, breath stealing clarity in the morning mirror not long after she'd returned from Italy. Piecing her life together by what made sense to her, not to others. Her words inadequate, making no sense in the air between them.

'I'm having this baby because I know I want to be a

mother. Just a mother, not all those other things. And, maybe that way, I might finally know my own mother. Somehow, in some small way.' Kate's hands squeezed her again, holding on, giving her courage.

'You don't know anything,' Hester told her, rigid in anger. 'You're a fool, you don't know the first thing about how to be a mother. You turn away the chance to raise children with a decent bloke and get yourself pregnant with that insane, useless fool, who will screw anything that moves, who thinks sex is a form of social interaction and doesn't know the meaning of intimacy or loyalty or responsibility or...' her voice rose to a screech.

Asha picked another bowl off the dresser and dropped it, saying as the noise shocked Hester back into silence, 'I said, nicely.'

'Now wait one minute,' Kate added. 'If you ever, ever, speak about Kit like that again you will feel the weight of my hand.'

'Kate, hush,' Elsa murmured.

'Oh, hush yourself,' Kate snapped before turning back to Hester. 'You don't know Kit even one fraction as well as you think, don't judge him until you do,' she added, raising her hand in a curt flick to silence Asha's attempt to interrupt her.

'And Kit can't...' Isabelle began to finish for her.

'And...' Kate interrupted her with a warning squeeze on the shoulder, '... Kit can't be here to speak for himself. And you will not speak a word against him while I'm here to listen. Not a single damn word. Is that clear?'

Hester snorted with disgust. Or was it contempt? Isabelle was struggling to decipher the depths of her loathing.

'You're making a huge assumption that it's Kit's baby,' Kate added. 'But assumptions do seem to be your forte.'

'Oh, I am so sorry,' Hester retorted. 'Please, go ahead and astound me further! Whose baby is it, Isabelle?'

'It's my baby.'

'Really, that's the best you can do?'

'It doesn't matter who the father is.' Isabelle fisted her hands in her lap beneath the table, trying to find courage. 'I'm doing this by myself. The father won't be involved, what does it matter?'

'What does it matter?' Hester asked her, stunned. 'Do you even hear yourself? You get pregnant with God knows what scumbag you had a one-night stand with, he zips up his fly, waltzes off into the sunset so you can come home and raise his baby, and you actually ask me, What Does It Matter?'

'It wasn't like that,' Isabelle protested, withering inside with the thought of what had happened.

'You stupid bitch. Did you never even consider that the child you're having might end up no better than that waste of space you screwed to make it?' Hester spat at her, rising out of her chair and putting her hands on the table as she hurled venom at Isabelle.

Isabelle felt Kate's hands tighten. Sensed Elsa flinch in shock. Registered Asha picking up another large round platter and dropping it from chest height to the stone floor with resounding and ricocheting effect. Little chips rebounding off the cupboards and dropping in a spatter effect of sound as Isabelle sat stunned. Empty of hope that there was any way she could make sense of this to Hester. She felt the fracture of the platter moving through James and Hester, on through Elsa and Kate. The wave of silence that followed it, until it reached her at the far end of the room, where she sat on the edge of its impact.

Always the outsider. The failure. The disgrace.

The one who had to get up and walk away in shame.

Run down to her workroom, or away to India, until she felt the courage grow to come back and make sense of her life.

Except now there was a part of something, of someone, growing inside her. A baby whose creation she might never comprehend, but whose existence made, at last, complete sense to her.

How could she tell this perfect family who the imperfect father was? That knowledge would make the situation ten times worse, not even a fraction better. Made it impossible that he would ever be openly part of the child's life. And she was grateful for that. She was grateful to be able to make these decisions for herself, and her child. To decide the course of her own life, their life. The wave of shame and disgrace, which started with the shattering platter, ripping through her family, ending in relief as it reached her.

Knowing that she stood, apart, always apart. In the same place that Moth stood. In his own reality that they would never understand. In the dust of the smashed china, she stopped trying to preserve what she'd never felt part of and let go the hope that she ever would. She could feel warmth radiating inside her belly, the strength flowing through Kate's hands into her shoulders, and that was all she needed.

'It doesn't matter,' she told Hester. Told the crisp brilliant dawn of this clear vision in that echoing room. 'It doesn't matter because it would never make sense to you.'

'What does that even mean?' Hester asked, her tone full of contempt. Looking about the room for vindication from the others.

'It means you, me, all of us,' Isabelle told her. 'None of

what you are makes sense to me, and vice versa. And I'm sick of pretending we share the same reality. That there's this one great game plan and I'm the only one not playing by the rules. Or maybe Kit isn't either. Or maybe Moth too. Don't *you* get it?' Isabelle put her hands to the table, pushed up, shrugging Kate off, standing tall. Her voice expanding to fill the space. 'What does it matter if your life, or mine, or anyone else's doesn't make sense to each other? It doesn't make it any less real.'

'What are you talking about? This has got nothing to do with your baby. You're evading the truth because you haven't got the guts to tell it,' Hester told her.

'It's got everything to do with it. Truth? Whose truth? My truth? Your truth? They're not the same thing. This... this... contempt you give. This hatred you hold. This morality you claim. That I'm wrong because God made a child and I wasn't ready for it? Well God said no to you four times and you're not ready to listen. But you claim the higher moral ground and condemn me? Same as Kit. Just because he's different. Dares to live his own truth and apologises to no one. Same as Moth.'

'What's Moth got to do with this?' Hester yelled at her. 'You're twisting it on to him to evade what you're doing. To evade facing the mess you're prepared to make of a child's life.'

'Because he's the same. Living a life you know nothing about. Running away because he thinks his truth doesn't belong here. Because you think someone made you keeper of the realm and you've the final word on what will or won't be acceptable!' Isabelle shouted back at her. Shocked at the words echoing through the room, catching a glimpse of a smile on Asha's face, raised eyebrows of respect.

'Isabelle, have you heard from Moth?' Elsa asked, struggling to keep up.

She drew her breath in, tucked her courage up inside her somewhere deeper than she'd ever found before, and kept her hand away from her belly. 'No. I haven't heard from him. I saw him. When Kit and I were in Italy. We both saw him.'

'You didn't say anything?' Elsa asked her confused.

'There was so much to say, I didn't know where to start,' Isabelle told her, standing in that horrible space where she knew what she was going to say would cause more pain than she had already but unable to keep it back. 'And he asked us both not to.'

'But is he alright?' Elsa asked.

'Now, yes, I think. But he wasn't when we met him. He was a mess. He'd been... beaten up.' Isabelle wanted to say, rape, he was raped, but she couldn't. Walking away from the table toward the back wall in discomfort, turning to look back at them. 'Kit got a doctor, and sorted the hotel, and a nurse. He was under a lot of medication, and he... he told us things he should have told us when he was here, but he couldn't, so he left.' Isabelle looked at Hester. 'He left and he may never come back. Because that's what we do isn't it? We don't allow what isn't approved, if it's not part of the one great sanctified Threlfall reality, and those who can't cope have to run away.'

Elsa stood up from her chair, tears in her eyes, and walked over to Isabelle who stood with her hands rolled into fists. She took her arm and guided her back to the chair. As though she was worried Isabelle might indeed run from the room.

'Well, if anyone's to blame for that I must be first in the queue,' Elsa said. 'Hester, enough, please. Whatever else you have to say will wait. I want to know this first. And Asha, you too, if you could refrain from breaking any more china, at least for the moment.'

Asha sat down next to James with relief. Hester stood before the table a moment longer, not wanting to let go of the personal battle she was waging, staring at her mother. Elsa glared back until she relented and sat down, arms crossed over her chest to hold in the bitterness. Protecting the right to her final say.

Isabelle hated the delay, longed for it to carry on. Felt she could never find the courage to tell them, that it was worse to speak than to stay quiet. To leave Moth where he was, in a place where he believed it would make no difference anyway. That the truth would taint him, or that people would not believe him. Yet, even if she lost all of them through anger or disbelief, if she didn't speak now, she'd never tried to give him the chance of an open route home.

'Isabelle,' Elsa prompted her, 'what did Moth tell you.'

She stared at the table.

'Isabelle, I insist,' Elsa said. 'I shall know no peace until you tell me.'

Isabelle thought there was no peace. There would be grief. Horror. Guilt. In place of the secrets and silence. But there would be no more running away. Not by her.

'Moth told me what happened the night his parents died. He told me that he and David argued that night. A massive row, about... what had been happening. He said when it was over David drank heavily, argued with his mum. That Moth heard them fighting, went to try and stop it.' Isabelle wanted to stop. She wanted to take the words back and the past back. In that moment she knew how hard it had been for Moth to speak. To her, alone, in the darkness of the villa room, doors sealed, curtains pulled.

'Isabelle, please,' Elsa nudged.

'David said they all had to go out. Sandrine was crying, and David tried to go upstairs and get Nat out of bed and Moth refused to let him. They fought but Moth wouldn't let him go upstairs. Said he was drunk, and no one should go in a car with him. In the end Sandrine stopped it by going out with David. Moth begged her not to go, tried to stop her, but he couldn't keep David from going upstairs for Nat and stop his mum from going. He said he knew they would never come back. He sat and waited all night, until the police turned up.' The weariness of each word seemed to get harder to pull out. Knowing all the time she was stalling, hoping there might be a way to take it back, to avoid the end of the story.

'Moth never said any of this to the police,' Elsa said.

'He didn't want to tell them what the argument was about,' Isabelle stammered. 'He didn't think anyone would believe him, and he said it didn't matter, because David was dead.'

'That could be a misguided sense of guilt talking,' Kate told her. 'He might be struggling to cope with the grief of it all. To argue that way, the night they died.'

'He doesn't feel any guilt,' Isabelle told them. 'Not for David. He doesn't think about his mother, because he can't work that out. But with David, he's glad he's dead. He doesn't care what people think of him for that because he's happy knowing... knowing that Nat is safe.'

'Safe?' Elsa asked. 'From what?'

'He told me what the argument was about.' Isabelle felt her words were weak, useless to the task, yet they would be brutal in their impact. 'He said David was abusing him. That it had been going on for years.' She couldn't look at them.

Staring at the worn surface of the wooden table, holding onto the grain of the pattern. 'Moth stood up to him that night. Told him he would go to the police. Said he'd told a friend at school about... about what David did to him. Moth would have run away before, but he wouldn't leave Nat. Standing up to his dad, threatening to expose him, was the only way he could think to protect her.'

She heard her own voice trail away into a vast and unbelieving silence. Whispering along the furrows of the table. She put her hand on the surface. Tried to find comfort in its solidity. She could hear Moth telling her. Could see the images seared into her mind, impossible to forget, that she knew she could never repeat.

'I don't know if I can believe this,' Elsa said, her voice the clipped edge of self-control. 'I'm not saying there might not be something we don't know about, but this, I don't know. I can't grasp it.'

'Who does want to believe such things,' Kate said in a weary voice. 'Let alone of our own children.'

'What do you mean, abused him?' James asked. 'You mean he used to hit him?'

'No. That's not what I mean,' Isabelle said. 'I mean abuse. Sexual abuse. What he told me, it, it's awful. I can't, I won't... But not just that, not what he did, but how he did it. He used Nat as a threat. Told Moth if it wasn't him it would be Nat, that it was his choice. Said his mother was cold since they'd been born. That he had to have it somewhere and it was up to him to choose. He had to take it like a man. Or his sister would.'

'Jesus.' Kate reached out to place a hand on Isabelle's. Warmth radiating through. Fingers wrapping underneath her palm and squeezing comfort into her cold hand.

'Isabelle,' James said. 'Isabelle, look at me.'

She did, looking past the others, scared of what she might find there.

'Are you sure about this?' James asked. 'Do you realise how bad this is? I mean, Moth could be making this all up. How can we know, for sure?'

'That's the point though,' she said in despair. 'Don't you see? It's a truth that we can't even grasp, and it was his whole world. He left because he knows no one wants to hear the truth, and he can't live the lie.'

'But what if it's not the truth?' James persisted.

'What if it is?' Kate retorted. 'He wasn't even fourteen when David died. Christ, how old was he when it started?'

'Ten.' Isabelle looked at Elsa, who was sat with her head hung, her arms barricading her chest. 'He said he was ten.'

'Perhaps it was the painkillers?' James said. 'You were abroad, you don't know what he was taking.'

Isabelle gave up. She could feel herself slipping away from the moment, failing to grasp it. She looked at Elsa, aghast and tight-lipped. At Kate, pensive and stern. Asha, who was watching Hester and frowning. Hester, rigid and pale, staring at the table in silence. Her mouth a thin line of clenched fury. Hands clutched into fists in front of her chest. Pushing away this vision of her adored older brother.

What had she hoped for?

There had been that brief time with Moth when life was peaceful and right. When he'd said everything he needed to, releasing it like a vein of poison until they had cleansed it. Now, here, she could only feel how wrong she was. How right he had been to keep his silence. How woeful an attempt she'd made to explain herself. It was all over. They would think worse of her. And they didn't even believe Moth. Isabelle closed her eyes and gave up.

Elsa was weeping and Kate had gone to sit beside her, hold her hand. The sound of it taking her back to Moth. It was a poor, keening echo. Moth had fought it. With rage, and anger, and hatred, and despair.

Isabelle retreated from the sound of weeping. She put a hand to her belly, wishing for the world to stop breaking. Astounded that she wanted them all to go. So they could be alone, her and the baby. In their own home. The new life inside overcoming the grief and settling dust in her kitchen.

KIT SWERVED AWAY from the cat's eyes, trying to keep an eye on the car close in front and type a quick text. Elsa had been insistent he let her know when he was twenty minutes away.

He glanced in the rear view. Three cars back Fred was in the van. Singing and dancing away like no one could see, let alone the entire three lanes of traffic crawling along the M4 at Swansea. Twentyish, bloody traffic, he typed and looked back at the road.

The car was about as comfortable to drive as a shopping cart. Why Elsa decided she needed a new car the week before Christmas was beyond him. The one she had was working fine. He was embarrassed to be seen in it. Skoda had never got cool, no matter how much it spent on marketing, and it wasn't even a particularly new version. Not what he'd have expected Elsa to upgrade to at all. He'd tried to get it delivered, but she'd insisted he bring it himself, and Fred had laughed and jumped in the truck when he tried to make him drive it. Lou, the bitch, had taken a photo of him getting in and threatened to post it online if he didn't give them extra generous Christmas bonuses.

Christmas. His first year in the market had been intense. Beyond intense. Lou was only part joking about the bonuses, he'd worked them to a pulp.

Pulling off the motorway, negotiating his way closer, he couldn't stop looking at fairy lights. The endless options, the limitations, the intricacies, the fixings, the colours, the impact. His latest obsession struck the team as hilarious. He found their glibness irritating. Along with Elsa's insistence he come now, before Christmas, when he'd managed to arrange all visits for after Christmas, when his work was done. She had insisted Fred come as well, to bring the chair she'd ordered last minute from the boutique in Bristol. Without asking him. All in all, Elsa seemed to be losing the plot. He wondered if it might be the onset of dementia. She was of an age for it, after all, and she'd be more prone to succumb than Kate.

Kit gripped the steering wheel tighter, puffing an irritated sigh out. Someone had strung multi-coloured lights along with white lights and ice blue, together, on a single tree outside their house. All on mis-timed flicker. A bare-branched deciduous tree too. Jesus would be turning in his crib.

He hadn't seen Kate. Not since her house-warming party at Riverdell. Not since Isabelle had gone home from Italy and rung to tell him she was pregnant. Not since he'd heard from Asha about the family showdown, or Isabelle spilling Moth's secrets in the middle of it. Not that he wouldn't have minded seeing Hester lose her cool completely and blame him for the baby, he would have very much enjoyed putting her right on that score, but work had been intense. And

Kate hadn't rung. Not once. The scarf and her note tucked inside his top drawer had proven impossible to move beyond. What did "don't be a stranger" mean? He didn't want to know, and he'd found the perfect antidote in Christmas.

Christmas was crystal clear. It was ostentatious, it was competitive, it was exaggerated, it was slick, it was elegant. It was blatant extortion. In fact, Christmas was downright glorious. Unlike this car, which was anything but. He tutted again, picking up speed on the way to the Mumbles, before realising he was speeding through a 40 limit. He glanced behind, saw he'd lost Fred. Never mind, he knew the way.

The street was packed when he got there, family doing their pre-Christmas visits. There were pre, during and post stages to Christmas. Kit knew this now. Some family you dealt with beforehand, some were prioritised to the main event, some were relegated to the glut period. Most of those visiting families who'd clogged up his parking options were of the 'duty done' brigade, heading home to spend Christmas itself with the family they really liked. He ended up squeezing the car in halfway down the hill. Leaving the only parking space outside the house for Fred.

He got out with relief. A Skoda hatchback, that was one he didn't want to endure again. Taking the steps to the house two at a time he admired his own handiwork in the wreath on the door, the scalloped lights hanging along the curved handrail, tweaking the odd bulb into place. He hung on the buzzer, tried the door, which opened, and walked in. The Christmas tree he'd sent over was visible through the open door of the rear living room, centrally located for prime viewing. It was a cracker. Fine blue spruce, chilled to preserve its needles, sprayed with a special solution. Elegant drooping branches, long fluttering spines. He frowned, who on earth had decorated it?

'Elsa?' he called, walking towards the living area and the tree when the study door opened to his left.

'You're here, wonderful,' Elsa said, appearing in the doorway, wrapped up in a fuchsia twin set, the perfect shade to match her vulva. He resisted a shudder. His visualisation capacity had been in overdrive with Christmas. 'I've got tea ready. Come on in, the fire's going, it's delightful.'

'I hope you've got something stronger than tea,' he replied. 'Who on earth dressed the bloody tree?'

'Nat did it. I had a feeling you wouldn't approve, but she had a lovely time.'

'Don't you dare let anyone see it until I've adjusted it. Where is everyone, anyway?'

'Oh, Nat's popped out for a walk, and Hester's at her art class Christmas party.'

'How civilised,' Kit said, walking into the study.

'Where's Fred?'

'He got lost in traffic, he's not far behind.' Kit threw himself down in a chair with relief, watching as Elsa poured him a cup of tea. 'Really, tea?'

'It's just gone 3pm, too early for a drink. It's not Christmas yet,' Elsa said with a light tone of disapproval.

'It's been Christmas since June for me.'

'That can't be much fun.'

'It's ridiculous fun,' Kit argued. 'I was out in China buying fairy lights while you lot were filling paddling pools. There's something illicit about it that suits me.'

'Well, it's certainly kept you busy,' Elsa said. 'And absent.'

'You took all my time up last year.' He could hear the edge

of a whinge in his own voice and deepened it. 'I had ground to cover at work.'

'You always made time for us before.' Elsa sat down in her chair, lifting her cup and saucer level with her breasts, crossing her legs in their tweedish skirt.

Kit recognised this pose. It was the pose she struck when something was going to be said. It took him straight back to his first year living in Riverdell. How many times had he been called into the study for tea and a chat? It reminded him of Ms Suzanne Harper, whose memory ran a long, cold nail down his spine, alerting him to the present danger.

'Have I done something?' he asked, sitting up. 'It's been a while since I was asked in for tea.'

'You've been absent,' she said. 'I think it's time that ended.'

'I did warn you I would be frantic until after Christmas,' he countered, scanning the room. Taking in the details of her settling in, more books in piles on tables, drawing pads on the floor by the fire. Elsa had added to the bare pistachio shades he'd painted the room. A warm rose in the cushions, with hints of old lotus in the patterned rug. Creating a lighter, warmer look than her old study at Riverdell. He wanted to complain, but it all felt astutely harmonious. 'It's a whole new face to the business.'

'It's got nothing to do with Christmas.' Elsa's eyes followed his wondering gaze from over the teacup.

How on earth she metamorphosed into this dictator over a cup of tea was beyond him. No wonder the Empire had been built on tea. It could turn this mild elderly woman into a despot. He searched the room for more distraction. Elsa had moved that hideous old chest from her bedroom down here, it weighed a tonne if he remembered.

'How on earth did you get that thing down here?' he

asked.

Elsa looked at it, looked back. She lifted her cup from the saucer, sipped, returned it with a clink. Her small finger tilting outwards.

'I asked the neighbour's two sons to help me,' she said. 'They're rugby players. I don't think they even noticed how heavy it was.'

'Well, at least you're making friends.'

'The street has been very welcoming,' she said. 'Nat has made friends with a girl four doors down and another lady down the road is part of Hester's art course. We've been really fortunate.'

'And how is Hester?' Kit asked, trying to turn her attention further away.

Elsa sipped at her tea, refusing to be distracted. 'I asked the boys to bring the chest down for a reason,' she said, returning the cup again to its saucer. 'It belonged to your mother, Kit, and it's time it came to you.'

'What?' he asked, sitting straight upright. 'You never told me that.'

'Hmm, yes, you must forgive me for that,' she said. 'Rose asked me to keep it until she came home, and I've kept it all these years on some odd hope it might one day bring her back. Foolish, I know.'

'What's in it?'

'I have no idea,' Elsa told him. 'She never told me how to open it.'

'Why give it to me now?' The trunk did not inspire confidence. It was an ugly thing, heavy, rugged and intimidating. He couldn't think of a single client he could sell it to if he could empty it without damaging it, or even a dealer who traded such things.

'I'm done with secrets,' Elsa said. 'If Isabelle has taught us anything as a family it is the damage done by secrets.'

Kit wished Fred would get here, this meeting was getting uncomfortable.

'Well, what have we got planned for the evening?' he asked with a bright smile.

She glared at him, lowering her cup an inch. 'I want you to take the chest,' she said. 'I want you to promise to open it. Since all this... family stuff, I can't help but think Rose left it for a reason, and perhaps we should have explored that before. Promise me, Kit, will you do this?'

'Haven't we had enough skeletons for one family?'

'Maybe, enough secrets, that's for sure.'

Kit didn't point out that Isabelle was keeping the biggest secret of all. Just how much Isabelle had told the family changed depending on which member present at the epic family teddy-throwing was telling the tale. Asha had been the most forthcoming but even she didn't know the full details.

'Promise me?' Elsa insisted.

'I'll have Fred put it in the van when he gets here.' She smiled at him and he swallowed the irritation of that happy coincidence. She hadn't given him any excuse to leave it here. The sly old bitch. 'I can't promise to do it anytime soon, but yes, someday I'll look into it. I don't know why you haven't knocked the lid off the hinges, it's ugly enough. I won't mind not keeping the chest.'

'That's your choice.' Out in the hall they heard the front door open and Nat's voice in the hallway. He cocked his ears to listen, but Elsa rushed on, clinking her cup down noisily in its saucer. 'Ah, now, as for this evening. I have a favour to ask of you. I wish you to take that car you've brought over to its new owner, and to give a friend a lift home too.'

'What?'

Elsa stood up, walked over to the doorway and opened it. Kit craned his neck round the chair wing to see what she was up to, but she had positioned herself between the door and the frame, blocking the hallway view.

'Hello darling, did you have a nice walk? Oh lovely. I left a snack out for you, go ahead, I'll be just one moment.' Her voice changed as Nat ran down the hallway, going up to a more adult level. 'We have a visitor. Would you join us?'

Kit felt his hands go clammy. What the hell was she up to? He stood up from his chair, put his cup down, turned towards the doorway. He watched as Elsa stood aside and pulled the door open. As Kate walked in full of her usual energy, saw him and stopped dead in the doorway. Her drawn breath, about to spread news and enthusiasm, stunned out of her. The hems of her trousers swishing a tide into the space they'd been expecting to move towards. Elsa pushed her forward and closed the door behind her.

'That car is for Isabelle,' Elsa told him. 'It's my Christmas present to her and the baby, they're going to need it. And Kate was due to go home on the train tonight, but I want you to take her back, please, Kit.'

Kate stared daggers at him. As though he had conspired against her.

'I didn't know you were here,' Kit said, hating how apologetic it came out.

'She summoned me two days ago,' Kate replied, composing her shocked expression. 'I didn't have much choice.'

'It seemed desperate measures were needed to make you two speak to one another,' Elsa said, standing guard over the door. 'Do you honestly think I haven't known what's what all these years? I can't say I always approved but I've held my peace over it.'

'You conniving cow,' Kate muttered at her.

'You're welcome,' Elsa told her. She looked from one to the other, heard the music of Fred's van arriving outside with a horn toot. 'Ah, here's Fred, I'll go put the kettle on.' Put her hand behind her, on the door handle. 'I'll leave you two to talk. Join us in the kitchen when you've made your peace, I won't bear this ridiculous silence. I have a grandson I need to find and convince to come home and a niece about to become a single mother. I need all hands-on deck. You two having an almighty lovers' spat is simply not an option.' She left the room and pulled the door too with a firm click.

Kit looked at Kate, who didn't move from her spot by the door.

'This is awkward.' Kit stepped away from his chair. 'Do you want to sit down?'

'I'm quite comfortable standing,' she said. 'You stayed away a long time.'

'You made it clear how you felt,' he countered. 'I didn't want to confuse the issue.'

'I had my reasons.' She unwrapped the throw tossed across her shoulders, smoothing its edge down her front.

'More bloody secrets?'

She grimaced at that, toying with the edge of her sleeve. The heat from the fire reflecting on her wind chased face. Her cheeks warming to a hue that he couldn't take his eyes off.

'Perhaps. But what's the point in going over old ground? I'm sorry Elsa dragged you here, I would never have let her.'

'I suppose she thought she was doing good.' He caught himself staring. Dazzled by the sudden presence of her, that had become a soft blue scarf of memory. Her skin glowing, her hair crazed from the sea breeze, rampant. Her eyes flashing with irritation. Looking like she had on the beach all those years ago. 'You look as beautiful as ever.' He took a step towards her.

'You look bone-tired and worn out,' she retorted. 'You've been working too hard.'

'Work made more sense.'

'More sense than what?'

'Anything?' he suggested. 'Anything at all that's happened in the past year.'

Kate took a step towards him. The imprints of her feet rising from the deep pile of the rug, the pointed toe and wide heel of her mules. The arching space between.

'It's been tough on everyone,' she said. 'Though it would have helped to have you around more. You abandoned us when we needed you.'

'I couldn't see what I could do.' He ate another footfall out of the space between them, crushing the lotus pile. He'd missed her shoes. How could you miss a person's shoes? 'Anyway, I thought I wasn't wanted.'

'Not wanted? By whom?' Kate asked, letting the last word fall in surprise, caught repeating words she'd spoken many years ago, when he'd first sworn to run away.

Kit watched her hand rise in protection to the exposed dent between her clavicles. He took one more step toward her. Riddled with longing, held back by the words on the card. He clenched his hands into fists, opened them, twisted his watch on his wrist, cleared his throat.

'You tell me,' he said, amazed that the words came out less confident than they had when he was a teenager.

They stared at one another across the space left between them. It was no more than a hand's reach.

ACKNOWLEDGMENTS

A writer is the spy amongst you. I am indebted to the many families who welcomed me into their homes and lives and inspired so many of my characters. Riverdell would not exist without that experience. I do hope no one is offended.

My greatest thanks go with this book to the readers of Book 1. The launch team members who not only gave me such thoughtful, incisive feedback but all said, 'Hurry Up with Book 2!' Here it is, I hope it satisfies, at least a little.

In particular my heartfelt thanks to Noels, Nat, Lottie and Lydia, for all your faith, hard work and honest feedback. Writing involves many, many hours alone, finding such readers who engage with me beyond the book is a joy I still cannot believe I am lucky enough to have found.

To all my readers, you are and always have been my only goal in being a writer. Thank you for returning to Riverdell.

THE THRELFALL FAMILY

Like all families, the Threlfalls are a complex bunch and introducing them all in Book 1 was a challenge for many readers. My early readers petitioned me for a family tree which was great fun to make and made beautiful by Amanda Hillier, the cover artist, to be included in all editions from now on.

Much has been made of the sexual relationship between James and Isabelle in Book 1. They are half first cousins, sharing one grandparent, not two, with their parents being half-siblings. It is worth noting that sexual relations and marriage between first cousins is legal and acceptable in many countries, including the UK where the book is set and the author resides. The inclusion of their relationship is as intentional as all the others in my work, seeking to explore what we find both comfortable and uncomfortable in our understanding of sexuality. If Book 1 raised your eyebrows, then this book should have fair singed them off. I suggest you read no further, for Book 3 includes Rose's story and she takes no prisoners.

ALSO BY MARIANNE ROSEN

Discover where the journey started with Book 1 of

The Riverdell Saga:

The Doors of Riverdell

And coming in November 2021...

Book 3 of The Riverdell Saga:

The Lights of Riverdell

Rediscover Isabelle, Moth and Kit as the years move on. It's 2016 and Isabelle has more to learn about the history of Riverdell as she considers her future, Moth is in Turkey avoiding both the future and the past, and Kit is confident he's master of both until a friend discovers his mother's diaries.

Meet Rose, the passionate rebel of the four friends as she explores the life of a single mother and the forbidden depths of her sexual desire. Watch Riverdell flourish in the strange new arms of its gloriously untraditional family.

Sign up to Marianne's newsletter at www.mariannerosen.com to keep updated with release details.

ABOUT THE PUBLISHER

Oriel Books Ltd is an indie publishing house dedicated to promoting the careers of indie authors.

Combining traditional publishing practice with modern digital vision we work to advance and promote the careers of dedicated, series-based authors at every stage of their journey.

If you have enjoyed this book consider joining us as a beta reader or advanced copy reviewer, working to help develop the stories of new authors in your favourite genres.

If you are an emerging author with a strong idea for a series of books, consider pitching your novels to us.

Details can be found at www.orielbooks.com